# 50 WAYS TO WIN BACK Your Lover

## KELLY SISKIND

 Montlake

Text copyright © 2022 by Kelly Siskind
All rights reserved.

Published by Montlake, Seattle

www.apub.com

Amazon, the Amazon logo, and Montlake are trademarks of Amazon.com, Inc., or its affiliates.

ISBN-13: 9781662505645
ISBN-10: 1662505647

Cover design by Caroline Teagle Johnson

Printed in the United States of America

# 50 WAYS TO WIN BACK
## Your Lover

# ONE

Despite what some people think, I'm not dead. I haven't been stranded on a desert island these past ten years. I didn't secretly join the priesthood or get stuck in one of those escape rooms. Nope. I'm here. Out in the world and alive.

At least I was alive, until the loudspeaker at the terminal gate crackled to life and uttered two words, one name—*the* name that has the power to cut me down at my knees: Delilah Moon.

Now? I'm definitely dying. Or is this a mini stroke?

My brain's gone on the fritz, unable to form a coherent thought other than *Delilah Moon, Delilah Moon, Delilah Moon.* I'm pretty sure if I move, my rubbery legs will fold, sending my frozen face on a collision course with the half-crushed Dorito on the retro carpet.

Delilah Lost-Love-of-My-Life Moon.

I scrutinize the departure area like a sniper who's inhaled a case of Red Bull: furtive reconnaissance with a frantic edge. Kids sit slouched, half sliding off their faux-leather seats, faces plastered to their phones. The adults aren't much better, thumbing their devices, eyes dilated in their Cell Trances. My brother Lennon is thankfully still off perusing the terminal's stores. If any of my brothers heard that name, they'd shout a list of reasons why I have to hide from Delilah Moon—if this is *the* Delilah Moon—and remind me we aren't allowed to talk to anyone from our pasts.

Heart racing, I lean toward the elderly woman beside me. "Did they just say the name Delilah Moon?"

She glances at the departure counter, magazine crinkling in her grip. "I believe they did. It's a lovely name, isn't it?"

It isn't lovely. It's downright *angelic*, but that name cannot be here. "Maybe they said Eliza Woon. It was tough to hear clearly."

"No." The man next to her leans forward, shaking his bald head at me. "Definitely Delilah. It made me think of dahlias, my wife's favorite flower." He winks at her.

A sudden flash hits me: Chasing a shrieking Delilah through the wildflowers on her property. Laughter, sun, carefree bliss. Scooping her up and tugging her down, her fingers threading into my hair, our lips connecting under a canopy of daisies and scarlet flax.

My stroke intensifies, but I still don't see her. Not one hint of the breathtaking woman who undeniably owned my heart. And my pulse? Still running a three-minute mile.

Unsure what to do, I reach for my sketchbook—any possible distraction—and proceed to cut my finger on a page. Because, of course. Blood beads along my skin. I suck on it, attempting to control my hamster-wheel thoughts. *It's not her, right? It can't be her. Nope. No way. Definitely not her. Life wouldn't be this cruel.*

By the time I glance up again, it's clear Life enjoys kicking me in the nuts.

My first and only love is hurrying up to the departure counter. Her curly brown hair is longer than I remember, her hips rounder, her body fuller. *Lush.* The girl I knew has transformed into a woman, and instantly, my eyes burn. I stand up. Sit down. I'm a malfunctioning jack-in-the-box. Which kind of sums up my current self, forever confined and controlled, forced to embody a different name and altered existence, because . . . are you ready for this kicker?

I happen to be in witness protection.

Delilah leans on the counter, angled away from me. From this vantage point, I can't tell if her lips still have that bee-stung look or if her blue eyes still undo me with one glance.

Another breath-stealing flash hits: Delilah and me, sixteen and inseparable, lying side by side in her barn, hay sneaking into uncomfortable places, her family's Arabians snorting and nickering while we take turns flipping comic book pages, her eyes so blue they're the color of summer freedom and Sonic the Hedgehog, the parts of my body touching hers on fire with a heady mix of love and lust.

The burning behind my eyes worsens.

"Why is your face red?" Lennon's holding a plastic bag with whatever he bought, his back to Delilah, clueless to the source of my overheating body.

"I'm not red," I force out, but my rushing blood isn't corroborating my lie. I lean to the side, desperate for another glimpse of Delilah.

She rotates, digs into her purse, searching for something.

I pull back and hide behind Lennon.

He tilts his head and rubs his beard, the cuffed sleeve of his plaid button-down slipping to his elbow. "There's a definite red tinge." He smiles at our elderly neighbors. "Doesn't he look flushed?"

The couple scrutinizes me. "I think it's the name," the lady *un*helpfully blurts. "The flight attendant said—"

"Nothing." I pop up, grab my satchel, and forcibly lead Lennon away from that couple and Delilah.

"Are we on a reality show?" Lennon says, getting up in my space. He's not as tall as me, but he's fit from his mountain biking and rock climbing. He'd tackle me if he knew Delilah was nearby. "Is this the part where we're given clues, and I have to figure out why you're being rude to senior citizens? What's up with you?"

"I mean, we *could* be on a reality show. Our asshole father did launder money for a drug cartel. Netflix would cream themselves to tell our story." Five boys forced into witness protection, ripped suddenly from their lives like pages from a censored book.

That shit would kill it in ratings.

Lennon smirks. "Michael Fassbender would play me. He's not as hot, but he can pull off the beard and reddish-brown hair."

"You're delusional," I say, ducking as Delilah leaves the departure counter. "He's not hipster enough."

Lennon scowls. "How many times do I have to tell you: wearing plaid doesn't make me a hipster. And you're acting weird. What was the lady saying about a name?"

"Nothing." I peek at Delilah again. She takes a seat beside some dude wearing orange jeans, thankfully facing away from us.

Even if she saw me, the odds of her recognizing me are slim. I'm twenty-seven, not seventeen. My Justin Bieber haircut is thank-fuck gone, replaced with shorter strands I struggle to tame, but at least I don't look like someone dropped a limp mop on my head. I'm taller and fuller, not muscled up like our three oldest brothers, but I run like my life depends on it, which it kind of does. The six-pack I didn't have when Delilah first took off my shirt has emerged. I'm now Brian Baker, not Edgar Bower—E to my friends back then—but I still have a telltale scar through my upper lip. She might notice that defining feature or see our treasure trove of memories swimming through my eyes.

Orange Jeans Guy smiles at her. She smiles back.

I clench my jaw, mentally talking myself down from doing something stupid like telling Orange Jeans Guy to take a hike.

Delilah Moon isn't mine. She hasn't been mine for ten long years, and if she knew I was within fifty feet of her, she'd probably use my face for target practice. (Delilah won Windfall's skeet shooting contest at age fifteen.) Leaving her without a word was bad enough. Ghosting her after we made love for our first and only time?

Forget skeet shooting. She'd probably launch a grenade at my crotch.

"Actually," I tell Lennon, struggling to inflate my lungs, "I am feeling off."

An ache has settled in my chest, my dormant love for her scrabbling to the surface. If I tell Lennon I'm stealing glimpses of Delilah's slightly sloped nose, wishing I could brush my nose against hers as our lips slowly meet, he'll forcibly drag me away from here. I'm not ready to lose sight of her again. Not yet.

"I'm having a Delilah Day," I tell him. A partial lie.

"Oh, yeah. Okay." His sympathetic tone doesn't ease my churning panic. "It's been a while since you've had one of those."

Delilah Days were my most morose days during our early years in WITSEC, a.k.a. witness protection and my messed-up life. I'd sit on social media obsessively, too nauseous to eat, my skin that translucent bluish color of an underground dweller who never saw daylight, reading Delilah's old posts over and over—worried messages that grew increasingly desperate.

*If anyone knows where the Bowers are, please contact me.*

*E, if you see this, call me. I'm freaking out.*

*E, I don't understand. Where are you?*

*How could you leave me like this?*

As you can imagine, I didn't cope well. Kind of like now.

"It *has* been a while since I've felt this intense," I say.

Lennon adjusts his plastic bag, then crosses his arms. "Something specific bring it on?"

"Nothing major." Unless you count seeing my former best friend and lover for the first time in ten years. "The departure counter called out the name *Eliza Woon*, which sounded like *Delilah Moon*. And this connector going through Charlotte is throwing me off, knowing we'll be close to Windfall."

He huffs. "I knew taking this flight was a bad idea."

We'd normally never have booked a flight going to Charlotte, so close to our former hometown, but my meeting with my agent in New

York got pushed back. We had to change our flights home to Houston and wound up heading there of all places.

"Anyway." Lennon rocks on his heels. "I know this is rough. I totally miss Windfall too. The festivals were a blast, and the hiking and biking trails are killer," he says wistfully. "But it's different for you with Delilah. Any specific memories coming back?"

A nervous laugh almost escapes me. "Nope. Nothing specific."

"Well, I'm here for you. Unless you drink my beer at home again. Then you're on your own."

"I don't like your hipster beers."

He holds up his middle finger. "I'll piss in the cans next time and seal them up. Maybe you'll like that better."

Living with Lennon and riling him up with hipster jokes is usually entertaining, but I'm a second from a nuclear meltdown.

I glance at Delilah's riotous hair, needing more from Lennon. *Something.* A hint of what I'm supposed to do. I mean, what if seeing Delilah out of the blue is fate trying to push us back together? "I was just thinking, wouldn't it be wild if I ran into Delilah here? Like, if she happened to be on our flight and I had the chance to talk to her."

"Not really," he says, his tone hardening, "since there's a death threat on our heads. If you saw Delilah, we'd run our asses away from here and book another flight."

"Ha, ha," I say stiffly. "I was just playing the what-if game."

Except this isn't a game. My chest aches from her proximity. Delilah's name is a love letter looping through my mind. If I tell Lennon she's here, I'll lose this tiny connection to her, even if it's fleeting. So, no, I haven't contemplated ditching this flight. I've barely walked ten paces from Delilah's orbit.

"Anyway," I say, going for nonchalant, "it's just a rough day."

But also kind of amazing. Seeing Delilah brings back our first kiss outside of Haddie's Diner, the taste of innocence and peach ice cream on her tentative tongue; sneaking into her room and leaving flowers by her bed; fighting with her over which comic book we'd read; cradling her all night after her father's heart attack, then again after the funeral; surprising her with a puppy—Dill Pickle—from Big Joe's litter; spending afternoons sketching her on our wildflower picnics; confessing that she made my heart feel like a hot-air balloon, so big and bright and full it could carry me to Mars. "You're not Delilah Moon," I'd tell her. "You're Delilah Mars. That's where my heart is. In Mars, stuck on you."

Lennon's talking about some book he bought, but I don't listen. Orange Jeans Guy is on his phone now, as is Delilah. I alter my angle to see her face better. She's too far away for me to absorb small details, but she's smiling while she talks. Her skin is more cream than tan, like she doesn't spend hours outside anymore. The intensity of her blue eyes isn't as clear from here, but her lips are as full as I remember, that Cupid's bow in the center teasing me with its feminine dip. Her jeans and white T-shirt are casual, perfectly Delilah, accentuating her fuller figure.

In two seconds, I'm addicted.

"Jesus." Lennon waves in front of my face. "You really are out of it today."

I blink at him. "Honestly, I'm fine. And dandy. Totally fine *and* dandy."

"Fine people don't say the word *dandy*." He narrows his eyes at me.

Unable to resist, I steal another look at Delilah . . . and Lennon starts to turn, intent on following my traitorous eyes. *Not good.*

I grab his shoulders and force his focus on me. "Tell me more about your book."

"You're evading."

"No, I really want to hear about your book."

"Likely story, Captain Weirdo. Something else is going on with you."

He twists out of my grip and turns.

My heart climbs into my throat. "I'm hungry. We should get a snack for the flight."

Ignoring me, he searches the departure area and doesn't seem to notice Delilah. Then he does a double take. "No, no, no. *No fucking way.*"

Face pale, Lennon whips back and drags me past a coffee shop to a different departure area. "That was Delilah."

"Are you sure?" I rub the back of my sweaty neck. "I'm almost positive they said *Eliza.*"

He points a furious finger at my face. "You *cannot* talk to her. You can't breathe near her or even look at her. We can't be here at all."

"*I* didn't plan this. I'm as shocked as you are she's here."

"But you lied about it, and in case you've forgotten, the cartel our traitor father testified against is still alive and well. Connecting with anyone from our pasts could paint targets on all our heads."

Like I need the reminder.

But Delilah Moon isn't just anyone, and it's been ten excruciating years of revisited memories, unbearable heartache, and frustration. As crazy as my story is, if I told Delilah the truth, she might even believe me. Learn to not hate me. The skeet-shooting-my-face thing might not happen. Hope thrums in my chest, hot and insistent, fogging up the rational side of my brain.

"I need to speak to her," I blurt.

"Nope. No. No, you don't." He waves his hands frantically. "Absolutely no way."

"Witness protection isn't a jail sentence. No one's forcing us to stay in hiding. We do this to keep each other safe, but it's not like I'm turning up in Windfall, where someone might be staking her out."

Lennon drops his bag between us and forcibly holds me, the veins on his corded forearms looking ready to pop. "I love you. I love our brothers and Mom. I know your relationship with Delilah was intense and special, but family comes first. You cannot speak to her. Jesus Christ," he mumbles. "We have to switch flights."

A few people shoot us curious glances. The loudspeaker announces a departure.

I attempt to battle Lennon's panic with forced calm. "We checked for other flights," I remind him, slipping out of his hold. "When I had to push back the departure date, you checked and said this was the only flight we could take, because you can't miss more work."

He glares at me. I scrub a hand down my face, hating that I can't see Delilah from here. Missing a second of her when she's this close is physically painful.

"Did you have fun in New York this week?" I ask, changing tactics. "The show we saw, checking out art galleries, eating a stupid amount of salted pretzels?"

He squints one eye at me. "I did."

"And why did I invite you to come along?"

His nostrils flare—annoyance as he picks up the clues I'm dropping. "I was having a rough week, and you bought me the ticket and said I needed a break."

Over the past ten years, Lennon shed his teen hippie tie-dye and bought hipster plaid and hipster skinny jeans and a collection of hipster hats, even though he claims he's not a hipster. He grew his reddish-brown hipster beard and started an adventure camp for kids, where he's upbeat and fun and a great leader, but he struggles to fill his programs. And some WITSEC days simply suck for the hell of it.

"I hoped the change of scenery would do you good," I say. "We all know how rough this gig is. I didn't need you with me to meet with my agent and publisher. I just wanted to see you happy."

He slumps and rubs his eyes. "You're not supposed to talk to her."

"I know, but what are the odds of seeing her here? And it's been ten years. If she doesn't know my new name or where I live, there's no link to us. There wouldn't be a digital trace. One quick hello so I can hear her voice, finally let her know I'm not dead." When he stays silent, I bring out the puppy dog eyes. "Come on, man. I *need* this."

He growls and glowers, shakes his head a bunch while mumbling, then jabs my chest. "You can't tell her about the cartel."

"Of course not."

"And you have to wait until we land in Charlotte. We don't interact with her on the plane. You talk to her quickly when we arrive, then we bolt to our connection. You don't see or speak with her again after that."

"No interaction on the plane, then we bolt," I agree, not mentioning the possibility of never speaking with her again. I can't offer that promise. Seeing Delilah feels like kismet. Like that asshole Life is finally shining a ray of hope on my face.

"I need to get my head checked," Lennon grumbles and pokes my chest again. "Not a word of this to the family. If they learn what's going down, they'll string us both up by our balls."

"That's why you're my favorite." I punch his shoulder, pulse thrumming. "I'll just stand near her until boarding is called. Without being seen," I add.

He huffs.

I spin and head for our gate. People pass me, oblivious to my swirling nerves. My limbs are twitchy and hot, my steps clipped. Delilah is on my flight for a reason. I feel it. A deep knowing in my bones. Once I speak to her in Charlotte, I'll somehow get the love of my life back.

I spot her easily, all that wild, curly hair impossible to miss. She's still on her phone. My heart attempts to make a break for it and race toward her. Swallowing hard, I stay put and soak in the gorgeous view, wondering how she'll react when she finally sees me. If she'll feel as lovestruck and overwhelmed as I do. Or just furious. She laughs at something, then lowers her phone and pulls up her purse. Her hand catches the light.

I squint and lean forward.

A slight glow flickers.

A flash on her left hand. A ring on her fourth finger.

A sparkling round diamond that means only one fucking thing.

# TWO

Life has a deviously twisted sense of humor. Not only do I have to fly on the same plane as Engaged Delilah Moon Who Loves Someone Else—I have to sit behind her on the flight. I don't mean the general vicinity of behind her, like some random seat in this tin can that will defy gravity and propel me through the air at three hundred miles per hour. I mean directly behind her, on flight 3432 to Charlotte, aisle thirteen, middle seat D. Swear to God.

I often wonder what I did to offend Life so thoroughly. Granted, I wasn't the perfect cherub of a child. I broke curfew on a whim, sneaking home after a night of stargazing with Delilah or after losing track of time while sketching or messing around with my best friend, Avett Lewis, in the old quarry. I bribed my brother Desmond to buy me vodka once, got wasted with Avett, and puked on Mom's azaleas. Actually, that happened twice. But if an elderly person gets on my bus or train, I give up my seat. Several times, I've paid for a person's groceries when they've been flustered and upset and couldn't manage the cash. I never litter and always hold the door open for others. I refuse to kill spiders, for fuck's sake.

Now I'm staring at the seat in front of me, aware of my every breath and twitch. I'm also wedged between Orange Jeans Guy, who doesn't understand the meaning of personal space, and Lennon, who's staring intently at the ceiling like doing so will eject us out of here.

He's had that same tense expression since I trudged back and told him Delilah's engaged. He flattened his lips while we rushed to get in line before her, ducking our heads to avoid recognition. He scowled while we shoved magazines in front of our faces as she neared our row . . . and then slid into the seat in front of us.

Now neither of us are talking, for fear Delilah will recognize our voices.

Shrinking into the confines of my seat, I attempt to hold my breath for the duration of takeoff. The experiment ends with me closed-mouth coughing while trying to avoid alerting Delilah to my presence. By the time we're cruising at thirty-five thousand feet, my stomach hovers somewhere at one thousand.

The flight attendant, with a seriously thick set of eyebrows, is pushing the drink cart toward our row. When he asks Delilah—who's one seat in front of me, in case you forgot that nut shot—what she'd like to drink, I immediately think: *Sprite without ice.*

"Sprite without ice," Delilah says.

My stomach lowers to eight hundred feet.

Delilah never liked ice in her drinks. She hated how it felt bumping against her teeth, claimed it got in the way of drinking. Apparently, some of her preferences haven't changed, and I hate that I know this about her. She probably still cracks her knuckles when she's stressed and loves the smell of a new book and looks at her boogers after she blows her nose. Her *fiancé* probably knows these details about her and more. New habits I never got to learn.

"Would you like pretzels or cookies?" the flight attendant asks Delilah.

I think: *Cookies.*

Delilah says, "Cookies."

Make that six hundred feet.

Unable to handle food or drink or anything sloshing around in my stomach, I wave off the flight attendant and his huge eyebrows. Orange

Jeans Guy beside me has usurped our shared armrest. Lennon is silently fuming over our fate. Delilah's wind chime voice assaults me from up ahead as she talks about the book her seatmate's reading.

Elbows held tight to my body, I debate pulling out my sketchbook, distracting myself with drawing wild creatures or working on my graphic novel, but I'll probably just draw Delilah.

Lennon shoves a magazine in my face and points to the Wi-Fi option while holding up his phone. He stares at me until I comply and receive his message on my phone.

Him: I hate you.

Me: Again, not my fault. I didn't plan this.

Him: We should've switched flights.

Me: YOU CAN'T MISS WORK.

Him: I still hate you.

Me: No you don't. You hate our life.

Him: I really fucking do. And I do hate you when you drink my beer, Brian.

I hate when he purposely uses my WITSEC alias, knowing it irritates me. Our US Marshal handler pushed us to choose our new names, each one starting with the same letter as our birth names for easier recall. Lennon is Logan. Callahan is Connor. Desmond is Daniel, and the oldest, Jake, is John. Since everyone called me E instead of Edgar, I was told not to use that letter. I grudgingly opted for Brian after one of my favorite illustrators, Brian Bolland.

While I've used our aliases aloud the past ten years, in my head I've refused. Thinking of my brothers as anyone other than who they were was a line I couldn't cross.

Thinking about the woman in front of me is pure torture.

Despising life, I resume texting Lennon.

Me: If you hit me really hard, I might pass out for the whole flight. Forget it ever happened.

Him: I hate this for you more than I hate you for drinking my beer.

Me: I hate our father more than any of that.

The money-laundering bastard who pulled the rug out from under us.

Frustrated with *everything*, I cross my legs, then realize I'm jostling Delilah's seat. I freeze. At least, my limbs freeze. My pulse thinks it's running the hundred-yard dash. When Delilah moves her seat back, leaning into my space, I grab the puke bag from the seat pocket and tuck it by my side. The last thing I need is to projectile vomit onto my lost love's head.

This is how I spend the next half hour: my body atrophied, each bone fused into immobility, worried one small breath will alert Engaged Delilah Moon Who Loves Someone Else that the guy who broke her heart is behind her. I also have to pee, but I'm terrified she'll see me, so I've crossed my legs so tightly my calves cramp.

Lennon is staring morosely out his window. Orange Jeans Guy spreads *his* legs, his knee hitting mine as he sprawls. I shrink smaller, too freaked out to speak and ask him to keep to his space. My voice is deeper than when I was seventeen. Still, Delilah might recognize it. Her voice has more husk than I remember, but her bright wind chime tone is unforgettable.

So I continue my impression of a fossilized Edgar Eugene Bower, with Orange Jeans Guy in my space, my bladder nagging at me, my calves nearing spasm, when Delilah says, "Oh my God."

As mentioned, I know a lot about Delilah Moon, including her gross booger habit. I also know the various levels of *oh my God*s she uses.

There's her this-is-the-best-thing-ever oh my God.

There's her you're-an-idiot-E oh my God.

There's her this-can't-be-happening oh my God.

Finally, there's her I'm-about-to-punch-you-in-the-dick oh my God.

The latter never happened to me, but Delilah dick-punched Freddie Lorimer (after saying *oh my God*) because he fooled around with her best friend, Maggie, then told everyone he slept with her, except all the moron did was cop a feel. Not that the lie mattered as much as the loud-mouthing, according to Delilah. No one messes with her friends.

Unsure which *oh my God* she just used, I perch on the edge of my seat, ears attempting to lengthen and twist, like they're periscopes able to inch closer to Delilah.

She says, "Oh my God" again, angrier this time, and it's no contest. That was definitely one of her dick-punching *oh my Gods*.

Lennon narrows his eyes at her seat. I'm ready to tear off my shirt like the Hulk and defend her honor.

"Is everything okay?" the woman beside Delilah asks. I can't see her face, but the concern in her voice has me liking her already.

"I'm definitely not okay."

I try to stand. My seat belt strains, keeping my stupid ass exactly where it should stay: away from Delilah. Whatever's going on with her, it's not my problem. She's no longer mine to defend or annoy or make laugh. I don't get to tease that intoxicating moan from her throat when I press my fingers *just right*.

Swallowing my groan, I shove the heels of my palms into my eyes, debating using the bathroom after all. I'm behind Delilah. She won't notice me if I stand.

My phone buzzes. With shaky hands, I check Lennon's message: Do not speak to her.

Me: Do I look like I'm opening my mouth?

Him: You look like you want to vault over the seat and fly her to a secret island.

Jaw clamped shut, I do not reply.

"We have another hour together," Delilah's neighbor says. "And I'm a good listener. Let me know if—"

"Apparently," Delilah says, "my fiancé took a job offer after we spent the past few days discussing it and deciding *together* it would be a disaster for us personally. Like, he'll be traveling a ton for this new consulting position when he likes his current job and makes a great living. But, according to his email just now, he simply couldn't pass up the opportunity."

Her seatmate makes a derisive sound. "That's not cool."

"Not cool is the fact that we've been in a long-distance relationship, and we agreed that I should sell *my* business and move *my* life to New York so we can finally be together, which I was excited for. Now he'll barely be home. I mean, does he think I'm the only one who needs to make compromises for our relationship to work? Did he just placate me by discussing the job offer, then decide to do whatever he wanted? Does he even *care* what I want?" She whispers the last part, livid.

Orange Jeans Guy stares at Delilah's seat, smirking, like her pain amuses him. I've morphed into a Malaysian exploding ant that can burst its own body at will to kill a rival. Only a selfish narcissist would disrespect Delilah so flippantly. My phone buzzes again, but I refuse to look at it or Lennon.

"Is this something he does often?" Delilah's neighbor asks. The calm to her fury. "Steamroll over your opinions to serve himself?"

"I don't know." There's defeat in her voice now. Resignation. "It's been a bit of a whirlwind relationship. Maybe I don't know him as well as I thought."

The kind neighbor's hand moves across the gap, reaching for Delilah. I'm so thankful someone nice is sitting next to her at a time like this. "From my experience, tigers show their stripes when they're secure and confident. They slink around and hide while stalking their prey, then drop the act when the kill's in the bag."

"That's a disturbing analogy," Delilah says, her tone inching from defeated to alarmed.

"I'm in the middle of a nasty divorce. But take it from me—make sure you know who you're marrying before you tie that knot."

Delilah sighs. I touch the back of her seat, wishing I could reach through, stroke her hair, hold her the way I did when her dad died. Let her tears seep onto my skin, her pain seep into my heart, a safe place for her to feel whatever it is she needs to feel.

Then she says, "Maybe it's me. Men always treat me like shit."

Now I need a safe place.

Over the years, I've tortured myself, imagining how hard my disappearance actually hit Delilah. I often picture her running to her chicken coop, glowing from our amazing first time together the night prior, wondering what was taking me so long. Then she's running to my house, pounding on my door, still smiling, wondering why no one's answering. Then she's calling my phone. No smile this time. The tears start. Then she's texting me and writing frantic messages on social media, terrified, devastated, completely confused as to why the one person she trusted and loved above all others vanished without a trace.

I have no clue how accurate those nightmarish imaginings are, but I now have this to add to my mental torture bank: *Men always treat me like shit.*

Lennon gives my thigh a squeeze, like he knows I'm dying inside.

"Don't you go taking all the blame," the nice neighbor says more forcefully. "It takes two to tango, and I have a feeling he's tipping the scales in his favor." When Delilah doesn't reply, she adds, "Just because you have that pretty ring on your finger doesn't mean you have to marry this guy. Moving on is hard, but ending things later is harder."

"Yeah, well." A heavy silence. A rough intake of breath. "I'm used to losing people in my life. If it comes to that, I'll deal."

Remember the puke bag I tucked beside me? I grab the flimsy paper and make a big enough production of shoving my face in it that Orange Jeans Guy finally vacates my personal space. I don't actually heave, but my insides torque so painfully I click off my seat belt and utter some weird sounds, insinuating I need out of our row stat. I avoid touching Delilah's seat on my way, then practically run to the lavatories at the back of the plane, thrilled there's no lineup.

*See, Life? Was that so hard?*

I try to yank the door shut behind me, but someone's shoving at it. Lennon sticks his hand through and joins me in the coffin-size aluminum box.

"Dude," he says, looking as bewildered as I feel. "That was intense."

"How could someone treat her like that?"

"Because that someone is an idiot. I hate this for her. And for you. You two . . ." He leans against the door and sighs. "You two were the type of couple everyone envies. Except *me*, obviously. But everyone else. Life is so fucking unfair."

I want to move, pace. Work off this frantic energy. I can barely blink without knocking into Lennon. "I have to tell her why I left."

"Nope." His spine snaps straight. "Bad idea."

"But I'm the guy who bought you a ticket to New York to make *you* happy, and you agreed talking to her once is fine."

"That was before."

"I don't care if it was during the Ice Age. She needs to know my disappearance wasn't her fault. She clearly blames herself."

As horrible as my years without her have been, I knew where she was and had a vague sense of what she was doing. Except for two blackout years of silence shortly after I left—otherwise known as utter hell, when she quit posting on social media—I'd search her name periodically and learned tidbits, like the fact that she opened a bakery in Windfall, the business she apparently plans to sell. I knew she was living a seemingly successful life.

All she knows about me is that I vanished. A FOR SALE sign went up on our property. Our handler, Agent Rao, told townsfolk we had to move for my father's work, but no one would have bought that vague bullshit. We were simply gone, leaving Delilah with a pile of questions and inescapable, painful memories. And maybe a few precious ones?

My suppressed love for her rises so keenly I have to brace a hand on the sink and catch my breath. Honest to God. I still love her so much I actually grip the nasty-ass bathroom sink, unable to support the weight of this crushing emotion. Emotion so big and thick there's no way I'll be able to stuff it back down. Not again. Not this time.

"I have to speak to her. Tell her she shouldn't settle for less than she deserves. I mean, *she's sitting right in front of me.*"

When Lennon stays quiet, I shift jerkily and knock knees with him.

We trade glares, breathing hard in each other's faces, then he sighs. "When I agreed before, you were wired, but you were calmer. Everything about you now reads 'desperate.' You're too emotional. Talking to her will only hurt you more, and you'll probably say things you shouldn't."

"I'm not desperate." I gesture to my face, hating how fast my pulse is racing.

He cocks his head and stares at me.

Yep. I'm totally desperate.

Groaning, I bang the back of my head into the wall. When that doesn't solve my problems, I jam my elbow into it too. Honestly. That asshole Life really has it in for me.

# THREE

Back in my seat, my heart still performing more calisthenics than I did in seven years of phys ed class, I do the only thing I can think of. I pull out my phone and creep Delilah on social media.

I haven't checked her status in over a year. She never used Facebook much and still has no personal information listed. There is, however, a recent post from her trip to New York. The photograph is of her with her fiancé on a typical New York street. Apparently, his name is Hugo. He's a white guy of average height (shorter than me) and looks as preppy and horrible as you'd imagine. Delilah's smiling in the picture, but it's not her solar eclipse smile, the one that's so bright it's hard to look at. This is more of a smile-for-the-camera smile.

Hungry for more of her, I scroll to her next post, one from a year prior. The bakery café she owns looms behind her while she points to the storefront's sign—SUGAR AND SIPS—a bigger grin lighting her face. It's an adorably clever business name. Sweet treats. Coffee sips. Out of morbid curiosity, I check Hugo's page next, but his page is listed as private.

Delilah sniffles from in front of me, and I freeze. She sighs, and I slump. Her neighbor is giving her space, an inch I'd like to cram myself into so Delilah can lean on my shoulder, cry on my shirt. She can even blow her nose on the soft cotton, then check her boogers.

Lennon has resumed his morose window staring. I close my eyes, praying for sleep or an aneurysm. What I get is a replay of my Top Ten Best Days.

Many people would struggle to pinpoint the absolute best days of their lives. Those lucky bastards probably don't obsess over their memories in the hope of retaining a part of their abolished identities. Me, I have a Top Ten Best Days list. Each one is written in my collection of journals. Tweaked and embellished when a specific memory surfaces, the details forever recorded, never to be lost. Not because I'm a glass-half-full, rainbows-and-lollipops kind of guy. After I relived my worst days ad nauseam until I existed in a perpetual fetal position, my brothers held an intervention and suggested I focus on the good memories. The special occasions. The unforgettable moments—so I never forgot who I once was.

Number ten isn't my memory, per se, but I've heard the story so often it feels like mine.

I was born Edgar Eugene Bower on a windy day in the Windy City, my horrendous names courtesy of Dad's great-grandfathers. That day, powerful gusts knocked out half of Chicago's power. A tree fell in front of my dad's car, causing another vehicle to rear-end him, forcing me to be born in the back seat. Mom said I was her only natural birth. No C-section like with Lennon or drugs used to dull the agonizing pain like with my other brothers, but the second I was placed into her arms, she said the pain disappeared. "You have power," she often tells me. "When people hurt, you absorb their pain. It's why you're so compassionate."

Or I'm just an oversensitive man who feels too much.

Emotional baggage aside, coming into existence is number ten on my list. Without that milestone none of the others, good and bad, would have happened.

Five belongs to the day I turned seven and my parents moved the family to Windfall, North Carolina. My accountant father praised Windfall's vibrant arts community and hiking and equestrian scenes.

He said he wanted to live somewhere with fresh air and lead a quieter small-town life.

Shocker of all shocks, Dad lied.

Windfall's massive tourism influx, its general stability and affluent visitors, along with the variety of cash businesses Dad could front—nonchain convenience stores, liquor stores, restaurants—made it a prime location to launder money and keep his cartel bosses happy.

So our oblivious family moved to a hobby farm with rolling hills and tall grasses, forests of oak and hickory cradling the tranquil property. There was a fence on our lot next to the neighbor's chicken coop, its sun-bleached wood stretching along our property line. Typical in all regards, except for the seven-year-old girl standing on the bottom rail, her curly hair wild and her face pinched, as she shouted, "Get off my land!"

I squinted at her pursed lips and shouted, "Get off my fence!"

She shouted, "Get a new face!"

I shouted, "Get a brain!"

A woman with similar wild hair ran over, interrupting our clever repartee. Smiling indulgently, she grabbed the mini tyrant off the fence and plopped her on the ground. "You'll have to forgive Delilah. She has a royalty complex. Thinks she's queen of Windfall. I'm Hayley Moon," she called to my parents. "We're thrilled to have new neighbors."

She went to chat with Mom and Dad while my brothers ran off to explore, leaving Delilah and I glaring at each other through the fence slats.

"Eat dirt," she said, channeling her best Maleficent.

"Eat worms," I replied, going for Jafar.

Then she gave me the finger and ran away.

It was an awesome day.

The fourth-best day of my life was the day of my truce with Delilah Moon. Being neighbors, we rode the same bus to school. She'd sit at the front. I'd sit at the back. For two years we ignored each other while perfecting our death glares, unless one of us felt creative. Those days we'd mumble jabs like *butthead* or *butthole* or *buttwad* as one of us would walk past. As far as I was concerned, Delilah Moon was an invasive species—a weed in my new life, popping up her vicious little head in the worst places.

The day of our truce, the fourth-best day of my life, we got off the bus at our stop. Just the two of us as usual, a couple of butt-insulting enemies on our rural road, while my brothers participated in after-school sports.

She walked ahead, holding a ceramic horse in her hands—her show-and-tell keepsake from class. Little Gracie had been her grandmother's figurine, acquired the day her grandparents moved to Windfall and bought their horse-breeding farm. Delilah's evil eyes had shone when telling the class Little Gracie was the name of the first Arabian her family owned. She'd explained how strong and kind and athletic their horses were, while I tried to burst her head with my laser-hate vision.

That afternoon, as she walked down the road, she held the figurine up toward the sun, watching the light refract off the brown glaze. My fingers twitched for some reason, the urge to draw that horse and her tanned hand pulling at me. I pictured my pencil dancing over a paper, smudges and lines growing into a picture. In that version, the horse was eating Delilah's head.

Then she tripped over a rock and dropped the horse.

I froze.

Delilah sucked in a sharp breath, followed by a quiet "No, no, no, no" as she gathered the useless shards in her hands. A sob racked her body, and something sharp jabbed at my heart.

It's a sensation that often plagues me when other people are upset, like my heart's a hollowed organ, the interior filled with jagged stones. That day, the stones grated, building into a hard-to-breathe kind of pain that made me want to cry. Cry for Delilah's grandmother, who loved that figurine. Cry for Delilah's mom, who probably loved the memento. Cry for Delilah, who I hated but who'd lost her special keepsake.

She glanced over her shoulder, her too-blue eyes full of sadness, not villainy, and I ducked my head, ashamed of witnessing her misery. Tears running down her face, Delilah hopped to her feet and bolted ahead, her short legs pumping, leaving Little Gracie broken on the dirt road and me with an aching heart.

*When people hurt, you absorb their pain.* My mother's words rang in my ears as I gathered the pieces Delilah dropped, unable to leave them on the road. I took them home, glued them back together, and left the mutated-looking horse in the grass by the chicken coop, where Delilah went first thing in the morning.

I hadn't memorized her schedule because I liked Delilah Moon. Enemies needed to keep track of their rivals' schedules. Ensure they didn't catch you by surprise. I certainly didn't like watching her mimic the rooster's crows every morning. I hated when she'd stop to watch the sunrise, the candy-floss glow breaking over her upturned face.

The morning I left Little Gracie by the coop and Delilah's head whipped to my house, her squinty eyes traveling up to my window, and she bit her lip, I definitely didn't like the swooping feeling in my stomach.

Later that morning, she caught up with me on the walk to the bus and said, "Edgar sucks. I'm gonna call you E."

Definitely a solid four on my Top Ten Best list.

Today, as I chew my cuticles bloody and test how deep I can dig my nails into my palm before my eyes water—the answer: as long as it takes to quit stumbling down Delilah Memory Lane—I do my best to blank my mind. This flight can't end soon enough. The second I get home, I'll be going for a three-hour run. Maybe a double marathon. But as the plane hits the runway and taxis to our arrival gate, I suddenly don't want to unclick my seat belt.

I pull out my phone and message Lennon: I don't want to leave her again.

He blows out a rough breath.

Him: I know. I'm sick about this for you.

Me: We were supposed to be forever.

Him: And you would've been. I have no doubt about that. I wish I could say something to help besides this sucks.

Being this close yet far from Delilah more than sucks. In mere minutes, this fleeting glimpse of her will be gone. She'll drive from the airport to Windfall, clueless to the fact that Lennon and I have been behind her for one hour and forty-eight heart-crushing minutes. We'll grab our connecting flight to Houston, where the US Marshals stashed us. A big city with big action, where a family with five pissed-off boys could vanish into thin air.

I don't want to go back to that fabricated life. I don't want to leave this narrow airplane seat that has zero back support and smells like an old lady's plastic-covered sofa. I'm behind Delilah Moon and don't want to go back to pretending I've forgotten her, when my memories and feelings are as strong as ever. Except that isn't quite right, is it? My feelings aren't *as strong as ever*. My love for Delilah is *stronger* than ever. Every precious memory has marinated for ten long years. Gained nuance, flavor.

The captain's talking, but it's tough to make out the words over the sound of my rib cage caving in. To make matters worse, it smells like Orange Jeans Guy applied Eternity on his last bathroom trip. No big deal, you might think. He could smell like Desmond's jockstrap after one of his football games. Wouldn't that be worse? The answer is a resounding *no*. Eternity is the same cologne I stole from Desmond to impress Delilah for our first time together—our final, perfect night. The absolute best and worst night of my life. And this space-invading guy is bringing it all back.

The seat belt sign shuts off. Passengers stand and reach for the over-head bins. Delilah's still sitting, saying something to her nice neighbor, and I make a flash decision.

I nudge Lennon and shoot him a message.

Me: I'm doing this. Talking to her after.

Him: We already decided you weren't.

Me: WE didn't decide anything. Not talking to her will make me feel even worse, and I'm calmer now.

Him: What about the fact that she's having a pretty shit day? You think now's a good time to be all . . . surprise, I'm not dead!

He makes an annoyingly valid point. One hour and forty-eight minutes of a flight, and I didn't spend one second of that time figuring out how to approach her without making this tough day tougher for her. I bounce my knee. Sweat gathers under my armpits. Rationally I should let sleeping dogs lie, but I just . . . can't. There's too much history to let this moment escape.

Me: Even if seeing me is rough, she'll finally have some closure. How can I deny her that?

Lennon grunts, then sighs.

Him: For the record, I think this is a mistake. Nothing good will come of it for you or her, but you're gonna do it no matter what I say. Just be quick and discreet.

Damn straight, I'm doing this. I'm going to speak to Delilah Moon after all these years. Say her name and see those blue, blue eyes up close. And this *could* be good for her. Insight into our past might give her clarity for her future.

Nervous but pumped, I try to come up with a killer opener so she doesn't crumble or dick-punch me. All I think is *gray*. Why did I wear my gray Coca-Cola shirt today? I don't even like Coca-Cola, and there isn't a worse color on this planet for sweat stains.

Thanks again, Life.

Delilah's up and quickly moving out of her row. Too fast for me to fall in behind her. I do the only logical thing and dive across Orange Jeans Guy. He curses. My hand touches something it shouldn't.

"Sorry, sorry," I say as I get into the aisle. "But serves you right for hogging my space."

He glowers at me.

I cut off the next person, who is four people behind Delilah. The man in front of me waddles at an injured penguin's pace. I dodge left and right, wishing I had extendable legs so I could clamber over Penguin Man and reach Delilah before she's gone. By the time I make it off the airplane into the boarding bridge, I don't see her. Not one strand of her curly brown hair.

With no other choice, I run, collecting dirty looks as I go.

"Excuse me." That was my elbow catching Penguin Man's arm.

"Sorry." That was my bag, hanging off one shoulder, bouncing violently into the nice lady who sat beside Delilah. I turn and give her the softest eyes I can manage. "You're an amazing person."

She looks weirded out. Rightfully so.

I hit a slow jog, my bag banging against my hip, nerves and adrenaline pumping my lungs.

One step into the departure/arrival lounge, I see her. Delilah. My girl. She's off to the side, tapping out a message on her phone, her eyebrows furrowed in angry concentration.

My heart is on a roller coaster, climbing up, up, up, happy and terrified at once, about to cross that scary line into we're-going-down territory, and I say, "Delilah."

# FOUR

As soon as I've spoken, I realize I whispered Delilah's name. She's still focused on her phone. I'm still on the up portion of the roller coaster, chug-chug-chugging toward the unknown. Swallowing through the sludge in my throat, I say louder, "Delilah."

She looks up. Her eyes scan the arrival area, pass over me, her eyebrows furrowing deeper. A second later, her gaze slips back to my face. Rests on me. She squints.

Sweat soaking through my gray T-shirt, I lift my hand and wave.

Her eyes widen.

My heart tips over its roller coaster edge, a rushing plummet toward the ground as I whisper "Delilah" again.

Delilah Lost-Love-of-My-Life Moon.

The fast-flip stages of shock play across her face: confusion in her darting eyes, denial as she takes in my non-Bieber hair and bigger body. Tears of utter relief and joy shine in her eyes, cutting me down and lifting me up at once.

Lips trembling, she says, "It can't be you."

"It's me." *It's us,* I want to say. *That guy doesn't deserve you. I was on your flight for a reason. We're meant to be.* My ribs might crack from the pressure of holding in all I'm not saying.

Then Delilah says, "Oh my God."

For those of you not following along, that was Delilah's this-can't-be-happening oh my God, and I'm a tad less worried about this roller coaster running off the tracks. But she repeats her "Oh my God," and this time it's definitely of the dick-punch variety.

I clasp my hands in front of my crotch and study her rolling carry-on bag, wondering if she managed to smuggle her shotgun onto the flight. Nope. Wouldn't fit in there.

She stares at me. I stare at her. The roller coaster in my chest barrels faster.

Spotting Lennon in my peripheral vision, I move close enough to speak to Delilah quietly, but my mind blanks. Nothing comes out.

Anxiety rising, I proceed to spew words without thinking. "My father was laundering money and we didn't know and we were forced into witness protection and I couldn't contact you, but I've thought about you every day for ten years. I'm not even supposed to be talking to you now, but seeing you brought everything back and I'm so sorry for hurting you and leaving you and . . . *fuck*."

I swallow convulsively, go to rub my eyes, but I don't want to miss a second of Delilah's gorgeous face, even if she looks like someone just told her we live in the Matrix and nothing she knows is real. "Delilah, I'm so sorry. I'm really not allowed to contact people from my past, so please don't tell anyone you saw me, but I couldn't let you walk away. Not this time. I just . . . I'm so sorry. I only left because I was forced to."

She blinks. Opens her mouth and closes it, like she's a fish lost on land. I want to be a lost fish with her. Or a pair of floating seahorses, mated forever, our tails tangled as our butts bump together with the tide. Her blue eyes go watery and red. Her breathing turns harsh and ragged. I reach for her—instinct, magnetism, my body drawn to its other half—and the moment shifts.

Her trembling jaw hardens. The water in her eyes solidifies into ice. "I have no clue what bullshit you just made up, but it doesn't matter. What we had is in the past. I'm engaged now. Getting married to a great guy. Like, really great. Someone who treats me like a queen. And I need to get going. Long drive home and everything."

Her eyes do another scan of me, from my toes to my much cooler hair. She gives her head a little shake. The chin trembling starts again. Abruptly, she shoves her phone into her purse and walks away from me. Doesn't even glance back. Her pace gets faster and faster until she's practically running.

My free fall begins, the death-defying race of my heart careening to the ground. Everything hurts. Breathing hurts. Blinking hurts. Existing hurts. I plant my ass on one of the lounge's faux-leather chairs and grip my head before it hits the carpet.

Lennon sits beside me. "I'm guessing it didn't go well."

"Excellent deduction skills."

"At least she didn't deck you." He rubs my back. "What lie did you use when explaining why you left?"

I stiffen. Right. That. "I *maybe* panicked and said some things I shouldn't have?"

He yanks me up by my chin. "What did you do?"

"I don't know." I nudge his hand away. "It all just rushed out— WITSEC, the cartel—but she doesn't know my new name or where I live. There's zero connection to our new identities, not that she believed me anyway." Our unbelievable life story only happens on sets like *Ozark* or *The Godfather: Part Forty-Three*, with directors yelling *Cut, try again, get it right this time.*

I'd like to try again. Have a second take. Say something less bullshit sounding and ease Delilah into the truth of my past ten years, but that fucker Life didn't install a rewind button.

"If it helps," I say, "you were right. I definitely made her feel worse. She even lied to me about her loser fiancé. Said he was a *great guy.*"

Lennon skewers me with a dark look, then plants his elbows on his knees. "First of all, I'm pissed you told her about WITSEC. Rookie move. You know better. The odds of it biting us in the ass are slim, but

God help me if any of us gets hurt. Second . . ." He scrubs his hand down his face. "If she lied to you about her fiancé, she did it because seeing you likely brought back a lot of intense feelings. She was just protecting herself."

I perk up on my seat.

Delilah didn't just lie to me once. She said she was engaged to a great guy (lie number one, according to that flight), then she repeated the *really great* (lie number two), then she said he treats her like a queen. Ladies and gentlemen, that's a triple-axel, spinning-through-the-air-with-a-leotard-riding-up-your-butt lie. Triple-axel lies only happen when someone is desperately trying to control a situation and their emotions. As WITSEC pupils, Lennon and I are well acquainted with that tactic.

Delilah lied to my face the way I lie to the people I meet. Self-defense. Protection mode. The critical need to keep my truths hidden. Her lies could equate to unresolved feelings where I'm concerned, a hint of affection hovering under all the hurt. There was at least one moment where she looked downright thrilled to see me, however brief.

Lennon massages his temples. "My nerves are fried. Meet me at the next gate. I need to mainline a gallon of green tea."

He trudges off, but I don't move. I keep trying to capture Delilah's image, memorize it to replay later, wondering if she really might harbor feelings for me.

Before I can reel in my hope, I'm reliving Best Day Number Two, meeting Delilah at the edge of her driveway, both of us sixteen, officially a couple, the fall wind kicking up dust and leaves.

She bounded toward me that day, at her usual speed of head-on. Grabbed me and hugged me, practically knocking me to the ground. "Good morning," she said, fitting her arms beneath my backpack.

I draped my arms over her bulky pack and kissed her softly, because kissing was a thing with us by then. "Morning."

She hummed against me, because humming was a thing with her. "I missed you."

"We talked all night."

"But not yet this morning. I always miss you in the mornings."

I missed Delilah always, even when I was with her. It was the strangest feeling I couldn't put into words. I imagined it was how astronauts felt, surrounded by everything—limitless infinity and beauty—unable to touch the universe. Delilah was all the stars in the galaxy, so big and bright I could never quite hold all of her. Couldn't fill my lungs all the way when she was near. "We should fix that," I said. "Tell your folks you're sleeping at Maggie's. Let's sleep outside and wake up together."

"It's fall, E." She stepped on a dead leaf, crunched it under her boot, punctuating her point. "We'll freeze."

"You don't trust me to keep you warm?"

She bit her lip and bounced her knee, then gave me her secret smile, the one that said *dare you*. "Okay, let's do it."

Pumped, I grabbed her hand, gave it a kiss, and walked us toward the bus.

"Did you finish your history paper?" she asked.

"Does drawing doodles in the margins count?"

"You don't draw doodles. You draw jaw-dropping creatures that should hang in galleries."

"Not according to my family."

She squeezed my hand. "Your brothers are a bunch of jealous jocks, and all parents cringe when their kids want to pursue art. All that worry about *stable futures*. I bet Stan Lee's parents told him to quit drawing and get a real job. Your artwork is *that* good."

"Stan Lee didn't draw his comics," I said, dodging her compliment. Most people didn't consider comics art. Most people thought what I did was a silly hobby. Except Delilah.

"Whatever Stan Lee did or didn't do," she said, "you still need to graduate." She knocked her shoulder into mine. "If you flunk the paper, you could flunk the class."

If I knew then what I know now, I'd have shrugged and said who cares. (I also might have kidnapped and caged my criminal father before he ruined our lives, but prison food wouldn't agree with me.) Art has carried me far in life. Sketching clears my mind, smooths the rocks that catch in my heart, and I earn a great living bringing my writing partner's graphic novels to life.

Back then I didn't have a crystal ball.

"I'll work through lunch," I said.

"I can help, if you want. I'm free at lunch."

"You're not free."

"Pretty sure I know my own schedule."

I swung our hands like we were a couple of grade schoolers. Swear to God, we were *that* cute. "You'll be busy daydreaming about our perfect night under the stars. There's no way you'll be able to concentrate on my history paper."

"You mean *you* won't be able to focus."

Delilah could always see right through me.

Already, I was mentally listing everything I'd need: sleeping bag, pillows, flashlight, hat, gloves, scarf, a thermos of Delilah's favorite blueberry tea. Halfway through math class, I caught myself smiling—seriously, smiling in *math*—fantasizing about holding Delilah all night, her big hair stuck in my face, our bodies tucked tight in my single-person sleeping bag.

By the time we'd lied to our parents and I had Delilah all to myself on the cliff overlooking Bear Lake, I was so full of anticipation I forgot how to breathe. Goddamn lungs trying to hold too much air, too much Delilah.

We'd fooled around plenty before that night. She'd had her hands down my pants, and I'd had mine down hers. We were both relaxed around each other, happy to experiment and test our boundaries. Sex wasn't on my mind, per se. I mean, I was a sixteen-year-old boy. Sex was always on my mind. But that night, while we lay in the sleeping bag like an overstuffed burrito, not talking, just staring up at the stars, the vastness overwhelmed me. Billions upon billions of tiny lights splashed across the blue-black night. Each time I took a breath, Delilah's body shifted against me, and it felt like I was inhaling those stars. Zillions of bright spots filling me up. Shooting stars in my arms. Exploding stars in my chest. A galaxy of stars glowing in my stomach, so endless and bright that I turned to Delilah, flush against her, her huge hair in my face, and whispered, "I love you."

She sucked in a sharp breath and turned her body toward mine. "I . . ." She swallowed, slow and hard, her Sonic the Hedgehog eyes more midnight in the dimness—full-moon midnight, reflecting the heat of my words back at me. "I love you," she whispered, her voice cracking. "God, I love you so much."

We kissed under the limitless sky, laughing haltingly, smiling against each other's lips, the galaxy inside me exploding like fireworks, as our bodies rubbed together in our cozy burrito.

We didn't take off our clothes. It was too cold, and we were too in the moment. We kissed and rubbed, whispering *I* and *love* and *you* between our panting breaths. She straddled me, rode my hips until she tensed. I held her down, grinding her harder on my erection, hitting her in that perfect spot, watching as her body shook and her eyelids fluttered. I wasn't far behind, shooting off in my pants.

I didn't care that I'd have to wake up like that and walk home with dried cum on my boxers. I didn't care that my feelings for Delilah were so vast they could consume me. I didn't care about anything except that I loved Delilah Moon and she loved me.

Surely her triple-axel lies mean she just needs time. Once the shock of seeing me wears off, those old feelings will resurface, and we'll finally get our second chance. Surely, this is another beginning, not another end.

Just as quickly, I deflate.

I'm doing it again. Fantasizing about the impossible notion of a rekindled romance. It doesn't matter if Delilah harbors feelings for me. She's still engaged to that idiot, and I'm still not allowed to be in her life. I have to quit letting my imagination and desires get the best of me. Stop reliving my Top Ten Bests. This flash of time will only ever be a new memory shoved under all those other suffocating moments I can't escape. Once again, I have to figure out how to live without Delilah Moon.

# FIVE

Fuck you, Life.

# SIX

No, seriously. Fuck you. As hard as my early WITSEC days were, I thought I was past the worst of it. Head down, jaw squared, I got on with living my life, building a career, functioning like a moderately well adjusted adult. This week, I've reverted to a state of morose paralysis.

When I say week, I mean that as literal time. 7 days. 168 hours. 10,080 minutes. Figuratively, it feels more like 9,372 years. I'm not sure if it's my insomnia or lack of appetite, but I've been walking around in a fog, not drawing, barely going outside, my body molding to my couch as I commune with late-night infomercials. (*Yes*, I bought the kitchen knife that can cut through metal.)

Even in the middle of the afternoon, I'm so zoned out I don't notice Lennon's in the room until he picks up an orange and beans me in the head with it.

Wincing, I rub my forehead. "What the hell?"

"I would say I told you so, that talking to Delilah was a bad call, but I don't have the heart. You have to find a way to put her out of your head and move on. You've been inside so long you're nearing scurvy levels."

I peel the orange and flick strips of rind at him. "Guess I better eat this orange, then."

He plops onto the couch beside me. "What can I do to help, brother of mine?"

"Not toss oranges at me."

He sighs. "At least put on different clothes. I can't invite people over with you like this."

"Your only friends are our brothers, and those idiots don't care if my sweatpants are ratty."

"If I *did* have friends," Lennon says, "I wouldn't be able to bring them here. And honestly, I'm getting Shower Incident vibes from you. You have to quit shutting me out."

I grit my teeth, annoyed he brought up *the Shower*.

That fun time was courtesy of social media and Delilah's sudden return to Facebook. After her initial pleas to find me, she went radio silent for two years. *Two freaking years* of me obsessing over what she was doing, terrified she was as devastated as me. I only found two pictures of her during that time. Not on her timeline. They were posts from her friends, tagging her. Parties somewhere, with her in the shot.

Then, on one of my weekly searches, there she was. Smiling with her best friend, Maggie Edelstein. Sunlight captured in a moment. They held up ghost-shaped cookies in their hands, Windfall's Halloween decorations splashed over the town square. Her eyes were crinkled—Sonic the Hedgehog blue, bright with happiness—and I let out the saddest sigh of sighs.

But there was a second picture. A horrifying photograph that had me seeing spots. Delilah was smiling again, this time with Andrew Chan, their arms slung around each other. My lungs backfired. My heart shriveled to the size of a dehydrated pea.

No one's arm belonged around Delilah Moon but mine.

I wound up huddled in the shower afterward, utterly *destroyed*, emotion ripping through me so forcefully I choked.

So yeah. It wasn't a fun time, and I don't want to revisit those dark days.

Determined to do better, I pop off the couch. "You're right. Let's get out. Do that hike you need to check out for your program."

He claps. "Now you're talking. We can grab snacks at Baker's on the way."

"Solid call. I haven't had their—"

Aggressive pounding comes from our front door.

We trade wary looks. "You expecting someone?" I ask.

He shakes his head. The next pounds are louder, followed by a stern "Open up!"

That deep voice is definitely our oldest brother, Jake. The last time he smashed his fist into our door was when we thought the cartel had tracked Mom through an online purchase of the rare Corkscrew Albuca plants she loves.

Lennon points at me. "You did this."

"I did *what*?"

"The cartel fucking knows," he whisper-hisses. "They found us because you *just had to* speak to Delilah. Jesus Christ, we're all gonna die."

"I hear you dipshits in there," Jake says. "Open up the door."

"Just a sec!" I holler, scanning our beige walls and open kitchen area, wondering if the cartel bugged the space. To Lennon, I say, "Don't tell Jake it was me."

"Oh, I'm definitely telling him. I warned you this would happen. It's your funeral, figuratively and literally."

"You're my least favorite brother."

Fuming, he marches past me and yanks open the door. Jake is there, big and brawny as always, but he's not his usual stoic self. He's smiling so wide I actually see his teeth.

"Did you win the lottery?" I ask.

"In a manner of speaking." He steps inside and passes his hand over his mouth. "Victor Becerra is dead. Whole cartel was wiped out."

"I'm sorry." Lennon is stone still, all but his pumping chest. "It sounded like you said the Becerra cartel was *wiped out*."

"Obliterated." Jake shakes his head and lets out an incredulous laugh. "The Quintero family went on a rampage at a Becerra wedding.

A feud over a recent killing. There's no one left to come after us. We're in the clear."

"Holy shit." Lennon whoops and punches the air. "Holy fucking shit."

I don't whoop and yell. I mean, I used to pray for this day: Victor Becerra dead, the rival Quintero family having eliminated their enemies. Allegiances would shift. The threat on our lives would end, and I'd finally be able to leave WITSEC. Go home and tell Delilah the truth. Reboot my life and start over. But there's no running to Delilah.

Delilah Moon is engaged to some dick.

"Dude." Lennon gives me a light shove. "Why aren't you celebrating?"

"I think I'm in shock," I say. It's all so much. Seeing Delilah recently, learning she's engaged, the possibility of my family's lives changing dramatically again. I press my hand to my stomach, worried the developing ache is an indication I have an ulcer. I press harder, try to stop the pain from cracking wider, spreading to my limbs. I close my eyes, force some deeper breaths.

Feeling like I'm tumbling out of control, I glance at Jake, our captain, the leader of our ramshackle troop. "I don't trust it."

He grips my shoulders—his standard oldest-brother move, holding us together—and says, "I felt the same, but it's true. It's over, E. They're all gone."

I crumple. Full sobs. A fierce wave of emotion that almost takes me under. It's not the confirmation that sets me off or the adrenaline crash of the shock. This, right now, is the first time in ten years anyone's called me by my real name, E.

Jake hugs me tighter and grips the back of my neck. "Tough decade, huh?"

I laugh, wiping my face. "I don't remember signing up for any of this."

He pounds my back and releases me. "Don't say a word to anyone yet." His voice hardens into its usual commandeering tone. "There are still details to discuss. I called a family meeting. Figured we'd do it here."

~

Thirty minutes later, everyone's in our beige apartment. Beige isn't just the color of our walls. Since being forcefully dragged from Windfall, all the Bower-turned-Baker boys live beige lives. None of us have close friends or girlfriends. There are no personal pictures or tasteful accessories in our homes, unless you count our vintage *The Invisible Man* movie poster on our wall. Lennon gets the credit for that next-level irony.

I fit myself onto our small end table. Jake's and Callahan's big bodies overtake the sofa. Lennon's hipster self is propped on one of the kitchen stools. Desmond, who disappears for stretches of time, is miraculously here. He's leaning his angry shoulder into the beige wall, his angry man bun sloppily piled on top of his angry head.

None of us speaks. We're waiting on Mom, who's taken up her family-meeting spot, standing in front of the TV. Between her auburn hair swept up into a ponytail and the dark circles under her lined eyes, she looks both younger and older than her fifty-nine years. The only person missing from this family gathering is our father. If you're wondering where that special brand of asshole is, here's a hint: we don't fucking care. Once we got settled in Houston and Mom regained her mental fortitude, she gave him the boot. There were no sentimental goodbyes.

"It's so nice to have you all together," she starts, her eyes flicking to Desmond.

His jaw pops. "Jesus, why are you looking at me? You called, I showed."

Our thirty-three-year-old problem child.

As much stress as my oversensitive outbursts (or as I like to call them, *in*bursts) have caused, no one took our upheaval worse than Desmond.

Before WITSEC, he was Windfall's golden boy—a former quarterback acing his first year of law school. Since then, he's given up on law. And on life. And on cutting his hair. The blue-splotched tattoo on his neck in particular pisses me off. The lion's face resembles a bloated, hairy amoeba, when I could've designed him something sharp and dynamic, or he could've found a proper tattoo artist who doesn't work out of a bar bathroom for cheap beer. This is the first time we've seen him in three months, hence Mom's eye flicking. He's as angry as ever, and I understand why. I may have loved Delilah madly, but he planned to propose to his girlfriend before WITSEC shoved our lives into a trash compactor.

"You're looking great," Cal tells him, always the peacekeeper. "Love the new piercing."

No, he doesn't. The ring in his eyebrow looks infected.

Desmond grunts.

Lennon gives his full-body hipster smirk: bearded chin tucked, right shoulder cocked, condescending eyebrows raised. "Peeing on needles doesn't sanitize them."

Des snarls. "Says the guy who has last week's dinner living in his beard."

"Says the guy who thinks vodka is a food group," Lennon shoots back, still smirking. "But it's great to see you."

"Vodka *is* made from potatoes," I say. Facts are facts.

"Good point." Cal practically gives me a thumbs-up.

"Enough with the heckling." Jake's strong voice cuts through our ribbing, the conductor of our rickety train. "Listen to Mom."

"Seriously," Des says, his lip curled. "I don't know what kind of emergency meeting this is, but I have somewhere to be."

I freeze midblink and shoot a look at Mom.

Chelsea Bower is an amazing woman. She used to do crafts like quilting and candle making and macramé, even though she sucked at them. She has three things she cooks well—grilled steak and mashed potatoes, grilled steak and roast potatoes, grilled steak and double-stuffed potatoes—and she loved nagging at us to "get our lazy butts into the kitchen to help clean up." She grounded us when we did things like puke on her azaleas (both times), and she gives the second-best hugs in the world. She also had no clue our father's influx of money came from drug lords, as opposed to his thriving "accounting" business. Yet, after learning of his deception, she never once broke.

But she doesn't meet Desmond's perpetual glare now. Neither does Cal, who's usually the first to offer a compassionate glance.

It hits me then—Desmond doesn't know.

They probably wanted him here, with his family, when he found out we don't have to keep hiding. That our lives are about to change again. Between his notorious benders and disappearances, telling Desmond I got a paper cut before my flight is risky. This? I chew my lip. Wait to see who volunteers to launch the grenade.

Jake, of course.

He stands, walks over to Des, and grips his shoulders. The move's totally predictable. "Victor Becerra is dead. Whole cartel was wiped out by the Quinteros."

Des turns to stone. "What?"

"Massive bloodbath, killing all of them at a wedding, which means we're in the clear. The Quinteros don't give a shit who ratted out Becerra's son."

Des drags his hand down his face, steering clear of the infected piercing. "Fuck me."

I watch him intently, waiting for him to lash out, but if I'm not mistaken, that was a hopeful *fuck me*, not an angry *fuck me*. I blow out a relieved breath. Mom gives Des a watery smile. Cal presses his fist to his mouth, choked up. Jake says something quieter to Des I don't hear.

Lennon slaps his thigh. "Knew this would end one day. You can finally shave the man bun, Des. Go back to being the cocky, obnoxious version of yourself—Most Likely to Rule the World."

I wince the second he finishes, silently cursing Lennon for not thinking before he cracks a joke. I sneak another look at Des. It's not good. His chiseled jaw churns into cement. His dark eyes turn deathly black. I can only imagine the sickness coating his gut at the prospect of returning home and seeing his lost love, Sadie. Facing her as a shadow of the man everyone expected him to be.

He pushes off the wall and shoves past Jake. "Doesn't matter. Nothing changes. My life is my life. I'm Daniel Baker, not Desmond Bower, and I don't give a shit. I'm not taking my old name back."

He glares at us, like we've made him this distorted version of himself, then he storms out, slamming the door behind him so hard the Invisible Man rattles.

Lennon scratches his beard. "That went well."

"I really thought he'd be relieved." Jake cracks his neck, then his knuckles.

The move reminds me of Delilah cracking her knuckles when she's stressed, and my mind is back on our flight, hearing her wind chime voice, seeing her in the flesh . . . then watching her run away from me. I blink hard, grapple to focus on the issue at hand: Desmond. Another punch to his gut.

Jake rubs his eyes. "I don't know how to help him."

"You do all you can," Mom says gently. "He just needs time to adjust."

"Exactly," Cal says. "Once he blows off steam and gets his head around it all, he'll come back."

Instead of adding my two cents to our pathetic collection cup scrawled with the words *bullshit lies we tell ourselves*, I shove on my boots and rush outside. I'm tired of giving Desmond time or space or whatever everyone thinks he needs. If he was messed up before, he'll be flirting with rock bottom now.

I jog into the parking lot, scan the cars, and find his decrepit ride. In high school, Desmond was voted Most Likely to Drink a Fifth of Vodka without Puking and Most Likely to Drive a Porsche. While he upheld the former prediction, instead of a Porsche, he drives a Camaro of the noncool, gasping-its-last-breaths variety in shades of banana peel and rust. He's sitting behind the wheel, staring at nothing.

I walk over and knock on his window. He jumps and swears. Doesn't spare me a glance, just puts his key in the ignition and turns it. His banana-mobile coughs to life.

I bang harder on his window, relentless pounding he can't ignore.

His car continues assaulting the ozone layer, but he rolls down his window. "What?"

"You can't leave. We need you."

He turns his face toward me, and I nearly stumble back from the self-loathing shining from his dark eyes. If I drew him, he'd be a villain who chews on his own fear and pain, then breathes that noxious gas into the world, razing every happy memory, person, and place he ever loved. "No one needs me," he says, flat.

"I need your dating advice just as much as I did when I was gawky and useless with girls." Except the only woman I want to date is engaged to some jerk. "Lennon needs someone to be the butt of his bad jokes. Jake needs to know he didn't run our train off the track. Callahan's probably rehearsing the right thing to say when he sees you again, one of his feel-good pick-me-ups. You know he lives for those moments. And Mom needs all of us, Des. She needs to know you're okay, or she won't be okay."

Desmond aims his self-loathing at his steering wheel and twists his hands around the rim. "Being around Mom won't bring her peace. I'm just a reminder of the asshole who ruined her life."

It's true. While we all look similar, with varying shades of brown hair, Desmond, with his thick eyelashes and darker eyes, resembles our father most. They also share a not-so-fun short fuse.

"What about the girl you once loved?" I say, trying to ignore the twinge in my gut at the thought of Delilah. "You had five years with Sadie. *Five years.* How can you pretend this news isn't game changing? You have to look for her, find out if there's still a chance."

He gnashes his teeth so hard I hear them scrape. "Sadie left Windfall. Within a year of my disappearance, she was gone. I have no clue where she is, and if you haven't noticed, I'm a drink slinger, not a defense attorney. A different name doesn't change those facts or that she's probably with someone else. Every time I sleep with a woman, I feel alive for a minute, then I feel sick. None of them are her, so I try again and again, but none of them are *her*. So if you think I'll ever go back to Sadie, to wherever the hell she moved, and let her see what I've become, just to spiral harder afterward, you're more screwed up than I am."

He puts his car in drive and peels off. Well, not quite peels. His rusted banana-mobile coughs and farts its way to the road, leaving me sucking on Desmond's supervillain-noxious fumes.

Lennon appears beside me and watches Des's car disappear. "I shouldn't have made the man-bun joke."

"No, but he would've wound up furious anyway."

We both sigh.

"At least your life's looking up," he says, nudging my arm. "You're not responsible for our murders, and you're finally free to contact Delilah."

"Delilah's engaged," I say thickly.

"Is she, though?"

I flinch. Lennon knows I don't joke about Delilah. "Do you not remember seeing her on our flight? Her engagement ring?"

"What I remember is hearing that her fiancé isn't worthy of her. If I were a betting man, I'd guess she gave him the boot."

It's possible. Delilah said theirs was a whirlwind romance. The excitement and newness might have snowballed into a proposal before she realized how wrong they were for each other. But what if my disappearance crushed her spirit? What if she's not strong enough to do what she should? Her men-always-treat-me-like-shit retort from the airplane has contributed to my sleeplessness since our flight.

Frustrated, I drag my hand through my hair. "She might still be with him. She doesn't list personal information on social media, and his account is private."

"Sure, but it's pretty clear she should ditch the guy, and you two were more than a couple, E. You were best friends. Seems to me she needs you in her life now more than ever. Also . . ." He grins at me. "I just called you E."

"Yes, *Lennon*." I mirror his grin, overwhelmed I get to use his real name. "I heard that, *Lennon*. I also remember hearing you tell me to get over Delilah this morning."

He swats at the air. "That was when I didn't want to be decapitated by crazed drug lords. My new vote is for you to return to Windfall. Quit moping around our place and win back your girl."

A brilliant idea, but Lennon never reads the fine print. "Did you miss the part where Jake said we still can't tell anyone about the cartel and witness protection? I may have blurted the truth to Delilah, but no one else there knows the story. I'd have to lie to everyone in town."

Including the friends I left behind, who for sure hate me.

While I was the artsy weirdo in school who often sat alone, absorbed in my drawing, I wasn't a total outcast. Ricky Sellers and his infamous garage band, the Tweeds, often asked me to video their rehearsals and make flyers for their gigs. The group of us also regularly hung out in his basement, where I had my first taste of weed (a.k.a. the night I was convinced we were surrounded by a SWAT team and my dry tongue was turning to dust).

Seeing Ricky again would be tough, but Avett Lewis was my closest friend a decade ago. The last time we hung out, a week before my disappearance, we stole the school's woodchuck mascot. He attached catlike whiskers with pipe cleaners. I added cat ears with Mom's crafting supplies, both of us cracking up the whole time. We tied it to the field's goalpost for the football team to find in the morning. The note pinned to the mascot's chest read, *Pussies*.

Then I vanished on him without a word.

I massage my temples. "Returning there wouldn't be easy."

"I didn't say anything about easy." Lennon picks a stray thread off of his plaid shirt and tucks it in his jeans pocket. He has a staunch no-litter policy. "I said your former best friend needs you. Isn't that reason enough to face Windfall's wrath?"

"She ran away from me at the airport."

"I think we can agree she was slightly shocked."

More than slightly, and he's right. Delilah and I *were* best friends. Before I disappeared, I was there for her on her worst days, offering her unconditional support, lifting her up with my unending supply of immature jokes. If she kicked preppy Hugo to the curb, she'll need a dose of my obnoxious humor. If she's still with him, she'll need someone to help her see how wrong he is for her, which means "easy" doesn't factor into this choice. I'm apparently no longer in hiding. I only need a computer, a sketchbook, and my creativity to work. Driving from Houston to Windfall is no hardship when the only place I want to be is wherever Delilah is, which means my old hometown will soon have a population increase of one.

I pound Lennon's back. "You're once again my favorite brother."

"You'll be mine when you move out and leave me your Bose speakers. But there is the family issue. If we can't tell anyone yet, they won't support this choice. There might be stipulations."

Yeah, no. I'm done with stipulations—being told who I am, where to live, what to do. If the cartel's no longer a threat, I'm no longer under anyone's control. "If it comes to that, they can't know I'm going to Windfall. I'll have to lie about where I am."

"Consider me your wingman."

We bump fists and head upstairs.

Back in our apartment, the circle of conversation has shrunk. Captain Jake and Compassionate Cal are still on our couch. Mom has taken my spot on the end table, her hands resting on her knees as she speaks quietly to them.

When I close the door, her head whips my way. "How is he?"

"Not good," I say, unable to sugarcoat the truth. "I predict a bender and thorough disappearance. Might not see Des for a while."

She passes her hand over her mouth, probably to hide the trembling. Jake shakes his head, muttering under his breath. Cal looks sad.

Lennon shoves onto the couch, jostling our brothers. "Maybe his next tattoo will say 'I Love My Mom,' but *love* will be spelled l-u-v-e."

Mom's muffled laugh slips through her fingers. Cal and Jake roll their eyes. I sit on the floor and face my family, pleased with Lennon's diffusing of the Post-Desmond Tension. Still, the rocks in my heart shift and grind. I hate leaving Des like that, and I hate possibly having to lie to my family.

I focus on Mom. "What happens from here?"

"They need to make sure there are no lingering Becerra supporters who might lash out at us with some kind of final revenge. And if you decide to leave the program, paperwork will need to be filed. It'll take time to get identification with your old name."

"The US Marshals move like a sloth colony," I say, struggling to control my aggravation. "That kind of paperwork could take weeks."

"More like months," Jake says.

Exactly why I have to lie. There's only one scenario in my future, and it leads me straight to Delilah's cute shop, Sugar and Sips.

Rolling full steam ahead with my plan, I take a calming breath. "It's fine. I can wait to go back to Windfall. I mean, it's already been ten years. What's another few months?"

Jake squints at me like I'm one of those abstract 3D posters, where if he stares long and hard enough, my true intentions will be revealed. "You can't go back yet."

"I heard Mom the first time."

"Seriously, you can't."

"That's times three, and it's just as clear."

I stand and stretch, inching away, attempting to dodge more questions, but Mom follows me to the kitchen.

"I know this isn't easy for you," she says, leaning into the counter. "Thanks for taking it in stride."

Guilt over lying rises, but Delilah is worth the fib. "I'm fine waiting to go back. I have work to do for my publisher. It's best if I hunker down for a while and focus."

"A new project?"

"A prequel to Sathya's series. We're on a deadline, and I need sketches for the whole thing done in a few months. I'll probably go work with her at her family's ranch. Use the time to get my head on straight, then figure out how to go back to Windfall and not scare the daylights out of Delilah by appearing out of thin air."

Delilah has already had the daylights scared out of her by yours truly, but the rest isn't a complete lie. I do have a deadline. Unfortunately, my writing partner, Sathya, isn't at her family's ranch. She's MIA. I have half her script for her prequel to our bestselling Gates of Ember series. It's been a killer few years of huge sales and rabid fans, mostly due to Sathya's vivid world building: a reimagined underworld with the haves and have-nots of purgatory, deception, unions, spies, workers, horned defenders fighting the spear-tailed demons who feed off their fear. The prequel was our publisher's suggestion. A way to milk more money from the successful graphic novels.

Sathya was on board. She wrote the first half of the script. Now she's off the grid, vanished without communication, which isn't abnormal. Unlike Desmond, she doesn't resurface with infected piercings and horrible tattoos. She returns with fantastically written pages. My agent is praying she returns sooner rather than later, with the remaining panels for the graphic novel outlined. My fateful trip to New York was a way to appease the publisher, let them know half of our production team is on track and on time. I've already knocked out the illustrations I can with the material I have, and I'll have a ton of work to do when Sathya resurfaces.

Until then, I have an abundance of free time, otherwise known as beg-Delilah-to-be-my-best-friend-and-hopefully-my-lover-again time.

"Work will be a great distraction," Mom says. "The time will fly."

"It will." Because I'll be in Windfall wooing the love of my life. "It would be awesome if we all move back eventually."

Her mood dims. "A lot happened there, and a lot of time has passed. Returning to a place with that many memories can hurt more than it heals. I'm not sure I want to go back."

Her warning takes a bite out of my optimism.

There are no guarantees where Delilah is concerned. Our chemistry might have fizzled. Our old scars might be as infected as Desmond's eyebrow ring, too damaged to heal. Delilah might be so upset about her (hopefully *ex*) fiancé she doesn't give me a chance. I'll also have to face Ricky and Avett and their animosity for vanishing on them too. But I can't shake the feeling that Delilah was on my flight for a reason.

So yeah. As soon as possible, I'm heading to Windfall and Delilah's shop, Sugar and Sips. Earning her trust won't be easy, but I'm up for the challenge. I was *built* to love Delilah Moon. Already, I start a mental list of ways to prove my faith, love, and loyalty to her—Fifty Ways to Win Back Delilah—beginning with my first three winners:

1. Be consistent so she learns to trust me.
2. Convince Delilah to believe my unbelievable WITSEC story.
3. Remind Delilah how well I know her by brewing her favorite blueberry tea.

Life's about to learn who's back in control.

# SEVEN

You know that special sensation when you revisit a place from your childhood or teen years, and nostalgia trickles through you like a sip of hot chocolate on a cold day? I experience none of that cozy delight. The second my truck passes the Windfall WELCOME TO PARADISE road sign, I sink lower in my driver's seat.

I'm a big guy. Not as jacked up as Cal or Jake or Desmond, who hit the gym to work out a portion of their angst. I run long and hard instead, letting the pounding of my feet drown the relentless pounding of my thoughts. While I'm not the beefiest Bower boy, I'm the tallest, and I tell you, hiding my six-foot-four frame while driving is no easy task. I'm slouched so low my knees are jammed against my truck's dash, my shoulders are hiked toward my ears, and the steering wheel is cutting off airflow to my lungs. Anxiety rising, I call Lennon.

"Miss me already?" he says after one ring.

"Tell me again this plan will work."

"This plan will work."

So easy for him to predict from the comfort of his armchair. "If someone recognizes me, word will spread that I'm back, and I might get accosted in Delilah's shop. Getting reamed out in front of her won't do me any favors."

"Maybe the gossip hounds aren't as voracious as they used to be."

"Do you not remember this town *at all*?"

Windfall isn't just the place where I met and fell in love with Delilah Moon. Aside from the farms and forests surrounding the area and the pretty multicolored houses brightening the historic downtown core, this is a town built on gossip, held together by back-fence whispers and did-you-hear-that-oh-my-God-I-swear-it's-true hearsay.

Honestly, the rumor mill in Windfall is *legendary*.

The time I cheated on my grade-five math test—because *math*—I got off the school bus thirty minutes later, thinking I pulled off the crime of the century. (An achievement Dad surpassed with zeal.) One step down our country road, my mother was there with her you-puked-on-my-azaleas face. Apparently, Lexi Davies saw me reading the answers I'd written on my hand, and she told Abby Jiang who told Zara White who told Taylor Hilroy who told her mother, who did quilting with mine, that I cheated. I had to clean the second-floor bathroom for four weeks. Five boys used the one shared toilet, and Desmond, who has lactose intolerance, insisted on eating grilled cheese regularly that month, the fucker. I still have PTSD.

That's why I'm driving with my eyes barely above my steering wheel, my tall body painfully scrunched. Word gets around this town faster than wildfire on a gusty day, and I need to talk to Delilah without angry townsfolk bursting into her shop with pitchforks.

"You should've come too," I tell Lennon. "I need a decoy to draw attention away from me."

"Um." He laughs haltingly. "Hard no. This is your thing. *Your* mission. I'm never going back to Windfall."

I park on Third Street, a residential road *away* from prying eyes, and frown at Lennon's comment. "You don't want to come back?" I ask, confused.

"No point," he says quickly. "My business is here, and Windfall's in the past." His octave rises, and I swear to God if I could see him, his eyelid would be twitching like it does when he lies to me.

"But you always say Windfall's the best town in the world. You love the hiking trails and town festivals. You complain about how hot Houston gets, and if you moved your business here, you probably wouldn't struggle so much making ends meet. The summer influx of second-home owners would eat up what you do."

"Whatever. I don't know what I said before. Just don't want to move again, asswad."

Hello, defensiveness. Lennon's so full of shit about his reasons for not returning to Windfall that our old septic tank would be jealous of him. If I had to bet, there's someone here he's nervous about seeing again, and there's no ex I know about.

Am I curious? Absolutely.

Do I have time to drive back to Houston and CSI his room for clues? Not even a little.

"I'm still worried," I say. "Showing up like this will be hard on Delilah. Maybe I should've called first. Given her a heads-up." It's been three weeks since I've seen her. Her anger and shock might have grown, not lessened.

"Nope. Calling would only give her the chance to tell you to fuck off. Shock and awe is the better tactic. *Ooh-rah,*" he adds, like he's in the marines.

I'm not sure why I rely on Lennon for advice on women. Goes to show how desperate I am. "I'll head to her shop before I find the apartment I rented. Not give myself a chance to chicken out."

"That's the spirit. I've got the family covered. They don't suspect a thing."

Duping them was the easy part.

We hang up, and I take a deep breath. *It's now or never.* I grab my satchel with my laptop inside, shove my sunglasses on my face, and walk toward Main Street.

I keep my head down as I walk. It may be the start of fall, a typical early-September day in Windfall, the perfect balance of warm and refreshing, but my steps are quick and stiff. If Delilah's best friend, Maggie, sees me, I'm sure she'll happily stick my face in Big Joe's grain grinder. Delilah's mother will probably help her hide my body. Then there's Mom's quilting crew and Cal's friends and Lennon's friends and Jake's friends and Desmond's friends, as well as Ricky and Avett. Yeah, a lot of people will have angry or shocked or confused questions.

If I do get accosted in Delilah's shop, I have my pat answers prepared.

My first winner is: *It's complicated.*

Followed by the brilliant: *There was a family emergency I can't talk about yet.*

Genius, right?

Instead of soaking in the quaint charm of this town I've missed, I keep my head down and hurry to Delilah's shop, hoping to avoid detection.

My pulse picks up as I near the small seating area outside Sugar and Sips. By the time I'm at the front door, my short breaths practically fog up the glass. I'm not wearing a gray T-shirt today. Black was the only call, in case my nerves get the best of me again. I wipe my damp palms on my jeans and remove my sunglasses. A mental kick in the butt later, I push inside.

The bell above me jingles. A coffee machine whirs. It smells like espresso and cinnamon and chocolate. My nervous stomach settles, but my focus jumps over every detail.

Delilah's all around me, in the welcoming pastel-colored decor, the hipster coffeehouse music Lennon would love, the pretty white tables, and the cushy yellow sofa chairs against the far wall. The succulents in the little clear vases at the center of each table are so Delilah. She loved succulents. Said they were resilient and badass, able to grow under difficult circumstances. Blackboards line the wall behind the counter, decorated with drawn flowers and the menu of the day, written in Delilah's looping script.

A punch of pride hits me at all she's accomplished, even though this job path surprises me. Delilah loved helping her mom bake when we were growing up, but it was just for fun. She'd turn up at my door with blueberry muffins or lemon scones or my favorite snack bars packed with nuts, dried fruit, chocolate, raisins, coconut, and puffed rice. I called them kitchen-sink bars, because they had everything in them but the kitchen sink. As much as she enjoyed baking, she never talked about it as a career, opening her own place. The last I knew of Delilah's hopes and dreams, she planned to run a day care or teach kindergarten. Another reminder a lot of time has passed and many things have changed.

Several tables are occupied with people like me, laptop carriers who like to work in a happy place that smells like Candy Land got taken over by Juan Valdez. I don't see Avett or anyone I recognize, but I still don't go to the counter. I'm so proud and amazed at what Delilah created that I'm frozen in place.

Then I hear Delilah's this-can't-be-happening oh my God.

She's mirroring my frozen pose, looking stunning and shocked and entrepreneurial with her clipboard and a Sugar and Sips apron over her T-shirt. Abruptly, she swivels and careens through the swinging doors that must lead to the kitchen.

Not the best welcome, but it could have been worse. In that split second before she bolted, I noticed (a.k.a. frantically analyzed) her ring finger, and guess what? Zero engagement ring.

I try to contain my relieved "Yes" and school my features. Of course Delilah had the strength to tell that loser where to shove his ring. Of course she realized she deserves to be treated like the amazing woman she is.

Assuming she'll come out again, I go to the counter and order a black coffee. Nothing fancy for me. Just dark and strong and robust. I peruse the sweets in the display case and do a double take. There, second row from the bottom, snuggling between the lemon ginger bars and the chocolate salted-caramel bars, are the kitchen-sink bars.

"Add a kitchen-sink bar," I tell the young man ringing up my order. The fact that Delilah kept the name I coined for her treat pleases me more than it should.

When my order's up, I collect my goods and head to a vacant table on the quieter side of the store. Assuming Delilah comes back out, I'd like some privacy for our inevitable confrontation. I'm not running to a connecting flight this time. She can't speed walk away from me, because she owns this adorable shop. Hanging around here also helps me mobilize number one on my Win Back Delilah list: be consistent so she learns to trust me. I'll show up here every day until she realizes I'm not leaving town and decides it's okay to sit and talk with me.

I take out my laptop and set up. Not because I'll be getting work done today. Concentrating while I wait for Delilah to gather the courage to come back out here is akin to concentrating while the president announces our first alien invasion. Instead I scroll through social media, looking at cute animal posts. Honestly, this one of the dog playing with the squirrel and the squirrel jumping on the dog's nose is adorable. I take a bite of the kitchen-sink bar while I scroll. The chewy goodness is so sweet and nostalgic I have to close my eyes and moan.

"Why are you here?" Delilah's beside my table, arms crossed, clipboard gone. She still looks shocked and angry and stunning, all that hair of hers piled up on her head, and . . .

Her ring finger's no longer bare.

There's a diamond on it, but it's not the diamond I saw the day of our flight. That one was a run-of-the-mill round-cut diamond. Pretty but unoriginal. This one's inlaid into the band and is a bit large on her. If I were a betting man, I'd say Delilah borrowed someone else's ring in the last few minutes so she could pretend to still be engaged.

Interesting.

"I'm here for coffee and this delicious bar and a quiet table where I can work," I say, incredibly pleased with this turn of events. Lying means feelings. Feelings mean anger, fear, worry, or nerves. Whatever the motivation, Delilah's in heart-protection mode, which indicates her heart is vulnerable to me.

She bounces her knee. "You're not working. Sandra behind you already told me you're doing nothing but looking at animal videos."

I swivel to see this Sandra character. She has pale skin, a pointy nose, and an eighties perm, and she isn't even pretending she's not watching me. Returning to face Delilah, I say, "Actually, I am working." Sort of. "Animals inspire my art. This is research. Just treat me like any other customer."

"Most customers," she says icily, "don't disappear from my life for ten years, then concoct ridiculous lies when they see me again, proving they're immature and spineless and a waste of my time."

Ouch. Not gonna lie. That hurts. But I can take the hits. I'll be Delilah's punching bag, if that's what she needs, but there will be no further untruths from me. She's had enough lies to last ten lifetimes. "Every word of that story was true, and the cartel who had a hit on us was recently wiped out by a rival group. So, to reiterate, I've been in witness protection for ten years and spent every minute of that time missing you, which is why the first thing I did with my newfound freedom is come here."

She sucks in a tiny breath and bites her plump bottom lip. Then she glares at me. "You seriously expect me to believe your dad was laundering money for some *cartel guys* and all this time you've been in hiding and that's why you vanished on me without a word?"

"Yes."

"*Yes.*" Her body's brimming with sarcasm.

"Glad we're on the same page, but if there's any doubt, search the Becerra cartel. If you haven't seen it on the news already, they were gunned down in a bloody massacre two weeks ago. Most articles mention my dad's involvement without using his name. And I don't know if you told anyone about my witness protection lockdown, but things are still being sorted. If you could continue *not* telling anyone, it would be appreciated."

Her eyes thin into calculating slits, her lips mimicking the suspicious line. She stares at me so long I become extra thankful I went with the black sweat-hiding T-shirt. "I don't know what you're up to, *Edgar*, but I'm busy with work and . . . planning my wedding. Go spread your lies somewhere else."

Wedding, my ass. But the Edgar dig falls like a stone in my gut. "I didn't realize sitting in here quietly would distract you so much."

"You don't distract me."

Oh, now this is fun. Delilah hates when I call her on her bullshit. So much so she invariably argues herself into a corner. "You just said I distract you."

"No, I didn't."

"Are you sure? I mean, you seem pretty fixated on me. You've basically hired a private eye to track my every move." I hook my thumb toward that Sandra character.

Delilah rolls her eyes. "Sandra's a retired busybody."

"Righto," I say in an overly dramatic English accent.

This was a thing Delilah and I used to do. We both played bit parts in our high school's rendition of *Oliver!* Not by choice. A couple of kids dropped out. Mom was friends with the drama teacher and forcefully suggested we fill in. Although we were told we didn't have to speak with English accents, Delilah was determined to breathe life into her one and only line. When it was her turn to scowl and say, "This soup is disgusting. I feel like throwing up," she sounded like a cross between a coked-up pirate and a congested Australian.

My favorite congested Australian fights a lip twitch, either from nostalgia, remembering how ridiculous we were during that time, talking in awful English accents on our walks home from school, or from annoyance with present-day me. I can't be sure which.

Unwilling to let the moment pass, I say, "Delilah, will you please sit down and talk to me?"

She eyes the free seat at my table, a slight quiver to her chin. "Why?"

I could tell her again how sorry I am, spew another rendition of my father's impossible-to-believe money-laundering story, that I never would have left her in a million years if the choice had been mine, in the hopes she finally believes me. I could tell her she's more beautiful than I remember and that looking at her bee-stung lips and slightly sloped nose makes my chest feel like a hot-air balloon again, too big, too full, so pure and bright I'm not sure how to breathe.

There are a million things I could say to Delilah, but I settle on the simplest reason as to why I'm here, asking for a moment of her time. "I miss you," I say quietly.

Glassiness sheens her eyes.

"If you really want me to leave," I continue, "I will. But I miss having you in my life. I'm hoping a small part of you misses me too."

She opens her mouth, closes it. I swear she looks about to cave and sit, then she says, "Stay here if you want, just stay out of my way."

*Thank fucking God.* "I think I will. Stay here and work, that is. Since I don't distract you, Delilah Mars."

She fumes at me, likely for using her old nickname, her mass of knotted hair sure to catch fire from the fury burning in her face. I don't know why I'm pushing her. Antagonizing Delilah isn't part of my Win Back Delilah plan. I've just missed our jousting banter so much, egging her on, watching the red rise to her cheeks, offsetting the blue in her eyes.

"If you call me Mars again"—she leans closer, her voice dropping in volume but increasing in venom—"I will get my shotgun from the back and use your nuts for skeet shooting practice."

I mentally review my Fifty Ways to Win Back Delilah list, debate crossing off "call Delilah by the nickname she hated but secretly loved," but she didn't tell me to get lost when she had the chance. One day soon, she'll appreciate our history, even that silly nickname.

Instead of lying and agreeing to her demand, I say, "Have a lovely day, Delilah Uranus."

"Oh my God, you're the—" That fire burns to the tips of her ears. "Nothing. You're nothing, and I don't care what you call me. Enjoy your coffee, *Edgar*."

She marches off, her lush hips swaying, like she knows each angry swivel hits me in the dick.

Yeah, I'll be working here every day for the next however long it takes for her to sit and talk to me like the friends we once were. She gave me permission. There's literally nowhere else in the galaxy I'd rather be. Pleased our initial confrontation is out of the way, I take another bite of my kitchen-sink bar and get lost in the memories it conjures.

"I cannot believe you're here."

I look up, surprised it took Maggie Edelstein this long to turn up. Almost one whole hour. Windfall's rumor mill must have a kink in it. "I'm here," I agree.

"You need to leave," she says, her voice as loud as ever.

All the patrons glance our way, and Delilah's cute blue sneakers peek out from behind the swinging doors at the back. She's for sure eavesdropping. With our first conversation successfully conquered, I'm less stressed about her witnessing this town hating on me.

"Delilah already said I could stay," I tell Maggie. "And I have no urge to vacate this seat. The back support on these chairs is exceptional."

"Well, *I* didn't say you could stay. You shouldn't be here or anywhere near this town."

I smile up at Maggie's face, amazed at how red she still is. Red hair, red freckles, red-tinged fair skin the shade of

I-am-a-vengeful-woman-who-will-mess-you-up. Her straight hair is shorter, hitting her shoulders, but she's as fiery as ever. "Are you mayor of Windfall?" I ask. "Did you pass a law banning me from my former hometown?"

"Are you delusional? Do you know the wreckage you left in your wake? Do you know what you did to that amazing woman? Do you know—" She slams her mouth shut, looking ready to launch her fist into my nose.

For the first time since I sat down, apprehension lurches in my gut. Did I ruin Delilah after all? Steal the fire from the girl who yelled at me to get off her land? And here I am, forcing her to face that pain all over again.

Maggie yells at me once more, marches away, pauses, then marches back. This time her reddening face has a different quality to it I can't pinpoint. "Is Lennon coming back too?"

"Why do you care what Lennon's doing?" As far as I know, Maggie and Lennon didn't hang out when we were teens. He rolled with the hippie crowd back then. She was one of the popular girls who walked through school like she owned it. Maybe Maggie is why he didn't want to return to Windfall, even though he loves and misses it.

"I don't care about Lennon," she says haltingly. "It was just a question." She makes a huffy noise and resumes her angry stomp to the swinging doors at the back.

I have no brain space to think about Maggie and Lennon. The smells of coffee and cinnamon turn rancid. Heat crawls up my neck. Hearing how badly Delilah actually suffered after I left catches in my throat like a string of rusty barbs.

Maybe I *should* go. Leave the past in the past. Finally move on with my life, even if that life doesn't contain Delilah. But, like Lennon said, we were more than a couple before I left. We were each other's unconditional support. I'm 99 percent sure she broke up with her fiancé. Even if my list doesn't lead to us rekindling our romance, I want to be Delilah's best friend again. Support her during this tough time. Make her laugh and forget her worries like I used to. I just hope this choice to stay doesn't make the next ten years of my life harder than the last.

# EIGHT

Day two in Windfall starts off low key. I've settled into my apartment, which came furnished and decorated with an alarming amount of pink. The fabric headboard on the bed is covered in light-pink and fuchsia flowers. The plastic shower curtain in the bathroom is an explosion of pink butterflies, and the walls are painted a softer dusty mauve. Even the sofa is a brighter magenta, which matches the kitchen counters and cabinets. I've progressed from a beige life to one draped in shades of Pepto-Bismol, but the location means I'm a short walk from Delilah's shop.

Unlike yesterday's head-down, no-eye-contact rush through town, today I stop and soak in this quaint haven I've missed. Plump pumpkins and fall flowers burst from antique wooden pushcarts, punctuating the seating areas on the wide cobblestone sidewalks. Even though the annual Scarecrow Scavenger Hunt isn't held until mid-October, elaborately dressed and sewed scarecrows are already affixed to the old-fashioned lampposts.

A man's walking his something-doodle beside the bench where I scratched in the words *I love Delilah Mars who is from Uranus*. We won't discuss how mad she was about that. Two women with strollers are talking and laughing by the mermaid fountain Jake used to piss in when he was drunk. The large oak in the center of the square's grassy park hasn't changed. Neither has Windfall's breathtaking beauty and picture-book charm. It's one of those towns that fills social media with tags like #NoFilter #CutestTownEver #LoveLoveLove #ParadiseFound.

But some upsetting things are different.

Haddie's Diner should be on the corner of this block. My ninth-best day happened there, tasting Delilah and peach ice cream when we shared our first kiss. A few other stores are unrecognizable as well. More than a few, actually. Dad had his hand in some of those missing shops, used them to launder cartel money. Maybe his irrevocable actions affected those small business owners. Maybe the books he was fudging fell apart when we disappeared. I'm uneducated on the minutiae of money laundering, aside from the fact that it ruins lives. His actions might have destroyed other local families too.

Shaking off that unpleasantness, I let the town's fall decor mellow me as I walk toward my favorite coffee shop. When I enter, Delilah's nowhere to be seen *yet*. But her private eye, Sandra, is at a table. She scrutinizes me, as do a few other patrons. I don't dip my head and try to hide my face. I order my coffee and pastry and set up camp. It's only a matter of time before Delilah breezes through here to talk to customers and her staff. I plan to wait her out and actually work today.

Since my writing partner, Sathya, is still MIA, I don't have panels to illustrate. Instead of watching more animal clips so pointy-nosed Sandra can narc on me, I pull out my sketchbook and my favorite Blackwing Palomino pencils, then relax as I focus on the page.

I often draw animal-inspired characters because animals are predictable and loyal and are generally better than people. Working with Sathya on Gates of Ember pushed my skills further, forcing me to expand beyond my turtle men and snow leopard women—the early sketches she saw when my local comic book store hosted a mini art show. I hadn't planned to enter my work for that exhibition. Cal was the one who saw the ad for the event and pushed me to draw and submit. The rest is history, as they say. Sathya and I started meeting, sharing ideas, planting seeds for Gates of Ember—the series she'd write and I'd illustrate.

I haven't worked on anything but Gates in years. These days, most of my work is digitally based. For some reason today, I have the urge to draw.

My pencil moves over the page, long legs taking shape, then sensual shoulders, the rounded curves of a woman's breasts, majestic wings, a gloriously ornate winged headpiece. I spend time on the feathers, sketching each barb flowing from its central rachis, tightly layered in some sections, sparse in others, adding texture, soft or coarse, depending on their positions. By the time I've drawn hypnotizing eyes and a full mouth, I realize what I've done.

This is Delilah as my albatross. My forever mate. Symbolism that shuttles me back to the number one day of my Top Ten Best Days.

Oddly, my best day started with a fight. While Desmond isn't what I'd call a male role model these days, back then, he had the confidence and lady moves I lacked. If I wanted manly cologne for my planned romantic night of nights with Delilah, I was stealing it from him.

Except I got caught.

"Get out of my stuff." Desmond was home from college, a weekend visit to see Sadie. He flicked my ear. "No cologne can mask your smell of desperation."

"Fuck you."

"If you want to fight, let Jake record me destroying you." He blocked the doorway with his big body. "That shit will kill it on YouTube."

"Remind me again how a Neanderthal like you got into law school?" He curled his lip. "I'm top of my class this year, cockwad."

Where young Delilah and I shared a love of butt insults, Desmond was all about cock slander.

Ignoring my annoying brother, I kept hold of his cologne—Eternity, by Calvin Klein—and tried to dodge him out the door. I was seventeen and scrawny. Des was a twenty-three-year-old football jock.

He caught me easily and launched me onto his bed. Clutching the cologne in a death grip, I bounced once, hard enough to feel something weird and sharp under my shoulder. When I recovered, I stuck my hand under the covers and found a small velvet box.

Desmond was on me in seconds, his knee digging into my ribs, nostrils flaring. "Give it here, cockweasel."

I knew the leverage I'd discovered. The secret Desmond hadn't shared with any of us. I could've used that velvet box as ransom for the coveted cologne. Shoved the box in my pants and told him to go fishing. But I wasn't aggressive like Desmond. I was me, and the feel of that soft box—its implications, the joy it would bring, and the nerves visible under Desmond's posturing—I couldn't reduce that meaningful box to a pawn.

"Sadie's gonna be so happy," I said.

The pressure of Desmond's knee lifted, the nervous flicker in his eye showing a rare hint of vulnerability. "You think?"

"I mean, I don't know why. You're an asshole, but yeah. She'll go nuts."

Desmond gave up holding me down, plopped on the bed, and scrubbed his hand down his face. "I think she'll say yes. Pretty sure, at least. I planned to propose when she was at my place last weekend, but I chickened out. Have no clue why I'm so nervous."

I thought about why I was stealing his cologne—my plan for that night: Delilah and I sharing our first time together, consummating our love, starting something deeper and binding—as I spun the soft box in my hand. "You don't have to worry. She's your albatross."

"If that's an insult, you're gonna eat my fist."

I opened the box, looked at the small diamond ring inside. Simple and tasteful. Perfect for Sadie. "There's some darker symbolism about albatrosses, but they also represent freedom, travel, and elegance. And they mate for life. They preen and rattle and bow, do these silly dances to win their partners' affection. But once they select their mate, that's it. They separate for times but always come back together. As long as they're alive, they're connected."

Des picked at his cuticles, then shoved my shoulder. "Put the cologne back when you're done with it. And if you want to set the mood, use the song 'Pillow Talk,' by Sylvia Robinson. Delilah will love it, and buy her a sweet treat."

Sadie never got her engagement ring. I found it in the trash at our orientation Safesite. Took it out and saved it for Desmond, hoping he'd get to use it one day. I still have it in my these-memories-hurt-me-the-most keepsake box.

Unaware our lives were on a collision course with heartbreak, I took the cologne and used Desmond's advice. Set up our barn with flowers and a blanket and bought the lemon macarons from Haddie's Diner that Delilah said tasted like sugary clouds.

Nervous for our impending night, I knocked on her door, then talked to her mother about their newest breeding program and how beautiful their roses looked. Around Hayley Moon, the ever-present rocks in my heart ground harder. She was sweet and warm and loved her daughter, but the sadness from losing her husband hung on her like the not-very-good quilts Mom made—squares filled with family memories, roughly sewed together, ripping in spots.

Then Delilah was on their stairs, floating down in jean shorts and a yellow tank top covered in tiny blue flowers, the same bright blue as her eyes.

"Hi," I said, mesmerized. My constant state around Delilah. My albatross and former nemesis.

She bounded down the last two stairs and kissed her mom's cheek. "I won't be late."

"Have fun, you two," Hayley Moon called, watching us from the door.

I turned once and waved. Hated the sad shine in Mrs. Moon's eyes, but I couldn't focus on those sharp stones in my heart for long. Not when I had Delilah's hand in mine.

Delilah tugged me along, hugging me from the side as she stuck her face in my neck. "You smell so good."

*Thank you, Calvin Klein, for inventing Eternity.*

Grasshoppers jumped around us, wildflowers and tall grasses tickling our legs. A nearby woodpecker tap-tap-tapped to the beat of my pulse. I stopped partway to the barn and touched the black string hanging around Delilah's neck. "You're wearing the necklace I made you."

Blushing, she dragged her fingers down the simple string to the hanging moon-shaped rock. The week prior, I had spotted the rock at the quarry and thought of Delilah right away. I drilled a hole in it at school and hid it in her locker with a note that said, *A moon for my moon.*

"I'm never going to take it off," she said, tracing the rock's curve.

"You've only had it a week. I'm sure you'll get tired of it."

She flattened her hand over the gift. "I'm sure I'll be buried with it."

God, what that girl did to me. "You get more beautiful every day."

"You're a romantic fool, Edgar Eugene Bower."

"A fool for you. But call me that name again, and I'll shove you in a manure patch."

She tilted up her chin, thick curls spilling across her back. "Edgar Eugene Bower," she crowed, a huge grin lighting her face.

"Now you've done it." I grabbed her by the waist, hauled her over my shoulder. "Hope these clothes wash well."

"Put me down, E. Don't be a turd."

She could call me whatever names she wanted, as long as she kept teasing me, kept smelling my neck, kept pounding my back, reaching to smack my ass. I carried her to my family's old barn, the dilapidated one at the back of the property no one used, laughing the whole way. But the second I stepped inside, my pulse jumped as fast as the grasshoppers dodging my feet.

I lowered her down slowly, every inch of her rubbing down every inch of me. Unsure how I was lucky enough to have Delilah Moon in my arms, I brushed her hair from her face. "We don't have to do this tonight. Not if you don't want. We can wait."

We'd talked about having sex, had planned that evening together. Still, it felt big. A signal of change between us.

Delilah pushed her hands through my Justin Bieber hair and said, "Do you love me?"

"What kind of question is that?" I held her closer, brushed our noses together. Seriously. We were that cute. "You're my muse. My artistic inspiration, even when you drive me nuts. I love you times infinity, Delilah Mars."

"I hate when you call me that."

"You prefer Delilah Uranus?"

"You're such a goof."

"A goof who loves you."

She hummed a flirty tune. "And will you, Goof McGee, be here for me tomorrow? Meet me at the chicken coop, toss grass at my face, and annoy me while I collect eggs? Be the same sweet idiot who did that awful job gluing together my horse figurine?"

"I'll annoy you tomorrow"—I pressed small kisses to her eyelids—"and the next day"—more kisses to her cheeks—"and the next day, and every one after that. There's no getting rid of me."

Let's hit pause, shall we? Put a pin in that promise. The super important one where I vowed to be there for the girl I adored, not love and leave her and ruin her life. It's a pretty vital tidbit, seeing as I'm now sitting in her shop, wondering if she'll decide to talk to me or to slip arsenic into my food.

Sadly, we didn't have a crystal ball that night, and Delilah gazed at me through teenage love goggles, brimming with undying trust, and said, "Then yes. I want to have sex with you tonight."

Even in the face of our mutual love, my confidence suddenly dried as quickly as my tongue on weed. "So yeah." I released her and wiped my dampening palms on my cargo shorts. "I brought a towel. I mean *a blanket*. Not a towel. The soft blanket from the truck that you like? But maybe I should have brought a towel. In case . . . you know."

Blood. I was thinking *blood*, wondering how I'd wash Delilah's virginal blood from the light-gray blanket laid out on the hay. Then I was wondering why the hell I was thinking about blood instead of kissing Delilah and why the hell I was talking about anything related to blood and pain before I took my girlfriend's virginity. But what if I hurt Delilah somehow? What if I got so into things I wasn't gentle and she hated sex and her first experience tainted intimacy for her forever?

"I have treats." I gestured to the lemon macarons beside the bouquet of wildflowers, grappling for a topic change. There were three condoms beside the sweets. I'd driven one town over to buy the small red packets, lest I risk Windfall's rumor mill catching wind of our extracurriculars and blasting them through the town square. "We can eat the macarons now or later, if you want. You know, after the sex."

I actually said that. The Sex.

I'd set out to create the perfect night for Delilah. Cologne, music, smooth seductions where I'd slowly peel off her clothes, getting her so worked up and ready I'd slide into her with one hot push. All I managed to peel off was a layer of my masculinity.

Determined to save myself from myself, I hurried to my quasi-romantic setup, which was becoming more quasi and less romantic by the second. I thumbed through my iPod, found Desmond's suggested song, and put "Pillow Talk" on repeat.

"E." Delilah's voice was close, like she was right behind me. "Why are you so nervous?"

Did I say I lost one layer of masculinity? Make that two.

Defeated, I dropped my head forward. "I just want this to be perfect for you. Tonight should be the best night of your life, and I'm fucking it up."

She wrapped her arms around my waist, resting her head against the center of my back. "You're not fucking up, E. The details don't matter. I don't need a fancy setup and romantic music. All I need is us."

Exhibit A: why Delilah Moon is my ideal woman.

Just like that, I relaxed. Turned around and pulled her down on the blanket with me, tucking one leg over hers. "You're right. I'm being my stupid neurotic self."

"You're being sweet. And neurotic. But that's why I love you."

Groovy beats played from my iPod. The setting sun from outside spilled through the barn slats, softening the light from butter bright to caramel mellow. I tugged her closer. "You love me because I overthink simple moments until I'm a frantic mess?"

"I love you because you care so much. Your heart's so big you worry about the details other people ignore. Makes you a bit high strung at times, but we both deal with each other's shit."

I give you exhibit B.

I stretched out longer, flattened my palm on the soft dip of her belly. "You also love me because of my six-pack, right?"

She snorted. "You don't have a six-pack, babe."

"I have an almost six-pack." In my dreams. The ones where I was a super smooth lover who didn't sometimes get neurotic.

"We'll call it a two-pack, but maybe I should count to be sure." She slid her hand under my shirt, traced my stomach. "I'm having trouble checking. I need a visual display."

"Your wish is my command, Mars."

"Shut it with that name, goof."

I sat up, grabbed my shirt by the back of my neck, and pulled it over my head. Delilah did the same, both our shirts landing in a wrinkled pile, her little blue flowers on top of my faded X-wing fighter. We lay back down, her fingers feathering across my contracting two-pack while I traced the edges of her lace bra, the contours of her hardening nipples. My skin tightened with need, as did my heart. A sharp squeeze that had my throat feeling thick. *Too much.* I suddenly wasn't sure my chest was capable of holding this much *love*.

Swiftly, she rolled on top of me, straddled my hips, and did that rocking thing where she rubbed herself just right, the fly of my cargo shorts pressing against her thick denim, pressure that had her eyelids falling heavy.

Anticipation pulsed through my body, gave my too-full heart another breath-stealing squeeze. Delilah kissed her way down my chest, got her busy hands on my fly, pulled down my shorts and boxers. Took everything off and flung my clothes to the side.

I tensed my thighs, terrified I'd come before she touched me.

She bit her lip. "I love looking at you naked."

Was she trying to murder me? "I'm feeling slightly underdressed. We need to do something about your clothes."

"Oh, this?" She cupped her lace-covered breasts. "Or these?" She placed her hands on the front of her jean shorts and did a little swivel.

I made a garbled grunting sound. Or was that a pathetic whine? Desmond was right. No amount of cologne could hide my desperation.

Getting to her feet, she swayed her hips and proceeded to striptease to "Pillow Talk" because Delilah Moon was the best girl of girls.

Bra, gone.

Jean shorts, dropped.

Her white underwear with the cute little bow, adios.

She grabbed a condom from my pile, but I took it from her, placed it behind me. "Let me touch you first." Make sure this was so good for her.

"Yeah, okay." Trust beamed from her as she lay next to me. She lifted her knee, giving me the access I craved, letting me work her up until she was panting. "Now," she said, sounding as desperate as I felt, gripping my forearm to make me stop.

Right. Yeah. *The Sex.*

I knelt between her legs, fumbled with the condom until she took it from my trembling hands.

She ripped the package with her teeth, held the latex circle in place, and rolled it on. "Like this? Does it feel okay?"

Riding shotgun in Jake's Charger felt okay. Cannonballing into Bear Lake on a scorcher of a day was okay. This? Everything felt enhanced, like I was a superhero with heightened senses, all my nerve endings sparking with the faintest brush. "Yeah, it's good."

She lifted her knees, pulled me closer. I lowered my hips and her eyes flared, then I pushed in, just a bit. Her breath stuttered.

"You okay?" I rasped.

She nodded. "Deeper."

I settled my forearms on either side of her head, making sure I had control. *Don't lose it and pound into her.* I pushed in another bit. She let out a taut moan, lifted her hips, a small move that had fire licking at my spine.

*Don't you fucking lose it.*

"More, E. Deeper. I want all of you."

She had more than all of me. She had the atoms that made up my bones and marrow, the veins that carried my pumping blood, the misfiring synapses fuzzing up my brain—all of me was hers. I eased in farther, couldn't believe how good she felt. This was a full-body buzz from my tense feet to my tingling scalp. Then she grabbed my ass and forced me flush.

She gasped.

I damn near shot my load. "I hurt you. Did I hurt you?"

"Just . . ." She swallowed, adjusted her hips. "It hurts a bit, but it's getting better. Start moving."

She didn't have to ask me twice. My hips were already pulling out, easing forward. Small moves that wouldn't shatter my barely-hanging-on composure. On my next retreat, I leaned down to kiss her, needing her lips, her breath, her tongue, even that messy clack of our teeth. Our tongues twirled in our usual rhythm, the easy slide perfected over the past two years, and I pushed into her harder, erasing all the space between us.

No matter how many times I replay this part of our night, it's hazy. A blurred tangle of groping hands and grinding hips and heat and love and those blue-blue eyes locked on me as she whispered, "I love you, E," a tear slipping down her face.

I was so full of *everything* I didn't know how to separate the hot grip of her body, the hard clench of my heart, the intensity of wanting the moment to last forever. She came first. Thank God she came first, and I wasn't far after, crushing her with my weight as my body shook and my vision blurred.

"Wow," I said into her hair afterward.

"Definitely wow. I wasn't expecting to get off our first time."

"Guess I'm a sex savant."

She laughed, the shaking of her abdomen forcing me from her body. "I got off because it's us, E. Because we're good together."

I dealt with the condom best I could, regretted not bringing a towel. There was blood on the blanket. Just a bit, but I wished I had a damp cloth to clean Delilah, take care of her beautiful body the way she deserved. I lay back down. "Pillow Talk" still crooned around us. I tucked Delilah against me, fed her a lemon macaron, laughing when she licked the crumbs off my chest.

We only used the one condom for one round of the Sex, and I didn't care. As far as I knew, we had a lifetime of sex and stripteases and crumb licking ahead of us.

If I'd known my kiss good night to her would be my last, I might not have called her Mars on her front porch. Or Uranus when she pinched my side. I might have told her again how much I loved her and that she was my albatross. If I'd known I'd get home to strange men and women in my house and my brothers forcing me into a van while I fought and yelled and told them I couldn't leave Delilah, tears spilling down my face, my throat raw from screaming, I'd never have promised her I'd see her the next day at the chicken coop.

# NINE

As per usual, memories have a habit of eviscerating my vital organs. My pencil is hovering over my sketch of Delilah the albatross, trembling with the beauty and pain of our last night together. My heart's beating so fast I have to remind myself that my and Delilah's story isn't over. I'm out of WITSEC. She's lying about being engaged *for a reason*. We're at the crossroads of a new beginning, not hurtling toward another viciously painful end.

But when I glance up from my sketchbook, I have the overwhelming sense that everyone in Sugar and Sips is staring daggers at me.

For example, Mrs. Santos, who used to work at the town variety store and would slip an extra pepperoni stick into my grocery bag, is standing a foot from my table, staring at me like I slashed her tires. I don't know the tween sprawled on the yellow armchair, but he's sending me an award-winning stink eye. The little kid with the braids who's holding her mother's hand? She's sharpened her tiny eyes into mini bayonets.

Some might call me paranoid, but I know dagger eyes when I see them, and I know Windfall. The rumor mill has churned all night and morning. Word of my resurrection and not-so-triumphant return has spread. Assuming Delilah heeded my plea and didn't share my story, as far as anyone in this town knows, my family left out of boredom, and I returned for shits and giggles.

Delilah finally makes an appearance, puttering through her shop, smiling extra wide at everyone who isn't me, stopping to talk to patrons, saying things like "How's Emilia's sprained ankle?" and "I'm so jealous you're reading *Next Year in Havana* for the first time."

She pretends like I'm not in the shop, dipping and diving around the daggers flying my way, but I catch her glancing at me several times. The second she knows she's caught, her eyes dart away.

Needing a distraction, I resume my sketching, but my skin prickles with awareness. When I look up again, she's wiping a nearby table while watching me. Instead of ducking her head this time, her attention lingers. Long enough for my heart to skip a beat. I swear I see softness around all that Sonic blue. Compassion. Like she maybe googled the cartel killings and knows I'm not lying. Then she's bustling, clearing tables, smiling extra wide at everyone else, as though I don't exist. I sigh into my coffee cup.

The front door chimes, announcing another patron. Mrs. Jackson, who used to lead Mom's quilting group, enters and scans the shop. She's a tall Black woman with a plentiful stomach. When she finds me, she approaches with clipped steps. "Where in God's name has your family been for the past ten years?"

On instinct, I clasp my hands on my lap, like I've been called to the principal's office. Mrs. Jackson has one of those voices that demand attention. "It's complicated," I say, my stellar planned reply.

"That nonsense doesn't fly with me. You vanished into thin air, not a word to anyone. Left that poor girl to—" She flattens her lips, gathers her purse close to her body. "I called your mother, but her number was disconnected. I even went onto social media when I don't do social media. I held our quilting sessions every week and listened to everyone's shock and worry, and still not a word from any of you. We thought you were dead, for heaven's sake. So, I'll ask again, where in God's name has your family been?"

With no other option, I fall back on my second planned answer. "There was a family emergency I can't talk about yet."

"Yet you're here, sitting in Delilah's lovely shop, pretending like you never left. What part of you thinks this is okay?"

"I'm sorry you worried," I say gently, unsure how to navigate this minefield. "My mom's fine, though. Still sucks at quilting and misses all of you."

Mrs. Jackson makes a grunting noise and blows out of the café.

I slump on my seat, rub my eyes. The bell chimes again. When I force my eyes open, Avett Lewis is looming over me, his jacked-up arms crossed. My former best friend has a trim beard now, his black hair not as dark as the spite in his eyes. He's bigger than when we'd slingshot beer cans in the quarry and get wasted on vodka and deface stuffed animals. He's Jake and Cal big, like he hits the gym regularly.

He looks like he wants to hit me now. "Where the hell have you been?"

"It's complicated," I say, but the line's getting old fast, and Avett deserves more than a pat answer. Even with the past two weeks to prepare myself, I don't know where to start. "It's great to see you," I say lamely.

He flinches. "We were best friends for eight years, and you dropped off the face of the earth. Didn't call, nothing. And all you can say is 'It's complicated'? Jesus. You left Delilah and—" He clacks his teeth together. "What you did was beyond messed up."

More insinuation that I destroyed Delilah, reiterations of Maggie's claims yesterday, and I'm no longer deflating in my seat. I've mutated into a cockroach-man, an invasive insect who deserves to be squashed. Stepped on. Sprayed with venomous hate. "There was a family emergency I can't talk about yet," I say, weaker this time. "But I missed you and wanted to call. Should've called when I got here, I just . . ." Didn't. I didn't, because I was a coward and could only deal with one major confrontation at a time, namely Delilah.

He gives me another angry grunt, shakes his head, then marches out of the shop.

Heat prickles my neck. Anxiety does the breaststroke through my stomach. That flashback to my Number One Best Day did me no favors. When your best day merges with your worst, bad things happen. Crying-in-the-shower things. Or in this case, mutated-cockroach-man things.

I still feel everyone's attention on me, including Delilah's. She's behind the counter, no doubt eavesdropping on every ugly word launched at me. And hey. I get it. I wasn't the catalyst that set this nightmare in motion, but it still feels partly my fault. My life. My disappearance. My repercussions to absorb. Every nasty look and dirty word adds rocks to my heart, a wall of jagged stones, building higher, cutting deeper.

I'm definitely a mutant cockroach-man, but not like Gracklin of the Black Waters—the underworld creature Sathya and I created for Gates of Ember. Gracklin has badass attributes: night vision, impermeable exoskeleton, the ability to survive for extended periods without food or water. The character is dark and creepy and was fascinating to develop. If I were to draw *my* mutated-cockroach self, I'd be the runt of the litter, weak shell, damaged immune system, one finger flick from rolling on my back and croaking.

I risk a glance up. Delilah's behind her coffee machine, peeking at me over the fancy apparatus. Instead of disgust and a serves-you-right smirk on her face, there's something else in her eyes. A slight tenderness that flays me.

Then she disappears. Literally drops out of sight, as though she ducked.

The door chimes again like I'm a contestant on the worst game show ever: *Guess Who Hates You Next!* Unable to avoid my fate, I glance toward the front door.

Shawn Harden, former drummer for the Tweeds, saunters in. His white skin's paler than I remember, his nose ruddy. Instead of yelling or glaring at me like I kicked his puppy, he slaps my shoulder and says, "Dude, you're back. That's so cool."

He smells as strongly of weed as he did when we hung out in Ricky's hot-boxed basement. I never thought it would feel this good to see him.

The next visitor isn't angry either. A friend of Callahan beelines for me, concern in his searching eyes. "I'm sure whatever happened with your family, it was intense. I'm here if you need to talk. Also"—he lowers his voice—"I speak Russian."

"Thanks," I say slowly, unsure why he's sharing his language aptitude. "I appreciate the concern."

He winks at me and mouths, *Russian*, again.

Delilah's cousin comes in next. He's angry and accusing and tells me I should be banned from town. A woman from Mom's quilting group follows. She slides a pamphlet toward me and says, "I know you wouldn't have left on purpose. If you start having visions, let me know. You are not alone."

The pamphlet is titled *Aliens Among Us*.

Three more confrontations over the next hour have me scratching my head and sinking lower in my seat. One guy asks if I can use my "hacking skills" to access the mayor's spending account, a second tells me he believes my family wouldn't have left without good reason while insinuating he can help me hide bodies. Delilah's hairdresser is a whirlwind of anger. Her hissed "get out of town before you hurt Delilah *worse* than you did the first time" has me queasy.

A man with any sense of self-preservation would have left already. Cut his losses and hid in his apartment with the blinds closed, but I keep replaying everyone's nasty or confusing words. The town seems to be divided into two camps: those less affected by my disappearance, who seem to have concocted a slew of stories as to why we vanished, and

Delilah's friends and family, who would like to see me beheaded with a dull blade, proving just how damaging my disappearance was to her.

The smells of chocolate and coffee are doing zilch to settle my stomach. There's a twitch in my right eye I can't shake. I need to go for a run. A marathon along the back roads—hard-packed gravel under my feet, fall air soothing my clammy skin, my blood pumping hard enough to dislodge the despair seeping through my veins.

I'll come back to the shop tomorrow, when I'm not a minute from breaking down. I'll be able to smile at Delilah, who deserves nothing but fresh-faced smiles.

I reach to gather my bag, but the bell chimes.

Someone mutters, "Oh, shit."

Cutlery clatters from behind the counter.

Unsure I can handle much more today, I pack faster.

Not as fast as the brisk steps nearing me. "You have some nerve."

Hayley Moon, mother to her only child, Delilah Moon, glares at me, her fine-boned features pinched. Her thick dark hair is still so much like Delilah's, but there's silver threading through the curly strands and murder in her eyes. When I dated her daughter, Hayley Moon was warm and kind and talked to me evenly, like an equal. She supported my and Delilah's young love. Now the heat of her seething anger practically singes my eyebrows.

"I'm sorry" is all I say. Not *it's complicated*. Not *we had a family emergency*. Whatever Delilah suffered after our disappearance, Mrs. Moon bore the brunt of it.

Her laugh has a maniacal edge. "When she told me you were back, I thought she was joking. I mean, what kind of narcissistic egomaniac would waltz into town after destroying the people he supposedly loved, like nothing ever happened?"

My pulse pounds harder, shooting heat through my face. I was wrong yesterday, thinking my reappearance would be good for Delilah. She's spent most of today hiding from me, and half the people on my game show from hell were furious on her behalf. My reappearance has done nothing but pick at old scabs.

I tilt up my chin, give Mrs. Moon my jugular. The vein is hers to cut if she wants. "I can't imagine wh—"

"I'm not done, Edgar Eugene Bower." She leans down, so close the smudged mascara under her lined eyes is unmistakable. Evidence of dried tears. "You have no idea what Delilah's been through. Your disappearance didn't just hurt her. You devastated my daughter. She has wounds that will never heal, and I will not stand by while you creep back into her life. I don't know why you're here, but I'm telling you that you need to leave. You—"

"Mom." We both look at Delilah, who's breathing hard, glaring at her mother.

Mrs. Moon steps back.

I blink the burn from my eyes, try to swallow. Nothing works. *Devastated. Wounds that will never heal.*

Whatever Delilah went through, it's miles worse than I imagined, and I can't breathe. I can't stand the suffocating heat and coffeehouse tunes and too-sweet smells. I'm up and rushing out of the shop as fast as I can move. Forget a marathon. I need to sprint back to Houston.

I make it half a block when I hear "E, wait!"

I stop on a dime. Delilah's voice has that effect on me, and she called me *E*, not Edgar. I don't turn, though. I don't want her to see me like this. My neurotic teen self, times ten.

She touches my arm. I know it's her by my body's reaction—a flare of warmth across my skin, that telltale tingling up my spine. *My Delilah.*

"It's true, isn't it?" she says. "That crazy story—your dad laundering money for some drug cartel. All of it's true."

I slump, relief loosening my bones. I'm still a mess. Shaky and sad and not sure I should be here, but Delilah's faith in my story is everything. "It's true."

We're getting looks from the people along the street. Even the scarecrow attached to the lamppost ahead of me is staring at us. His stitched face is droopy. Straw pushes out from the top of his shirt, his cuffs, and the bottom of his pants—jagged pieces he can't keep contained. It's like looking in a mirror.

Instead of forcing me to turn around or hugging me from behind like the night of nights when Delilah took pity on me while I fumbled setting up our lovemaking scene, she walks around me and stops in front of my face.

"Did you want to leave me that night?" Unshed tears turn her blue eyes into twin pools of pain.

"Delilah." I reach to touch her cheek, a magnetic need, desperate for my first feel of her skin in way too long. I drop my hand. "Everything exploded so fast—the cartel learning my dad was an informant, us being loaded into a van and driven away. Leaving you was the worst thing that's ever happened to me."

"You didn't call." The choked words are accusatory but also a confession. *I wanted you to call. I waited. Why did you make me wait?*

"They didn't let me."

"You could have tried harder."

"And risk people getting hurt?"

Angry puffs of air flare her nostrils. "So, all this time, you've been in hiding, wishing you could be with me, but you were forced into witness protection and couldn't call or write or reach out in case this cartel found you."

"No, not in case they found *me*. Not like that."

Unable to keep my hands to myself any longer, I reach between us and slip one finger under hers. Subtle enough that our audience doesn't see, but feeling her skin against mine sends a blast of desire through me.

Her breaths deepen, her finger twitching against mine.

I'm so addicted that I risk slipping a second finger under hers. "If I called and told you what happened, even if the call wasn't traced, you wouldn't have been as upset. The cartel might have assumed it was because you knew where I was. They might have hurt you to find us. And later, I was just scared. Everyone told me the less you knew, the better. So *no*, I couldn't risk reaching out, putting you and my family in danger. How could I live with myself if someone hurt *you*?"

She blinks, tears finally falling as she murmurs, "Jesus." She glances back at the shop, then down at the slight join of our hands, at the fake engagement ring on her finger, then back up at me. "I'm so sorry, E. I can't imagine what this has been like for you."

I don't want her sympathy. Well, maybe a little. Those few words cauterize a portion of the wounds from today's verbal attacks. Enough that thoughts of sprinting to Houston flee. "Can you come over tonight? Or I can come to your place." When she jerks her hand away, I add, "Just to talk. I'm sure you have lots of questions. I have plenty of my own, including why someone asked me if I could hack the mayor's firewall."

"This town," she murmurs and shakes her head. "Everyone has theories on why you all left. Alien abduction. Russian spies. Hackers hiding from the CIA. There's a money-laundering camp too."

"Which faction were you?"

"Honestly . . ." She rubs her face. "Nothing really made sense, but some businesses your dad worked for assumed he was messing with their books and stealing cash. They figured he left before he got caught, and the rest of you went because you were either helping him or were horrified about what he did. I thought I knew your family too well to believe all the ridiculous stories, but that one seemed the most legit."

"It's closer than alien abduction," I say softly. But not as terrifying as a drug lord threatening your life. "So can we go somewhere to talk? I'd like to explain more."

She nibbles her lip, wipes her lingering tears. "Yeah, sure. I'll come to your place."

This is how I find myself tidying my small apartment, trying to make it look more like a cool bachelor pad and less like a six-year-old girl's birthday-party palace, while ignoring Mrs. Moon's threats to leave her daughter alone.

# TEN

I'm starting to regret suggesting Delilah come to my non-manly apartment, but I've conquered number two on my Fifty Ways to Win Back Delilah list: convince Delilah to believe my unbelievable WITSEC story. Having her in my place allows me to implement and tackle number three on my list: remind Delilah how well I know her by brewing her favorite blueberry tea.

There's a knock at my door. I glance around, decide there's zero I can do to give this bubblegum space a dude vibe, and open my door.

Delilah's wild hair is piled on her head. She's still in her white T-shirt and jeans from work, but she's not wearing her apron. Her lack of uniform gives me a prominent view of her full breasts stretching the cotton of her shirt. My body reacts the way it always did around her, *insistently*. Already, my jeans feel tight.

"Thanks for coming," I say.

She gives a noncommittal "Yeah."

I back away from the entrance and fan my hand, inviting her in. Her steps are hesitant. Mine are less so. I follow her like the lovesick puppy I am. She stops in the middle of the space, leans to the left, glancing into my flowery bedroom. She pivots to the right, taking in the Pepto kitchen and small open living-eating area. "I don't remember you loving pink this much."

"Oh, I adore pink. Hands down my favorite color. You should see my assortment of boxers."

She turns and scowls at me. "I'm not here so you can flirt with me." She raises her hand. "I'm engaged, E."

I call bullshit.

Still, I appreciate her effort to keep me at a distance. I have a long way to go to prove myself to Delilah. A plethora of numbers to cross off my list. "I have some blueberry tea." Her absolute favorite. Hello, list item number three. "Can I make you a cup?"

She scrunches her nose. "I don't drink that anymore. Do you have bourbon?"

Fuck. No, I do not. Delilah didn't drink bourbon back in the day. She didn't drink alcohol at all, even when I'd offer her a sip of my illegally procured beer or vodka. This change not only screws with my remind-Delilah-how-well-I-know-her tactic, but the awareness of our ten years apart shakes me. I don't know this Delilah—what she's been through these past ten years, how time has shaped her. She might hate Sonic the Hedgehog and cannonballing into Bear Lake. I mentally rearrange my list and add: play twenty questions with Delilah until I know all of her.

Unlike bearded Hipster Lennon, who drinks obscure beers with ironic labels, I'm more of a cheap-and-easy guy. I walk to my fridge and grab a couple of tried-and-trues. "Will Coors Light do?"

"Sure," she says. Then, "Seriously, what's with all the pink?"

I should have at least repainted before inviting her here. "The place came furnished."

She makes a *huh* sound and sits on my offensively bright couch. Her knees are practically glued together, her hands clasped daintily on top. The Delilah I knew didn't sit like a demure debutante. She was a lounger, with her legs shoved into my space, commandeering the entire couch. She also said she'd never remove the moon necklace I made for her, but her neck is bare.

I hand her a Coors, hoping our fingers brush again. Sadly, they don't.

I sit to her right on the flowery love seat, perched on the edge, trying to shrink the gap between our knees. "I'm sure you have questions. Ask anything you want."

She fiddles with her beer bottle. Her fake ring clacks against the glass. "There are so many. I don't know where to start."

"My favorite question is, how could my father have been such a lying prick?"

Her attention snaps to me. "Did your mom know?"

"Not a clue. Remember Staci Wilcox?"

"Your dad's secretary?"

The seemingly sweet woman who'd come by the house with wine and magazines for Mom, books for me, and sports gifts for my brothers. "Turns out her real name's Grace Balsam, and she acted on behalf of the cartel in North America, managing some of their affairs. She's the one who brought my dad into the fold, molded and trained him."

Delilah's eyes are saucers. "Seriously? She seemed so nice and quiet."

And my dad seemed like a regular middle-aged accountant, not a mastermind criminal earning dirty money. "When the trial happened, like, a year and a half into WITSEC, Dad's testimony took her down. It also sent Victor Becerra's son to jail." Luis Becerra, known hit man and drug lord. Great company, my father kept.

Delilah gives her head an incredulous shake. "I remember something about a trial. Vague news stuff."

"The proceedings were held in closed court to protect the witnesses, so you wouldn't have heard details about my dad or Grace, but you might have heard Becerra's kid was killed in jail later. After that fallout"—my gut still clenches remembering those terrifying days—"Becerra made it clear he planned for my father to suffer the same fate: seeing his kids murdered. WITSEC became more intense after that."

"Jesus." She searches my face. "Do you still talk to him?"

"Dad?" The grunt I make is pure loathing. "None of us do. Haven't seen or talked to him in ten years. We stayed together as a family for the first six months leading up to the trial. It was the shock more than anything, I think. All of us functioning in a daze—navigating WITSEC orientation at a designated Safesite until they set us up in Houston. Once we had our IDs and understood what our lives had become, Mom lost it on him. Kicked him out. We were all pretty relieved to see him go."

"I can't even imagine."

I don't want her to imagine. I don't want her to endure a fraction of the pain I experienced. "We made it through. Except Desmond. He's the most messed up these days."

"He's not a lawyer at some fancy firm, driving a Porsche and rubbing it in your face?"

I love that she knows the old Desmond would have revved his Porsche engine with a shit-eating grin, but thinking about how far from that guy he is deflates me. "He didn't finish his classes. Works at random bars now, disappears for stretches of time. He even has a man bun and a horrible collection of bad tattoos."

Her mouth drops open. "*Desmond* has a man bun."

"And he drives a rusted yellow Camaro."

"No way."

I spin my beer, moving my thumb through the condensation. "He was gonna propose to Sadie. I saw the ring and everything. Then, at the Safesite orientation place, I found it in the trash. He just loved her so much. Losing her sucked the life out of him." I lift my eyes to Delilah's, unsure whether she can read my pain. I'm talking about me now, not Des. Bleeding my heart is easier like this, pretending my pain belongs to someone else. "He barely made it through each day. Obsessed over social media, freaking out when Jake would take his computer away. He didn't know losing someone could hurt like that. I think it broke something inside him, irrevocably."

I don't bother swallowing past the Everest-size lump in my throat. Delilah has a couple of tears on her cheeks. She doesn't wipe them away.

"He was a mess," I go on. "Couldn't stop imagining how hurt Sadie was. He didn't eat. Barely slept. He looked like utter shit and couldn't even—" Draw. I was about to say *draw*, but I don't. I keep playing this game of It's Not Me, It's Des. "He loved Sadie more than anything in the world, and when he lost her, he lost his light. Struggled to make new friends. He couldn't figure out how to be happy without her. He's living his life now, getting on the way we all do, but he's not the same. He misses that light in his life."

Delilah dashes at her face, then puts her beer down on my coffee table and rubs her hands down her jeans. I don't know if she's reading the true meaning behind my words—*I lost my light. I'm not the same without you*—but when she focuses back on me, I see the little girl who yelled at me to get off her land. Fierce Delilah, full of fire and emotion.

"Sadie loved Desmond more than anything in the world too," she says. "When she lost him, she spiraled, could barely eat or sleep. She didn't know loving someone could hurt so badly. She was a shadow of the person she was, and she didn't want to get out of bed. She didn't want to go on with her life."

"Delilah." I cave forward, plunk my beer on the floor before I drop it. Hearing from others that she suffered was brutal. Hearing it from her?

I want to scream or vomit or upend my furniture, punch the pink wall. I'm furious at what she endured, the time we lost, the fact that we have to share our emotions through secondhand stories because everything else is too damn hard. Did she try to hurt herself because of me? Did she do something drastic to make the pain stop?

I search her wrists, her arms. I see no telltale scars. "Whatever you went through, I'm so sorry."

Her shoulders droop. "It's not your fault, E. It's neither of our faults."

"I know, but I'm the one who vanished. Even though my father did this, it feels like I'm partly responsible." Wherever we go from here, I'll replay my verbal lashings today. Exist with barbs of guilt scratching under my skin.

Furrowed lines sink between her brows. "You know how I knew your wild story wasn't a lie?" When I shake my head, she rubs at her frown lines. "You always felt so much growing up. When someone got hurt or their dog or cat died, you got this devastated look on your face like someone reached into *your* chest and ripped out your heart. When I broke my horse figurine, you fixed it, even though we hated each other. No matter our history, you couldn't stand seeing me upset. I used to think you were an empath, like your mom used to say about your birth—that you had this ability to absorb other people's emotions. But I decided you were just the best person I knew."

Her last line inflames this deep missing of Delilah in my life, makes me ache to move beside her on the couch, wrap her in my arms.

Her gaze drops to her knees. "You were never good at hiding your emotions when we were kids, and you're still not. You absorbed everyone's anger today like you deserved it and didn't once defend yourself. These past years, I built you up in my head, imagining you cold and callous. But I saw how much those words hurt you, and I knew. This isn't a game to you. What you went through hurt you deeply, and you took that backlash like the old E would have, like it was your penance."

"If they need me to be their punching bag, so be it. If *you* need me to be your punching bag, then please take your shots. I knew you were hurting back then. I saw those early social media posts, but hearing from everyone and your mother—I didn't realize the full repercussions of my disappearance." Our knees are too far to touch. I do the next best thing and move my foot until my socked toe nudges the tip of her blue running shoes. "Please tell me about that time. I need to know what happened."

The blackout years. Zero social media posts, aside from two pictures on other people's timelines. In one, Delilah was grinning, sandwiched on a couch at someone's house. In the other she was blurry and off to the side, holding a SOLO cup, eyes drooping like she was tired.

Like those suffocating days, I need to learn the extent of Delilah's downward spiral. I need to understand how hard I have to work to replace those bad memories with better ones.

She presses her hand to her stomach, closes her eyes briefly. "I'll say this once, because it needs to be said. Then I don't want you ever asking me about that time again. No questions about those couple of years after you left."

It's a tough ask. I've spent a decade obsessing over the possible what-ifs of that time. Her mother's fury only inflamed my need to understand what Delilah endured, but if this is what she needs to let me back into her life, I don't have a choice. For now. "You have my word."

She nods once and focuses on my face. "Losing you wrecked me. Not knowing what happened to you broke something inside of me so epically I shut everyone out. I started partying, drinking a lot, and making a lot of bad decisions. I wouldn't listen to my mother, and my grades dropped. I—" She firms her jaw. "It wasn't good. What happened wasn't your fault, but it's hard for me to separate all that pain from the relief and happiness of seeing you alive and well. I'm not sure why you came back here, but if it's for us, to rekindle what we had, I can't go back there again. It's too hard for me. *And* I'm engaged. Happily," she adds, punctuating the comment with a smile that doesn't reach her eyes.

I understand her engagement vehemence. She clearly needs this boundary to deal with my reappearance, but adding the happy part and fake smile is overkill. She's forcing cheer. For her sake or mine, I'm not sure. Either way, my abdomen hollows out to make room for her confession, a place for her upsetting admission to sink in—Delilah drinking, lashing out, hating everyone and everything because I vanished from her life.

I have no doubt I'll relive those details and how firmly she said *I can't go back there again.* I'll give those moments their fair due and run later like my life depends on it. Right now I need to erase that broken look from Delilah's face. Which makes this the perfect time to cross off numbers four and nine from my Win Back Delilah list:

4. Reinstate our BFF status.

9. Unleash my endearing humor to make her laugh.

Clinging to the one positive thing from her confession, I say, "So you're relieved and happy I'm okay?"

She sniffles and rolls her eyes. "Of course you focused only on that."

"It was the best part of what you said."

"I'm engaged, E."

"I know." Even though she's lying now, that ring at the airport was real. She loved someone else enough to offer him forever. The awareness is another boulder shoved into my hollowed stomach, as is the fact that I can't console her. If we weren't playing her I'm Still Engaged game, I'd tell her she made the right choice. She deserves better than a man who steamrolls over her and usurps their relationship.

Since she needs this safety net, I say, "It's a lovely ring."

She doesn't reply, just keeps her eyes on the fake jewelry. She looks a bit angry and a lot sad and hasn't even sipped her beer.

Keeping my distance from her is one of the hardest things I've ever done. Distance I need to bridge. "The past ten years, I've learned how precious time is. I know being around me again is hard. And trust me when I tell you: being everyone's human dartboard is no fun. But after seeing you at the airport, I couldn't go back to pretending you don't exist. I can't continue living that lie. If you're happy with your fiancé"— if she's happier being without *me*—"then I understand. I won't pretend I don't want more. I wish we could try again, see if there's still something between us, but I won't push for that. Not while you're engaged. I will, however, push for this."

I drop down to one knee and hold out my hand for hers.

Have you ever watched those horror movies where the main character realizes the scary dude on the phone is actually in her house? That's the best way to describe Delilah's horror-struck expression. And I love it. I still have the power to take her mind off her sadness and replace that pain with indignation.

Doing my best impression of a nineteenth-century nobleman, I say, "Would you, Delilah Mars, do me the honor of being my friend again?"

She fumes my favorite fume, gives me her squinty face—like she hates that nickname and the stupid stunt I'm pulling—but she doesn't tell me to take a hike. (Exactly why I left "call Delilah by the nickname she hated but secretly loved" on my list.)

She stands, ignoring me on my bended knee. "I should get going."

"But you barely asked me any questions."

"Yeah, well. It's been a long day."

I jump up when she moves. Both a bad and excellent decision. Light headed from jumping and having Delilah this close, I stumble. Delilah tries to dodge me and winds up grabbing my arm. Some might call this an awkward kerfuffle. (Mostly ninety-year-olds who love watching *I Love Lucy*.) I call it Life finally giving me a break. My hands come to Delilah's hips, steadying us both. Her hands move to my chest. She breathes harder. I barely breathe at all.

"Be my friend," I whisper. "Please."

Her fingers move over my pecs. Just a smidge. And yeah. She's feeling my body, the harder lines that weren't there ten years ago. Abruptly, she shoves past me, her cheeks pink. "Fine, E. We can be friends. I'll see you around."

It doesn't take her long to reach my door and yank it open.

I, of course, can't leave well enough alone. Even after our tough conversation, my default setting is Flirt with Delilah. Before she leaves, I call, "Just so you know, from one friend to another, I have a six-pack now."

Her "Oh my God" lingers as she cranks the door shut. If I'm not mistaken, that was a why-does-he-have-to-be-so-endearing oh my God.

# ELEVEN

For those of you who took a bathroom break, Delilah Moon and I are now friends. My grueling run last night helped burn off some of yesterday's anxiety. I'm feeling a tad more optimistic. Still, I didn't sleep great. I spent half the night reliving Delilah's confession about drinking and partying and losing control. I have the distinct impression she shielded me from the brunt of what she suffered. Most people who yelled at me yesterday mentioned Delilah in a stilted way. Like they wanted to say something they couldn't. My best guess is they know about her broken engagement and they blame me for haphazardly sending her on that path.

Not only is Windfall's rumor mill top notch—they also protect their own.

When I walk into Sugar and Sips this morning, Mrs. Jackson is in front of me in line. She clucks her tongue at my appearance, then gives me her back. I don't take it personally. All this hate means Delilah protected me. Even when she didn't believe my unbelievable WITSEC story, she didn't confirm anyone's wild guesses about my past. So yeah. Half the town still has bets on whether I'm a spy or hacker or alien abductee. The other half is Team Delilah and despises me for hurting her. But Delilah no longer hates me.

She's behind the counter this morning, loading more muffins into her display case. When she notices me, she pauses. I'm pretty sure her focus darts to my abdomen and the six-pack she can't see. Then she's working, organizing her fancy baked goods, wiping the counter, stepping out of the way when the two baristas hurry to grab supplies.

Mrs. Jackson takes her turn at the counter and says loudly, "Melody showed me your wedding invitations, Delilah. They're absolutely beautiful."

Delilah freezes. Her eyes slide to me, then back to Mrs. Jackson. "She did a great job, didn't she?"

"Gorgeous. I can't wait for the big day. You deserve all the happiness." Mrs. Jackson tilts her chin, making sure I hear that last line.

I hear it, all right. That's why I'm in this town, intent on proving how happy *I* can make Delilah Moon.

A shorter woman I don't know, with dark skin and an impressive collection of facial piercings, pops out through the swinging kitchen doors. "Wait until you see the cake I'm baking for *the wedding*." Her pointed gaze falls on me when she emphasizes *the wedding*. "It'll be epic."

If I knew I'd be getting an impromptu *Masterpiece Theatre* production of *Delilah's Getting (Fake) Married* with my coffee and pastry, I'd have brought extra cash for tips.

The pierced baker disappears as the front door chimes. I tense, wondering if today will be a repeat of yesterday's game show from hell.

Maggie saunters in, struts past me with a sneer, then makes a show of handing Delilah a small box. "I picked up your resized *engagement ring*," she says, raising her voice as she speaks. "It should fit now, so you can give that temporary one back."

"Oh, wow. Thanks." Delilah smiles sweetly at Maggie and accepts the box.

I am seriously impressed. Not only do I love this town for being all mama bear, protecting Delilah from the imagined predator that is me, but she must have taken acting classes since her congested Australian performance in *Oliver!* If I didn't sit behind her on the plane and hear what a dick her fiancé was, I'd believe this little vignette.

"Put the new ring on," I say, playing along. I've always wanted to take improv classes. "Let us all see it."

Delilah narrows her eyes, but she doesn't hesitate. No joke. Is the Academy watching this performance?

She removes the oversize inlaid ring from her finger and gives it to Maggie, who is positively gleeful. Then she extricates the new square-cut diamond from the box. It's small and pretty. Different again from the real ring she wore on the plane and the absolute wrong engagement ring for Delilah. If I ever get to buy her an engagement ring, there will be tiny sapphires lining the band—the color of her eyes—and the central diamond will be pear cut, elegant and unique for this one-of-a-kind woman. Not round like the ring the self-centered jerk bought her.

The moment this new ring is on her finger, everyone in the shop oohs and aahs and showers her with compliments. Each over-the-top "It's gorgeous" and "It fits perfectly" and "You're so lucky to have such a great guy" is punctuated by a hard look at me.

I try not to laugh.

When Mrs. Jackson moves to collect her coffee down the counter, Maggie shoves her freckled face in my way. "You need to leave here and never come back."

I could tell her it's not her choice. Delilah's the only person who can ask me to leave, and she said I could stay, but this improv thing's been really fun. I've been bitten by the acting bug.

I cock my head. "Oh, I think that's my phone ringing. It's the same ringtone as the song playing, and I didn't notice it."

Maggie curls her lip. "The ringtone on your phone is a coffeehouse version of Carly Rae Jepsen's 'Call Me Maybe'?"

"It's a fantastic version." I pull my phone from my bag and make a show of answering it. "Hey, Lennon. You'll never guess who I'm with." I smile at Maggie. "You should say hi to Lennon."

I hold out the phone. Maggie mimics Delilah's the-killer's-in-my-house face and abruptly marches away. I guess my acting skills have gotten better since *Oliver!* too. Must be all the lying I've done the past ten years.

"Exciting morning," I tell Delilah when it's my turn at the counter. She's at the cash register now, freeing up her baristas to do barista things.

She holds up her hand and admires her sparkly diamond. "It really has been. Anyway, what can I get you?"

"I'll have a large coffee, one of those strawberry-and-cream muffins, and an appointment with you tomorrow at four o'clock."

Her fingers freeze on the cash register screen. "We don't have that last item on our menu."

"Funny." I point to her looping writing on the chalkboard above, gesturing to the tagline under today's specials. "I thought your motto is 'If you can imagine it, we can make it happen.'"

"That applies to pastries, E." She composes herself, pastes on a smile. "Anything else I can get you?"

I glance behind me. We have our usual audience—Delilah's acting troupe, including narc Sandra—watching me, but there's no one in line. I lean my hips into the counter and lower my voice. "I have to do something tough tomorrow afternoon and didn't want to do it alone. Figured since we're friends now, I'd check if you could come."

She fiddles with the ring on her finger, looping it in a circle. "Fine. Meet me here tomorrow."

"Delilah." The pierced baker is back, looking none too pleased. "The dishwasher's not working again, and Leon can't get here until Tuesday."

Delilah groans. "Why does equipment always break on weekends?"

Because Life has a twisted sense of humor, but Delilah's dilemma surprisingly works to my advantage. "I can fix it."

She whirls on me. "No, you can't."

"Actually, I can. I worked in a restaurant for a bit washing dishes." More like four years. Easy mindless work before my publishing contract, when I couldn't handle school or anything requiring focus. "The machine I used was old and broke constantly. I eventually learned how to fix it. Depending on what's wrong, I might be able to get yours working."

Delilah nibbles her lip.

The pierced baker scrutinizes me, like I somehow sabotaged their dishwasher, then she sighs. "On top of the regular work, we have to bake those sample cakes for the Rothman wedding. Without a working dishwasher, we'll be here all night."

The only Rothmans I remember lived near the old quarry and used to chase Avett and me away when we'd blast music from my iPod. "Who's getting married? Aaron or Kim?"

Delilah's eyes go soft. "Aaron, next month. He's having a short engagement and an intimate wedding at that fancy resort at Sheldrake Falls."

I don't remember Aaron well. He was quiet and kept to himself, but I like talking about *real* weddings. Real commitments instead of reprising our *Masterpiece Theatre* roles. Delilah needs reminding that some people find true love. "Who's his lucky bride?"

She grins so wide I find myself grinning too. "Ricky Sellers."

"*No* way."

"Yes way."

"Ricky Sellers of *the Tweeds* Ricky Sellers?" Our high school's famed garage band, the crew who gave me my first toke and let me hang around like the lanky outlier I was.

"The one and only."

Forget grinning. I'm a prize-winning jack-o'-lantern. Ricky dated girls during high school. No one for long, and he didn't wax poetic about female celebrity crushes while we lounged in his basement, but I wouldn't have guessed he was gay or bi. Granted, I had a limited view of sexuality when I was younger, but I'm genuinely surprised and happy for him.

Unfortunately, the happier I feel, the more my jack-o'-lantern dims. This news is another example of how much I've missed. I wasn't here to support Ricky when he came out. I wasn't here to congratulate him on his engagement or help plan him a wickedly embarrassing bachelor party. All my old friends have grown up, dealt with their own challenges, moved on with their lives, and I missed every second of it.

"I'll have to reach out to him," I say. Hope he doesn't riddle me with hate bullets like Avett and half of the town. "And my offer still stands. If I fix your dishwasher, you won't have to work all night and be too tired for our appointment tomorrow."

I'll also be able to cross number twenty off my list: find ways to help Delilah in her everyday life. This is a big list item. One I'm happy to cross off again and again. I want to make Delilah's life easier. Happier. Lighten her burdens any way I can.

She moves the pens on the counter to the right, then realigns them to the left, then returns them to the right. "Fine. I also have *my* own wedding stuff to do, so this will be a big help. No charge on your order today. I'll also pay you. Just track your hours."

"The free coffee and muffin are enough." I walk around the counter, toss a suck-on-this smirk to that narc Sandra, who's no doubt trying to mastermind ways to bring me down.

I follow Delilah into her shop's kitchen. She takes one look at the batter a young guy is mixing and winces. "Leif, did you use salt instead of sugar in the brownie batter?"

He frowns at the mixer, then his eyes slide to the salt container beside it. "Oh, *shit*. How the hell did I do that?"

"Kitchen rule. Always double-check your ingredients. No exceptions. Dump the batch and start over. Also . . ." Her tone softens. "Great job on the scones this morning."

He nods, relaxing as he dumps the messed-up batter. I blink at Delilah's profile, impressed at how well she handled that screwup. She was stern but kind, keeping her employee in positive spirits.

"Stay focused, Leif," the pierced baker reinforces and gestures to me. "E's here to try and fix the dishwasher. Our usual repair guy isn't free."

Instantly, a heart-pumping flash assaults me: Delilah in my room, saying she was curious about porn, asking if we could watch some together. I was hard in seconds, cueing up a video as quickly as possible. The piece we watched was old school and crass, with lots of pubic hair. We laughed through the first two minutes, then we were all over each other, grinding on my bed, using our hands to get each other off as we panted and kept our *fuck*s and *yes*es and *so good*s quiet.

The opening line to that exceptional piece of filmmaking was *You're not my usual repairman.* Hence my immediate hard-on and muffled laugh at her baker's "Our usual repair guy isn't free."

Delilah swivels toward me. "Don't you *dare* say that line."

See? Did I not tell you we were meant for each other? This woman can read my mind. "I have no clue what line you're talking about. I'm just here to replace your *usual repairman.*"

I wink. Seriously. This material writes itself.

She flattens her lips, but there's no hiding the amused twitch. "The dishwasher's over there, *Edgar.* I'll be out front, then in my office. If you need anything, let me know."

We've reverted to Edgar, but I salute her, thrilled to help her and her business.

∼

Not only do I save the day and fix the loose wire in Delilah's dishwasher, but I manage to get drenched when washing my hands with the sink's pull-out sprayer. I'm wearing my light-blue "Life's a Bitch" T-shirt. By some magical twist of fate, the threadbare fabric goes semitransparent when wet.

"All fixed," I tell Angel of the plentiful piercings.

"You're a lifesaver," she says like she doesn't actually hate me. "I'll get Delilah."

I run my wet hands through my hair, getting the non-Bieber strands messy and damp, then I strike a pose—one hand propped on the vanquished dishwasher, the other on my hip. My wet shirt is plastered to my body, showcasing the edges of my six-pack.

Leif, the scrawny employee redoing his salt-laden brownies, full-on guffaws. "Dude, you're pathetic."

I see no lie here. I am fully, 199 percent pathetic when it comes to Delilah Moon. I know the hell of having her ripped out of my life, the sharp crack of hitting rock bottom. I have no intention of revisiting that fall. In about thirty seconds, I'll be crossing off number twenty-seven on my Win Back Delilah list: tease her with a hint of my new and improved abs.

On cue, the squeak of her running shoes signals her arrival. The second she sees me, her eyes perform a routine that would earn a ten on *Dancing with the Stars*: flare, drop, drag right, drag left, slide up, slide down, blink, blink.

"Is it fixed?" Her body and face are rigid, cast in stone, lest she twitch and drop her gaze again.

I may run and do sit-ups and push-ups for my mental health, but there's a silver lining to all that hard work. It glimmers like a tense and flushed Delilah. "This baby's purring like an overworked, waterlogged kitten."

"Great. Awesome. That's just"—down-up-down-hover-slide-blink-slide—"really great. I'll get my checkbook."

"Honestly, no need. It's my pleasure. I'm just happy I could"—wait for it—"fill in for your *usual repairman*."

Her cheeks burn the color of Maggie's red hair. I flex my stomach muscles. She spins away from me—a move that's becoming a habit with us—and marches toward her office.

"See you tomorrow," I call after her.

Leif methodically wipes down the stainless steel counter. "I didn't give you enough credit. Never seen her flustered like that."

"She was annoyed, not flustered," Angel says pointedly. "Delilah is *engaged*."

Funny thing about that. Angel's wearing the inlaid ring Delilah first flaunted when I showed up to town. I grin at her. "I'm aware of Delilah's relationship status. We have a history together, but we're just friends now."

No point broadcasting my intentions to one of Delilah's many accomplices. If Delilah knows I know what game she's playing, her walls will go up faster than Desmond can say "infected piercing."

"They're really happy," Angel says, her tone revisiting antagonistic territory. "A fantastic couple."

If by *fantastic* she means Delilah's fiancé belittled her and broke her trust, then sure, we'll go with that. "I'm sure he's wonderful. Delilah deserves nothing but the best."

We have a stare off, but I don't give it my all. I've done what I came here to do. I've helped Delilah's business, showcased a hint of my abs, and procured an "appointment" with her for tomorrow. There's a chance I'll be pulling out a doozy for our rendezvous. Number thirty-two on the list: inflame her memory with a few spritzes of Eternity cologne.

# TWELVE

Today, I'm rabidly impatient. It's two p.m., and I'm meeting Delilah for our special appointment at four, the one I convinced her to attend by telling her I have something tough to do. Did I use my painful past to my advantage when suggesting this upcoming appointment would be hard for me? Definitely. Did Fake-Engaged Delilah worry about me and offer her support? She absolutely did. I don't feel bad about the slight fib. Choosing the right dog to buy is tough work. It also crosses off two points on my Win Back Delilah list.

> 34. Show Delilah I'm still a compassionate animal lover.
> 42. Prove to Delilah I'm here to stay.

Dogs thrive on routine and stability. Owning a pet will prove I plan to stick around, and, more to the point, I love dogs and want a furry companion. My parents weren't big into us having pets, but I loved going to Big Joe's farm and picking out a puppy for Delilah as a surprise for her.

Her father had died the month prior to that day, and I hated seeing her so sad. They had also lost their barn dog recently. I thought having a puppy around would be lively and fun and help distract her and her mom from their pain. Joe suggested I take one of the big robust puppies yapping and nibbling and acting like adorable pests. But there was a runt, with black-and-white patches on her face, feeble and sad, and I thought, *you need Delilah as much as she needs you.*

The solar eclipse grin on Delilah's face when I handed her Pickle—Delilah ate pickles like they were a cure for cancer—could have powered a rocket.

I don't know if she still has Pickle or if she still eats lots of pickles. More blanks about Delilah's life I need to fill in, but that memory has me reconsidering my list. Most of the items have been focused on me and my desperate need to win her back. As badly as I want us back together, resuscitating her solar eclipse grin is even more important. I mentally change number thirty-four from "Show Delilah I'm still a compassionate animal lover" to "Lift Delilah's spirits by playing with adorable dogs."

Needing to pass the time, I take my sketchbook to Sugar and Sips. Everyone here is firmly on Team Delilah. They still hate me, except scrawny Leif, who nods at me when he bustles out from the kitchen with a tray of M&M'S-topped cookies. They look warm and gooey and smell like chocolate crack.

I order a coffee and one of those mouthwatering cookies, then take my usual seat. Narc Sandra isn't behind me. She must have found some other innocent victim to investigate.

As I sip my coffee, a pretty Chinese woman enters. I don't recognize her, but she nods to a barista. A moment later, Delilah hurries out with a smile and hug for the newcomer. "Ally. So glad you could make it."

Delilah leads her to the free table near me. Delilah glances at me and nods, the corners of her lips lifting slightly. Pleased she acknowledged me, I wave and mouth, *Hi.*

She blushes, then she's intent on Ally, her hands clasped on the table. "Last year's bake sale was great, but I have an idea to make this year's hospice fundraiser bigger."

"I'm all ears." Ally deposits her purse on the table. "We can use all the donations we can get."

"What do you think of a balloon pop?"

"I'll tell you once I know what a balloon pop is."

Balloon pops are a mystery to me too. I squint at the duo, wondering if this is another of Delilah's impromptu acting vignettes, but she's focused on her friend, not paying attention to me, and Ally isn't launching exaggerated looks my way.

"I read about it online," Delilah says. "We ask local businesses to donate prizes and write them on papers, then stuff them into balloons. For the event, we fill a room with the balloons and sell needles to pop them for the prizes. It would be fun for kids and adults."

"Oh, I like that." Ally nods as she talks, while I eavesdrop like the Delilah-fixated man I am. "We could use the high school gymnasium and still do the bake sale after."

"The bake sale is a must," Delilah says. "Mr. Shavez told me he'll boycott my café if he can't buy my chocolate strawberry truffles."

Ally laughs. "Mr. Shavez gave Diane at the garden store the same threat, demanding they get his favorite mulch back in stock. But I have to agree with him on this. The fact that you only make those truffles for the fundraiser is criminal."

"It's about driving up demand and price," Delilah says brightly, then scrunches her nose. "So you think the balloon pop is a good idea?"

"I think it's a brilliant idea," I say, piping in. Their heads whip my way. "I'd spend money on that."

Delilah's brow knits, like she thinks I'm messing with her. What I am is *impressed*. Her ideas are smart and fun, and she obviously loves helping her community. "If your strawberry chocolate truffles are as good as everything else you make, I'd also pay a week's salary for them." I take a bite of my M&M'S cookie and moan.

Delilah's attention drops to my mouth.

Ally tilts her head, appraising me. "Aren't you a charmer?"

"No, he's not," Delilah says, but there's no fire in her voice. "That's Edgar. He's . . . a friend."

"Edgar *Bower*?" I may not know Ally, but she's apparently heard of me. She clasps Delilah's hand on the table. "I can't thank you enough for all your work. We have lots of time to organize, so let's talk about it more next month. And I cannot wait for your *wedding*." She cuts me a pointed stare.

I almost give her a standing ovation as she leaves.

"It's lovely everyone's so excited for your wedding," I tell Delilah. This thespian town is hell bent on pulling the wool over my eyes.

She gets up and lines her chair under the table. "It's nice to feel supported," she says, focused on her fake ring. I expect her to hurry off, but she lingers. Her attention flits to me. "Thank you."

"For what?"

"What you said about my idea."

"I said it was a great idea because it was. Ally seemed to agree."

Wistfulness seems to blanket her expression. "Thanks," she says again, like she's not used to receiving compliments. Like her idiot ex did worse things than disregard her opinions. "Guess I'll see you later." She grips the chair back tighter, shifts on her feet, then returns to the kitchen without sliding me another glance.

I watch the kitchen door swing shut, wishing I could bust through it, sweep Delilah into my arms, tell her over and over how amazed I am by the woman she's become. I settle on eating my cookie with the reverence it deserves.

With more time to kill and pumped by our pleasant interaction, I debate looking up Avett's number and calling him. Try to find better words to explain my disappearance without telling him exactly what happened. Truth is, there are no better words. Fixing our friendship might have to wait until Agent Rao gives us the all clear. Ricky Sellers, however, might take my reappearance more smoothly. We weren't as close, and the former front man of the Tweeds had a magnanimous quality that always made him easygoing and well liked.

Before I chicken out, I search his name online and luckily find his number.

He answers after two rings. "Hello?"

His voice sounds the same as I remember—lazy yet congenial. "Hey, Ricky. This is gonna sound nuts, and I really hope you don't hang up, but—"

"Holy shit, E. Is that you?"

I guess I sound the same too. "Did the rumor mill reach you?"

"Of course it did. This is Windfall. I just can't believe you're back. Where the hell have you been?"

He sounds more curious than mad, which is a testament to his good nature. "It's a long, complicated story I can't share at this time, but I wanted to reach out. Delilah told me you're getting married, and I wanted to say"—*sorry I missed all your moments, sorry I dropped out of your life, sorry I smoked your weed and didn't replace it*—"congratulations, man. So thrilled for you and Aaron."

"Thanks, E. Means a lot."

"I'm also sorry I smoked your weed and never replaced it."

He laughs. I don't.

"I'm sorry I wasn't here for you," I go on, "especially if there were times when you might have needed me, and I'm sorry I never contacted you or anyone. I'm just really sorry about a lot of stuff, but I'm also really happy you're happy."

A weighty pause stretches, then Ricky sighs. "Your disappearance was intense. Messed with a lot of people, Delilah in particular—" Muffled angry words interrupt him, someone shushing him before he says whatever he was about to say. I once again have the distinct impression more went on with Delilah during her social-media-black-out-drunk-partying phase, and it's not sitting well.

"Delilah went through a tough time," he says, giving me nothing. "It upset a lot of people. I'm guessing your return has had a less than welcoming reception, and I have no interest in making it worse. The past is in the past, man. If you're here with good intentions, then it's great to hear from you."

"I am," I say, saddened again by the trauma my disappearance caused but touched he's willing to let the past lie. "I've missed Windfall a lot."

A comfortable silence descends. The type of lull full of forgiveness and old friendships and fresh starts. I spin the cookie-less plate on my table. "I still can't believe you're marrying Aaron Rothman. That guy can't sing to save his life. Remember when he did that Bieber song for the school talent show?"

"Says the guy who strutted around with Bieber hair."

"That hair was awful."

"The worst. And . . . give me a sec." More muffled voices, tones rising and falling. "Sorry. Aaron's here, and we were wondering if you wanted to come to our wedding."

I scrub a hand over my mouth, too moved by his kindness to speak right away. I didn't dare expect this much generosity. The only event I imagined being invited to was my wake. "Are you sure? My presence has a tendency to cause drama. I don't want anything to take away from your big day."

"It's my party, and I get to invite who I want to. Plus, the Tweeds will be playing. We can't go on without our roadie."

I cross my arms, hugging my chest, unsure what to do with all this warmth ballooning inside me. "Yeah, sure. That would be great."

After a bit of light chitchat, we hang up, and I breathe more freely than I have in a long while. Maybe I can build a fresh-start life in Windfall after all, beyond winning back Delilah. Rekindle my friendships, find a way to face Avett again, walk into a store and not be assaulted with accusations and conjecture. The prospect is still daunting.

That bastard Hope, like Life, never did me any favors these past ten years, but I can't deny the burst of positivity buoying my mood.

With a bunch of time to kill before my meeting with Delilah, I pull out my sketchbook and pencil and stare at my last drawing—Delilah as my albatross, majestic wingspan, fairy-tale eyes, a mass of curly hair cascading around her.

Without thinking, I jot down a line: *Get off my land.*

I'm not sure what happens next, if I've been sucked into a portal to another dimension, or if a restless spirit has taken over my body. I scribble lines and rough sketches as the outline of a story spills from me. My story. Delilah's story. *Our* story. Crude doodles and notes, snippets of our Top Ten Bests followed by our worsts, reimagined in a bird-inspired world.

Delilah is the albatross, obviously. Using my typical realist style, I've drawn her and the other characters as mostly human, with avian accents on their lower bodies and elaborate wings extending from their backs. I'm a stuck-in-the-past great curassow, whose jaunty crest resembles a bad eighties perm—a nod to the Bieber mop. My father and the Becerra cartel are bullying grackles. Mom is a small but mighty wren, capable of surviving dark, cold winters. Desmond is a hoatzin, known for its pungent body odor; Lennon is a Dong Tao chicken because the bird is obscure enough for his hipster self and has gnarly thick legs that are a blast to draw; Cal is a comforting barn owl; and Jake is the all-powerful eagle who grips everyone's shoulders and takes charge.

Here's the thing about my art. I don't write stories. At least, I haven't written or imagined a plotline since entering WITSEC.

Before I lost Delilah, I'd muck around with graphic novel ideas like a bowlegged hero who could walk over cities. I'd plan action sequences, imagine dark villains with sad pasts who didn't choose their villainy. I'd give my heroes obstacles they could only conquer if they faced their personal demons. Then Dad happened. My world became too dark, too cynical, too much like the unbelievable story lines I wrote. I kept sketching, but for the life of me, I couldn't imagine a hero beating a villain. I couldn't write an action scene without imagining myself standing over my father with a bloody knife in my hand.

Meeting Sathya at that comic exhibition was kismet. She doesn't draw, but her brilliant mind is full of off-the-wall, larger-than-life stories. We came together, feeding off each other: her stories, my art. I didn't have to imagine impossible worlds. She didn't have to draw stick figures. We've both made a solid living combining our forces.

Now, suddenly, I'm writing. Imagining. Telling a story again for the first time in ten years.

"Do you still have that appointment?"

I slam my book shut. The fact that I was so absorbed in my plotting I didn't notice Delilah's approach shocks me to my core. I grin at her. "*We* still do, yeah. A tough, important appointment. Let's get to it."

She's not in her usual work attire. Darker jeans cling to her curves, and her light-blue sleeveless top complements her eyes. Little buttons run down the front—buttons that would be so fun to undo—the soft-looking fabric hugging the generous swells of her breasts, finishing in a casual tie at her waist.

I need a minute before I stand.

Once I'm up and less hypnotized by Delilah's beauty, I lead the way to my new truck.

The day before I drove to Windfall, I purchased the truck. Something about being in my hometown and driving my blend-in-with-the-crowd Nissan Altima didn't sit right. I love big trucks: their power, the country vibe, the flatbed where I can snuggle with Delilah while we watch stars pop in the sky. Unwilling to be beige in this new life I'm rebooting, I bought myself a used Ford F-150 truck in my favorite color, blue.

I'm parked behind the clothing store that's under my apartment. When we get there, Delilah gives my new purchase an approving nod. "This is the exact truck I expected you to drive."

The simple comment winds me. Proof I'm no longer as invisible as the generic name Brian Baker on my driver's license. "I've spent so long pretending not to be me, it's like I'm learning who I am all over again."

Delilah steps closer, the lines of her face softening. "It can't be easy, but I'm glad you're finally finding yourself again."

"It helps having you back in my life."

Her gaze drops. I hate not having her in my arms.

Playing it as cool as my noncool self can manage, I open her door and breathe in her sweet bakery smells of cinnamon and chocolate. She twists as she gets into my truck and—I swear this is not my imagination—she leans in closer and sniffs my neck.

Eternity still delivers.

I hope the nostalgic scent shoots her back in time to us on that soft gray blanket, me whispering "Let me touch you first," getting her ready for our first time.

Her chest expands. Her eyelids flutter. Then she's clambering into the passenger seat, attention dead ahead. She buckles her seat belt with a hard click.

Once we're on the road, I make a decision. I do not blare "Pillow Talk" from the stereo. Yes, playing that blast-from-the-past tune is number seventeen on my list, but it's too soon to unleash that secret weapon. She's seen a suggestion of my abs. She's sniffed my cologne, but her knees are slammed together like the time she got her period in the middle of English class.

Better to save the big guns for later.

Instead of playing our song from my phone, I fiddle with the dial and find a classic rock station. Steve Miller Band's "Take the Money and Run" fills my truck's cab. I bet Dad loves this tune.

"I told my mom," Delilah says.

Colorful Windfall homes, bright and well maintained, stretch down the side streets. I glance at her, then back at the road. "Told her what?"

"Why you left town. I didn't tell Maggie or anyone else, but she needed to understand why you're here out of the blue. Why I've let you back into my life."

Being the glutton for punishment I am, I've replayed Hayley Moon's seething anger more than is healthy, dissecting her "you devastated my daughter" and "she has wounds that will never heal" umpteen times. All I ended up learning is how crappy I can feel. "Yeah, sure. I get it. She probably still hates me, though."

"She does."

There should be a magic pill that cures I-hurt-a-great-woman's-daughter nausea. "Maybe one day she'll forgive me."

"What happened wasn't your fault, E." Delilah's even more vehement than the other night. So emphatic a portion of my guilt ebbs.

There's hardly any traffic in Windfall. It's a neighborly town where drivers stop for pedestrians and slow for cars that need to merge. With Delilah this close to me, I wouldn't mind a standstill or two. "Was the dishwasher fine this afternoon?"

"Yeah. Thanks again for that." She's being polite. Cordial but stiff.

Time to play twenty questions. "Do you still eat pickles?"

A quick glimpse shows her side-eyeing me. "Yes."

Guess who'll be buying ten jars at his next grocery shop? "What's your favorite show you've seen the past ten years?"

"*The Punisher*. It's so intense." She fiddles with her seat belt. "Yours?"

"That's so wild," I say with as much fake enthusiasm as possible. "Mine's *The Punisher* too."

Even from the corner of my eye, I catch her headshake. "You're so full of shit."

Busted. "*The Marvelous Mrs. Maisel* is up there, and I recently watched *Gilmore Girls*, which was adorable."

"And . . . more shit."

"It's rude of you to make fun of my digestive system."

"It's rude of you to ask me a simple question you're not willing to answer."

"But I did answer. I love Mrs. Maisel's hilarious antics, and the cute town of Stars Hollow reminded me of living in Windfall." Delilah's silence indicates she's not buying what I'm selling. I get it. Before witness protection, I loved binging *Sons of Anarchy* and *Breaking Bad*. After, not so much. "I can't watch anything with crime and twisted deceptions. Kind of sets off my tendencies to fantasize about torturing my father with a set of rusty pliers."

Harsh, I know. You try having your life torn apart and hastily glued back together with corrosive lies.

"Wow, E," she says quietly, then swivels toward me more fully. "You seriously love those other shows?"

"Have you seen the outfits on Maisel?"

She laughs. "Only you, Edgar Eugene Bower."

I ease my foot off the gas, slowing us down. Whatever it takes to keep us in my new used truck for a few extra seconds. "Do you do any of the baking at your shop?"

While I feel her attention on the side of my face, I don't check if I'm getting a can-I-risk-trusting-him-with-personal-details perusal or if it's more of a what-does-his-six-pack-feel-like perusal. Either way, my whole right side buzzes.

"I made all the food the first couple years," she finally says. "Never took time off. When the shop started earning enough to hire a baker, I found Angel. She does most of it now, with Leif or whoever's hired at the time."

"Those kitchen-sink bars are still my favorite, tied with everything else you make." She doesn't reply with a snarky or light comment. Her silence lingers so long that I glance at her. "What?"

"Being around you brings back a lot of memories," she says, her voice hesitant.

There's no way she has me beat on memory consumption. I'm so drunk on ours I need a fifty-step program. "Good memories?"

Another pause. "You were my best audience when we were young—laughing at my bad jokes, telling me my failed baking experiments were the best things you've ever eaten, lying to my face. I missed that about you."

"You missed me lying to you?"

She shoves my shoulder playfully. "I didn't miss your obnoxious humor, but you always went out of your way to lift me up. Like when my dad died, I was such a mess and you wouldn't leave my bed. You kept your arms so tight around me, but—"

"I had to pee," I cut in. Fuck, did I have to pee. "I mean, I *didn't* piss the bed, to be clear."

She laughs under her breath. "You were bouncing your knees and I couldn't figure out why, then I asked if you were stiff or thirsty, and you started going on about how water wasn't allowed to be discussed and that you might have a bladder infection from not peeing and a bunch of other nonsense I don't remember, but I remember laughing. Laughing so hard on the toughest night of my life, all because of you." She sighs and sinks back into her seat. "You worry about others before you worry about yourself, and you always went out of your way to cheer me up. Those are rare qualities. I'm happy you haven't lost them."

I do my best to keep my focus on the road, not on how her words please the heck out of me . . . and the way they gnaw at my gut. The guy she planned to marry didn't lift her up. Hugo tore her down, made her feel insignificant, and I want to say something. Offer comfort. With her engagement ruse, my lips are sealed on the topic. Unless I don't mention specifics.

I turn off the main road, loose gravel rocking my truck as I drive toward the town's dog shelter. "After what my father did, it wasn't easy keeping a positive outlook. I dissected every interaction we had—conversations, times we laughed together, times we fought. I was convinced

I did something to push him over the edge, that I maybe begged too much for a certain video game, complained about a bike Avett had that I wanted too. I thought my badgering him to buy me things might have pushed him to take a risk, earn more cash, provide for his family. In the end, I learned a valuable lesson."

"That he's a disgraceful human and nothing was your fault?"

I love the vicious undercurrent in her tone, how protective she is of me. Exactly how I feel about her. "I learned that Taylor Swift is a genius."

She snorts. "First *Gilmore Girls*, now you're a Swiftie?"

"Don't knock Taylor. Like she says, haters gonna hate, and more to my point, selfish pricks are always gonna be selfish pricks. Some people don't have the emotional capacity to consider how others feel. All they think about is how choices affect them. If one moment doesn't show their true colors, another will. Whatever choices my father made, he didn't make them because of anything I did."

The repercussions still affect my life, but this monologue wasn't about me. I steal another glance at Delilah, try to gauge if she's absorbing my intent. *What your idiot ex did wasn't your fault. The asshole steamrolled over your feelings because he's a steamrolling asshole.*

Her eyes are fastened on her "new" fake engagement ring. She runs her fingers over the small diamond, back and forth. "That's a great way to look at things."

Truth? I want to ram my truck into Hugo's house. Show him how it feels to have *his* walls crumble. But Delilah doesn't need an avenging knight. "I know we're in a weird place, that it'll take time for you to trust me and for us to rebuild our friendship, but I'm still here for you. I'm still the guy who wants to put you first and make you laugh when you're upset. I hope you give me the chance to really prove that."

She doesn't answer right away. I grip the wheel tighter, readying for her to cut me down. Tell me she was wrong and our history is too painful. We can't be friends after all. As much as I push, the final call is always hers. If she asks me to disappear from her life again, leave her alone for good, I'll do as she wants, even if it kills me.

I feel her attention shift back to my profile. "I know I'm going to regret saying this, because you *are* a pain in the ass, but . . . I'm happy you're back in Windfall. I'm glad you were your relentless self and didn't let my anger run you out of town."

I blow out a relieved breath. "Do you still read comics?"

"What kind of idiotic question is that?"

A diversion tactic. A way to get us to happier topics. "It's been a while since I've seen you. Maybe you only read the *National Enquirer* now."

"I only read that on weekends," she says dryly.

"Knew it." I glance at her again, every stolen glimpse saved for later, when I'll pull them up in bed, reliving our day in a montage I'll call "Delilah and Me and Eternity."

She taps her knee to the rhythm of the music. "You're still a pest. But, yeah, I still love comics and graphic novels. You got me hooked, and I love the escape, getting lost in a completely different world. Have you read the Gates of Ember series?"

I slam on the brakes and shove my arm in front of Delilah, bracing for impact.

"What the hell, E?"

"There was a large squirrel." There was a *small* squirrel, but her question shook me more than the darting rodent. Now my heart's beating in my throat and my arm's pressed against Delilah's soft breasts. I don't move. She doesn't ask me to move. And, no word of a lie, she's arching her back, pressing more firmly into me. Predictably, my body *takes notice.*

Before this gets weird, I ease my arm back and pull over to the side of the road. I need to be stationary for this conversation.

"I know Gates of Ember well," I say carefully. "What do you think of it?"

The song on the radio shifts to Foreigner's "I Want to Know What Love Is." It's nostalgic and romantic, and I'm suddenly shy, facing Delilah, so curious what she thinks of my graphic novel, worried she doesn't love my work. Worried she *does* love my work and I won't be allowed to kiss her, run my nose up her ear. Whisper how much her opinion means.

"How can you even ask?" Her voice brightens with excitement. "That series is amazing. Like in my top five, for sure. I reread them all the time."

"And . . . you like the artwork?"

She shifts, angling toward me, her face pensive. "The word *like* is too small for the art in that series. The work is raw and vivid. Sometimes almost painful to look at, but that's the point, I think. A lot of the characters represent our darker urges."

The energy waves just tracked on North Carolina's Doppler radar weren't unexplainable atmospheric changes. That was the intense blast of my joy. "I never told you my new name while in witness protection."

She tilts her head. "You didn't."

Instead of explaining who I am, I grab my wallet, dig out my driver's license, and hand it to her.

She side-eyes me like I'm up to something nefarious, but I'm not crossing off an item on my list or teasing Delilah the way I know she secretly loves to be teased. I watch as she reads my fake name—Brian Baker—and wait for it to click. There's no reaction at first. It's a pretty beige name, like everything in my life the past decade. Then her eyes widen. "Brian Baker, as in Gates of Ember Brian Baker?"

I nod.

"Oh my God." She grips my forearm excitedly, saving me from having to interpret this *oh my God.* "You're *the* Brian Baker."

I laugh, too overwhelmed and relieved and happy about her reaction to say much.

"E." She gives my forearm a squeeze. "I can't believe I didn't realize it was you. How could I not have known?"

Her eyes turn glassy. Foreigner's "I Want to Know What Love Is" fills the small space around us, too romantic and too sensual when I can't kiss the woman in front of me.

I move, though, reach out and cup her cheek. "I always hoped you'd read it. Putting it out into the world felt like a way to be connected to you, even if the hope was delusional." A tear slips from her eye—a sparkling blue diamond. I brush the moisture away with my thumb. "I swear, you were somewhere in every sketch I drew."

She leans into my touch, presses her palm over my hand. "Maybe that's why I love the series so much. Maybe, subconsciously, I knew those amazing illustrations came from your talented hands. I always knew you'd do something special with your art."

Because she was the one who encouraged me most growing up.

We're on an emotional seesaw now, staring at each other with stacks of memories—beautiful and awful—between us, pushing us back and forth. I'm quickly reminded how fragile this new beginning is. We don't know which memories or new tidbits learned are heaviest, which will tip us into the "Delilah and Me and Eternity" montage, or into the "Delilah and Me and Her Mother Yelling That I Ruined Her Life" montage.

Delilah releases my hand, but the move is tentative, slow. Like she knows how fragile this is too.

There's no one on this quiet road yet. There's still so much to say. So much to learn about her. "Before I left, you used to talk about teaching kindergarten or owning a day care. You never mentioned baking as a career. Why'd you make the switch?"

Instantly, her face shutters. She readjusts on her seat and faces the windshield. "I told you not to ask me about that time."

The seesaw's tipping in the wrong direction, but I can't stop myself from leaning into the unknown. She's hiding things from me, not giving me the full truth about those rough years. "I'm just curious about your career."

She cracks her knuckles one at a time. Her stressed-out habit. "It's hard for me to talk about."

"Not knowing about that part of your life is hard on me."

She makes a growly sound. "You're relentless."

"Didn't you say before that you *liked* my relentlessness?"

She rubs her face, blocking my view, but I'm guessing an eye roll is happening. "Like I told you, my grades slipped. I wasn't in any head-space to go to college, and I doubt I'd have gotten in. I started baking more at home. Following recipes got me out of my head, and Mom had saved for my tuition. Instead of investing in school, we decided the shop was smarter." She turns her hard stare on me. "Happy?"

No. Not even a little. I'm struck anew by the fallout from my father's actions. My disappearance didn't just change the course of my life. If I hadn't left, Delilah would probably have gone to college. She might have gotten her teaching certificate and could be molding young minds as we speak. Not that there's anything wrong with her current career. Sugar and Sips impressed me the second I walked in. Her shop appears successful, and Delilah seems happy there. It's just not the path she envisioned for herself.

A song I don't recognize rocks out from the stereo. Loud and inva-sive. Delilah stares out the passenger window. I can't think of a thing to say. There's no apologizing for running a person's life off its track, and my father's the one who owes a mountain of apologies. This growing tension is also exactly what we should avoid. Delilah needs fun in her life, not reminders of the ugly parts of our past.

With no words to duct-tape our widening chasm, I fumble with my phone and do the thing I decided I wouldn't do. I hit play on "Pillow Talk."

Delilah groans. "You did not just do that."

"It's not me," I lie. "There's something wrong with my phone."

"Honestly, E. There's something wrong with *you*. I'm engaged and already regretting saying that I'm happy you're back in town." She sounds more exasperated than mad.

I can work with exasperated.

# THIRTEEN

As my truck nears the driveway to Windfall's animal shelter, Delilah leans forward and stares at the passing welcome sign, then swivels toward me, her jaw unhinged. "You told me you needed me for something important. The words *moral support* were used."

"Yes and yes," I say.

"And we're at the dog shelter."

"Again, correct."

"If the important thing you told me you needed moral support for has anything to do with adopting a dog, you are so dead."

I ease my truck into one of the vague parking spaces in the gravel lot. Once I've killed the engine, I pat my chest and thighs. "Seems like I'm still alive."

She gives me her adorable squinty face, then crosses her arms, resuming her role of Exasperated Delilah. "I'm not going in there with you, so don't take long. I need to get back."

My earlier question obviously hit a tender spot with her, as did my knee-jerk reaction playing our song. Two steps forward with Delilah, ten steps back. I could drive her home, apologize for the slight deceit, but I changed number thirty-four on my list to "Lift Delilah's spirits by playing with adorable dogs" for a reason. Delilah loves dogs. With all she's going through, I want her to have some fun.

I rub the scar on my upper lip, debating the best way to convince her to join me. Pleading? Unleashing my puppy dog eyes? I settle on my childhood tried-and-true method of persuasion. "You're right. It was wrong of me to mislead you. I won't be long. I'll play with all the cute dogs without you. Let them lick my face and climb all over me. It'll be awful. You definitely shouldn't come in."

She mutters something as I leave. I don't pause and break character. I've learned a *ton* from our improv sessions.

Embodying my role as Reverse Psychology Champion, I march for the entrance like I don't care if Delilah joins me or not. Once inside, I don't see any dogs, but yipping and yapping carries from somewhere in the back. I feel a little thrill. One of those lonely pups won't be lonely for long. One adorable girl or boy will soon have a forever home, and I'll have a forever friend. Another portion of my life will be less beige: new blue truck, a dog I choose because I want a dog.

There's no one at the reception desk, but I spot a bell on the counter. Before I step toward it, I hear the front door open and close.

Delilah walks in and stands beside me. "I'm not here because you want me here."

"Of course not."

"And I won't play with the dogs."

"I wouldn't dream of asking you to do something so horrible."

"And just so we're clear, this isn't fun for me."

She's really sticking to her guns on this one, but I play along. "Petting dogs is a hardship, and I thank you for your support. Nothing at all cute will happen in this building."

She gives me her famous headshake. "You're too much."

Or just enough. Only time will tell.

I walk to the counter and ding the bell. Delilah's all sharp angles— shoulders pointed toward her ears, elbows edged out, her stiff hands shoved into her jeans pockets. An older woman I recognize as Andrew Chan's mother hurries out and smiles at us.

At the sight of her, I tense.

"Delilah, hey!" Mrs. Chan beams. "It's so nice to see you."

"Hi, Mrs. Chan. Great to see you too."

For those of you with less Delilah-fixated memories than mine, Andrew Chan accompanied Delilah on her return to social media, signaling their relationship status with his arm latched around her waist.

Mrs. Chan doesn't seem to recognize me. I don't sense any stewing resentment or the stirrings of pity. She also has no clue the photo of her son was responsible for my crying-in-the-shower episode I'll never discuss with Delilah. She simply shifts her pleasant smile to me and says, "Are you dropping off or adopting today?"

"We're adopting," I say.

"*He's* adopting," Delilah says, firm.

Righto.

"Excellent." Mrs. Chan shuffles through some papers. "There are forms to fill out. Let me know when they're done, and we'll visit our sweet dogs." She slides me a clipboard and pen, like this is the most normal thing in the world. Like filling out a dog adoption form doesn't turn me into a human stress bomb.

"I'll be right back." Mrs. Chan walks around the corner.

I take the clipboard, pen poised at the first question—a simple line any dog-adopting adult can fill out in two seconds.

NAME:

I have to write my name at the top, and I don't know which name to use. Technically, I'm not Edgar. I don't have any ID confirming that identity. My driver's license says Brian Baker, as does my truck's new registration. Filling out the dealership paperwork didn't pull the ground from under me the way it's teetering now. Delilah wasn't standing beside me that day. I didn't feel like I was straddling a fault line, two halves of myself separating, with my legs about to do a very awkward, very uncomfortable split.

Delilah presses her hand to my back. "The only ID you have is with Brian, right?"

I clear my throat, hating that the pen's shaking. "Yeah."

"Then use that. Mrs. Chan doesn't remember you. It's just stupid papers that'll be filed. No one will ever look at them again. We'll tell your dog your real name. That lucky pup won't know the difference."

She gives me an encouraging nod, her hand rubbing slightly on my back, and I realize I didn't stretch the truth when asking her to join me on this excursion. I truly needed her support.

After the forms are filled out, Mrs. Chan returns and motions for us to follow her. "What type of dog are you looking for, Mr. Baker? A puppy or an older companion?"

"Not a puppy." I shudder to think what a rambunctious puppy would do to all the pink in my apartment. They also tend to find homes easily. "An older dog who can run with me."

"We have several who fit that bill. You can walk through the pens, see who catches your eye, or I can set you up in the playroom and choose a few to bring in one at a time."

I shoot Delilah a questioning look.

"Definitely the playroom," she says, then adds quickly, "but it won't be fun."

"Agreed. It will be horrible."

"Playroom it is." Instead of commenting on our odd banter, Mrs. Chan slides an affectionate look to Delilah. "It really is nice to see you looking so well. Andrew still asks about you."

I stiffen at the remark. I have no clue when or why those two split up, but Andrew Chan still has the ability to crawl under my skin like he's Dinoponera from Gates of Ember, the hulking demon commander who has the power to shrink into ant form and burrow under his enemy's skin, driving them mad. Sathya comes up with some insanely dark characters.

"Well, give him my best," Delilah tells her.

A phone rings down the hall.

"Sorry." Mrs. Chan swivels and starts hurrying back to reception. "I'm waiting for a call from a dog food supplier. I'll just be a minute."

The second she's gone, I say, "Didn't Andrew Chan get caught jerking off behind the bleachers during the girls' soccer practice?" Jealousy is an ugly beast.

"Ugh. No." Delilah makes a face. "That disgusting moment was courtesy of Freddie Lorimer."

Right. That loudmouthed prick who Delilah dick-punched, defending her friend. "Why did Maggie ever hook up with him?"

"I'll never understand and prefer pretending it never happened."

Like I prefer pretending Delilah never dated Andrew Chan or Hugo or any other guy. Except I don't want to be *that* Neanderthal. Delilah isn't my possession. She's a strong, independent woman who led a full life while I was gone.

"Andrew's a good guy," I force out. "I'm glad he was there for you after I left, even if being with him was a letdown after being with me."

I at least get points for trying.

"You're such a child. And how did you know we were together?"

"I'm twenty-seven, not a child, and there was a Facebook post."

She crosses her arms and juts out her hip. "So you've been creeping me on social media?"

My deterioration into Obsessive Delilah Moon Internet Searcher is not on my list of today's chitchat topics. "As hard as I searched, I didn't find any nudes."

She flattens her lips. "A twenty-seven-year-old man-child."

"With a six-pack," I add, grinning.

A heavy door opens at the end of the hall. Barking and yipping spill out, along with none other than my former best friend who now hates me, Avett Lewis.

My smile drops.

He strolls from the back area with a skinny, timid dog on a leash. When he notices us, he freezes and narrows his eyes. Even under that baleful look, I recognize my fellow misfit and underage drinking buddy, whose tolerance was shockingly worse than mine. I see the guy who once took the fall for me when I got caught cheating in math (yes, again) so I wouldn't get suspended, the two of us always covering for each other.

I'm not sure what he sees when he looks at me, but his harsh "Why are you here?" doesn't bode well. He's Team Delilah all the way.

She gives him a small wave. "E's adopting a dog."

"Is he now?" His hard stare has me wanting to search for cover, but the stark hallway has zero furniture. "The shelter only adopts dogs to competent, caring households. Not sure you qualify."

Yeah, that hurts. Delilah winces. Luckily my cockroach armor has hardened since my verbal stoning at her shop, and I didn't replay any grueling memories this morning. Avett's insult makes a dent in my exoskeleton but doesn't penetrate.

"I'm sorry," I offer again. Useless, pathetic apologies. "I'll grovel if it helps. Even do karaoke and let you choose the songs. Whatever it takes for you to believe I didn't want to leave back then. I didn't have a choice and wasn't able to contact anyone. I can't explain why yet, but if we were ever friends at all, maybe you can find it in your heart to not hate me."

His brow crinkles. The timid dog tucks tight into his side. Instead of replying to me, Avett looks at Delilah. "After everything, how can you be friends with him?"

Her hand finds my back again, the dip where my spine's threatening to curve into a defeated slump. I want her hand there always, rubbing my back, maybe sneaking under the cotton fabric, whispering its comfort over my skin as her lips find my neck and I press my thigh between hers and . . . *fuck*. I really am a forever man-child, unable to last a minute without fantasizing about my first and only love.

"What happened wasn't E's fault," Delilah says, her palm still supporting my spine. "Messed-up stuff went down with his family, and condemning him for it isn't fair. His disappearance was as hard on him as it was on us."

Now I want to hug her. Platonically. Warmly. Thank her for being the best person I know.

Avett's bearded jaw flexes. He rolls his wide shoulders back, pops his knee a few times. I'm about to give up on reaching a truce, when his stance softens. "If Delilah says you didn't have a choice, then I guess you didn't have a choice, and I'm sorry for whatever you've been through."

"Thanks, man." I rub my sternum, unsure why my ribs feel bruised. "That means more than you know."

He shifts on his feet, as do I, both of us doing an awkward are-we-friends-now shuffle.

"Are you here for a dog checkup?" Delilah nods to the scrawny dog plastered against Avett's leg.

He gazes fondly at the pup. "One of her canine teeth was infected when she was brought in. I pulled it last week and wanted to make sure she was healing well."

"You're a dog dentist?" I ask.

He smirks. "I prefer the term veterinarian. I work at a clinic, but I do some community work here to help out."

"Wow. You're a vet." I swear I'm not always this dense. But when I look at him, I still see the kid who scrawled *Pussies* on a piece of paper, snickering as he pinned it to the woodchuck mascot we defaced. "I hope none of your patients are aware you have a history of mutilating their kin."

His smirk widens. "I've had my record expunged. What about you? Have you progressed to vandalizing larger zoo stuffed animals?"

"Not far off. I draw creepy animal-inspired humans."

We share what feels like a moment. Mutual understanding. An agreement to coast over the hard stuff and progress into a less awkward we're-sort-of-friends-now shuffle.

The dog by his legs whines. I walk closer to them and crouch, getting down to her eye level. She's so skinny her ribs protrude through her short brindle coat. One ear is flopped and the other stands upright. Her tongue lolls out of her mouth, likely due to her missing canine tooth, and her dark eyes are so innocent and fearful my heart breaks. "What's her name?"

"She came in without tags, emaciated and covered in ticks. For now, we've been calling her Candy Cane for her brindle stripes."

Scratch that. My heart didn't break before. That was just a crack. The organ's shattered now. Candy Cane is a dog version of me, her true name unknown, her life-giving sustenance denied—in her case food, in mine Delilah.

I hold out my hand for Candy Cane, give her my gentlest face, hoping the scar through my upper lip doesn't remind her of any bad humans. She leans forward. Just her upper body and face at first, keeping her legs close to Avett. Eventually she ventures closer, one step, then two, then she's sniffing my hand with her wet nose, extending her neck to smell me. She doesn't freak out and dash back to Avett. Like the other woman in my life, she must love the scent of Eternity. I let her test her boundaries as we assess each other's malnourished souls. She shifts closer. I run a gentle hand over her head. When I pull away, she puts her paw on my arm, like she doesn't want me to go. My heart gives a persistent thump.

In an instant I know: She's my dog. I'm her human. We're meant to be.

"How's my Candy girl?" Mrs. Chan is back, standing next to Delilah, holding another four-legged heartbreaker by a leash.

Avett urges Candy Cane back toward him. "If she passes this checkup, she'll be ready for adoption."

"Fantastic." Mrs. Chan fans her hand toward the playroom door. "Let's get you situated so you can meet your forever friend."

I don't need to meet other adorable homeless pups. Candy Cane is clearly mine. I mean, look at the shattered innocence in those glossy eyes? But this was supposed to be a fun outing for Delilah, who's had a rough few weeks. "I'll join you in a second. I just want to have a word with Avett."

Delilah scrutinizes me. I grin and give her a wave. "In private, if you don't mind."

She huffs out a breath and follows Mrs. Chan into the playroom.

Immediately, I corner Avett. "Tell Mrs. Chan not to put Candy Cane up for adoption. I want her."

"Then why'd you say you wanted to meet more dogs?"

"That's more for Delilah than me. She's been through a lot lately and needs a pick-me-up."

He widens his stance and crosses his arms. "You know about her ex."

"Of course I know about her ex. Do you honestly think I'd insinuate myself in her life if I thought she was happily engaged to be married?"

He gives me another hard stare, followed by a heavy sigh. "No. You wouldn't put her through that. But tread lightly, man. A lot went down after you left. She's been dealing with her recent breakup well, but—"

"She has? You've talked to her?"

He sneaks a peek at the playroom door and lowers his voice. "We got closer after you disappeared, stayed pretty tight. And yeah, I never liked the guy. She met him when he was vacationing here, and most of their time was long distance. He just always seemed too . . . perfect. Not genuine. Always steering conversations and boasting about himself. She even admitted as much after they split. Aside from feeling hurt, I think she's more relieved it's over than sad. But like I said, there are a lot of scars where you're concerned."

"I have a few scars of my own," I mutter. Inches deep, running straight through my heart.

He shakes his head. "You two, man . . ."

"Us two, what?"

He eyes the door again and fiddles with his leash. "There was this, like, aura around you two in high school. I didn't fully get it then. Was a bit jealous of how in tune you were to each other, but I get it now. You guys loved each other in this pure wholehearted way you don't see every day. So yeah, it wasn't a surprise Delilah went off the deep end when you vanished. I honestly don't think she ever fully regained her spark, which is why half the town hates you and means you can't push her too hard now. She's fragile where you're concerned."

"I'd never push Delilah."

He cocks his head, reading me plain as day.

"Fine," I concede. "I might push a bit, but I'm letting her lie to me, pretending the engagement's still on."

He chuckles. "Gotta love Windfall, right? You two and this ridiculous ruse are the talk of the town."

"Oh, trust me. I'm aware. So"—I adopt my most innocent tone—"when you say Delilah has a lot of scars because of me, what exactly do you mean?"

"No way, man. Not my story to share."

"Yeah, I get it." No one in this town will crack.

"Anyway, I gotta head back to the clinic after this checkup." He gives my shoulder a light punch. "But this was nice. I still have a ton of questions, but looks like there's time for that."

As long as that twisted devil Life doesn't play dodgeball with my face again. "We'll make plans. As will we," I tell Candy Cane.

She pants heavily, which I interpret as unbearably excited.

Pumped to adopt the dog of dogs, and relieved Avett and I breathed a few CPR breaths into our old friendship, I walk into the pale-blue playroom, ready to help Delilah find her missing spark.

# FOURTEEN

Dog toys and a couple of dog beds are scattered around the playroom's easy-to-clean, for-sure-peed-on linoleum floor. Mrs. Chan crouches next to the big bruiser on her leash, who looks like a cross between a yellow Labrador retriever and Albert Einstein.

Delilah sits on the couch against the far wall and promptly levels me with an all-knowing wizard stare. "Anything to share with the class, E?"

I sit cross-legged on the floor. "I ate Raisin Bran this morning?"

Now she's an exasperated wizard. "Whatever." To Mrs. Chan, she says, "Tell us about this cutie."

"This here is Caramel. He's been with the shelter for a month. He's wonderful with kids and other dogs and loves licking faces. Don't you, Caramel?"

On cue, Caramel lunges for me. He's a big guy, all gangly in that goofy big-dog way, pushing at me and licking my face until I'm lying on my back, covered in slobber. That's when I hear my favorite sound in the world: Delilah's belly laugh. The one that turns her face bright red and pushes tears from her eyes.

I turn my head toward her, not bothering to move from my prone position. "I feel violated. He didn't even buy me dinner first."

Another laugh. This one brings the shoulder shakes. When she recovers, her wide smile brightens the wattage in the room. "He looks like he wants to swallow you whole."

"Must be the cologne. Everyone goes nuts for Eternity." I waggle my eyebrows.

"Child," she mutters.

I maneuver back to sitting, hugging and rubbing Caramel as he pants his hot breath on my face. "He needs a shot of mouthwash, but this brute is definitely a contender."

I twist to ask Delilah's opinion, even though I don't need it. Candy Cane is the only dog for me. Instead of finding her on the couch, she's pulled some impressive ninja move and is now facing me, cross-legged on the floor.

"He's definitely a contender." She gives him a fierce rub, scrunching her nose, waiting for the assault. Caramel doesn't disappoint. His big tongue licks the length of her face, and there's that wattage again, big and bright, filling the room and my chest.

"Shall I bring in another?" Mrs. Chan asks.

Delilah and I share an excited glance and nod simultaneously. The second Mrs. Chan leads Caramel out, I wipe my face. "That was awful."

Delilah shudders. "Why do people even *like* dogs?"

Seriously. I need to find out where she takes her acting classes. "Do you still have Pickle?"

"No." She runs her finger along the seam of her jeans. "Lost her a couple years ago. She had cancer."

I think back to sitting behind Delilah on the plane, hearing her desolate *I'm used to losing people in my life*. Pickle was a people. Delilah lost her father, then me, then her dog, that bastard Life doling out loss unfairly. "Delilah, I'm so sorry."

"It was tough. She was a great dog."

Heeding Avett's warning not to push Delilah implies she's not ready for a sympathy hug from me, but Delilah and I *did* exist in our own bubble during high school—the aura Avett mentioned—always aware of each other's moods, offering tender touches if one of us seemed off. I can't hug her the way I want, but I extend my hand, palm up, hoping our simple connection eases her now like it once did.

She doesn't move at first, and I have to be honest, if she leaves me hanging, it will be a blow. I don't want to push Delilah for too much too soon, but she pressed her hand to my curving back when standing up for me with Avett. I need to offer her the same support.

Her fingers twitch, a small spasm, like she can't decide if she wants to curl her hand into a fist or stretch it out and reach for me. I'm braced for her inevitable brush-off, when she slowly extends her fingers and fits her hand into mine.

I black out. Or I've just closed my eyes. All my senses zero in on the softness of her skin, the gentle slide of our fingers, basic contact with a woman who was my first enemy, my first best friend, my first love, and my first understanding that another person could mean more to me than my own life.

She looks at our joined hands, her shoulders softening on an exhale. "Everything's changed, but some things don't."

"Which things?" I ask softly.

She flexes her fingers against mine. "This."

No other words are needed, just *this*. The miracle of a touch that inexplicably heals.

I thread our fingers firmly, bring our joined hands to my mouth, and press a soft kiss to her knuckles. Her breath stutters. My lungs don't recall how to function, and the hungry look on Delilah's face *slays* me.

"So," Mrs. Chan says brightly as she leads another dog into the playroom. "Here we have Sophie."

Delilah doesn't yank her hand away from me as I expect. We hold on a second longer, her heated gaze locked on my face, darting briefly to my lips. She pulls back first, because I'm not that strong, and angles her head at Sophie. "Aren't you adorable?"

She really is. We play with Sophie, messing up her mop of long hair, squeaking toys in her face, taking turns giving her hugs.

"Dogs aren't fun at all," Delilah says when Mrs. Chan leaves to get contestant number three.

"They're the worst," I confirm.

Dog three is as adorable and heartbreaking. Smaller and rambunctious, she's all floppy ears and cute button nose. By the time we shower her with love and Mrs. Chan leads her away, I'm picturing my small apartment filled with a menagerie of pups.

"You can't adopt them all," Delilah says, mind reader extraordinaire.

"But I'd buy them all pink collars. They'd match my apartment perfectly."

"Sure, but I *know* you won't adopt them all. I already know which dog you're choosing."

"You can't possibly know." But I suspect her all-seeing-wizard self does know. A development that works in my favor. Delilah loves nothing more than proving I'm wrong. I love nothing more than upping the ante.

"I definitely know," she repeats.

"You definitely don't."

"Let's each write down a dog's name," she says. "Then we'll show each other and prove you're wrong."

Bingo. Now it's my turn. "Okay. I'm in. But there has to be a wager."

She drums her fingers on her knee. "What do you have in mind? And if you say anything in relation to your cologne or that song you played in your truck or your supposed six-pack, you can count me out."

"Why are you always stealing my thunder?"

She purses her lips.

I sigh in defeat—there's my stellar acting again—and say, "Fine. If you win, I'll clean your place of residence for a week. If I win, you'll clean mine."

I can't lose this bet. Both outcomes end with me spending one-on-one time with Delilah.

She strikes a thinking pose, fingers propped under chin. "Does this include all aspects of the residence or just the visible areas?"

"All aspects?"

"Then you have yourself a deal." She looks like she just planned a coup to overthrow the government, and I have a sinking feeling I've walked into something less enjoyable than tidying Delilah's underwear drawer. She procures a pen from her purse, scans the room, then snags a dog magazine from a shelf against the wall. She opens it and rips out a page.

I mock gasp. "That's vandalism."

"Says the guy who tortured and tied a woodchuck to a goalpost."

"A stuffed woodchuck."

"You also graffitied my chicken coop."

"That was art." Created after our truce, but before we were a couple. One Delilah-obsessed night, I spray-painted a picture of a fox-woman with Sonic blue eyes and full lips . . . and big boobs because I was fourteen and boobs were everything back then.

She scribbles on her torn page, rips the paper in half, and hands it to me with the pen. I write Candy Cane in looping letters on my section, excited to drive that girl home and give her more love than she can handle.

"Ready?" Delilah says.

To clean her house and hold her hand when she's sad and tell her selfish pricks are always gonna be selfish pricks? "I was born ready."

We swap. She whoops. "Told you I knew. And the timing couldn't be better. Something died in the vicinity of my sink. You get to locate the dead critter before I asphyxiate on its rotting-carcass fumes."

I'd curl my scarred lip at the prospect, but I'll happily suffer through dead critters if it means I get to hang out with Delilah. "The pleasure will be mine. And I'll bring Candy Cane, since I can't leave my fur baby alone. Gotta be a stand-up dad." Unlike mine.

An odd look passes over Delilah's face. She returns the vandalized magazine to its original spot, probably regretting her choice to deface it.

"Sorry I took a while. Those phones don't answer themselves." Mrs. Chan returns and clasps her hands. "Have you made a decision?"

"I have," I say, but my phone rings. The flash of Lennon's name has me darting my eyes around, worried he's calling because my brothers heard I'm in Windfall, where I shouldn't be, with Delilah, who shouldn't know I still exist. I swear to God, if that narc Sandra traced my alias and ratted me out, I will hire a *real* hacker to infect her computer so it displays nothing but cute animal videos.

I give Delilah my best I'm-cool-as-a-cucumber smile, but I'm pretty sure I look like I just bit into a habanero pepper. I clearly need more acting classes. "Delilah can let you know my choice. I need to take this."

Delilah frowns as I jump up and hurry into the hall. Once outside, I strike a pseudocasual pose, like my family can see me. "Hey, big bro."

"Hello there, Edgar Eugene Bower. How goes the wooing?"

"Slowly. Why'd you call?"

"It's so nice to speak to you too."

"Sorry." I give myself a shake. "It's great to hear from you, I'm just in the middle of something with Delilah. What's up?"

"I ran into Sathya at the grocery store. She was acting odd and told me not to tell you I saw her, so I obviously called to tell you I saw her."

Well, now, that can't be good. Sathya going MIA when on deadline isn't new. Purposely avoiding me? I sense some painful calls with our agent in my future. "Thanks for the heads-up. Does the family suspect I'm here?"

"Nope, but I'm debating letting it slip. I love watching Jake's face turn purple."

I'm about to threaten him with shaving off his eyebrows, when I remember I have leverage. "It's just *wild* being back in Windfall. So many old friends and faces, including one uppity redhead who asked about you."

He's breathing so hard I hold the phone away from my ear. "Maggie asked about me?"

"She did."

"What did she say?" Lennon's going for calm, but I know that tight tone. His eyes are for sure bugging.

I lean into the wall, cross one ankle over the other. "How badly do you want to know?"

"Don't be a dick, E."

My level of amusement is high. My level of curiosity is even higher. While I'm akin to emotional flypaper that sticks to everything, Lennon is Teflon: emotionally unruffled, unaffected. Yet here he is, ruffled, affected, and sticky as hell. "I'll answer, if you promise you won't tell Jake I'm here."

He scoffs. "I had no intention of ratting you out. It's just fun messing with you."

At least I don't need to shave his face. "Maggie asked if you were coming back too. I told her no."

"And what did she say?"

"She glared at me and flew away on her broomstick. What the hell happened with you two?"

"Nothing," he says abruptly. "And FYI, looks like we'll have the all clear soonish—getting back IDs with our old names for whoever wants them. But not a word to anyone else until then. Should only take a couple more weeks."

I won't lie. I'll be thrilled when this town stops glowering at me like I steal babies in my spare time, but there's no point getting my hopes up. "A couple more weeks" in US Marshal speak often winds up being a couple more months. "Keep me posted, and keep your mouth shut about where I am. Oh, and I'll tell Maggie you say hi." I swiftly hang up.

My phone rings, then it buzzes with texts.

Pleased with my efforts to unhinge Teflon Lennon, I hit mute. I don't have time for his secret flypaper life. I have a dog to adopt and a girl to continue winning back, but Delilah's quiet while we organize Candy Cane's adoption. She doesn't say much on the drive back to town. She spends most of the time either staring out her window or checking on Candy Cane in the truck bed, answering my continued twenty questions quietly without her usual sass. I feel like I took a wrong step on this outing, that something got messed up between playing with the dogs and me answering that call, but I have no clue what it was.

# FIFTEEN

Candy Cane and I have an understanding. If I don't pet her too vigorously or love on her too much, she lets me stroke her ears and upper chest. But if I get greedy and go for her body or try to hug her, she shies away or puts up a paw with wide uncertain eyes, asking me to stop. I listen every time. It's clear she has scars I can't see and was at one point harmed by humans. Not unlike Delilah, who's progressed from light improv to emotionally submersed Method acting.

Candy Cane is tied to my outside table, where I'll be sketching this morning. Instead of ordering my coffee and treat right away, I spot Delilah wiping down a table.

Refusing to let her acting deter me, I join her inside. "I can come to your place tonight, put on my hazmat suit, and search for the dead animal."

She continues wiping the table, even though the surface is sparkling clean. "I'm meeting with my wedding florist today. We're having trouble deciding on flowers."

Three days ago she was having trouble with the caterer. Two days ago she needed to meet with her mother about the seating arrangements. Yesterday was a dress alteration. I consider most of our dog-adoption outing a success. We talked about things that mattered and things that didn't. We laughed and got licked by adorable dogs, but she's been extra distant since our ride home, and her Method acting has become intense.

As far as I can guess, a specific memory hit her she can't shake. Emotional quicksand I understand. In my early WITSEC years, I'd get yanked under at unexpected times. I'd suddenly remember Delilah running at me for one of her attack hugs, slamming me so hard she'd knock us over. Or dangerous, more tantalizing flashbacks would strike: me kissing my way down Delilah's belly, spreading her thighs, tasting her for our first time, inflamed by her heady musk, loving the hard pull of her hands on my hair.

I'd sink into those sultry memories, play them over and over until my only option was to jack off to the imagined taste of her. I'd crash after. Lie in bed for days at a time or go for exhausting runs. There wasn't much my family could do, except make sure I knew I had support if I needed them. They kept showing up, forcing me to get outside, encouraging me to draw. Without them, I wouldn't have pushed harder at my art, discovered my career. Learned how to breathe without Delilah at my side.

While I've been careful not to push for more than she can handle, I want to show up for her. Nudge a little harder. Help her any way I can. Like Avett said, our teenage love was pure and wholehearted—the type of unconditional affection that might help light the spark she lost after I left.

Instead of wishing her well with her wedding planning, I say, "I don't welch on bets, and I owe you an apartment cleaning. I'm sure you won't finish late with the florist. I can come by after."

She continues her useless wiping. "It's hard to say. We'll do it another night."

And she'll have another excuse.

I press my hand to the cloth she's got in a death grip, stilling her obsessive wiping. "We could take a rain check, or I could come by tonight, no matter what time it is. I'm a night owl. If we don't do something soon, that dead animal might stink you out of your place."

Her cheek hollows, like she's nibbling on it, her focus locked on our hands. Our fingers aren't touching, but my pinky is a hair from her index finger. I move mine slightly, just enough that we're resting against each other. "Please let me come over."

She hesitates another moment. When she looks up at me, the emotion swimming in her eyes hits me so hard it's like she's launched one of her attack hugs, wiping me off my feet.

"Okay," she says softly.

"Okay?"

"Ask me to say it again and the answer's no." There's my feisty girl, sassing me the way I love to be sassed.

"Gotcha. Important question, though. Where do you live?"

She snatches her cloth from under our hands. "Here."

I glance around the shop. Half the tables are full. Everyone is, of course, watching us, including Sandra at her usual stakeout location, sporting her immovable eighties perm. While I still get the odd set of daggers launched at me, the surveillance has taken a turn from vindictive to entertained. None of these jokers need cable or Netflix. I'm providing them with a continuous live airing of *Edgar Gets Shot Down*.

Not today, suckers.

I refrain from bowing to our audience and face Delilah. "Those sofa chairs look comfortable to sit in, but I bet they're murder on your neck when sleeping. I also offer massages with my rodent-exhumation services."

She doesn't jump at my selfish offer, but the hint of dimples in her cheeks indicates suppressed amusement. "I own the building and live in the apartment upstairs."

"You own this whole place?"

She ducks her head and blushes. "I do."

"Delilah, I can't believe you own a historic piece of Windfall." I want to hug her. Lift her up. Show her how impressed I am. Instead I say, "What a great accomplishment."

"I don't illustrate an insanely popular graphic novel, but"—she glances around this amazing space, twisting her cloth, pride in the lift of her chin—"I often forget it's all mine. Well, kind of mine. Mom ran the breeding program for a bit after Dad died, but her heart wasn't in it. She eventually sold the horses, then the farm. She lives in town now and helped me buy this building."

She's being modest, acting like her efforts in this endeavor barely mattered. "Getting help doesn't diminish what you've created. You designed the shop with your vision, built a happy, welcoming place for people. Your mom must be proud."

"Yeah." Her cheeks pink again. "She is."

"And she still hates me."

Delilah sighs. "She does."

Undeterred by that fact, we plan to meet at eight, after her "wedding" errands. I'm not frustrated by her continued lies. I'm too pleased this episode of *Edgar Gets Shot Down* ended with a surprising twist. I'm even given a dog treat with my black coffee and scone.

Once outside, I smile at Candy, loving how this small town is the opposite of Houston. Never in a million years would I have tied my dog to a table leg in the city, left her alone while I bought a coffee inside. Here? If the wrong person snatched Candy's leash, ten people would perform a citizen's arrest. At least, I hope they would. My standing in Windfall still hovers at pond scum levels.

I crouch next to my girl and hold out her treat. "For you, my sweet lady."

She takes the cookie, gentle as can be, and munches happily. She looks up at me after, her eyes brighter, that cute tongue lolling where her canine tooth used to be, and she licks my face.

"Oh my God." I glance around, needing to share this momentous moment.

The older man at the other outdoor table, who's been reading Tom Clancy's *Code of Honor* while spying on me, narrows his eyes.

"My dog licked my face," I tell him. When he doesn't look impressed, I add, "She doesn't lick faces."

A woman I've never met walks by us, and I can't keep in my good news. "My dog licked my face," I say brightly.

She touches her purse, like she's debating whipping out her phone and calling 911.

I'm about to share my thrilling news with the next passerby, when I realize the approaching redhead is Maggie. "Hello, Margaret."

"I heard your dog licked your face."

What did I tell you about Windfall's rumor mill? "She's a dog prodigy."

"She's adorable, and that's the only action you'll be getting in Windfall, so I suggest you enjoy it. Oh, and stay away from Delilah."

And let that quicksand drag her under? Not on my watch. "Should I tell Lennon you asked about him again?"

She snarls at me and sashays into the shop.

I settle into my seat, with my awesome, face-licking dog at my side, and open my sketchbook and laptop. With Delilah's Method acting and Sathya's continued avoidance, I've had so much time to sketch I've worn my pencils down. Not only have I fleshed out the characters in my life story, but I've blocked out the main turning points in the script.

In my early days working with Sathya, her scripts were incredibly detailed, every facial feature outlined, down to the length and directional flow of a character's eyelashes. Later, as we learned to trust each other's processes and instincts, a panel description would read as simply as *Ceuthon stabs Argus with a bolt of fire.* She trusted I'd illustrate the tension in Ceuthon, capturing his turmoil in killing the giant he once loved.

Writing my own graphic novel based on my life takes this minimalist approach to the next level. The panels are piling up in my head, details nagging at me to bring them to life. Instead of planning each chapter and the number of panels per page, I push my sketchbook aside and open a fresh Clip Studio document. Sathya isn't here to guide me with her plotting. There's no contracted script length I need to reach. I just have this tremendous need to purge my story, get it out of my head for the first time.

While I've designed the characters as avian-inspired humans—Delilah living on Earth, my family shipped off to Mars—they mostly resemble their human counterparts. I've changed our names, though. Delilah's name is Delilyn, and mine is Edgren. And yeah. My lack of creativity in the name department is why I've never been the writer of my publishing duo, but I don't let the name stumble thwart my progress. I can change those details later. I'll also add color when the whole thing's done. For now, I just need to draw.

The first couple of panels flow quickly, starting with young Delilyn's "Get off my land," her wingspan stretched wide, an attempt at intimidation, followed by my brilliant comebacks in this birding world. I spend extra time on her face, capturing the details from my memory—the indignation in her eyes, the wind whipping her curly hair. In later frames, I add the moon necklace I gave her that she for sure torched to dust. In each frame, I leave enough room for her dialogue bubble, the balance of written space and imagery second nature to me now.

Two hours later, when my phone rings, I have a full page of panels done.

I cringe at the sight of my agent's name, but there's no point putting off this conversation. "Hey, Margot."

"Brian. You sound well."

"Best I've felt in a long while." Margot is well acquainted with my deep dives into despair. Over the years, there have been a few less important deadlines pushed. "I'm guessing you haven't heard from Sathya?" I ask.

"Not a word. She won't answer my calls. What about you?"

I could lie, respect Sathya's wishes to drop off the grid, but I don't like that she's avoiding me. Her choices affect my career as much as hers.

"I haven't heard a thing, but my brother ran into her. She told him not to tell me he saw her."

"That's not good."

"Yeah. No clue what's up with her." While Sathya and I have spent a ton of time together, our relationship is mostly professional. WITSEC made me extra introverted, and she likes her privacy too. With her odd behavior, I regret not getting to know her better. "If we have to delay, how pissed will the publisher be?"

"It depends how this ends. This is their big summer release. They've booked advertising with some major players. Pushing the deadline won't go over well, but they'll find ways to adjust. If you don't actually finish and pull the project completely, they might take it to their lawyers."

The latter is not a good option. I've spent a chunk of my advance on my new truck, new apartment deposits, and daily living expenses. The rest of my cash needs to stretch until we start earning bigger royalties on this next release. "I'll try to get ahold of her again."

But we both know how that'll go.

Margot doesn't reply. A car slows on the main street, window rolled down so the smiling driver can chat with the person crossing the road. Two little girls run ahead of their mothers, giggling, aiming for the town's grassy central square, like they're going to vault into the stone fountain at the center.

I'm about to end the call, take a break from working and enjoy the heartwarming sights and sounds of Windfall, when Margot says, "You really do sound great, Brian. And your illustrations so far for the prequel have been phenomenal. Your best yet. You're insanely talented."

*Phenomenal. Insanely talented.* I don't have Candy Cane's enhanced canine sense of smell, but I can smell Margot's I'm-about-to-suggest-something-you-won't-like flattery from across the country. "That's so nice of you to say, Margot. Do your other clients lap up this kind of overinflated fawning?"

"You know you're good, Brian. I'm just reminding you of your exceptional talent. So, you know, if Sathya drops her side of the contract, then your talented fingers and creative mind can pick up her slack."

Oh, hell no. "I'm not writing the last half of Gates. This is Sathya's baby. Her world she created. I won't do that to her." Both our names may be on those novels, but as far as I'm concerned, Gates of Ember is her intellectual property. Haters are gonna hate. Cheaters are gonna cheat, and I am not a cheating traitor who will swindle Sathya out of her creation. Still, things are clearly worse than I expected. Margot wouldn't suggest I work solo if she wasn't freaking out.

I leaf through my sketchbook, the personal characters and story filling the pages. I have no interest in selling this project. Delilah wouldn't want our painful history blasted into the world, and it's too emotional for me. But I've never heard Margot this flummoxed. If she thinks there's a fallback plan—even a phony one—she'll bug me less while we wait for Sathya to surface. "I'm actually working on something else. A project I'm doing on my own."

"A spin-off series?" Margot's voice perks up.

"It's more personal than that. Kind of based on my life. Nothing as fantastical as Gates of Ember, but if I get it done soon and we're in a pinch, we could pitch this to the publisher as an alternative."

"That's a nice offer," she says, decidedly less perky. "But I doubt an illustrated life story will appease them. Just find Sathya and get the work done."

Sounds like a plan to me.

When we hang up, I call Sathya. No answer. I send her a text, even though I doubt she'll reply. As I flip over my phone, Delilah comes outside, and my mood lifts. She hums while wiping down a table, seeming more relaxed. She smiles and talks to the older woman at the table across from me. The new customer has taken up the space where the Tom Clancy reader sat. Instead of using a book to camouflage her espionage, she's knitting, pretending like she hasn't been watching me.

"Gorgeous day," Delilah says to her. "But it's getting cooler at night. I need to buy one of your scarves."

"I'd be delighted to knit one for you, dear. What's your favorite color?"

"Blue," I say loudly. Or is that just mine?

Delilah cuts me a stern look, then turns back to the knitter. "It's blue, but whatever you prefer would be lovely."

The knitter stares at me and purses her thin lips.

Ignoring my rapt attention, Delilah waves at Ally, her hospice-fundraising friend, who's jogging toward her.

"I've got the high school lined up for the winter," Ally says.

Delilah high-fives her. "I found a donor for the balloons. We should ask Celia to DJ."

"Oh, great idea. Can you take care of that?"

Delilah taps her temple. "Already added to my mental spreadsheet."

I sip my coffee, marveling at how capable and assured she is. Creative and smart. So goddamn sexy in her confidence.

"You're a lifesaver," Ally says. "Any fun plans for tonight?"

"Yes. I mean, *no*." Delilah's attention darts to me, then to her shoes, then to every person on the street. "Nothing much. Just, you know . . . wedding stuff. Then a thing after."

"Right. *The wedding*." Ally slides me a perusal, but the scrutiny isn't as cutting as usual. "Best of luck with all that."

"Delilah doesn't need luck," I say. "She's the master of her fate. And her life."

All she has to do is tell me she's single, and I'm all hers.

Delilah stares hard at me, like she's trying to read my mind, then she hurries inside.

I munch on my scone, pleased with her initial yes to Ally's question: *Any fun plans for tonight?* That yes could only pertain to our impending get-together, which means she's actually excited to see me later.

Another dog walks by with his owner. The pooch tugs and barks at Candy Cane. My girl sniffs the air and turns her head. Like Delilah, she's above the antics of desperate, loud men. Which gives me pause. I should try for subtlety tonight. Not overwhelm Delilah with my six-pack and musings on life. Focus instead on reviving her lost spark. As I've done often, I mentally rewrite number twenty-three on my list, crossing off "Find a reason to remove my shirt while in Delilah's apartment," adding instead "Make Delilah laugh so hard she pees."

# SIXTEEN

Respectful of Delilah's wedding-planning lies and our agreed-upon meeting time, I spend the afternoon huddled in my apartment, hippocampus deep in my novel. Voices and images crowd my head, like vivid memories of my late teens are in straitjackets, thrashing around, desperate to get out. I've never produced work this quickly. I also lose track of time.

It's 7:45 p.m.

Which is not good.

I planned to shower and shave, eat dinner, and feed Candy Cane, then take her to do her bathroom business before knocking on Delilah's door. The bathroom business and feeding of Candy aren't optional, which means my other plans are a no-go.

I dump food in Candy's bowl and rummage through my clothes, tossing shirts willy-nilly, until I find a clean T-shirt and jeans. Without the shower, I reach for Eternity to cover any lingering sedentary-illustrator-in-creating-mode aroma, but the bottle doesn't spritz. Frustrated, I loosen the lid and screw it back on. I angle the bottle and finally force it to spritz . . . and now I'm drenched in Eternity. Down my shirt, covering my jeans.

Honestly. Why can't I catch one freaking break?

I snatch one of my towels, rub at my clothes, and sniff the air, unsure if the bulk of the odor is hovering around me or sinking *into* me. When Candy whines to go out, I decide on the former. She needs out, and I need to get to Delilah's. A few minutes outside will surely disperse the smell.

By the time we get to Delilah's, ten minutes late, I'm exceedingly aware how wrong I was. My mouth tastes like it's full of Calvin Klein, and my eyes sting.

Delilah opens her door, smiles for half a second, then winces. "Jesus, E. Did you bathe in Eternity?"

I force my eyes wide, trying to keep them from watering. "I don't know what you mean. I didn't use cologne tonight."

"Is that why I might faint if I don't get a gas mask? The smell of death in my place is less offensive."

I hang my head. There's no adequate joke to save myself. "There was an incident."

"Did it involve the child version of you thinking there's no such thing as too much when it comes to cologne?"

"More like I got caught up in my work and blew through dinner and my planned get-ready time, and the Eternity bottle decided to explode on me." My stomach grumbles, corroborating my story.

"Honest to God. Only you." Instead of sending me packing, she bounces her heel, mutters something to the ceiling, then firms her jaw. "Just . . . get in here. But you have to use my shower, and my ex . . . *tra nice* fiancé has some clothes here." Her eyes have that fearful look Candy gets, wide and wary. "You can wear something of his."

She's worried I caught her slip, turning *ex* into *ex . . . tra nice*. News flash, Delilah Moon: I know your dirty little secret. "That's a splendid idea. Is it cool if I let Candy off her leash? She doesn't get into stuff."

Delilah rubs her nose, leaning away from me. "Of course. How's she doing? Good at night?"

I glance past Delilah into her apartment. The layout is similar to mine, but there's significantly less pink. Her place also has a homey quality mine doesn't, with vibrant throw pillows on her couches and bright artwork on her walls. The space feels happy, which makes me happy for her. Then I notice the awkwardly glued figurine of Little Gracie, the one I fixed for our truce, sitting on a lovely shelving unit.

I go from happy to downright moved.

I clear my throat. "Candy's usurped the bed, leaves me about an inch of space. Steals all the covers. So I'd say she's doing pretty well."

Delilah laughs, then wrinkles her nose and sneezes.

I would kick myself for ruining this night, but I don't. When life gives you lemons, you make lemonade. Or in my case, when that asshole Life gives me too much Eternity, I reinstate number twenty-three on my list: find a reason to remove my shirt while in Delilah's apartment.

I follow her into her cozy abode, grabbing my Eternity-soaked T-shirt by the back of my neck, taking it off as I go.

"The bathroom's through my bedroom. I'll find you clothes and fix you something to eat." She spins as she talks and stumbles, making a needy sound that has Candy Cane's ears perking up.

My stomach clenches at Delilah's lusty perusal. My jeans sit low on my hips, exposing my briefs, and I feel every contact point of my clothing: the denim scraping my hip bones, the elastic of my black briefs cutting across my abdomen. Unlike at the wet T-shirt contest I hosted in her shop, Delilah doesn't force eye contact, pretending she's not taking an eyeful. Her heated perusal is thorough, and my body stirs.

I want her hands on me, her mouth. I want to sink so deep inside her I forget I ever lived without her in my life.

I hold up my shirt. "Do you have a plastic bag to secure this for the night? Preferably something nonporous." Although my question is decidedly unsexy, my voice is back-road rough, dragging over the two feet between us.

"Yeah, sure." Hers is back road with a dash of honey. She meets my eyes, licks her lips. "I guess you need a clean towel."

"Either that or I can air-dry while eradicating your apartment of the stench of death." Not that I can smell much beyond the Eternity shrapnel and the pheromones wafting off Delilah.

Her eyes flare, doing another impromptu *Dancing with the Stars* number—drop, drag, slide, slide, blink, blink, slide. She's in bare feet, wearing worn jeans and a threadbare T-shirt with the words *Baking Queen* across her breasts. There's no missing her pert nipples through the thin blue cotton, the deepening of her breaths, and that sexy flush on her cheeks.

Every inch of me flexes with the goal to contain. Hold it together. *Do. Not. Kiss. Her. You. Desperate. Fucking. Asshole.*

"I'll get you a towel." Her honey-gravel voice turns extra husky, but she doesn't move.

I sure as hell don't move. I need three words from her. One admission. *I'm not engaged.* Once she gives me that gift, she can have me any which way she wants me, as long as I get to taste her lips.

She blinks again, touches her hair as though a strong wind blew through here, and is that . . . ? Yep. She subtly rubs her thighs together. "I'll toss together a salad. Something light, assuming you eat light to maintain"—she gestures vaguely at my body—"all that. You can eat after your shower, before the dead-body hunt, *while* you're wearing the shirt and pants I provide. Sound good?"

"Sounds perfect." Minus the shirt and pants and dead-body-hunt parts.

She gives a sharp nod and breezes past me, stomping around louder than necessary as she extricates a fresh towel from a hall closet. She tosses it at me and speed walks into her open kitchen, leaving me to decontaminate.

I take my time showering. I mean, this is Delilah's shower. It smells like her, clean and fresh and feminine, and I can't help picturing her under the hot spray.

A steamy flash hits: Delilah and me crammed into her tiny shower, those days before we were ready for sex but were insatiable for each other, wet bodies and lips sliding desperately, my throbbing erection digging into her stomach, slipping lower, teasing us with the possibility of slipping all the way in. Greedy hands. Sluicing water. Delilah falling apart, then stroking me until I shot my load onto her breasts and belly in a mind-blowing rush.

Showering alone isn't as fun.

I towel off and examine Hugo's clothes left for me in Delilah's room. His threads are as boring and posh as I expect: green collared golf shirt and khaki pants. No joke. How could she have fallen for this guy? I get dressed in the loser's clothes, which are snug, and I give the room a cursory glance. The space is as bright and lived in as the rest of her place, pillows piled on her bohemian-style duvet cover. A pretty quilt is draped over a side chair, and her distressed dresser has books stacked on top. As tempted as I am to poke around, I don't feel right snooping.

One day I hope she invites me in here to toss her pillows on the floor, mess up her sheets, sleep curled around her, and snoop to my heart's content. Today's not that day.

I leave the room and don't make it two steps. Mellow folk music plays from a stereo. Candy's made herself at home on the couch, and Delilah's swaying slightly, her back to me, humming while cutting up a salad. Nothing to get worked up about. But the scene is so domestic, like we're a couple again, about to eat together on a regular weekday night.

I blow out a rough breath, swallow past the *I wish* and *I miss* and *I want* lodged in my throat. "The Eternity has been eradicated."

She looks at me over her shoulder and snorts. "That is not your best look."

True. My ankles are poking out the bottom of the dorky pants. I lift the shirt's collar, going for full preppy mode. "I kind of dig it. Might wear it to Ricky and Aaron's wedding."

Her arms go rigid. "They invited you?"

"Ricky needs a roadie so the Tweeds can play. Or he took pity on me. Likely the latter. Guess we'll both be there?" In three weeks. At Sheldrake Falls. The gorgeous cottage-style inn with canopy beds, overstuffed duvets, fireplaces in each room, the smell of wilderness and romance in the air.

"Guess so." Her shoulders lower, and she grabs the cucumber by her cutting board. She starts peeling off the skin the way she knows I like.

Taking this as a positive sign, I go for casual, waltzing over to the living room side of the kitchen counter. I lean against the edge in my too-tight, too-preppy shirt and catch a whiff of something distinctly deathlike wafting from the kitchen. The reason for tonight's invite. First, I have a more pressing matter to address. "Is your fiancé coming in for the festivities?"

"Hugo? No." She peels faster. "He's super busy with work."

"We should drive down together."

Her peeler stills, just a second. Then she's meticulously stripping the cucumber naked. "Sure." She glances up at me shyly. "That would be nice."

My stomach flips. And growls. Her easy agreement has me leaning heavier onto her counter. "Thanks for cooking for me. No clue how I lost track of time."

"Must be amazing when you're that absorbed in work. Is it another in the Gates of Ember series? I heard something about a prequel."

"We're halfway through that piece, but Sathya, who writes it all, has gone MIA, which isn't odd for her, but this time feels different. I'm not sure what's up, and my agent's getting twitchy. For now I'm killing time with a new book, actually writing the script too." Writing *our* story, giving it the ending it deserves. "Something more personal."

"I'd love to hear about it, if you don't mind sharing."

I'm not exactly sure why I started writing our story, but I think I'm documenting it for Delilah. For her to understand what the past ten years were like for me, how integral she is in my life, even like this, as a friend who cuts me up a salad because I'm hungry and asks me to share my work and tells me I look ridiculous in preppy shirts. "It's early stages, but if you're willing, I'd love you to be the first to read it. When it's ready."

"I'd be honored," she says, swaying to the relaxing tunes. "Do you still use those Palomino pencils?"

"Blackwing Palominos, yeah. Although I've almost worn mine down to nothing, and they're out of stock in town and online. I'm impressed you remember, though."

She glances at my hands, heat in her eyes, like she recalls my lead-smudged fingers dragging up her thighs. "I remember . . . how much you loved those pencils. And how talented you were," she adds.

Delilah Moon, always boosting my art ego. "You know, you're partly responsible for the Gates of Ember series existing."

"Not sure how you figure that."

"When we were growing up, you were the one who gushed over my drawings. Kept telling me how amazing my stuff was. Cal and my family pushed me to keep drawing during WITSEC, but your encouragement is why I stuck with it as a kid."

She grabs an avocado, turns it over in her hand. "I think you're partly why I have my shop."

"Not sure how you figure that," I say, repeating her retort.

"I baked sporadically growing up, but you're the one who made it *fun*, always telling me what I baked was the best you ever tasted, goofing off when we cooked together. I think, unconsciously, baking after you left was a way for me to stay connected to those better days." She slices her knife through the avocado, making a clean circular cut. "To stay more connected to you."

She doesn't glance at me, but her admission spreads heat through my chest.

We settle into a comfortable silence as she cooks and sways her hips to the music. I catch the singer's lyrics and recognize Jack Johnson's "Better Together." Feeling like it's a sign, I make a mental note to add this song to the road trip playlist I'm already planning. I'll insert it before "Pillow Talk" and after "I Want to Know What Love Is."

Ricky's wedding can't come soon enough.

"So." I smack the counter and stick my nose up in the air. "From what I can deduce, something most definitely died in here. Of the rodent variety. Good thing I came with my own personal dead-rodent detector."

I round the island counter into the kitchen and open all the lower cabinets. Yep, something died in here. The smell's worse than my Eternity bomb, and it's way stronger with the doors open.

"I've already searched the cupboards," Delilah says. "Taken everything out. No dead rodents."

"You didn't have Candy Cane with you when you did that, did you?"

She shoots a soft look to my girl, who's panting on Delilah's couch. "I did not."

I whistle and click my tongue. On cue, Candy jumps off the couch and trots over. Instead of coming to me, she follows the death trail, shoving her cute nose into the cupboards. In five seconds she's nosing a box, whining and pawing at it. I follow my brilliant dog's lead and pull out what looks like a boxed fondue set. "Did you have a fondue party with a rat?"

"Actually, I did."

The annoyance in Delilah's voice has me pausing until I realize her double meaning. She ate fondue with that belittling rat, her ex-fiancé Hugo. Best to stay on subject. "Let's investigate, shall we?"

When I place the box on the counter, Candy whines louder, clearly intent on our mission. Delilah joins our investigative team, her brow furrowed as I open the lid and blast us with a stronger stench of decay.

The second it's open, Delilah says, "Oh my God," of the I-can't-believe-it oh my Gods.

I curl my lip. "What *is* that?"

What it is *not* is a dead animal. What it is, is a baggie filled with some kind of noxious brown liquid.

"Oh my God." She covers her face with her hands and cackles so hard Candy runs to the safety of the couch.

I grab Delilah's wrists and remove her hands from her face. "Explain yourself, Mars."

"I . . . we . . ." She's laughing too hard to talk. The sound's so unabashed and contagious that I laugh too. The harder I laugh, the harder she laughs, until she's losing it so thoroughly she tips forward and presses her forehead into my chest. I hold her like that, the two of us shaking, my cheeks sore from smiling. It feels as perfect as you'd imagine.

Eventually I pull back and brush a giddy tear from the corner of her eye. "Tell me honestly, Delilah. Did you poop in a baggie and forget it in the fondue pot?"

She half cackles again but reins herself in. "We took the pot to Avett's for dinner months ago—a double date with him and Naomi—"

"Naomi James?" While we didn't socialize in the same circles, Naomi sat beside me one year in math and helped me pass the class. She also had no issues calling me out for not wearing deodorant as often as I should have, and she loved teasing me for eating peanut-butter-and-potato-chip sandwiches. I like the idea of her dating Avett and giving him a hard time.

"Yeah," Delilah says. "They hooked up a few years ago, took off on a wild backpacking trip for, like, eight months. They're married with a kid now."

"No way."

"They're so cute together."

Jesus Christ. I missed so much.

"Anyway," Delilah goes on, "we made beef fondue and I brought my set, and we had some leftover raw meat. I guess I forgot Avett packed it in the pot for me to take home. It's been in there for four months."

Apparently, after four months, raw meat at room temperature turns into a toxic liquid. Apparently, after ten years, a person misses all the important stuff in everyone's life. But I won't dwell on all I've missed. There's too much, and my time with Delilah is too precious.

"Plug my nose," I tell her.

"What?"

"We need to transfer this toxic meat soup to your garbage, then take that bag to the metal bin behind your business. I'll grab tongs to extract it, but I need you to plug my nose. You know how sensitive my gag reflex can be." Hence the times I puked on Mom's azaleas, but my true goal is laughter. Lighting Delilah's faded spark with my antics.

She bites her lip, like she's fighting one of her solar eclipse smiles. "Good plan."

She grabs a pair of tongs from a drawer, hands them to me, then pulls out her garbage so it's ready for the dumping. She plugs my nose. "Be quick."

"The quickest." Bending awkwardly so Delilah can maintain her grip, I use the tongs to lift the baggie out of the fondue pot and launch it into the garbage bag. We're a synchronized SWAT team now. She grabs the plastic bin, while I tie off the bag and lift it, then both of us race for the door and run down the stairs, an excited Candy Cane hot on our tail as we rush outside to dispose of the offensive bag.

When the lid to the large bin slams shut, I face Delilah. "I can't believe you pooped in a baggie and hid it."

"It was the meat."

"Right." I wink. *The meat.*

"You're such a pest." She shoves me playfully, and we start laughing again, snorting and unleashing a slew of unattractive sounds. "God."

She wipes her eyes and catches her breath. "I haven't laughed this hard since . . ."

We lock eyes, both grinning our faces off. "High school," we say in tandem.

We stare at each other a beat, something deeper filling the moment. Then we make our way upstairs, joking and chatting and acting like ten long years didn't tear us apart. That's when I do the scariest thing I've done in ages. I dust off a smidgeon of the hope I buried under my Top Ten Best Days and imagine a real future with Delilah Moon.

# SEVENTEEN

"I can't believe it took me this long to watch this show." Delilah's kicked back on her couch, sprawled the way she sprawls, her hand mindlessly petting Candy Cane. "It's so cute."

Delilah's the one who's so cute, hanging out in sweatpants and a T-shirt, no makeup on. No pretense or primping. Just us being us, like we've been most nights this past week.

The day after the Eternity Incident and the Toxic-Meat-Bag Extraction, she welcomed me into Sugar and Sips with a solar eclipse smile, visited my outdoor table a few times, fussed over Candy Cane, and dished about the latest Windfall drama: much to the dismay of some residents, this year's Scarecrow Scavenger Hunt planner asked to change the after-party music from classic country to—*gasp*—something modern.

Gotta love small-town drama. And a foot in the door.

The conversation led me to reminding Delilah how cute the show *Gilmore Girls* is with all its small-town turmoil. Then Sandra, who was spying on me as per usual, piped up to tell us the only small-town show worth watching was *Schitt's Creek*. Neither of us had seen the sitcom, and we agreed to watch an episode together, which turned into two, which turned into seven. Aside from an evening I spent drinking beers and catching up with Avett, Delilah and I have had dinner together every night this week, followed by our cozy TV viewing.

"I would kill to have a coffee date with David Rose," I say. I'm on the other side of Candy, who's in a love sandwich between Delilah and me. My perfect doggo is much more relaxed these days, letting us both pet her. I occasionally let my hand brush Delilah's, getting off on the rush of heat making me light headed. Even better? She never once pulls away.

"As fun as David would be," she says, "I'm all Moira. Her theatrics are too good."

"She reminds me of our English teacher—Mrs. Bozic? When she took that year off in England and came back with an accent?"

Delilah laughs. "Remember when Avett was caught imitating her? He got in so much trouble."

"Those were good times," I say, letting my fingers roam toward Delilah's, brushing my thumb over her knuckles.

She watches our hands and moves hers slightly, still petting Candy, but also allowing our hands to flirt. Gentle bumps and soft touches. When she slides her thumb over mine, tracing the half moon of my nail, I experience a full-body shiver.

I stretch my fingers wider. "I'm insanely impressed, by the way."

"With what?"

"With everything you're doing—running your business, being a tough but fair boss, making time for fundraising."

She sighs. "Feels like I'm playing catch-up most days, but Maggie's grandmother died of cancer a while back, and the hospice team went above and beyond. They made Millie's last days as comfortable as possible, while offering grief counseling for the family. I'd go weekly with Mags, to be there for her, and I loved her *bubbe*. Fundraising afterward made me feel like I was helping other families too."

"Like I said, insanely impressive."

"Thank you." She blushes and adjusts on the couch.

Her shifting twists her T-shirt's neckline. My eyeballs zero in on the tease of visible skin—because *Delilah, skin*—then I freeze. I don't blink.

A black string I hadn't noticed hangs over her collarbone, dipping below the cotton of her shirt. It could be any black string. Any necklace, but my heart beats faster. So damn fast I can barely talk. "Is that . . ."

She frowns. Follows my line of sight, then bites her lip and presses her hand over the center of her chest. "It is."

The moon necklace I made for her. The one she said she'd never take off.

The one I assumed she destroyed in a blaze of fury.

Neither of us is petting Candy now. Delilah watches me. I watch her. I'm not sure what wearing my necklace means, but it means something. "I figured you threw it away."

Swallowing slowly, she traces the shape of the moon through her shirt. "I got rid of most of your stuff, had a bonfire while Maggie cursed you and squirted gasoline, but some things . . ." She shrugs, giving me a sad smile.

She doesn't need to finish that sentence. She kept this necklace and the reglued horse figurine. Even though I broke her heart, a part of her still cared enough to save pieces of me.

Maybe she always hoped I'd come back.

"May I?" I reach for the string but wait for her to give me the okay to touch it. To touch *her*.

She nods, and I fit my fingers under the string, can't help grazing her collarbone and silk-soft skin. Heat spirals through my stomach. Goose bumps erupt along her neck.

Loving her reaction, I pull out the pendant and run my thumb over the smooth rock. "I like seeing this on you."

"I don't know why I put it on. I mean, it's not like we're *us* anymore. But you were my best friend, and it's been so nice spending time together. And I—"

"Delilah," I cut in.

"Yeah?" She's breathing harder, so many emotions swimming in her eyes.

"I don't care why you're wearing it. I'm just glad you are."

She blinks and nods. We resume petting Candy, our fingers brushing again but lingering more. The extended contact makes my blood rush. My heart becomes a fireball burning up my chest. She focuses on my mouth, her eyes falling heavy, and I nearly launch myself at her.

"I should probably go," I force out. I don't want to leave or move, but I'm offering her an opening. A chance to tell me to stay, to confess she's not engaged and ask me if we can give our relationship a second chance.

She traces my nail again, turning the area into an erogenous zone. "Probably best." Her finger slowly leaves mine. "I have an early start."

"Yeah, sure." I deflate slightly and hate standing up, but she's wearing my necklace. I'll take that as a win. I'm also turned on from the finger flirting and don't attempt to hide it.

I adjust myself best I can and look up to catch Delilah focused on the bulge behind my fly. My cock twitches. Pink sears her cheeks. I'd kill to see that pink steal across her chest and breasts, stain her skin with desire as I peel off her underwear and give her a filthy lick.

I grit my teeth and give my butt a hard clench.

At the door, with Candy doing her impatient dance, I linger before leaving. "I can make curry for tomorrow, if you want."

"You make curry?"

We picked up food a couple of nights this week and alternated cooking the other evenings. Simple, easy meals like pasta, grilled chicken, and Cobb salad. I've been waiting to cross off number forty-seven on my list: make Delilah my orgasmic lamb curry.

"Sathya had me over to her family's for dinner once, and I begged her mother to share her recipe." Although I make mine with far fewer green chilies. "My spice collection is off the charts."

"I love that you love to cook."

I love that Delilah still loves things about me. "Aside from drawing and running, cooking was a great way for me to get out of my head. Kind of like baking for you—the simple tasks of following recipes shifted my focus. And if my food was good enough, it would shut my brothers up for longer than two minutes."

She inhales deeply, attention hazy as if lost in thought. "I miss your loud family."

"Yeah." I rub the back of my neck, remembering my last sight of Desmond, his self-loathing as he gripped his steering wheel, saying he never wanted Sadie to see what he's become. "I miss them too."

More specifically, the people we were before my father ruined our lives.

"I'd love to try your curry," Delilah says gently, like she knows my mind skittered off track. "I'll come to your place this time, bring something for dessert?"

I ache to hug her, hold her, remind myself I'm in control of my future now. Not my father. Not the US Marshals. I have TV nights with Delilah and the dog of dogs and my own graphic novel in creation. "Dessert would be great. And we'll watch *Schitt's Creek*."

More than tenderness seems to soften her eyes. "So much *Schitt's Creek*."

We linger by her door another moment. Delilah slides her teeth over her bottom lip. I shove my hands into my jeans pockets so I don't do something stupid like haul her in for a kiss.

"Tomorrow it is," I say and leave, feeling light and heavy. Hopeful and down.

I'm thrilled we're spending real time together, but Delilah still doesn't trust me enough to tell me about Hugo or the full story of what happened to her after I left. I feel like everything's linked, that her lies are born from that devastating time—the story Avett wouldn't tell me and everyone in Windfall seems to know. But there's no point dwelling. Not when I get to cook my orgasmic lamb curry for her and share another night hanging out.

Tomorrow will be our eighth evening together, which leaves thirteen days until we're listening to my killer road trip playlist, on our way to the idyllic romance of Sheldrake Falls. If all goes according to plan, Delilah and I will be sharing one of those plush poster beds while the woodsy fireplace crackles.

# EIGHTEEN

The next morning, I wake up to barking. And banging. Not the good kind of banging, with me thrusting hard and deep into Delilah, the bed shaking, my fingers digging into her hips as I slam into her. This is who-the-hell-is-trying-to-break-down-my-door banging.

I have morning wood. Similar to the perpetual wood I'm often adjusting around Delilah, but I'm wearing briefs, and I'm too tired to adjust or pee or do anything but stumble out of bed and drag my ass to the door. I don't bother checking who it is. I don't care that my dick's tenting my briefs like he's on the camping trip of his life. I pet my excellent guard dog, who's now smiling at the door, tail wagging, instead of growling.

Yawning, I unlock the door and swing it open.

"Thank God you're—" Delilah's gaze drops to my blatant erection. She flushes red, mumbles a swear, then swivels around. "Can you please get dressed?"

"Can you please not interrupt my sleep? I was having a fantastic dream. You happened to be in it," I add, because I'm cruel like that.

Another mumbled swear drifts toward me. Then, "This is serious, E. I'm guessing you haven't seen the news?"

I'm suddenly very awake and much less amused. "Give me a sec."

Back in my room, I toss on sweats and a T-shirt, brush my teeth quickly. Delilah isn't sitting when I get out. She's pacing, making Candy Cane antsy. I'm antsy. "What is it?"

"Your story's out."

I glance at my sketchbook and laptop on my dining table, freaked for a moment that I accidentally sent my work-in-progress novel to someone. That type of slip doesn't seem possible, and I haven't used our actual names. I used the brilliant cover-ups Delilyn and Edgren.

"What do you mean, *it's out?*"

She quits pacing in front of me and grips my shoulders. This is Jake's move. His I'm-here-to-hold-you-together arm clasp.

I'm now rightfully freaking out. "Delilah, what the hell happened?"

"Your dad wrote some kind of book, a memoir about his time working with the cartel. It's exploded on social media."

"I'm sorry, what?" I must still be sleeping and dreaming. It's the only explanation.

"He didn't mention your aliases or where you live, and I didn't see anything about you boys specifically, but he used his real name. Half of Windfall will remember him and put two and two together. The other half will hear the gossip through the grapevine."

I replay her words, a strange tingling spreading at the base of my skull, hoping I misunderstood her. But nothing about her factual explanation was vague. "Just so we're clear, you're saying my father decided he'd take it upon himself to tell our story to the world without our approval, before we're even allowed to have our lives back, so he can use the evil shit he did to make even more blood money? And now everyone here will know *his* version of the hell that is my life? Is that what I'm to understand?"

Her face slackens. "I'm so sorry."

I'm not sorry. I'm *furious*. I'm the raging lava river in Gates of Ember about to hit tsunami levels. How could he do this? How could he hurt his own family over and over and over without a thought to the repercussions, our feelings, the fallout? I'm beyond shaking. My heart's punching at my ribs as hard as I want to punch my father's face, and I don't want Delilah here for this.

"Can you take Candy Cane for a pee? I need a moment." Or fifty.

"Yeah, sure." She presses the flat of her hand to my chest, must feel the hard jabs of my heart. "I'll be right back, okay?"

I nod, unable to form a reply. She pauses at the door, glances back at me.

I force a tight "I'll be fine," even though I'm anything but fine. The second she's gone, I find my phone and power it up. As expected, there are a slew of texts from my brothers, this time in a group chat, minus MIA Desmond.

Jake: I will fucking kill him.

Cal: He's not worth our energy.

Lennon: I'll help Jake hide the body.

Cal: No one's hiding anything. He kind of did us a favor. Now everyone we hurt will know we didn't do it on purpose.

Jake: Did you just defend our scumbag father?

Lennon: I'll make room in the grave for Cal.

Cal: No one's killing anyone.

Jake: If he makes Mom look bad, or hurts her in any way, I will personally dismember him.

Cal: If he hurts Mom, I'll cut him and throw him in shark infested waters.

Lennon: Dude. Who took over Cal's phone? Did the cartel get to him?

Cal: No one fucks with Mom.

I tap out a furious question, the only one that matters.

E: Did his dipshit move ruin our chances to leave WITSEC?

Jake: No. We're clear. Agent Rao just called Mom. They were gonna give us the news today. There are no lingering threats. Whoever wants their old IDs can have them soon. Until then, we're technically free to tell people our real names.

The chat goes on, with Cal and Jake saying they'll likely resume their old names, Lennon saying he's not sure, even though they're already using our birth names in the chat. They curse Dad in between speculation and toss out a few worries about Desmond. I'm shaking too much to join the conversation. The relief in knowing the cartel's no longer a threat gets burned under my rage. Any kind of tell-all book will devastate Mom, drag her through this mess all over again. And Desmond. The last thing he'd want is to have any aspect of his life splashed across a book, written in permanent ink.

The walls feel like they're swaying, my vision clouding around the edges. All I see is hate. Red-hot fury, searing me alive as I picture the people I love hurting.

I storm into my room, toss on my running gear, and jam my feet into my sneakers. I'm running before I get outside, pushing my legs to go, go, go. I don't have a plan. I just need to move before I end up experiencing one of my *in*bursts, barricading myself in my room, unable to face the world and all it's heaped on my shoulders.

I hardly feel the pavement under me, barely notice the passing streets. I'm running without seeing, furious thoughts whirling at a dizzying rate. So much pain for Mom. Worry for Des. Sadness for all my brothers, who, like me, are nothing but marionettes in Dad's extravagant theater production of *My Family of Pawns*.

My lungs burn. My thighs and calves ache. The muscles in my face hurt from glaring. I have no clue how long I've been running, but I find myself on the gravel road to the old quarry.

The massive rocks still hold sentry, guarding my memories: Avett and I messing around; Delilah and I sitting on the stone ledge, lying on our backs, legs dangling over, holding hands while we talked about how much she missed her dad, how much we hated acting in *Oliver!*, how much Desmond annoyed me, how much I loathed math and science, how excited she was to be a teacher one day. I find myself in the same spot, on this shitty day of days, my legs dangling over the edge, rocks digging into my spine as I lie back. The sky is so blue and clear I'm sure a bird will fly over and crap on me, as per Life's MO. I press my hand to my sternum, unsure if this relentless pain will ever cease, kind of drifting off into a haze.

Tires on gravel alert me to someone's arrival, followed by the sharp crack of a door being slammed.

"Knew you'd be here." Avett's voice sounds strange out here, in this place of memories. Too mature and weighted for the boy who used to crack up when I'd shove rocks down his shorts.

I stay lying on my back. Avett sits on the ledge beside me. "I had no clue, man. I obsessed over a ton of reasons why you might have disappeared, talked to Delilah about your dad maybe stealing cash from businesses he worked for, wondering if you were too embarrassed to reach out. And witness protection *was* on my radar, but with the hacking theory, not money laundering, since Jake was good with computers and could've gotten your family caught up in high-level drama. But having cartel hits on your heads?" He blows out a long breath. "Can't imagine what you've been through."

There isn't much to say besides the obvious. "It was rough."

He picks up a small rock, launches it into the gaping quarry. "The tell-all book can't be good news."

"I don't know why he can't just leave it alone. Actually, that's bullshit. If I asked him, I have no doubt he'd say he had an opportunity and he took it. That's exactly what he said, by the way. I cornered him once, demanded to know how he could launder money and risk our lives. With zero emotion, he said, *I had an opportunity and I took it.*"

"Fuck, that's cold."

My angry snort doesn't begin to cover my feelings on the matter. "The man is a narcissistic egomaniac who deserves to spend his life behind bars, but here we are," I force myself to sitting and sigh. "How'd you know I was here?"

"Our vet tech told me about your father's book deal and the money laundering, and she saw Sandra at Sugar and Sips, who said she saw you running in this direction on her drive to town. I had a break and thought I'd check here, needed to tell you how awful I feel for yelling at you the way I did."

Of course it was Sandra who sleuthed out my location. "The rumor mill is as legendary as always. And you don't have to apologize. We were all hurt by what my father did."

"You didn't deserve that parade of hate, E. Not when what happened probably hurt you more than it hurt us. But you're right about the rumor mill. I also heard Delilah's frantically looking for you."

My heart kicks back into cheetah-sprinting speed. It's already midday. I didn't plan to be gone this long. "I should've left a note or something. It just all hit me so hard."

"Yeah, you should've." He crosses his arms, banging the heels of his boots into the rock wall. "You showing up here makes more sense now—turning up out of the blue, insinuating yourself back into Delilah's life. You lost her as suddenly as she lost you. I assume she hasn't told you about the ex yet?"

"She's Fort Knox. Her dedication is impressive." While there haven't been fake-wedding meetings the past week, and she hasn't let another "ex . . . *tra nice*" blunder slip, this stunt of mine, taking off without considering her feelings, might have set us back. I don't know what I was thinking, not talking to her first.

Avett rubs his chin. "I'm not surprised she hasn't cracked, and what I said still stands. A lot went down after you vanished. I'm rooting for you two, but you need to give Delilah whatever time and space she needs. The idea of being with you again won't be easy for her." I open my mouth to ask *again* what everyone's keeping from me, but he holds up his hand. "Don't ask. It isn't my story to tell. But don't you dare disappear on her again, even for a run or mental health moment, especially when you've been hit by a grenade like this crap your father pulled. She'll assume the worst, and I will lose it on you. If you hurt her, I hurt you."

The Avett of my youth wasn't this much of a badass. Aside from stealing booze from his father and mutilating stuffed animals, he was a bookworm who read more than he spoke. I appreciate his badass-ness, though. I love him for protecting Delilah, even if it means protecting her from me. "I hear you loud and clear. Any chance I can get a lift back?"

My mind isn't as on fire as when I left. There's still a lot to process, like imagining the exact ways I'll torture my father if I ever see him again, but I want to be with Delilah while I decompress, have her hand pressed to my chest, easing the pain of the rocks scraping my heart.

"I can drop you at home," Avett says. A sentiment that winds me. *Home.* Delilah and Windfall are once again my home. "But roll the window down. You smell like shit. I'll call Delilah and let her know you'll be back soon."

~

By the time I'm standing at my apartment door, my neck and back are clammy from the dried sweat on my body. Or is that the sense of impending doom sucking the heat from my blood? My shins certainly hurt from me kicking myself repeatedly for leaving here without a word.

Delilah will be furious. She *should* be furious.

How could I have been so insensitive?

Steeling myself for the worst, I ease the door open. Candy Cane's already at the entrance, tail wagging, body wiggling, ready to forgive me for running without her, zero grudges held. Dogs really are the best. Actually, no. Delilah is the best—the woman who rolls with my stupid jokes and makes life hopeful again. She turns me on with one flirt of her fingers, inspires my creativity, and sasses me the way I love to be sassed. She's part of all my Bests and all my Worsts. She's everything I want, and when I see her sitting on the couch—deflated, not angry, sad, not furious—my gut caves into a sinkhole.

"I shouldn't have left like that. I was just out for a run, needed to burn off my frustration, but I ended up at the quarry, and . . . I don't know. I just couldn't move. I didn't think about how leaving without a word would affect you. I should've thought. I'm so sorry, Delilah."

She leans her elbows on her knees and rubs her forehead. "It shouldn't be a big deal, but it is. With our messed-up history, it really is." She looks up, fire in her eyes. Like she's the winged albatross in my sketches, regal and fiercely courageous. "You can't disappear like that, E. Not when you've been dealt a blow like this morning and I have no clue how it'll affect you. Letting you back into my life has been hard, but you're here." She jabs at her chest. "You're *in here*. And thinking you might have taken off, out of anger or frustration or whatever—I can't go through that again."

As much as I want to go to her, hug her and tell her I'll never be this dumb again, I heed Avett's ever-present warning and give her space. Plus, I smell like ass.

Instead of infecting my pink furniture with my odor, I sit on the floor cross-legged. Candy Cane plops down beside me—man's best friend, regardless of my stupid choices. "You have my word. I won't disappear on you again. I don't always deal with family stress well, and I don't like the idea of you seeing me lose it, but you're my best friend, Delilah. Always have been and always will be." I swallow roughly and drop my voice. "I promise I'll treat you with the respect you deserve."

Tears glossing her eyes, she nods. "Are you okay?"

"No. Not really." There's no point lying, not when I need to earn her trust.

"I hate him for hurting you like this. And for what? To earn some cash?"

I pick at a rock lodged in my sneaker's sole. "I'm somewhat numb when it comes to my dad, but I'm sick for my mother. I don't know what this book will unearth, if he'll talk about wild cartel parties or reveal that he had an ongoing affair with Staci Wilcox." The supposed secretary who introduced him to the world of money laundering and betrayal. After learning of her involvement, I couldn't help but wonder if she used sex to lure him in. Not that it matters now.

I rest my elbows on my thighs, feeling too heavy to support my upper body weight. "I think, when the dust settled, that part hit Mom the hardest—feeling gullible, never realizing her husband was a mastermind criminal. And I'm sick for Desmond, who already hates himself. If Dad brings us into the book, talks about our toughest early days when he was still around, I'm scared what it'll do to all of us, but Des in particular. So yeah. I'm furious with my father. I hate him for the shrapnel his choices caused, the fallout that still lingers. His actions hurt so many people in so many ways."

Delilah presses her fist to her mouth, like she's struggling to keep it together, then she wipes her eyes. "He caused a lot of damage. Things he'll . . ." Her voice falters, cutting me deep. "He'll never grasp the repercussions of his actions. But I'm here for you," she says more firmly. "Seeing you hurting hurts me too, and I want to help any way I can."

Instantly, I know. Whatever she's still hiding from me, she's not staying quiet just to protect herself from reliving the details. She's worried the details will hurt *me*. That I'll melt down and run off again, like today. Which means I need to get my act together. "Can I still make you my famous orgasmic lamb curry? Tomorrow instead of tonight?"

She lets out a watery laugh. "I'd like that."

All I'd like is more of Delilah in my apartment, giving me hell for my bad choices, offering me comfort just by sitting on my couch. "Can you believe how messed up my life is?"

Me with cartel ties and a fake name, Delilah pretending she's engaged to make sure we take this reunion extra slow.

Her lips part like she's about to reply, but both our phones ring. We stare at each other a moment, then she grabs her phone from the coffee table. I stand and hurry toward mine on the kitchen counter.

It's my agent. Cursing under my breath, I answer. "Hey, Margot."

"Brian, hey. Just wondering if you've heard from Sathya yet. I got another fishing email from Josh."

My frustrated editor. I drag my hand down my face, wondering if this call is good timing or bad. I settle on: it doesn't matter. "I haven't, but there's something you should probably know."

My father may not have blasted out our names or aliases with his social media bomb, but when his book comes out next year, the world might learn who I am. Who I *was*. That I've been in WITSEC for ten years. Gossip from Windfall might slither its way onto the internet sooner than that. Margot and my publisher will need this information, in case it comes with professional repercussions.

Delilah's still on the couch, rubbing her forehead like she's having a painful conversation of her own. I don't like seeing her stressed, but I love that she's here. That she didn't hold my screwup against me. Talking quietly in the kitchen, I give Margot the lowdown so we can wade through this mess: I have two names, one of them might gain notoriety shortly, and I have no clue what it means for my career.

When Margot stays silent, I check the connection. "You still there?"

"Yes. Yeah. Sorry, I'm just floored." She exhales heavily. "So you've been in witness protection the entire time I've known you?"

Honestly. The story that is my life. "That would be accurate."

"And this tell-all from your father—it can't be easy. How are you holding up?"

"I'll be fine. Just don't know what happens when I get my old ID back. How it'll affect our contracts and such."

"I'll have my lawyer look into it, but . . ." Her pause lingers. "Last time we spoke, you mentioned your new project—a graphic novel about your life. Is it about your father and the cartel and what it was like being in witness protection?"

I tense. I know where this bread crumb trail leads, and I refuse to follow it into a gingerbread house that will be laced with arsenic. I go into my bedroom for privacy, followed closely by Candy Cane, who launches herself onto my bed.

"That book's off the table," I say. "I'm writing it for me and for a woman I hurt when I disappeared. I only told you about it because I figured Sathya would be in touch soon and it would never need to be used."

"But you suggested I tell the publisher."

"Only so you wouldn't worry about the contract being dropped. I figured if you had a backup plan, you wouldn't ask me to write the rest of Sathya's script again, and when she resurfaced, none of it would matter." She's so silent, I go rigid. "You didn't tell the publisher, did you?"

"Josh called this week, and I needed to do damage control. I suggested you had this other story, that if the worst happened, we could use it. I didn't know then what I know now, and Josh didn't seem impressed. He didn't mention it again in tonight's email, but we'll have to tell him about your history. Once he puts two and two together, he'll be salivating for this book."

There's that bird crap I was waiting for, falling directly on my head. "Then you tell him no. I'm not my father. I won't sell our story."

"You're sure?" Margot pushes.

"I'm sure. Please don't ask me again." But I know she will. This is her livelihood, and she smells a big payday. As will my editor.

"Fine. It's up to you. But just so you understand, if Sathya doesn't come through with that script, we'll be short on choices."

When we hang up, I make another big decision and send a text to Sathya, telling her to check out Raymond S. Bower's book announcement, adding the juicy tidbit that he's my father and that my real name is Edgar. My regular "please call me" and "where are you" texts have gone unanswered. I'm guessing this shocker will get her attention.

"Everything okay?" Delilah's at the entrance to my bedroom, arms folded around her middle.

I drop my phone on my bed, far enough from Candy not to freak her out. "Drama with my agent." The concern on Delilah's face reinforces that I can't sell our story. Not when I know her wounds are deeper than she's letting on. I'll have to find a way to deal with my publisher. "What about you? You looked stressed on your call."

"Staffing issues. Leif quit, so I'm down a dishwasher who also helps with the prep."

Well now. That unfortunate situation comes with a silver lining. "Luckily you know a former professional dishwasher, and I might be able to help with some of the other stuff."

"That's sweet, E. But today's been rough for you."

I step toward her. When she wrinkles her nose, because I once again smell offensive around her, I step back. "The grunt work will be good for me. It'll get me out of my head. As long as I can take breaks to walk Candy, I'm ready and willing."

She shifts on her feet. "You have your own work to do."

"Delilah, let me help you." *Let me love you. Let me be with you. Let me pick out the shrapnel from your wounds until there's nothing left but scars I'll kiss better every night.*

She unlatches her arms from around her waist, then fiddles with her moon necklace. "If it'll help you, then I'd appreciate it. Just until I find a replacement. But"—she makes a face—"you have to shower before showing up tomorrow."

"No need. The sweat stench will dissipate when I sleep, and I'll spray on some Eternity in the morning."

The corner of her lips quirks up. "I doubt there's any left in the bottle."

"Good thing I bought in bulk."

Laughing, she walks to my door, pausing before she leaves—a familiar move these days. She launches a wistful glance over her shoulder, like she's in a perfume ad of her own, a new Calvin Klein scent meant to conjure sexual tension and desire and the stirrings of rekindled love. I'd call the signature scent Longing.

When she's gone, I lie on my bed next to Candy and call Mom.

She answers swiftly. "Hey, honey. How you holding up?"

"Me?" My mom may be a subpar quilter and an unimaginative cook, but she always puts her kids first, even when she shouldn't. "Don't worry about me. How are *you?*"

"I've had better days." Her voice has an edge to it, the sound of exhaustion and defeat turning it hard.

"He's such a fucking asshole."

"He really fucking is."

We both laugh—the tired kind of laugh that makes you sigh. I rub Candy's side, letting her softness mellow me. "Jake said Agent Rao called and we're clear of danger. As far as you know, are there any lingering threats?"

"Any Becerra family members who held a grudge are gone. The marshals just wanted to make sure the associated families wouldn't step in and keep old feuds alive. From what I know, those involved shifted allegiances. They have bigger concerns than a dead man's vengeance.

Your father apparently found out before us. That's why he went public with the memoir when he did."

How smashingly kind of him. Still, relief finally hits me, a bone-deep heaviness that has me sagging deeper into the bed. The official end of any threats. No more backlash that could hurt the people I love. I stroke Candy's velvet ears. She licks mine.

"I'm in Windfall, Ma. Been here over two weeks."

It feels more like two months, every minute with Delilah stretching into endless moments I hoard and replay in my evening montages. Tonight's will be titled "Delilah and Me and Longing."

"I know you're there, E."

I glare at my pink ceiling. "Did that traitor Lennon tell you?"

"Lennon didn't say a word. I know *you* and know how much you cared for Delilah. I knew you wouldn't wait."

A mother always knows. "Why didn't you yell at me?"

"You're twenty-seven, and you've spent your adult years on a leash—told what you can and can't say, where you can and can't live. Seeing what these years have done to you boys has devastated me, and I won't stand in the way of your free will any longer. If Delilah and Windfall are what you want, then you better do whatever you can to fight for her."

If she saw my list of fifty ways to win her back, she'd know I'm not giving up easily. "Have you thought any more about coming back? Mrs. Jackson and the quilting girls miss you."

She pauses. I pet Candy, hating myself for taking off on my sweet dog like I did. Living the past ten years in relative isolation has done me no favors, like Mom worries, but maybe in different ways than she expects. I'm not used to caring for others, putting their needs before my own.

"I'm thrilled you're there," Mom finally says, "but there's so much negativity associated with that place for me. Your brothers are a different story. They all say they won't go back permanently, but I think they want to. They're just nervous. They've all left a lot of unfinished business in that town." All of it packed in their these-memories-hurt-me-the-most keepsake boxes. "I hope they find their way there, but they're not as strong and determined as you."

A strong man wouldn't tear off for the morning and leave his girl and dog without a word. A strong man wouldn't fall apart at some shitty news he should have come to expect. He should make sure the woman he loves knows she's supported at all costs. I better start carrying my weight around here.

# NINETEEN

Washing dishes is familiar work to me. It's a head-down job where chefs and waiters often ignore you, dumping dishes in the sink with a messy clatter, while they bustle around with their more important work. Delilah's café has a more pleasant vibe and manageable speed, but everyone's acting weird.

Delilah's pierced baker, Angel, carefully puts a mixing bowl in the sink, like she's worried any quick movements will have me hitting the floor, on the lookout for stray bullets. She then pats my shoulder the way I petted Candy Cane those first few days, tentative and gentle.

"You're doing a great job," she tells me.

Of course I'm doing a great job. I have four years' experience under this apron. "I'm aiming for employee of the month."

"You'll be a shoo-in."

Two shoulder pats later and a few pitying looks from the working baristas who pass, I have the distinct impression everyone thinks being in WITSEC means I'm made of glass. I mean, I get it. If I was on the outside looking in, I'd be fascinated, studying me like I'm a science experiment, one wrong ingredient from blowing up or shattering. I'm just not used to everyone knowing my business. For ten years, I've been a version of Lennon's Invisible Man poster.

With another session of dishes tackled, I grab the bus bin and push out the swinging doors to clear tables. The front door jingles. By the time I round the service counter, Mrs. Jackson's standing in front of me, holding her purse close to her stomach. "Edgar, I had no idea. What your mother—what your *whole* family must have gone through." She pats my arm. "Just horrible."

I'm starting to wonder if dogs actually like all the petting. Maybe it makes them feel overcoddled and insecure. "Thanks, Mrs. Jackson. It's been tough, but we're glad it's all over." Or just beginning again. It's hard to tell with Dad's tell-all on the horizon.

"I'm terribly sorry for my harsh words," she says, empathy in her dark eyes.

"It's okay. Everything that happened was pretty messed up."

She tuts. "When I'm wrong, I say I'm wrong. But if I see your disgrace of a father, God help him."

I picture Mrs. Jackson torturing my father by quilting his body, forcing him to wear little squares on his skin, each one a symbol of the damage he caused. "I'll be sure to give him your address."

Another arm pat later, she goes to order her coffee and pastry. I get the table clean as the door chimes again, announcing the arrival of two unfamiliar teens. The girls scan the café and stop when their eyes land on me. Whispers ensue, along with staring and pointing, like they're a couple of expert birders who've happened upon a rare species of endangered fowl. I imagine myself a great potoo, a neotropical bird who can simply close its eyes and camouflage with a tree.

I close my eyes. When I open them, I'm pretty sure I never camouflaged.

Mrs. Jackson bustles away from the counter, take-out coffee in hand, and marches for the birders. "This is a place of business, girls," she says in her school-principal tone. "Not a zoo. Get going or order up."

Rightfully chastised, they tuck tail and run. Narc Sandra catches my eye and salutes me. Through coffee shop chitchat, I've discovered she used to work at a security firm, hence her vigilant surveillance of me. With my WITSEC past blasted around Windfall, she must think

I'm one of her people now. A fellow undercover person with links to the law.

I attempt to clean another table out front, but the bell chimes again, announcing the arrival of Delilah's cousin who yelled at me on the first episode of *Guess Who Hates You Next!* He apologizes and pats my arm. Delilah's hairdresser comes in on his heels, with another—*you guessed it*—arm pat. Callahan's friend finds me and asks if I'm sure we aren't Russian spies, while patting my arm.

When he's gone, Shawn Harden, drummer of the Tweeds, saunters in and switches things up. He goes for the arm punch. "Dude, you were in WITSEC. That's so cool." He still smells like weed.

"It was something, all right."

He nods absentmindedly and lopes toward the counter. I find myself tensing. If this parade continues like last time, I'll eventually be faced with Delilah's mother again. I'm pretty sure she won't pet me like I'm Candy Cane. She'll probably come armed with a shotgun.

I wipe the table slower, bracing myself for her arrival, but she doesn't show. As should be expected. My WITSEC news isn't new to her.

More people enter, some of them scanning the shop, eyes widening when they see me. I used to like visiting zoos, sketching the animals and walking the leisurely paths, but I'm starting to sympathize with my caged and scrutinized brethren. Without the ability to camouflage, I beeline for the safety of the kitchen and slump against the sink.

Angel takes one look at me and disappears down the hall.

She returns moments later, with her boss in tow, and says, "I told you it was bad."

Delilah hurries over and doesn't offer an arm pat. She threads her fingers through mine. "I should've realized everyone would want a piece of you. I'll kick the lurkers out."

"And ruin all this extra business I'm bringing in? I'm gunning for employee of the month." I give her hand an affectionate squeeze.

Angel's attention zeros in on our connection, the tender way Delilah's running her thumb over my knuckles. Spoiler alert: it feels *sensational*. Instead of talking loudly about Delilah's wedding and reminding me she's off limits, Angel removes the dishcloth tucked into her apron tie and tosses it on the prep table. "I'm due for a break. Be back in ten."

She marches out loudly.

First a salute from Sandra. Now Angel's basically giving me her blessing to marry Delilah. Strange happenings are afoot.

Using my free hand, I tuck a stray curl behind Delilah's ear. "Hope I'm doing an okay job."

"You're such a huge help. I put an ad up today. Hopefully I'll find someone soon."

"However long you need me is cool. Dinner might just be a bit later tonight. I need time to bring my curry up to orgasm level."

"E, quit being a pest." She says this with a playful smile, still holding my hand.

I adjust our hands, giving myself space to lean toward her ear. "Do you still like your food spicy, Delilah?"

Her hot breath brushes my neck, sending shivers down my spine. "I do."

"How hot do you like it?" *How hot and wild do you like your sex?* is what I want to ask. She never hesitated during our teenage exploits, loved pushing our boundaries, but it's been ten long years. I've had occasional flings with other women. She's matured, been with other men. A desperate need to know her preferences and deepest desires has my fingers tingling to explore her new curves.

"However you make it is fine." Her voice thins, turning breathy.

Mine's all gravel again, navigating this back road, going extra slow for this singular woman. "Do you experiment like you used to? Get excited to try different things?" Like watching porn on my bed.

"Yeah." It's just one word, but the way she says it—*yeah*—half moaned, half whispered, her breasts arching toward me, I know she knows what game I'm playing. Tempting her, pretending like I'm talking about food instead of sex, letting her know I'm ready whenever she is.

"I'll make it extra special for you. They'll hear you moaning down the street."

She whimpers. My body temperature rises.

And the swinging doors bust open.

A barista drops dirty cutlery in the sink and gives me a pitying look. "Maggie's here to see you." She dashes back out.

Delilah rubs her eyes. "Honestly, this town needs to get a life. I'll tell her to go away."

"Thanks, but don't bother. If I don't talk to her now, she'll only badger me later. As long as taking a break doesn't affect my standing to get employee of the month."

Delilah gives me her stop-being-so-cute look.

I push through the swinging doors and don't dally out front this time, inviting gawkers. I spot Maggie outside the entrance and haul ass to get there. "Don't you usually barge into the store like you own the place? What's with sending the messenger?"

She grabs me by the elbow and drags me away from my ever-present audience. We're now on the street, standing between two parked cars. "Is Lennon okay?"

Maggie, with her fire engine hair and fiery personality, always fills a room with red, but I've never seen her red like this: red-rimmed eyes, the tip of her nose red and raw. Whatever happened with her and my brother is the Mystery of the Century. "He's okay-ish, like the rest of us. Except Desmond, who's rough. But Lennon and I have been living together, and he runs a kids' adventure camp with outdoor activities. He doesn't have much of a life outside of work and family, and his business isn't as booming as he'd like, but he gets by."

Her nostrils flare, and she looks down sharply. A moment later, the Maggie I know returns, haughty and almighty. "Don't tell him I asked. It's just all so nuts, and I was curious. Anyway, I'm *maybe* a little sorry for being such a bitch to you."

"Wow." I clutch my chest. "How could I *not* accept such a heartfelt apology?"

"Shut it, E. Just tell me one thing—do you know?"

She doesn't need to specify her meaning: *Do you know Delilah's not engaged?* Her eyes are all judgy, and she was the weak link in their *Masterpiece Theatre* number. "Oh, I know."

She purses her lips. "Knew it."

"But I don't want Delilah to know I know."

"I would never tell her you know."

"So we both know I know, and we know Delilah doesn't know I know. Where does this leave us?" I'd probably excel at speaking in code. Or pig latin.

She sniffles and narrows her eyes at me. "You two always had this *thing* that was weirdly special, but also gag inducing. I won't get in your way, but if you hurt her, I will sneak into your apartment and fill it with murder hornets and seal you in."

That was disturbingly harsh. "Glad you're on board. And if you ever want to talk about why you don't want to talk to Lennon, I'm here. Unless I've been attacked by a raging swarm of murder hornets. Then I'll be dead."

"You were always an immature child."

"I'm not the one who fooled around with Freddie Lorimer."

Her mouth drops open, her face flushing raspberry red. With an imperious sniff, she swivels and storms off. A much easier Maggie to deal with. Aggravating each other is our normal, but that's another person who's given me their blessing to woo Delilah. I'll have to make tonight's curry extra orgasm-y.

# TWENTY

Nine hours later, my apartment still looks the opposite of manly, but it smells like a Michelin-starred Indian restaurant. Scents of sautéed onion and garlic linger in the air, along with diced tomato, a heaping of cilantro, and my secret concoction of aromatic spices. The thick sauce pools around simmering meat, each morsel tender enough to cut with a spoon. Thanks to Sathya's mother, this Bangalore phaal—a lamb curry that's been in their family for generations—is the definition of food porn.

My cell rings from the counter. At the sight of Sathya's name, I wonder if my cooking her mother's recipe conjured her. I snatch up my phone so fast I almost send it flying.

"Where the hell are you?" I say, far past pleasant greetings.

"*Who* the hell are you?"

Yeah, I kind of deserve that. Sathya's the closest thing I had to a friend the past ten years, and she never knew my real name. "It's a long story."

"I cannot believe my writing partner has been in witness protection this whole time, hiding from a drug cartel. And your father? Screwing you over like that? Brian, this is *insane*."

She hit the proverbial nail on the proverbial head. A few select news stations have glommed on to Dad's story, focusing on the money laundering and cartel connections. They talked about his evidence that sent the notorious Victor Becerra's son to jail, a known hit man and drug lord, where he was found one afternoon, stabbed seven times, lying in a pool of his own blood. They're praising my father, holding him up as a martyr who sacrificed his former life to help bring down a monster, like he was an undercover spy working for the FBI that whole time.

The only monster I know is the man who lied to his family for years, putting them in jeopardy, all because he had an *opportunity he couldn't pass up.*

Agitated, I yank at the back of my hair. "I'd love to catch up and chat about my absurd life over cocktails one night. Right now, I'd love to know where you are and why you've been avoiding me."

"I feel awful for disappearing," she says, stealing my line, but her tone is sad. "I've been trying to write. I swear I have. I thought if I dropped off the grid, like I have in the past, got rid of the pressure to produce, I'd get motivated and feel inspired, but . . ." She's so quiet I press the phone harder to my ear. "My mom's sick."

I slump and rub my eyes. I only met Sathya's mother once, but she welcomed me into her home, fussed over me and made sure I tried all her homemade food. She boasted about Sathya with pride, shared stories about her family in Bangalore, and gave me her amazing recipe afterward. She's a bright light and a kind woman, and I hate that she's unwell.

"I'm so sorry," I say gently. "Is it serious?"

"Breast cancer, but we caught it early and her prognosis is great. I've just been helping my parents out more at home, and when I do write, I can't focus. Everything I've gotten down is garbage. The harder I try, the worse it gets. Like I'm trying to force a world that doesn't want to exist, because my world's too overwhelming. And, if I'm honest, I never wanted to do the prequel. It doesn't feel natural for the series."

Her frustration makes me think of how hard I've been pushing Delilah, showing up in her life daily, adding pressure, whispering about food disguised as sex. Forcing a world that maybe shouldn't exist when her world was so recently unsettled. Except she's been happier since we've been hanging out. There's no hiding her easier smiles and the blush on her cheeks. If Delilah didn't want me in her life, she'd have told me by now.

"You need to take care of yourself and your family," I say, focusing on Sathya and her mother. "And if you don't want to write the prequel, that's an issue in and of itself."

"I think I need to tell Margot, talk it out with her. Her messages have gotten intense. I hate leaving you both in the lurch like this."

I sink into my dining room chair and lean back, legs sprawled, grappling for the right thing to say. I want Sathya to write this script, for both our sakes, but creativity doesn't thrive under threats and coercion or family stress. I'd know. I haven't produced a story of my own for ten years. I'd also never dictate how someone else lives their life. Nothing good comes of that.

"Talk it all out with Margot. If you need to cancel this contract, I'll deal with the fallout. Find the money to pay back my portion of the advance."

"I feel stupid," she says, her voice shrinking. "It's just words on a page. I should be able to put words on a page, even with all this stress."

I don't like hearing Sathya, creator of a fantastical graphic novel, sounding anything but strong. "You're smart and talented and are the reason I've had success the past five years. I owe you more than my support."

"I still feel like I've failed you and Margot and the publisher."

"The worst person you can disappoint is yourself." Unless you're my father. Then the disappointment pool is quite large. "You've tried to write, Sathya. I know you and know you wouldn't walk away from this project unless you simply couldn't produce. Give yourself a break. Be there for your family. Take a breath and quit trying so hard. You'll either realize the trying was what was thwarting you, or you'll feel free."

Assuming the latter is where we end up, I'll have to shore my defenses. Find more firm ways to tell Margot I can't sell my story. I'll have to earn cash another way.

"Thanks, Brian. *Shoot.* Sorry. I mean Edgar."

"Call me whatever you want, as long as you call me. No more of this avoidance nonsense." A knock sounds from my door. Instantly, the heaviness in my chest lifts. My sweet Delilah. "Talk soon. And give your mother my best."

After we hang up, I stand and shake off my melancholy, a full-body bounce that has Candy dancing around my legs. Ready to focus on the love of my life, I strut to my door and reach for the knob, but I pause. I replay my advice to Sathya. *Quit trying so hard. You'll either realize the trying was what was thwarting you, or you'll feel free.* I'm about to cross off number forty-seven on my Win Back Delilah list—make Delilah my orgasmic lamb curry—but maybe the list is part of the reason she's holding back. Maybe I need to chill out and let us evolve naturally.

I mean, I'm me. I'll always be an obnoxious flirt who shamelessly shows Delilah she brings me to my knees, but relationships aren't checklists you can tick off. Love isn't something you win. It's something you earn. My desperate need to rekindle my relationship with Delilah has been so focused on *me* and *my* aching need for her I haven't given her space to take the lead too. Allowed us to build new moments together, letting us unfold organically.

If I want us to have a chance, I need to quit my Top Ten Bests and Fifty Ways to Win. Free us from old expectations and confining lists. Turn this relationship into a two-way street.

Rolling out my shoulders, I open the door and smile at Delilah, who's still wearing my moon necklace. "You look lovely."

Already, I'm super suave. Mr. Act Natural. You could churn ice cream on my level of cool.

She lifts a brown bag. "I brought us dessert."

I openly peruse her hot-as-sin body, caressed by her worn jeans and another of her threadbare T-shirts. "You certainly did."

"Glad to see you're as blatant as ever. Even though I'm engaged."

*Engaged. Engaged. Engaged.* She's like a pit bull who won't release her favorite toy, but I digress. I'm now chillaxed E, letting our relationship blossom naturally. "Some things never change, except the fact that I've become an exceptional cook."

I stand back to let her in, but she doesn't budge. Shyly, she holds up another brown bag. "This is for you."

"A gift?"

"No. I mean, not like that. It's not a big deal, just something you needed."

Curious, I take the bag and peek inside. My heart grows three sizes. "You found my pencils."

"Like I said, it's no big deal. I was picking up supplies in Ruby Grove, and they have a great art store. Figured I should check for you."

No big deal, my ass. I doubt Delilah regularly visits art-supply shops, and she knew I couldn't find my favorite Blackwing Palomino pencils.

"Thanks," I say as my stomach does a happy spin. "I'll put them to good use."

She ducks her head and crouches to pet Candy Cane. Not too vigorously. Candy still backs away if humans get too in her face. Delilah's learned how to navigate my dog's boundaries—when to remove her hand, when to go in for the under-the-chin scratch or the coveted butt rub. "She's so cute."

Both my girls are.

I leave them to it and putter around my kitchen, fluffing my rice with a fork, giving the curry a final lime squeeze, extricating bowls to plate my masterpiece, extra touched Sathya's mom shared this recipe with me. I'll have to send her a thank-you/get-well note.

Delilah sits on the other side of my kitchen counter, chin propped on her hands. "It's like I have a front-row seat to *Top Chef.*"

"Good thing I'm used to being observed, otherwise I might slip and add too much chili. Burn you out of here."

Her eyebrows pinch. "I hate the media for turning you into a sideshow."

"I'm used to living with drama."

"Doesn't make it okay. If we have more lurkers tomorrow, I'll kick them out."

"And let someone else win employee of the month? I think not." I fill our bowls and place them on the counter, where we can eat side by side, small dishes of yogurt raita and mango chutney between us. "Dig in, but if you moan too loudly, remember that Sandra probably has my apartment bugged."

"How many times do I have to tell you? Sandra was a receptionist at the security firm where she worked, not a private detective. She's harmless."

"But she for sure picked up a few tricks of the trade. Wait until she unearths your plot to eradicate Windfall of margarine in favor of butter and exposes you to the world."

"You're right." Delilah contorts her face into a villainous scowl. "Sandra's a menace. But she's also a dog lover. You should ask if she'll watch Candy while you're at Ricky and Aaron's wedding."

That's actually not a horrible idea. Sandra's resourceful and wily. If Candy got into any kind of trouble, Sandra would sleuth their way out of it. "I just might."

Delilah takes a bite of her food and does actually moan. "Oh my God, E. This is *amazing.*"

"I'm glad you approve."

"Maggie and I went to a Bon Iver concert in Wisconsin and fell into this tiny Indian restaurant. I thought that was the best curry I've ever eaten, but this." She lifts a spoonful of lamb and sauce, closing her eyes as she inhales the aroma. "This is magic."

My cheeks heat. "Honestly, people enjoying my food is half the reason I cook."

The way we're sitting beside each other, my thigh is flush against Delilah's. The close position's not a tactic. My counter's small, and my legs are long. Not that I mind. She hums while she eats, dropping a few more *oh my Gods*. I smile as I chew.

"We should cook together," she says. "Instead of taking turns. I'd love to learn this recipe."

"Cooking theme nights." I nod and drink some water. "I'd be down with that. You can teach me how to bake, since that's not my strong suit."

"Only if you promise not to eat half the raw batter. I have no clue how you didn't make yourself sick when you used to do that."

I loved those afternoons, chasing Delilah around her kitchen, trying to steal the bowls from her grasp. "I actually did get sick once, but it was worth it."

She quirks an eyebrow. "Eating raw cake batter isn't worth getting sick."

"No, but it made you laugh." I nudge her leg with mine. "Anything's worth making you laugh."

I'm close enough to hear her tiny intake of breath, notice the subtle way her eyelashes flutter, like she's watching the fast flip of a memory.

She takes a deep inhale, then lets it out slowly, her attention flicking to me. "How do you stay in such good shape?"

I frown at the sudden change in subject, not that I mind the topic. "Have you been thinking about my six-pack?"

She rolls her eyes. "I'm just curious. There's still so much I don't know about you."

The sad truth of our history. "I exercise daily, but I don't do gyms. Running, sit-ups, push-ups. Sweating helps me manage my stress."

"Do you still stargaze?"

"Nope." But I'm enjoying this. Delilah peppering *me* with questions for a change. "Too many lights in Houston."

"I'm guessing you've watched *Star Wars* a billion times by now."

"Not far off. I've for sure surpassed fifty."

She takes another bite of her food and chews thoughtfully. "If you could have a superpower, would you rather be able to walk on water or walk through walls?"

"Through walls, no question. I wouldn't have to worry about losing my keys."

We eat and talk, Delilah leading most of the conversation with her adorable questions. She occasionally leans her body into me, a friendly nudge while she makes a joke. I nudge her back. Tease her to my heart's content. She tilts her head and moans loudly a few more times, hamming it up, praising my food, either unaware of how my breaths deepen and how my jeans grow unbearably tight, or getting off on this torture.

When we're done, our bowls empty and bellies full, she squeezes my thigh. "Thanks again for cooking for me. It was amazing."

"Thanks for eating with me. It's no fun cooking for one."

Her touch lingers, growing lighter but not leaving. "The past ten years," she says hesitantly, "have you dated much?"

Her question tumbles in my stomach, mingling with the heat of my spice mixture.

Aside from casual hookups, I dated a few women the past decade, but I had a three-date limit. For the first three dates, it was okay to focus on the present. Jobs. Apartments. Friends. Foods I liked. Foods she liked. Hobbies I liked. Hobbies she liked. After date three, women got inquisitive. They—*gasp*—asked actual questions. That's when I started to lie.

*I'm from Houston.*

*I hate the countryside.*

*The color blue sucks.*

*I don't remember much about my teen years.*
*I've never been in love.*

It wasn't just lying that made dating tough, though. None of them were Delilah.

"Dating's hard when your life's full of secrets," I say, pressing my leg harder into hers. "There was no one who really mattered."

If this was an ordinary friendship, this is where I'd ask about her love life. We'd bond over shared stories of heartbreak, but Delilah's my only worthwhile story, and I don't want half truths from her. When I ask her about Hugo and how she fell in love with him and accepted a proposal, I won't be able to pretend he's a great guy who doted on her. When I ask those tough questions, I want her honesty.

I nudge her arm. "What would you like to do now? Call it a night or watch TV, or we can play a game?"

The old me would've suggested naked Twister. New me is all about stepping back, giving Delilah control. Also, her hand's still on my thigh, and I did not place it there.

"Can we watch *Schitt's Creek*?"

"That sounds perfect. I'll just clean up first."

"You cooked, so I'll clean." Slowly, she removes her hand from my thigh, killing me with the tingling drag.

I steady my breaths. "I'm the professional dishwasher here. I'll do it myself."

"Or we can do it together and finish in half the time."

"Sure," I say, liking the idea of Team Delilah and E working side by side. "Let's do it together."

We settle on my couch afterward, in our usual formation—Delilah at one end, me at the other, our lower legs overlapping. Partway through the episode, Delilah stretches out farther, and her foot nudges my ass. I adjust on the couch, grab her foot, and massage it the way I used to do when we'd watch TV in her basement. She moans, and I give her all

I've got. I dig my thumbs into her arch, pushing outward, moving in smaller strokes, then longer drags.

Her face is blissful at first, a slight smile touching her lips. Then her eyelids droop, her breaths slowing. Before I know it, Delilah Moon is sleeping on my couch, her moon necklace resting over her heart, and I can't do anything but stare, feeling incredibly lucky to have her so relaxed and trusting. There was a time I thought I'd never see her again.

Careful not to wake her, I shift my body and stand. I grab the gray blanket I bought to offset the flood of pink in this place and lay it over her, crouching as I tuck it up to her chin. I press a gentle kiss to her forehead, a slew of emotions gathering in my throat.

"I love you," I whisper, my eyes burning along with my throat. "There couldn't be other women when my heart's been on Mars this whole time, stuck on you."

# TWENTY-ONE

Delilah and I pull up to the inn at Sheldrake Falls, and no word of a lie, the heavens shine down on us. It was a dreary drive getting here, cloudy the whole way, the last leaves of fall drifting into my truck bed as we drove. Inside the truck was nothing but sunshine. My Win Back Delilah list is locked in my keepsake box. I've stopped planning ways to woo her. We played I spy and sang along to my cheesy playlist, except when "Pillow Talk" came on and she punched my arm. (I wasn't about to redo that mix from scratch.) We joked. We watched the passing farmland in companionable silence. Now we're driving up to the definition of romance, and the clouds have broken.

"I forgot how pretty this place is." Delilah leans forward, stretching her seat belt, gazing out the window.

Sunshine spills through the gap in the clouds, painting the white-washed inn amber. "I bet they have chickens that lay golden eggs here," I say.

She grins. "I bet they have a chocolate spa with chocolate water."

"I bet the beds are stuffed with unicorn hair."

"Oh, yeah." Her face goes dreamy. "That."

Delilah and I used to play "I bet" while walking home from school. Hands linked, birds chirping, grins so wide we were the envy of tooth-paste ads everywhere, we'd one-up each other with ridiculous lines, like

"I bet Mr. Vogel lives in a house built of little children's teeth" and "I bet the old quarry hosts late-night rock concerts by Jimi Hendrix."

We don't hold hands while we walk up to the inn today. Mine are full of our bags, and Delilah's too busy marveling at the pretty pumpkin garden and the vine-covered trellises.

Told you the air around here was filled with romance.

"E! As I live and breathe." Ricky waves at us as he jogs over, leaving an older couple who look like his parents. "Can't believe it's actually you."

I drop the bags. "In the flesh. And look at you, all mature and shit, getting married."

When he reaches me, we don't do an awkward are-we-friends shuffle. He grabs my extended hand and yanks me into a hug. "Missed you. Not sure why, but I did."

"I'm the only one who laughed at your jokes."

"Naw. I sucked at math and science, but you sucked worse. With you gone, I didn't have anyone to make me feel smart."

We laugh, pulling back, sizing each other up. Ricky still has reddish-blond hair and kind eyes, but he's fitter than when he was a pot-smoking teen. "You're a handsome devil now," I say. "I dig the beard. Aaron's a lucky guy."

"You don't look so bad yourself, for someone who's been in witness protection the past ten years." He shakes his head, passing his hand over his mouth. "Still have trouble believing it."

"It's pretty unbelievable."

As is seeing Ricky like this, not sprawled on his couch, stoned, strumming his guitar, creating lyrics to themes I suggest. My favorite was his impromptu "Watermelon Song," after we gorged on watermelon:

> The seeds are in my stomach
> Growing into a tree
> With leaves and fruit
> There's a watermelon in me

Man, we were deep. "Excited to hear you play again."

"The weekend will be a blast. There's a casual welcome dinner tonight. Tunes, food, booze. Make sure you come." Then he's all over Delilah, hugging her, kissing her cheeks. "Sorry for the delay. It's been a while with E."

"Trust me, I get it. And you'll die when you see the cake." She gives an excited little shake, like a human Candy Cane wiggle. "Angel outdid herself."

"Can't wait." He waves to someone behind us and moves toward them. "See you two tonight."

I watch him for a minute and feel a twinge of jealousy. He looks so happy, glowing with this weekend's celebration and love for his future husband. I so badly want to be openly in love again with the woman at my side. I want to glow with it, shout my feelings to the world, not pretend like she's still engaged. Alas, patience is my lot in life.

Bags in my hands, we walk inside the magically romantic inn and run into another blast from my past: Kaitlyn Moore, the bass player from the Tweeds. While I hung around with the band plenty, we were never particularly close. She's lounging in the inn's reception area with the band's drummer, perpetually stoned Shawn. When Shawn spots me, he elbows Kaitlyn. "Dude. Our roadie came."

Kaitlyn is half-Filipino and half-white, with deep brown eyes that always seem sleepy. She gives an old-school fist pump in the air. "Glad to have you back, E. Crazy shit the past ten years."

"The craziest." I'm not sure how normal people feel about high school reunions. Seeing Ricky was a rush. Finding my feet with Avett has been tough and important and has given me the lift I needed. With my history blasted into cyberspace, seeing surface friends like Kaitlyn is akin to walking around naked.

"I can't imagine how nuts it was," she says, staring at me like I've grown a third arm. "Did you actually meet those—"

"Can't wait to hear you guys play," Delilah interrupts, dodging Kaitlyn's incoming missile attack of questions like a souped-up submarine. She grabs her bag from my hand, sticking close to my side. "We're on a schedule, though. Cake and wedding stuff. Catch up with you later?"

Not waiting for their reply, she steers us to the front desk and smiles at the attending agent. "We should have two rooms, one under Moon and one under Baker."

First, she saves me from painful reunion questions. Now she's uttering my fake name without hesitation, rescuing me from fumbling like when I adopted Candy. Except now I'm thinking about Candy Cane and worrying about my perfect girl.

I grab my phone and text Sandra, who agreed a tad too easily to watch my dog while I'm gone. She could have an ulterior motive.

E: How's my girl?

Sandra: I'm fine.

E: I mean my dog. Does she miss me?

Sandra: She hasn't mentioned anything.

Even when she's on my side, Sandra lives to antagonize.

E: Don't you dare make her do reconnaissance work.

Sandra: Have a nice wedding.

I squint at my phone, debating calling and threatening Sandra so she doesn't get Candy tangled in any nefarious dealings, but Delilah says, "That can't be right."

Phone forgotten, my eyes do a pinball number, bouncing between the front desk agent's apologetic expression and Delilah's wide, fearful, the-killer's-in-my-house eyes.

"What can't be right?" I ask.

"We've somehow lost Ms. Moon's reservation." The agent clicks through her computer screen, frowning. "And we're fully booked."

"That can't be right," Delilah repeats, agitated. At the same time, I say brightly, "That's no problem. She'll just bunk with me."

Here's the thing. I didn't plan this. Getting stuck in a shared room isn't on any list I wrote, but I'm suddenly a staunch believer in the whole letting-go speech I gave Sathya. Finally, Life is giving me a break. Finally, luck is on my side, and you better believe I'm going with this flow.

I drop my head to catch Delilah's eye. "I'll sleep on the floor or wherever. It's no different than us crashing on each other's couches." Except it is. Neither of our apartments has a roaring fireplace, a canopy bed, or a mattress made of unicorn hair.

Still, our recent sleepovers have been *fantastic*.

Three times in the past two weeks one of us has accidentally crashed while hanging out. Our evenings have remained platonic, comfortable nights of shared dinners and TV watching, plus a couple of late-night talks where she asked more about my life the past ten years and I asked about hers, neither of us broaching Hugo or revisiting my romantic history, just catching up. I've given up on analyzing every twitch she makes, planning my moves ten steps ahead, but waking up in Delilah's apartment with her humming while drinking coffee and surfing the internet, a blanket over my stiff body as I realized where I was and who I was with . . . well. Utter perfection.

Now we're here, in the romantic inn of inns, and there's only one room.

"I guess it's the same as at our apartments," Delilah says, drawing out her words, as if by the end of her agreement, the agent will have miraculously found a vacancy.

She won't. I feel it. Not only has no one at Sugar and Sips asked Delilah about her wedding in front of me recently, but I've received numerous encouraging smiles. The winds have shifted in my favor.

"We don't have any cots left," the agent says, "but we can send up extra sheets for the couch."

"Yeah, okay." Delilah fumbles around in her purse. "Do you need a credit card for a deposit?"

"We have one from when Mr. Baker booked. Just need a signature here and you can be on your way. Will you be needing one key or two?"

Delilah shouts, "Two." I say, "One."

The agent smirks and hands us two keys. "If you need anything at all, don't hesitate to call."

"How about a second room," Delilah mumbles as she yanks the handle of her bag and hurries to the elevators.

Once we're sealed inside, I press the button for the third floor. "This will be fun. Like when we used to sleep outside under the stars."

"I have a fiancé, E."

"And I have a couch to sleep on. I doubt he'll mind." And he's the last person I want to talk about right now. "Are you sure Candy's okay with Sandra? What if they're on a stakeout and things go south?"

"The worst that'll happen is Sandra dresses Candy up with a cute bandanna around her neck."

I didn't consider a disguise. "What if she dresses her up as a devil with horns and a spiked tail, and the other dogs make fun of her?"

"You're too much, E."

I open my phone and scroll through some pictures: Candy smiling outside Sugar and Sips with her tongue lolling, Candy smiling in the park with her tongue lolling, Candy smiling on my bed with her tongue lolling. "Is it weird that I miss her already?"

Delilah sneaks a look at my phone and *awws*. "I'm sure she misses you too."

"If this is me as a pet owner, imagine how pathetic I'd be as a dad."

The elevator opens on our floor. I'm two steps out when I realize Delilah's not beside me. I glance back and frown. Her face is slack, her attention locked on the floor, analyzing it for God knows what, as the elevator starts sliding shut. I lunge forward and shove my hand between the doors, then gently guide Delilah out. "You okay?"

"Yeah, sorry," she mumbles but won't meet my eyes. "Just had a freak-out moment. Thought I forgot to remind Angel to bring the extra gluten-free cupcakes for tomorrow. Then I remembered I did tell her. So, yeah, no big deal. Just a momentary memory lapse." She does an awkward jazz-hands move. "I'm all good."

She bolts ahead of me, but I'm not fooled. She's panicked about us sharing this room. I get it. It's so romantic here only monks would resist getting naked and fornicating in all that luxury. Or maybe they wouldn't. But, as per usual, I won't push Delilah for anything she can't handle. We'll take this at her pace.

When we find our door number, I fan my hand toward the electronic sensor. "You can do the honors, milady."

An eye roll later, we're in romantic heaven.

Fireplace? Check.

Decadent hot tub? Check.

*One* canopy bed, complete with unicorn mattress, furry throw blanket, and chocolates on the pillows? Check, check, check, and check.

I curl my lip. "This room is awful. Has anyone even cleaned in here?"

Delilah loosens her death grip on her bag. "I bet the half-burned motel we passed on the highway is more hospitable."

"I bet sleeping on a bed of rocks would be more comfortable than *that*." I gesture angrily to the plushest bed I've ever seen.

"I bet there are cockroaches in the sinks."

The only cockroach in here is me, enjoying this banter way too much. While I love this shared-romantic-room circumstance, I'm not sure Delilah's ready for it. She's still playing the engaged card. I refuse to ask her about Hugo and why he's not here, making her feel worse for lying. With only one option, I drop my bag and sit on the edge of the bed. Definitely unicorn fur. "I don't have to stay on the couch. If sharing this room is too uncomfortable for you, I'm sure I can crash on Shawn's floor."

She firms her grip on the suitcase handle, studying the splendid room. Then she slackens. "Shawn smokes pot twenty-four-seven. If you stay there, you'll be high the entire time. He'll hot-box the room."

"It could be fun. I haven't been high in a while."

"You hate being high, E. It makes you feel like your tongue has shriveled and fallen out of your mouth, and you get super paranoid."

God, I love how well she knows me. "I could sleep by the lake. Hope no bears come to mate with me."

"Just shut up and unpack. You're staying here."

I don't argue the point. I offered to leave; she declined. The rest, as they say, will be history. "I can unpack your bag if you want. Lay your undergarments next to mine. Let them commingle."

"Child," she mumbles, marching to claim her drawers.

# TWENTY-TWO

The welcome dinner has started, but I'm in my room alone, having an uncomfortable conversation with my agent. I've avoided Margot's calls the past week, but another "send to voice mail" wouldn't have been kind. Hence my tardiness.

"It's not me," she says for the second time. "The publisher's pressuring Josh. He's in a tight spot, as is Sathya."

After Sathya called me, she spilled her guts to Margot, told her she wants to cancel the contract for the prequel. Understandably, Margot is hovering at DEFCON 3 stress levels. Canceling the contract reflects poorly on her. She loses money just like us. She asked me to talk to Sathya before she makes such a rash, irrevocable decision, but I did no such thing. Sathya is of sound mind. Gates of Ember is her baby. She birthed the world, grew every plot point and character in her brilliant head. I'm simply the vehicle through which her visions come to life.

I scoured my finances and have enough savings to cover my end of the canceled contract. It will hurt. I'll need a day job on top of finding another illustration project, all while finishing my book, which has been pouring out of me faster every time I sit and focus.

I'm okay with Sathya's decision, but I get a feeling this "tight spot" she's in isn't a reference to her mother's illness. "If something else is going on with Sathya, she didn't tell me about it."

"She feels bad enough about this contract. She didn't want to worry you with other issues, but her mother's bills are more than expected. If she pays the advance back, things will be tough. I didn't mention anything to her about your original offer—your new graphic novel—but if you give the publisher your story, I think I can convince them to publish that first and rework the rest of the deal to include another new project from you as a team, which Sathya is keen on exploring. Something fresh on a looser timeline."

I picture Sathya buried under bills, worrying about affording proper care for her mother, and the rocks in my heart catch. I picture her and her family stressing over their everyday expenses, and those jagged edges scrape. In seconds, I'm not gradually giving in. I'm caving so hard I'm practically a professional spelunker.

"If this is even a possibility," I say, rubbing my chest, "and I mean a huge *if*, I can't do anything without talking to some people first." My mother. My brothers. Delilah most of all. "The publisher would also need to hire outside colorists. I won't have time to add color with this deadline."

"It can be arranged."

And this is all happening way too fast. "When would Josh need an answer?"

"If I tell them you're considering it, it'll buy us time. A month. Maybe two."

"I'll speak to Sathya and think about it. I'll let you know."

"That's all I can ask."

I send a quick text to Sathya, asking about her mom and telling her we need to chat, then I'm rushing to the welcome dinner, dark jeans and a dress shirt on, stressed about that call but excited to spend the night with Delilah. Except I don't get to spend the evening with Delilah.

As stunning as the dining room is with its massive wood beams, cathedral ceiling, rustic-chic decor, and charming wagon wheel chandeliers, there are no free seats next to her. She's beside Maggie and a woman I don't know. Avett waves at me, inviting me to the free chair next to him, on the other end of the massively long table from Delilah. Such is my fate.

But it's cool. I'm sharing a room with Delilah. We'll have plenty of alone time in our fairy-tale suite. This way I also get to make Avett uncomfortable by gossiping about him to his wife.

"So, Naomi," I say when I sit. "Do you remember that time the fire alarm went off in school and no one could find Avett for, like, three hours?"

Avett angles his big body, trying to block me from seeing his wife. "You are not telling that story."

"Oh, he definitely is." Naomi shoves Avett back and leans in front of him. "Do tell."

"Leo Whitaker decided to mess with your boy and stole all his clothes after gym, along with the towels. Avett got out of the shower and—"

"I think we've heard enough." Avett pushes forward again, attempting a human shield.

"I missed your wedding," I say. "The least I owe Naomi is a special gift."

Naomi covers Avett's face with her hand. "Go on, E."

"As I was saying, Avett was as naked as the day he was born, and the older guys were coming in next. He didn't want to be ridiculed, so he pulled the fire alarm, ran out, and hid in the closet."

Naomi's dark eyes widen. "He did not."

"Oh, it gets better."

"No, it doesn't." Avett's sulking now.

I'm in my element. "Being the crafty guy he was, he found a pen and paper and slid a note out for someone to find. It read, 'Tell Edgar Delilah's in the closet waiting for him.'"

Naomi knocks her husband's chest. "Good thinking."

"The best way to E was always through Delilah," he mutters.

It still is. "Unfortunately, Maggie was the one who found the note, and she knew Delilah was in our *Oliver!* practice, so she was the one who opened the closet door to find Avett buckass naked, with a mop held in front of his penis."

Naomi smacks the table and cracks up. "How did I not know this?"

Avett slants a bitter look at the far end of the table. "I bribed Maggie to keep quiet by doing her English homework for a month, but she told Delilah, and Delilah obviously told E."

Because back then Delilah and I didn't keep secrets from each other.

If my Spidey senses are correct, Delilah's sharing a secret with her best friend right now, the two of them whispering, heads bent close. Delilah's as fidgety as when she came off that elevator, shooting occasional glances at me. I wish I had Sandra's surveillance equipment. Or I could've brought Candy Cane, hooked a microphone to her collar, and sent her on a mission, instead of sitting here like a shmuck who's hopelessly aware two girls are whispering about him. This is grade school all over again, but instead of discussing if I have cooties, they're probably dissecting the odds of me walking around Delilah's hotel room naked. The answer is *high*.

They glance at me again. I grin and wave. Delilah ducks her head, like I might not see her. Then they're off to the races again, whispering furtively.

That's pretty much how my night goes. Delilah avoids me. Maggie has a date I don't know. She spends half her time dancing with him and half of it dancing with Delilah and some other girls, all drinking and laughing and having a good time. Instead of intruding, I catch up with Avett and Naomi and make them show me all their pictures of their little girl, Simone. She's beyond adorable.

"Thank God she looks like Naomi," I tell them.

"Amen to that." Avett pulls his wife in for a kiss.

I melt into the crowd, giving them alone time, but when I'm unoccupied, I'm more aware of the fact that people I don't know keep staring at me, pointing, whispering. *Birding.* I'm the endangered great potoo again, caged, studied. I don't like it. The one person I *do* want staring at me is rehearsing for her forthcoming role in the for-sure-to-be-Academy-nominated *Edgar Eugene Bower Doesn't Exist.*

When groom-to-be Aaron has a free moment, I slide in and congratulate him. Other people vie for his attention, so I don't linger. I try to camouflage myself along the outskirts of the room, feeling out of sorts and alone, when for the first time in ten years the people around me know my real name and my secrets.

Shockingly, stoned Shawn sees me through my attempted camouflage. The weed must give him laser-sharp vision. We shoot the shit, and I swear to God, the guy's apparently an accountant. Didn't see that one coming. Kaitlyn joins us, the two of them joking about a concert I never got to see. I morph into my teenage pre-Delilah self, awkward and insecure. A square peg in a round hole. With one last look at the back of Delilah's head, I leave the festivities for the quiet of our room.

But I can't sleep.

The lights are out, and I'm under the sheets on the couch, which is surprisingly comfortable. Must be the unicorn hair. Still, my mind is on fire. I keep replaying tonight, trying to understand why my mood felt so weighted, why I couldn't relax and have a good time. My best guess: I may have my old name back, but I'm not the same E from high school. My experiences changed me, robbed me of the shared memories everyone else enjoys with smiles and laughs. Events like tonight's are designed for quick catch-ups and bromance back pounds. There's no quick catching up about US Marshal Safesites and WITSEC. There's no surface conversation that can coast over my life in a couple of minutes before someone calls, "Let's do a round of shots!"

I thought returning to Windfall would finally give me the sense of home I've missed. But I'm realizing Windfall's not my home. Delilah in my kitchen is my home. Delilah on my couch is my home. Delilah rolling her eyes at me is my home.

The door snicks open, and I hold my breath. I don't know what time it is, but Delilah's quiet as she moves around. Drawers open. The sound of a zipper lowering has me biting my cheek and flexing my thighs. Her dress hits the floor in a soft whoosh.

I stay facing the couch back, force my body to stay put.

Her feet pad toward me and stop. Her breaths are heavy, growing deeper as the seconds pass. Then her fingers land in my hair, stroking so tenderly shivers slip across my neck. Her nose follows, a deep inhale that spreads the tingling down my spine. The light kiss she places on my temple nearly breaks me. Not as much as her whispered "I love you."

My body freezes, but my heart doesn't. The love-starved organ's pounding so hard I'm sure they hear it on Mars. She's gone in an instant, doing her evening routine, brushing her teeth, removing her makeup, applying her night creams.

Killing me softly with her whispered admission.

I could jump up, tell her I love her so much I'm sick with it, but she's been drinking—and sometimes confessions are meant for the confessor, not the listener. Still, resolve hits me.

In the morning, this ends. Delilah is my home, and my home needs to stop lying to me. We need to say all the things we haven't said. I'll give her tonight, let her sleep off her drinks and wake up fresh. Tomorrow I'll tell her I was sitting behind her on that flight, and we'll finally unleash the romantic fumes hot-boxing this room.

# TWENTY-THREE

When I wake up, Delilah isn't in the room. Also, unicorn hair is less comfortable than first surmised. My neck twinges, my shoulder throbs, and my back hurts. I'm twenty-seven going on ninety-eight. I gingerly stand and stretch, rub at my messy hair, and scan the suite. The bed-sheets are askew. Our suitcases are beside each other against the far wall, and our toiletries have claimed their His and Hers sides of the sink. The domesticity of it would please the hell out of me, if I hadn't spent the night on the couch.

Downstairs is a replay of last night's high school reunion, except with more bloodshot eyes and hungover winces. The greasiest food on the breakfast buffet is disappearing fastest. I load up on eggs and bacon and find a seat by the large windows, trying to relax and wake up. This place really is stunning. Sun sparkles on the lake, late-fall trees guarding its borders. Maybe Delilah and I will have our she's-not-engaged talk under the pagoda on the whitewashed dock.

Avett sits beside me with a mug of coffee. "A few of us are heading out fishing. You should come."

As fun as fishing sounds, I'm on a mission. "Have you seen Delilah?"

"Angel just got here with tonight's desserts, but there was a lem-on-tart mishap. They're doing damage control. Baking more, I think."

A lemon-tart mishap doesn't fit into today's plan, but helping Delilah comes before my emotional needs. I also excel at dishwashing. "Rain check on the fishing. I have stuff to do."

Avett blows on his coffee and takes a sip. "Is that stuff related to a blue-eyed woman you can't leave alone?"

"No clue what you're talking about."

He laughs. "Likely story. Godspeed, my friend."

He doesn't warn me to move cautiously this time. A positive sign I'm willing to run with. I shovel in my food, then offer morning pleasantries to the hungover guests as I head to the kitchen. Most go like this:

"Morning, Kaitlyn."

She winces. "Yeah."

"Gorgeous day, Billy. Isn't it?"

He grunts.

"Morning, Maggie," I say extra loudly by her ear.

She gives me the finger.

I nose around until I find the kitchen. The inn staff are cleaning up from breakfast service, clanging and clomping as they go. I spot Delilah toward the back, hairnet over her curls. She disappears into a walk-in cooler, her face grim. My girl needs me. I squeeze past the busy cooks and come face to face with lemon carnage. Several crushed boxes are tossed on a table, bright-yellow guts squeezing out. Delilah pushes from the cooler, her arms full of egg trays and butter.

I salute her. "Reporting for duty, Captain."

"Turn the oven on and get me the flour. Angel's gone out for the raspberries we need for the garnish. We have to make three tarts, and they have to be perfect."

"Oven and flour and perfect. On it."

She places her armful down and pauses. "Thanks for helping, E."

"Anytime." I give her a reassuring smile.

Her gaze lingers on my face, searching—for what I have no clue—then she's in baker mode, moving around the large kitchen like she owns the place. I sift flour and cube butter and wash dishes. When Angel returns, she joins our platoon.

Occasionally, I grab a cloth and dab Angel's forehead, telling her things like "You've got this. This is the home stretch."

She laughs and high-fives me.

When I do it to Delilah, she swats me with her cloth.

Two hours later, we're standing around a stainless steel counter, our aprons speckled with flour, admiring three perfect lemon tarts. Their golden crusts and glistening curd are more beautiful than a Windfall sunrise.

"They're too pretty to eat," Angel says.

"No such thing." I smolder at Delilah. "Beauty is meant to be enjoyed."

She blushes the color of the raspberries in her hand. "They're just missing these." She holds the bowl of berries out to me. "You do the honors. We couldn't have finished this fast without you."

We're Team Delilah and E again, and I'm pleased as punch, which is an expression I never understood. Does it mean fruit punch is so delicious it's pleasing? Or is it a reference to the thrill of punching a jerk like Hugo in the neck?

I accept the berry bowl. "Can I make a smiley face with them?"

Delilah snatches the bowl back. "You just lost your privileges."

I pout at Angel. "Mom's being mean again."

Angel cackles. "You two are worse than my parents."

"Oh, we need the mint garnish too." Delilah hurries to the fridge.

Angel quickly faces me. "I know I gave you a hard time when you showed up in town, but that's because I love Delilah. She's an amazing boss and even better person. If you hurt her, I will spike your food with laxatives, but . . ."

"But?" I ask, not keen on the idea of spending this weekend locked in the bathroom.

"*But* as long as I've known Delilah, I've never seen her this happy."
She bumps her elbow into mine. "You're good for her, so consider me
a fan."

"That means a lot. I'm also a fan of you and your baked goods, *and*
the fact that you support Delilah, even if it means dosing my food."

Smirking, she points two fingers at her eyes, then points at mine.
"I'm watching you."

Noted and approved.

The second Delilah's back, Angel grabs sanitizer spray. "Excuse me
while I clean the mess we made so the cooks don't sabotage our beautiful
desserts."

Pleased Angel's given us privacy, I convince Delilah to let me help
her line the raspberries on our tarts, perfect rows circling into the center.
I'm glad I was here to do damage control. I'm happy Angel confirmed
what I believed: Delilah's been happier with me in her life. I'm also
thankful I have more confidence than my seventeen-year-old self, who
got flustered setting up our lovemaking scene.

"Delilah," I say, my eyes on her beautiful profile. "We need to talk."

She freezes, raspberry poised midair in her hand. "It's a busy day,
E. I have to shower and get done up, then make sure all's good with
the wedding cake and cupcakes and other desserts." Hand shakier than
before, she places the last raspberry in its home.

I take Delilah's hand—*my home*—and say firmly, "We need to talk,
in private, today. It's time. I can't keep pretending I don't know you're
not engaged."

She closes her eyes and caves forward. An eternity passes before she
says quietly, "I figured you knew. You wouldn't have flirted so much
otherwise. It's just been easier this way. For me, at least."

"It was easier for me too." That truth surprises me. The lies allowed
us to slowly rebuild our friendship and spend time together. Pressure-
free time. "But pretending you're engaged isn't easy now. Can we go
for a walk?"

She studies our perfect tarts and wipes her chin, leaving behind an adorable smudge of flour. "Yeah, sure. You're right. We can't keep going on like this."

Together, we set the tarts in the large kitchen fridge and thank the chefs who gave us space to work. We drop our dirty aprons and cloths in the laundry bins and walk into the beauty of this fall day. Leaves crunch under our feet, sunshine dancing in Delilah's unleashed hair, the smell of fresh-cut grass and second chances in the air. We walk out onto the whitewashed dock, then sit side by side on the picnic table under the pagoda. The lake's gentle lapping drifts below us, so much history binding us together.

I start at the only place I can. At my rebirth. "Lennon and I sat behind you on the plane."

Her eyes snap to mine. "What do you mean *behind me*?"

"Like, in the seat directly behind you."

"Oh my God." She rubs her face, slumping slightly. "You heard everything, then—Hugo taking that job, treating me like I didn't matter."

"Everything," I confirm. "I couldn't believe another man was lucky enough to have forever with you, then I couldn't believe he was stupid enough to throw it away."

Rings disturb the water's surface—a fish finding food, clueless to the humans baring their souls. Delilah's jaw knots, then relaxes. "It never would've worked between him and me."

I could tell her how much I hate him for making her feel small. I could write a thesis on the subject. But we're finally being honest, and I need to understand. "Did you love him?"

She grabs a dead leaf from the tabletop, spins it by the stem. "I met him at a tough time in my life. I was lonely and tired of being lonely, often falling into random funks of sadness. He was in Windfall on vacation, and he made me laugh. Swept in with his polo shirt and khaki pants. Not my usual taste, but I don't know . . . I liked that he wasn't my type. I thought maybe I just needed different, and I liked his attention. He was good at that, making me feel special when we were together. He took over conversations when I wasn't in the mood to speak. He made plans when I didn't want to plan. He was a doer, and it was easy to get sucked into his orbit."

I think about our nights, how easy they are, whether talking or watching TV or goofing around. The comfort in our silences. Neither of us plans much or takes over. Not since I abandoned my list. We work together naturally. "So, you fell in love with him?"

"I fell in love with the idea of him." She stares off into the distance, her face contemplative, the tip of her nose red from the chilly air. "With the idea of a fresh start somewhere else without the memories of my dad and Pickle and you. I thought leaving would make me happy, and he offered me a new life in New York. New friends. New memories to be made. But we were apart for most of our relationship, and he proposed quickly, which makes sense in the aftermath. He's a spontaneous pleasure-seeker who does what he wants when he wants."

The crisp air fills my lungs, while Delilah's confession fills me with sadness. "I wanted to say something, comfort you. I hated not saying anything."

She lets out a weary sigh. "His disregard of me and my feelings hurt, but being long distance made the break easier. And I knew it was the right choice, ending things." She slides her gaze to me. "Then you turned up."

"Then I turned up." I brush the backs of my fingers across her breeze-kissed cheek. "Your acting's improved exponentially."

"You mean better than this . . ." She screws her face into a scowl. "This soup is disgusting. I feel like throwing up."

There's my favorite congested Australian.

"Miles better. You should teach classes." I take her hand and run my finger over the fake engagement ring. "You should also take this off. I don't like seeing it on you."

She pauses a moment, then pulls the ring free and places it on the table. We stare at the simple piece of jewelry, a symbol of change, our future shifting as we sit here on the edge of a sparkling lake.

"Please give me a chance," I say, my focus on that monumental ring. It represents her past, our reunion, a perfect future I'm still terrified won't happen. "I want more. I want you. I want us." I face her and cup her cheeks. Tilt those gorgeous lips toward mine. "Losing you destroyed me, and having you back in my life is everything. Please trust me. Please trust I won't hurt you again."

She blinks, the press of her eyelids pushing a tear free. "This isn't about trust, E. I know you. I hate what you've been through and know you didn't hurt me on purpose."

"Then what's holding you back?"

Her hands find my chest, palms pressing flat. "You know I went through a rough time when you left, but you don't know the extent of it, and I don't want to relive it. I don't want to see your face when you find out what happened. I don't want to live with the knowledge of what it will do to you."

I'm racking my brain, trying to figure out what this terrible, awful secret is. She admitted she went off the rails—drinking, drugs, reckless behavior. Did she get into prostitution? Did she get sucked into some illegal gambling ring and has a mountain of debts to pay? Did she hurt herself like I once suspected, taking pills to numb the pain? There are no good possibilities. Already, I'm breathing hard, feeling ill. Wishing I could hold her and kiss her and promise her all scars heal. More than anything, I need to show her I can handle heartache.

"I lived through my father's betrayal and ten years of witness protection. I'm stronger than you think."

"Are you forgetting your disappearance the day I told you about your father's book deal?"

"Sure, but . . ." There are no buts. I was a selfish prick that day, and it's coming to bite me in the ass. "I came back and we're good, right? I

221

didn't let it fester. I worked in your kitchen and helped you today and made you an orgasmic curry?"

She laughs, smoothing her palms down my chest. Gradually, her hands fall to her lap. "Tell me again why the idea of your father's book upsets you so much."

"Besides the fact that he's earning money from our misery?" Saying it aloud pisses me off all over again. His betrayal's also a reminder there's no way I can sell my story and help Sathya without everyone's approval. A hurdle that can wait.

"Besides that," Delilah says.

I cover her hands with mine, needing a connection. "It wasn't about me. I'm worried about my mother and Desmond and how his latest stunt will affect them."

"Exactly. You absorb everyone's pain, and I don't want you to absorb mine."

We're back to her thinking I'm an empath again, feeling too much, on the cusp of *in*bursting at the slightest provocation. She's not completely wrong. I've proved once how selfish and oversensitive I can be. Which leaves one option. "Then don't tell me."

She frowns at her lap. "It's not that simple."

"At least give us time to try again. Time to decide, together as a couple, if we're worth whatever pain I'll suffer. Can you give me that? The chance to decide for myself? Or am I not worth it?"

She meets my eyes, her chin trembling. "You're worth everything, E."

"Then don't tell me yet. We'll put a pin in that conversation and save it until we're stronger. But I can't go on pretending we're not perfect for each other."

More tears fall down her cheeks, so many I'm worried the lake will rise, swallow us whole, drown us in all this painful history—then she's dashing at her cheeks and nodding. "Yeah. Okay. Let's do it. I want to try. Just don't ask me to talk about it, okay?"

"I won't." I cup her cool cheeks, inject as much sincerity as possible into my voice. "I promise."

We don't dive in and devour each other like I imagined we might. My heart beats in my fingertips. Her lips part in what can only be described as a decade's worth of longing. We meet achingly slow, share each other's breath and brush noses as our lips touch in a tentative graze, testing, savoring the closeness, the promise we've made, until I'm dizzy with wanting her.

Finally, I slant my lips over hers, tasting all I've missed—my Delilah. Our tongues graze and slide. I groan so loud the birds nearby dart for cover. Her lips are softer than I remember, her moves less tentative. She's pushing into me, gripping my hair so tight my scalp stings, moving until she's straddling me on the bench, grinding her hips down, and I'm a goner. I can't believe this is happening. Even with the weeks we've spent together, I'm in awe. Engulfed in heat. An inferno in my veins. Fire gripping my balls. Flames burning up my heart. I'm a fire-breathing dragon, last of his kind for ten years, discovering he's finally not alone.

"Fuck, Delilah." I kiss her deeper, twirl our tongues in a heady rush.

Two blinding kisses later, she presses her forehead to mine, panting. "If we don't go to our room, we're gonna give Windfall enough gossip for another ten years."

"If I stand up and try to move, my dick might break."

She laughs against my lips. "That's not possible."

I glance down between us. "It's never been this hard. It could happen."

"Well." Her whole face is red now. "We can try to make a run for it and hope for the best, or we can quit while we're ahead and save this for later." She swivels her hips as she speaks.

I'd rather break my dick. "When we stand, move in front of me."

"We're too far away for anyone to see your erection."

"My chest and six-pack aren't the only things that have filled out the past ten years."

"Such a child." Eyes flashing with mischief, she slides off my lap and grabs the fake ring from the table. She slips it into her pocket and does me the kindness of standing in front of me so I can reach into my jeans and readjust. Then we're holding hands and walking briskly, shooting each other searing looks, going for cool when all I want is to break into a run.

Maggie sees us and gawks. I wave at her with my middle finger. Ricky notices us and nudges Aaron. The two of them smile our way. Other people gape and whisper. Instead of feeling like a caged zoo animal, I puff up my chest and strut. When we get inside the elevator, I revert to my seventeen-year-old self and maul Delilah.

I crush her against the wall, my mouth on her neck, sucking, biting, kissing. I press my thigh between hers and grab a handful of her breast. "Your body will be the death of me."

She tries to shove her hands up my shirt, but I'm too close. "I almost died when you took your shirt off in my place. I need to feel the six-pack."

I give a silent nod to my dearly departed Win Back Delilah list and that stellar move. The elevator slows too soon. The doors open. Reluctantly, I release her and turn to see Aaron's parents, who were always on the conservative side, frowning at us from the hall.

Behind me, Delilah mumbles, "Shit."

"I was checking Delilah for lice," I say. "Her head was itchy, and you can never be too careful." They look unconvinced. Delilah pinches my side so hard I see spots. "Can't wait for the ceremony," I add as we scoot past them.

The elevator seals Aaron's parents inside, and Delilah pinches me again. "Now everyone will think I have lice."

"It was a panic move. But back to that part about you wanting to get your hands on my six-pack."

She gives me a gentle body check with her side. I wrap my arm around her, loving the fit of her tucked close while I walk awkwardly with the situation in my jeans. I'm desperate to teleport to our door, strip Delilah, and defile our bed, but I find myself slowing.

I stop when we reach our room and spin her toward me. "If we go in there. You won't be a virgin any longer."

She gives me her get-real-E look. "You took care of that ten years ago."

I sure did, with a spritz of Eternity cologne, a soft blanket, and "Pillow Talk" playing as we fumbled with the condom. "I mean there's no going back. If we go in there now with that fireplace and the unicorn bed, sex will happen. Are you okay with that?"

Like our first time, I ask if she's sure. I won't risk us rushing if it means a setback.

She threads her fingers through my hair, playing with the strands in a sensual way that makes my eyes drift shut. She leans forward, rubs her nose up my neck, then presses a soft kiss to my skin. "Fuck me in that room, E."

# TWENTY-FOUR

This is definitely not like our first time. We're older. Wiser. *Dirtier.*
And I'm more confident. At least, I try to be. It takes three swipes for
me to get our door open—*smooth as ever, E*—then I'm all over Delilah,
kicking the door shut, grabbing handfuls of her ass, knocking her into
the bedpost. I pull up her shirt and toss it on the floor.

At the sight of her, I groan and go still. My hungry eyes consume
all that smooth skin, her full breasts encased in black lace, my moon
necklace resting in her cleavage, the soft dip of her stomach. Everything
I've imagined for years but have been denied.

"Your body makes me angry." I give my aching dick a hard rub.

"You're no longer fascinated with boobs?" Playing the role of vixen,
she undoes her bra clasp and lets the lacy fabric hit the floor.

The sound I make is savage. "I can't explain it. You're fucking beautiful, but I feel wrathful when I look at you. Angry I missed ten years
of this."

"*You're* angry?" She takes fistfuls of my shirt and yanks it up and
over my head. Her sigh as she palms my abs undoes me. "You've been
tormenting me with these for *weeks*. Being this hot should be illegal."

Loving her as much as I do should be outlawed.

I tug her to me, groaning at the skin-on-skin contact. "Bet they feel
better like this, rubbing all over you."

Her body trembles against me, and I can't get enough of my hands on the velvet-soft skin of her back, the hard crush of her breasts against my chest. My dick throbs with the pressure of all this desire. I wasn't joking earlier. I've never been this hard. The desperation to be inside Delilah flays me with its ferocity. Like I'll wake up any moment, too late, and she'll be out of reach again.

Forcing myself to slow down, I dip my head and take one beautiful breast into my mouth. I'm rewarded with a sensual moan. I lavish her with my tongue, coax more sounds from her throat, stroke that pretty pink nipple. Relearn the weight of her, the soft give of her flesh. She's a woman now—fuller, softer, fiercely addictive. I kiss her sternum, her ribs, on a mission south.

She cups my jaw and stops my descent. "E . . ."

Her hesitancy breaks through the lust clouding my thoughts, leaving room for a sliver of anxiety. Instead of kissing my way lower, I drop to my knees and gaze up at Delilah in all her glory, worried she's having second thoughts. "Do you want to stop?"

She shakes her head. "It's just, I have a scar. I don't want you to be surprised, and I don't want you to ask about it."

Here we are then. The crossroad of the promise I made: *Don't ask me to talk about that time.* There's only one answer. "Scars are beautiful. They mean you're a survivor, and I promise I won't ask."

She bites her lip and nods, then pops the button on her jeans. An invitation. Confirmation she wants this as much as I do.

I take over, slowly unzip her fly, part the material, and freeze. "Delilah."

I don't know what I was expecting, but it wasn't an angry line on her abdomen, running from hip to hip. The type of scar that implies surgery . . . or, *fuck*. My mom has one of these, from her C-section with Lennon. She used to remind him of it when he'd do something stupid like getting caught skipping class, saying things like "I have scars from giving birth to you. Why do you have to add emotional scars?"

It can't be that. Delilah would have told me something so important. She's so rigid, I'm not sure she's breathing. As usual, I'm breathing too hard. I run my thumb over the puckered skin, force a rough swallow and look up at her. *What happened?* I'm dying to ask.

Her jaw stiffens, like she knows how much this is killing me, how close I am to breaking my promise. Whatever type of surgery she had, it hurt Delilah deeply, and I'm not sure how to stay silent. I sit back on my heels, fist my hands. Try to figure out how to love her the way my body's urging me to, while ignoring this scar when it scares the shit out of me. I grip her hips, press my forehead to her abdomen, can't help the tortured sound that escapes.

"I'm sorry," she says, her voice breaking. "I know it's ugly."

Jesus. Is that what she thinks? That anything about her body's ugly to me? Instantly, I know. I don't have a choice. I can't break my promise. I need to worship her body the way she deserves, show her how gorgeous she is, scars and all. And I can't risk losing her. Not again. I need Delilah like I need art and oxygen and running and my family—the life rafts in the turbulent waters of my life. She promised me time. In return, I owe her this.

I give the terrifying scar a kiss and look back up at her. "You're the most beautiful thing in the world to me, all of you, inside and out."

Her eyes well. "You must not get out much."

"A hermit for ten years," I say, both of us smiling sad smiles, but we're smiling, and I'll take that over tears. "All of you is gorgeous, Delilah. These tits, though." I lift up enough to pull the tip of one lush breast into my mouth, showing her how much I love her body. "These make me downright furious."

She arches with me, her hands dragging through my hair, her nails scraping along my scalp, sending shivers down my spine as I worship her. I don't pause at her scar this time. I know it's there. There's trauma in her past. Our past. There's also blazing attraction, two bodies and souls meant to merge, best friends under all this passion. I help her out of her jeans and underwear, and yeah. I have to pause again. I need a second. A wrinkle in time so I can memorize Delilah like this, her body bared to me: the soft curls covering all that wet heat, wider hips, fuller thighs, creamy skin that begs for my hands. She's the definition of feminine allure.

I'm the definition of dumb male.

I no longer remember either of my names. I'm here for someone's wedding, but I have no clue whose. I'm moving, one hand molded to Delilah's ass, the other dipping between her thighs, spreading her open, teasing her with little circles as I walk her to the bed.

She doesn't let me take her over the edge.

"Get these off." She's fussing with my jeans. Fly. Briefs. Denim. It all goes down.

I somehow step out of the tangle without getting a concussion. Then naked Delilah Moon is on her knees, holding my steel shaft, stretching her lips over the head of my dick, and I buck. It's uncontrollable and rough. I think I grunt too. Or scream her name. I sink my hands into all that thick hair and move with her. Not forcefully. I let her lead. There's too much pleasure twisting at the base of my spine as I watch my rigid flesh sinking into that mouth I love so much, making me angry again. So in love and angry at all I've missed I'm worried I'll be too aggressive.

"Not like this," I choke out. "I need to be inside you. Please."

I'm not above begging.

She releases me with a twist of her tongue that drives me wild. I'm a teenager again, on the verge, unable to control myself around her. I grip my shaft. Give it a strong squeeze.

"There's a condom in the top dresser drawer," I rasp.

She doesn't go for it, though. She stands and rubs her hands all over me, exploring my back, bringing our naked bodies flush. My dick is trapped against her stomach, pleasure gripping me in hot pulses.

"I've been tested," she says, trailing kisses up my neck.

I may be in dumb-male mode, blinded by lust, but I'm not a complete idiot. I understand her meaning instantly, and here's the thing. I was wrong before. My dick's never been *this* hard. One wrong move and it actually might snap. "So have I. I've never been with anyone bare. You're on the pill?"

"It's fine," she says, wrapping her hand around my length, cutting off my ability to think.

Yeah, sure. It's fine. I'm fine. Sinking into Delilah Moon bare, with nothing between us, won't short-circuit my brain.

She leads us to the bed and crawls into the center, beckoning me to follow. My dick listens. My whole body listens. My shaft is heavy with the weight of expectation, my balls drawn up tight. Every inch of my skin is oversensitive, like I could conduct electricity with every hard, sharp pulse of my heart. Delilah takes charge, rolling on top of me, sliding her wet pussy down my cock, biting my nipples the way she remembers I like, charting my developed six-pack, nipping at my hip bones, then guiding me to her entrance.

I grip her hips. Because yeah. I need another moment, a breath to calm down before I embarrass myself. Delilah settles her hands on my pecs, runs her fingers through my sparse chest hair, then rocks her pelvis slightly, trying to lower herself. The tip of my cock is right there, nudging her, barely pressing through her hot flesh, and my dick pulses. Along with my full-body buzz, emotion crowds my throat, stings the backs of my eyes. I push in an inch farther, and I have to bite my tongue.

"E." My name whispered from my girl. "Go all the way in."

I'm not sure she understands what she's asking. I'm losing myself here, remembering so much, clinging to the past and locking her into my future. Once we're flush, she's mine. There's no going back, no matter her troubling secrets. And I can't hold out any longer.

I thrust up as she pushes down.

"Fuck." I think I came a bit. She's so hot and wet, contracting around me, obliterating my senses.

"Jesus." She moans. "You *are* bigger."

"I . . ." Am having trouble forming words other than *fuck* and *yes* and *so hot*. "I wouldn't lie about something so vital," I finally choke out.

She looks down at me, something like mischief sparking in her eyes. "We're having *the* Sex, E."

I always knew she'd remember that line, but we never had the time for her to tease me about it. It's even better like this, being inside her, both of us comfortable enough to joke the way we joke, no fake veneers or roles left to play. "We're not having the Sex yet, Mars. This is foreplay." I alter my angle, push deeper, grind harder. A blast of heat sears my thighs.

"God, yes." Her lips part in a sexy pout. She sets a rhythm and angle that allows her to rub against my pelvis, her hands gripping my chest, her body undulating, taking me deeper. I tense my thighs and rock with her, using the bed's bounce in our favor.

"I'm close." Her eyes flutter shut, her movement getting looser, faster. "So close."

I don't break the rhythm. I want her falling apart around me, rubbing herself all over me, covering me in her scent so I can walk around like a caveman telling every living soul Delilah Moon is mine. She doesn't shout when she comes. Her body coils tight, her pussy clamping so hard I almost shoot off, but I don't. I'm not ready for this to end.

When Delilah opens her eyes with a blissful smile, I say, "Now we're about to have the Sex."

I flip us over, lift up on my knees, raising her pelvis with me. I plunge back in. We both cry out. The bed bangs the wall. I'm beyond making love. I'm fucking Delilah Moon because Delilah Moon asked to be fucked in this bed, and a good woman deserves to be thoroughly fucked. I'm also in love and still angry and so thankful, a thousand emotions pouring out of me as my hips slam into hers, bouncing her tits, our skin slapping as we grunt.

I drop my weight on her, needing more. Us, closer. Lips. Tongue. Teeth. Messy kisses with our hands tugging at each other. Her breathing picks up. My vision clouds at the edges, points of pleasure gathering so tight I can't contain them. I feel her come again—that contracting pulse of her inner walls, her body going rigid, the quietest "God" panted in my ear—and I lose it. My orgasm barrels down on me, shakes my body, pouring out of me in violent bursts I can't control.

I'm panting afterward, sweaty, propping my weight slightly, but I'm all over Delilah, kissing her again. Desperate, hungry kisses like we didn't just have the most intense sex of my life. When it comes to Delilah, I doubt I'll ever have enough.

# TWENTY-FIVE

Thank you, Life.

# TWENTY-SIX

Honestly. I have no clue what tipped the scales. Life is not only on my side, but the bastard has become my wingman, obliterating obstacles left, right, and center, giving me a clear path to my end goal: Delilah. Like right now, there is literally a clear path between me and where Delilah's standing. The wedding invitees are milling in the reception area beyond her, waiting for the outdoor ceremony to commence. She's talking to a waiter about cakes or tarts or cupcakes or cuptarts. I don't care. All I know is there's nothing stopping me from walking up to her in front of every single person here and kissing her silly.

Except I'm not sure it's cool.

We made love two more times this afternoon. The last time melted my brain. It was the type of slow sex where each breath-stealing drag burns you up from the inside out, neither of us moving faster, just rocking together in the sexiest slow dance in the history of slow dances, with me coming in long hard streams from the sheer force of our connection.

Delilah claimed she needed to primp afterward, to shower and make herself pretty. I told her it's impossible to be any prettier and received a naughty kiss for my efforts, then I went for a run while she got ready. Did I think about her scar while I ran? Of course. Will I ask Delilah about it? Of course I won't. I made a promise to let her set the pace on this. I trust her to open up when she's ready. But I haven't seen Delilah in forty minutes, and I now understand how Candy Cane feels.

The deranged excitement she exudes, wiggling and smiling her face off when I leave the room for two minutes and—*poof*—reappear!

It hasn't even been an hour, and I can't believe Delilah's still here. I want to wiggle all over her, lick her until she screams my name. But I stay put. It was one thing holding hands while we made our mad dash to our room earlier. Only a few guests were around. This reception area is filled with Windfall folks. While I'd like everyone to know Delilah Moon is my lover and best friend, I'm not sure she's on the same page. We didn't discuss public protocol.

She says something to the waiter she's talking to, then she spots me. Instantly her eyes soften—an expression that hits me in the heart—and her lips quirk with mischief. I know that look, understand her decision the second it's made, and I do the only smart thing. I brace my legs. But she doesn't launch the attack hug I expect. She seems to check herself, the mischief in her expression shifting to a polite smile. I get it. Attack hugs are our thing. They remind me of our earliest days as a couple, when we were carefree, no worries but school tests and buying a new comic before it sold out. We're not that carefree yet.

Instead of running at me head-on, she approaches slowly until I wrap her in my arms. When that's not close enough, I stuff my face in her neck and inhale her intoxicating scent. "You smell amazing. And you look . . ." I step back and whistle. "That dress is stunning with you in it."

The fabric's the same Sonic blue as her eyes, snug around her breasts, flitting jauntily about her thighs because it knows how lucky it is to touch her.

She straightens my blue tie, which matches her dress and eyes. "You clean up well, handsome."

I drag her closer, brush her nose with mine. We may not be ready for attack hugs, but I can't pretend I don't want to devour her. "As long as you approve."

"The suit won't stay on long after the party, but it's a good look on you."

I guess she's done pretending too. "Keep saying things like that and we'll be defiling the walk-in cooler. I have it on good authority there's lemon carnage in there that would taste amazing licked off your body."

She nips my ear. "That would be hot."

I hug her close, so she can feel how turned on I am. "You're hot."

"You're both nauseatingly adorable." Naomi grins at us and tugs on Avett's arm. "Aren't they adorable?"

I have no clue where they appeared from, but I grin back. "You two are also adorable, but less so when you sneak up on me while I'm seducing this gorgeous woman."

Delilah straightens her dress strap. "He wasn't succeeding anyway."

I gawk at her. "You were putty in my arms."

"Guess you don't know when a girl's faking."

She did not just go there. But yeah. Of course she went there, and I love her for it. Avett, the traitor, snickers. Naomi high-fives her.

I lean into Delilah's ear. "I'll be running scientific studies later to test if you're faking. Multiple experiments. I'll be analyzing results. Be prepared."

Delilah's cheeks and neck redden. Mission accomplished.

Naomi sighs. "I'm so happy to see you two together." She elbows Avett. "Doesn't it remind you of us, babe? When we couldn't keep our hands off each other?"

"It does because you keep reminding me how cute they are and that we apparently aren't as cute as them anymore."

I shine my knuckles on my suit jacket. "Be jealous."

"I'm not jealous that you were seducing a girl who's like a sister to me."

"Or any girl," Naomi adds.

"Of course any girl." Avett leans down and gives her a filthy kiss. "See? We're still cute."

"Yes, my man." She beams up at him. "We certainly are."

They really are a handsome couple. Avett's all done up in a dark suit similar to mine, but trendier, with a shadowed gray pattern I'd never be able to pull off. The years have been kind to Naomi too. In high school, she was a studious kid who wore baggy clothes and spent her lunch hours in the computer labs, never speaking up much in class. Now she's all confidence, working as a teacher, like Delilah once dreamed, her olive skin glowing against her purple dress, her long brown hair flirting with her shoulders. And they have an adorable daughter.

If one of us is jealous of the other, I'm jealous of them.

Naomi hooks her arm with Avett's and leads us to the other waiting guests. As expected, when Delilah and I strut that way, all eyes shift to us. I'm not sure if it's my notoriety drawing continued attention or our open display of affection. Either way, I don't care tonight. With Delilah on my arm, I'll happily flash my feathers for the crowd. We mingle briefly, everyone chatting about the gorgeous day and the fishing or hiking or whatever it was they did. I don't say much since I did Delilah all day and don't feel it's polite conversation.

Maggie saunters over with her date, a tall Black guy with an Ivy League vibe: broad shoulders, strong jaw, thick glasses. She fans her hand my way and says, "Thomas, this is Edgar Eugene Bower. When we were kids, he was caught feeling up a mannequin in Mrs. Talbot's old ladies' clothing store."

Avett drops his head back, cracking up. "I dared him to do that."

"And I never back down from a dare. I've heard the same about you, Margaret."

"You . . . *what?*" Maggie's wearing a healthy dose of makeup. Even under that bright blush, there's no missing how her face pales.

"Dares," I say, unsure what has her ruffled. "Like the time Delilah dared you to drink a thirty-two-ounce bottle of Gatorade at Desmond's college football game and you peed your pants on the drive home." But I suddenly recall that Lennon loved playing truth or dare as a kid.

Was actually kind of obsessed with it. His crowning moment was when he dared lactose-intolerant Desmond to eat a brick of cheddar during my toilet-cleaning punishment, on top of Desmond's regular grilled cheeses. Good times had by all.

Maybe Lennon and Maggie played their own version of truth or dare, some kind of game that has them both acting odd. I could ask her outright, but tormenting her is more fun.

She laughs haltingly at the Gatorade-peeing incident, like she's relieved I didn't mention anything more embarrassing but worried I know her secrets. She latches harder on to her date's arm. "It was a fun day. Delilah was imitating Edgar's awful acting in *Oliver!* and I was laughing too hard to ask him to pull over."

Thomas chuckles with the group, but he's eyeing me curiously.

I'm getting used to the attention. Mostly. But this close and intense isn't as easy to brush off. "Do we know each other from somewhere?" I ask him. It's possible. I don't have the best memory for faces other than Delilah's.

He looks at Maggie, who shrugs a shoulder, as though giving him some kind of permission. He beams. "I'm a Gates of Ember fan. Mags told me you're the illustrator. Your work's awesome."

"Wow, thanks." And because compliments make me uncomfortable, I deflect to Maggie. "I had no clue you were a closet fan too."

She crinkles her freckled nose. "I don't read comic books."

"Graphic novels."

"Exactly."

"You're working on a prequel, right?" her date says. "I'm dying to read it."

"I am, but things are . . ." I wave my hand vaguely instead of finishing the sentence.

Cancellation of the prequel isn't public knowledge yet. I'm waiting to finish my current project before I broach the subject of publishing it with Delilah and my family. Sathya and I still have to talk out our options, but the more I think about selling my story, the less I hate the idea. Helping Sathya's family in a time of crisis is a factor, but there's a revenge component I can't deny. Father Dearest is publishing his version of our life. I have no doubt it will be overflowing with his expert subterfuge as he panders to his ego, building himself up as the martyr.

My story has our hard truths wrapped in fantasy: Delilah turning her back on her princess heritage, fighting through her pain when I disappear, then working her land on Earth in disguise, sowing, tilling, feeding people the food she grows until they recognize the princess behind the cloaked shawl. I'm on Mars during this time, slaving for our captors, finding solace drawing murals of my lost love, spending hours upon hours trying to hatch a plan, escape back to Earth, with my family's suffering woven in.

I don't know yet how the novel ends. The urge to live out my deepest desires through my art is strong. Revenge writing. The torture and suffering of my father when his greed invariably brings him down. Or I'll write a fairy-tale ending with Delilah and me running to each other in the attack hug of hugs, the two of us finally on the same planet, my father forgotten because he doesn't deserve to be remembered. Or it'll be a film-noir-style novel, where nothing changes, the bad guys win, and we go on with our lives in relative peace, knowing justice wasn't served, having tasted freedom, only for Delilah's secret to tear us apart again.

The last possibility has me frowning.

A violin carries in from the patio outside, where the ceremony is to be held. Everyone moves toward the sound, but Delilah holds me back. "What's going on with the prequel?"

While I won't share that information with Maggie's random date, I have no problem trusting her. "Remember that call from my agent the night your dishwasher quit?" She nods. I go on, "Sathya told our agent she can't finish the prequel. She doesn't want to write it for several reasons, which means we're in breach of contract, unless one of us produces something else quickly, and Sathya's mother is sick. She can't focus right now, which leaves me."

"E, you should've said something. I'd never have let you wash dishes if I knew you needed to work."

I thread our fingers together, pulling her closer. "Don't do that."

"Do what?"

"Make decisions for me. I did what I wanted to do, and I've been fitting work in." Earlier mornings after I walk Candy Cane. Free minutes between dishwashing and spending my nights with Delilah. I lift her hand and kiss her pulse point, the direct line to her heart. "Let me put you first for a change."

She softens against me. "Fine, but not always. I want to support you too. Can I still be your first reader when your novel's done?"

"I'm counting on it." When I know the shape of our story and how it ends. Then I'll give it to Delilah and my family and let them decide if it gets published or not.

"Also . . ." Her voice drops shyly. "Will you be my date to the Scarecrow Scavenger Hunt this year?"

"Didn't you used to plan that as a girl's day with Maggie?"

"I did, but I'd love to be there with you this year. And I worry about how much you're working. This would be a fun way for you to get a break."

I wrap her in my arms, overwhelmed by her offer. This is more than us having amazing sex and flirting openly. This is Delilah wanting to care for me as much as I want to care for her. "I'd love nothing more than to be your scavenger hunt date."

We kiss chastely, then join the festivities outside. Colored leaves float down in the breeze, ivy and white flowers spilling over a wooden pergola. We take our seats next to Avett and Naomi and hold hands while the music plays. We keep holding hands while Ricky, then Aaron, walks down the aisle and says their vows, the two of them sharing their love with us all. We hold tight while I picture Delilah and me up there, pledging ourselves, overcoming the odds, kissing like Ricky and Aaron—sweet and sensual and a little filthy. When they hug intensely, emotion sears my throat, and Delilah squeezes my fingers.

So yeah. I cry at weddings. Shocker, I know. Delilah looks at my face and blubbers. Maggie turns around at the sounds I'm making trying to hold it all in.

She mouths, *Baby.*

I whisper, "Let's play truth or dare."

Her face shrivels, and she whips back around.

Inside the inn's cathedral-ceilinged room, champagne flows and pretty appetizers are passed around. The mood is downright vivacious, everyone toasting the newlyweds and grinning broadly. The buffet dinner is fantastic. Delilah's by my side for most of the night, but she's with her friends too. I enjoy those moments almost as much. The way she laughs and talks with them, then searches the room, her eyes finding mine, sparkling that electric-blue sparkle that snaps across my skin. We share silly winks and secret I'm-going-to-defile-you smiles, and when our lemon tarts join the stunning desserts she and Angel created, I feel a hit of pride.

The pièce de résistance is when the Tweeds take the stage.

I assume my role of roadie like a seasoned pro, helping set up after the DJ clears out. Shawn smells like he smoked ten ounces of weed. Kaitlyn doesn't listen when I ask her to test her bass. Ricky's drunk and doing some weird dance onstage, making everyone laugh. For the first time since returning to Windfall, it's like nothing's changed.

They rock out. Loud and proud and awesome. I slam dance with Avett like we're fourteen and stupid. I holler and cheer until my throat's hoarse. I do the chicken dance for Delilah until she almost pees herself, then I drag her close and dirty dance with her because I can. Yeah, it's a great night.

Delilah and I are among the last to leave. Ricky and Aaron are slow dancing with some stragglers around them. Shawn is passed out on the floor with a crushed cupcake in his hand and smeared icing on his face, like he hit the floor midbite.

Not gonna lie. I'm pretty drunk. As is Delilah. We're leaning on each other, sleepy and smiley, and I do my drunken best not to sit down in the elevator. If I do, I'll be snoring in seconds. We help each other to our room, fumble with the keycard five times. Nope . . . make that six. Then we stumble inside and plow onto the bed. Fully clothed. No washing up. We don't have sex or even kiss. I tuck her against my chest, spooning her aggressively—one of my legs wrapped over hers, both my arms latched around her stomach, my face squished into her thick hair. I hold her, scared about how happy I am. How good I feel. How perfect everything is.

# TWENTY-SEVEN

"It's definitely the Sandpiper's Nest," Delilah says, crowding me to read the paper in my hand. "The bird reference is obvious."

I have no doubt she's right, but I haven't participated in the Scarecrow Scavenger Hunt in a decade. I'm enjoying dragging out the late afternoon, watching Delilah's face light up when we find a hidden mini scarecrow. It's been two weeks since the wedding, and she was right about me needing a break from work. Thanks to her, today has been the perfect breather.

Participating tourists and locals have been running around town all day, one of ten different papers in hand, each with eight clues to find eight scarecrows, all in mixed-up orders to spread people out. Once again, Windfall will be splashed over social media with hashtags like #CutestTownEver #MiniScarecrowsForTheWin #SoMuchFun. More people will come. This small town, which runs on gossip and protecting its own, will thrive.

Most participants started much earlier and have finished their hunts. They're congregating at the beer garden now, purses and backpacks filled with mini scarecrows, sharing stories and smiles in the town square. The barbecue tent smells amazing, and it appears the organizers opted to stick with country music for the after-party—the band setting up under the tapestry of strung-up lights are sporting impressive cowboy hats.

Since Delilah and I couldn't follow our clues until her shop was quiet enough for her to leave, we're some of the last stragglers hunting scarecrows. I move behind her and wrap my arms around her stomach, tucking her close as we reread the clue.

*Find me where birds of a feather flock together, protected by a castle, with four minus one sentries guarding me.*

"The bookstore is a good guess," I say, running my nose along the slope of her ear. She shivers, and I drop a soft kiss to her temple. "But lots of birds shit on the mermaid fountain. It could be over there."

"Except Yvette's obsessed with all things medieval, and she owns the bookstore. The castle and sentry part has to be her." Delilah nuzzles into me, neither of us caring if anyone is watching. "I also really love it when you flirt with my ear."

"Like this?" I blow a soft breath on target. As amazing as being openly affectionate at the wedding was, standing in the middle of town, with Delilah telling me what turns her on, beats that awesome weekend.

She moans softly and presses her ass against my growing erection. "Seems like you enjoy flirting with my ear too."

"I enjoy all of you all the time. But this dress?" I slide my palm across her abdomen, quickly realizing this game we're playing is not public appropriate. Her blue dress is thin and soft and patterned with tiny peaches. "You look edible," I murmur.

A guitar strums. Laughter erupts down the street.

Delilah pulls away from me and adjusts her dress, her face beautifully flushed. "So, the clue. Birds. Castles. Sentries."

I can barely focus on blinking, let alone clues. "I'm not sure about the 'four minus one sentries' part of the riddle, but I know where one sentry is, and he's standing at attention." I point to my dick.

Delilah bites her lip, which makes me want to bite her lip, her collarbone, the swell of her full breast, the soft skin of her inner thigh. I release an animal grunt. I'm not sure if my face looks as ferociously covetous as I feel, but she grabs my hand before I cause more town gossip and drags me toward the Sandpiper's Nest.

The bookstore is brighter than I remember: soft-yellow walls, sections organized by themes, not just genre. I walk stiffly at first, my body still primed for Delilah, but the happy space eventually distracts me. Yvette Lozano waves at us, then continues chatting up two older ladies at the cash register.

"When did Yvette buy the shop from her parents?" I ask.

"They retired a year ago and returned to Mexico. She's already revamped the place. Added a cute reading nook for kids, and she hosts knitting nights where she reads aloud as people knit."

More changes since I've been gone, but the awareness of what I missed no longer saddens me. Not when I'm holding Delilah's hand, having fun chasing scarecrows and riling her up.

"Four minus one," Delilah mumbles as she slowly scans the shelves. "With the castle and sentry references, I'm guessing she has three historical or fantasy books stacked somewhere, but one of the series will be missing. Like right there," she says, her voice rising in excitement.

She yanks at my hand, intent on her mission, but I don't budge. We're in front of a graphic novel section, and my book is facing front. It's the first in the series, with Ceuthon's serpentine face front and center, the fiery gates of hell pulling at him from below.

Delilah follows my gaze and squeezes my hand. "It must be so cool to see your work in the wild."

I wrap my arm around her shoulder and tug her into me. "That day in my truck, when I told you I was Brian Baker, I wanted to kiss you so badly. What you said about my work meant a lot."

She flattens her palm on my chest, her blue-blue eyes sweeping over my face with wonder. "I meant every word, and I wanted to kiss you so badly too."

"Really?"

"Not kissing you was killing me."

I study her and chew my cheek. "I honestly couldn't tell if you were fighting our pull as much as me or just being kind. I mean, I *hoped* you were into me, but it was tough to read you with all the fake fiancé stuff."

She traces my jaw, then the scar through my upper lip. "After I saw you at the airport, I couldn't stop thinking about you. I was with Hugo, stressed about our relationship, but all our memories flooded back. I think that's what gave me the courage to end my engagement."

I kiss the tip of her finger. "How so?"

"As wrecked as I was when you left me, seeing you again reminded me that when relationships are good, they lift a person up. A partner should make you feel like the best version of yourself, and Hugo didn't do that for me. We weren't right for each other. Then you showed up at my café, and . . ."

"And?"

Eyes full of a bookstore's worth of emotion, she threads her fingers into the curled ends of my hair. "And every second I held you at a distance was torture."

"Worse than the time Lennon dared you to eat a live worm and dropped it on your hair?"

She shudders dramatically, still mooning up at me. "Even worse than that."

"Guess it's a good thing we can touch and kiss whenever we want now." I lean down and kiss her, soft and slow and chaste. We sigh in tandem, rubbing our noses together. When Delilah opens her eyes again, they're shining with unshed tears.

I tilt her chin up. "What's wrong?"

She smooths her hand down the front of my newly purchased "Life Is Good" T-shirt and tangles her fingers in the hem. "I'm just so happy."

"Isn't that a good thing?"

She nods and gifts me with a watery smile, but something darker is shimmering in her gaze. Fear. The secret she hasn't yet shared glinting below the surface.

In case you're wondering, I haven't pushed like the pusher I can be. As requested, I haven't asked Delilah for answers to my many questions. Fact is, I'm in this for the long haul. Every time we have sex, I finish with a kiss on her scar. A kiss to let her know she's beautiful. A kiss to remind her she needs to open up one day. A kiss to promise her story won't change anything between us. She stays quiet every time, which is okay. I want this time together as much as her, unfettered by more drama.

"I'm happy too," I tell her and run my knuckles down her cheek. Not just happy. Busting with so much emotion that my chest often aches. "And if we're confessing stuff, that day in the truck, when I told you my alias, I didn't hit play on 'Pillow Talk' by accident."

She rolls her eyes and blinks away the darkness. "Shocker. Now let's find this scarecrow so we can dance under those fairy lights."

"Excellent plan. The sooner we get to the party, the sooner I get you home and out of that dress." I wink at her.

She gives her skirt a saucy flick, then skips ahead to the stack of books she spotted. She yanks them aside, expecting to find mini scarecrows behind them, but there are just more books.

She slumps. "Must be a different series."

She scrutinizes the rows of novels, heading to the kid's reading nook. There could be a series about kings or queens or castles in there. I'm about to join her, when I spot an adorable dog.

I've always been a dog lover, but since having Candy Cane, I've become a dog freak. Any and all furry friends must be petted and given love. Since my girl is at home—busy festivals aren't her speed—I crouch and give this pooch an extra dose of attention.

"I bet you've seen it all," I tell the old-timer while rubbing his graying ears. He's a wiry dog a bit bigger than my girl, with extra weight around his middle.

"That's Perci," Delilah calls. "He's a sweetheart. But not as sweet as Candy, obviously."

"Obviously," I say, loving how much Delilah loves my dog. "But Perci is a good name. Isn't it, boy? Like Sir Percival, gallant knight of the round . . ."

*Table,* I don't say as my clue-solving mind kicks into gear. Not only is Perci named after a knight, but his donut-shaped dog bed is decorated with a castle motif. I squint at the pup, then pull out the clue and reread it.

*Find me where birds of a feather flock together, protected by a castle, with four minus one sentries guarding me.*

Birds of a feather could easily be this store: the Sandpiper's Nest.

Protected by a castle: Perci is curled up in a cute castle.

But I don't see the tiny scarecrows.

Yvette might have forgotten to replenish the found scarecrows, or she could've hidden them really well. Either way, the "four minus one sentries" is a conundrum. Unsure I'm on the right track, I move to lift the edge of Perci's bed. He stands before I get far, shoving his nose at my jeans pocket. He adds in some paw action and whines. I laugh and nudge his nose away, remembering I have Candy's treats on me.

Hitting pause on my scarecrow search, I extricate a treat, hold it out, and gasp. "He's missing a leg."

Delilah joins me and scratches the pup's head. "He came to the shelter with three. But it doesn't hold you back, does it, Perci boy?"

Perci takes the treat and munches happily, unperturbed about his lack of limb and unaware I'm basically Sherlock Holmes. "He has *three legs*," I tell Delilah emphatically.

"I think we already covered that."

"Three legs—*four minus one sentries.*" I gesture at his bed. "He lives in a *castle.*"

She hitches her shoulders and grabs my forearm. "You found it! But where are the scarecrows?"

I curl my lip dramatically. "If they fed Perci the little buggers and we have to wait until he poops one out, the planning committee will be getting a strongly worded letter from me."

Delilah smacks my stomach, then gets on all fours to search under the bed. Perci, of course, thinks this is great fun. He licks Delilah's face and ear until she's cracking up, fending him off. While they're occupied, I drop back to my knees to lift the edge of his bed. Lo and behold, there are a couple of mini scarecrows.

"Victory!" I call, holding our spoils in the air.

Delilah shimmies over on her knees, the two of us grinning silly grins while Perci tries to grab our treasure. We kiss over him, then add our scarecrow to Delilah's purse.

"I think it's dancing-under-the-fairy-lights time," she says.

"*After* we gloat to Maggie that we finished our hunt faster than she predicted."

"And *after* we gorge on barbecue." Her stomach rumbles as we stand.

"Food first, dancing after. And more hand-holding time in between." I grab hers, linking our fingers firmly, happy to sink into this fun day.

❧

Maggie's at the barbecue tent when we get there. She's with Thomas, the same glasses-wearing guy from the wedding, but she has a hazy expression on her face, like she's half listening to whatever he's saying.

When she sees us, she beams at Delilah, then her face neutralizes, as though liking me goes against her DNA. "Did you skip the last couple clues?" she asks me.

"Nope. I'm just a scarecrow-hunting champion."

"I call bullshit. I wrote half those clues, and most people took twice the length of time."

Maggie works for the town, helping run festivals and events. While I could tell her how great the event is and how fun the clues were, she would assume I'm being condescending. "Living in WITSEC gave us all superpowers. I have problem-solving powers, and Lennon reads minds now, even from a distance." I tap my temple, then point knowingly at her. "If I were you, I'd be careful what you think."

Her green eyes narrow into slits.

I grin broadly. "Also, this was a great event."

"I don't need your attitude, *Edgar*."

Exactly why I should've kept the compliment to myself.

Ricky and Aaron join us. Instead of boasting about their scarecrow finds, Aaron stares glumly at a gnarly one pinned to his chest. The tiny bugger seems to be covered in blood, and every time Ricky looks at him, he almost falls over laughing.

Ricky finally gathers himself, wiping at his eyes. "We found the scarecrow at Hatcher's butcher shop, and he made Aaron pin it on his shirt and he . . ." Ricky cracks up again, leaning into Aaron, who looks resigned to being ridiculed. After a few calming breaths, Ricky says, "Hatcher pointed at Aaron with his bloody cleaver and told him not to take it off, so now Aaron thinks he'll get axe murdered if he removes it."

I snort out a laugh. "I guess Hatcher the Hatchet is as scary as ever."

"He's always bloody," Aaron says and shudders. "Like, *always*. Blood on his clothes. Under his nails. I think he drinks the stuff. And no one knows what happened to his dog. One day that mutt was just *gone*."

"It's true," Delilah says and pats Aaron's shoulder. "Don't mess with Hatcher. If I were you, I'd wear the scarecrow for at least a week."

Ricky moves behind Aaron and mouths, *A month*, to Delilah.

"A month," Delilah corrects quickly, keeping a straight face. Honestly, her acting is unreal. "Definitely a month."

Aaron stares morosely at the creepy scarecrow as Avett and Naomi join our group. Their daughter, Simone, is sleeping cuddled on Avett's chest, oblivious to the music and loud chatter in the square. We gather food and sit at a picnic table under the tent, plates laden with pulled pork sandwiches, mac and cheese, and a beet salad made with Windfall's delicious farm-grown beets.

Delilah's pressed up beside me, practically leaning on me, eating quietly. She steals looks at Ricky and Aaron laughing together, at Avett running a hand down his daughter's back while Naomi whispers in his ear. Delilah's eyes then flick to me, that same happy but fearful expression lingering.

Wanting to perk her up, I grab one of the fall-themed cupcakes Maggie brought to the table and take a massive bite, making sure the orange icing gets on my face and nose. Schooling my expression, I turn to Delilah. "Do I have something on my face?"

She takes one look at me and cackles. "Is this your first time eating a cupcake?"

"No. But it's my first time doing this." I cup the back of her neck and dive in for a kiss, smearing the icing on us both.

"Oh my God." She laughs and shrieks, shoving at me so hard I fall off the end of the bench to the cheers of our friends. It's okay. I don't mind lying on the grass, looking up at Delilah's shocked and indignantly amused face. Not when she used her signature you're-an-idiot-E oh my God.

"You taste good with icing," I tell her.

"You're one wrong move from waking up with snails in the bed."

I recoil. I developed my fear of snails when Desmond thought it would be funny to hide a few shell-less slugs in my open bag of Cheetos. Delilah was there for my flailing freak-out.

"Honestly. Don't even *joke* about that."

"I see no joking here." Her evil-mastermind expression doesn't bode well.

"I'll never smear icing on you again," I say as I rush to my feet and gather some Wet-Naps. "You'll only get clean kisses from me for the rest of your life."

Our friends shake their heads at us and leave to mingle.

Happy for the privacy, I wipe Delilah's face gently and finish with a clean dry napkin, ensuring there's no icing left behind. "See? Like it never happened, which means there's no reason whatsoever to retaliate."

She opens a fresh Wet-Nap and drags it slowly over my nose and mouth. "What if I don't want *only* clean kisses from you?"

Yeah, okay. My body hums to life, but I pitch my voice low. "Do you want to experiment with dirtier sex, Delilah?"

Her slow drag of the cloth suddenly feels electric. "I think I might like dirty talk. The guys I've been with have always been quiet in bed, so I don't know. And . . ." She looks up at me through her lashes. "I'm not sure *I* want to do the talking, but I think hearing it would turn me on."

"Well." I swallow through the lust drying my mouth. "I think we can work on that."

"What about you?" she asks, shifting closer. "Is there some secret desire you're curious about?"

Every second with Delilah is enough for me, but her blue eyes have darkened with intensity, like she's dying to know what I fantasize about. Like she's *desperate* to make my wants a reality. "I've never had sex in public."

"As in . . . you might like it if other people watch?"

"Fuck, no." Even the thought has my jaw hardening. "The only person who gets to see you gloriously naked is me. But something about the possibility of getting caught might excite me."

Her nostrils flare, and she bites her lip. "Okay."

This conversation is more than *okay*. Not only am I dying to growl naughty words to Delilah, but I love that we no longer have to disguise our desires, talking about spicy food instead of sharing our true fantasies.

Feeling impatient to have her in my arms, I let her clean the rest of my face, then pull her into me under the fairy lights, at the outskirts of the grassy dance area. She rests her head on my chest. I splay my hand possessively on her lower back, the two of us swaying to the band's slow song. I honestly love this woman. Talking openly with her, teasing, joking, stoking each other's desire with nothing but a few whispered words. I also love being here, in this town full of memories, surrounded by friends and townsfolk who no longer want to chase me with pitchforks.

The fiddle's gentle tempo weaves with our steps. The fairy lights cast a magical glow over the crowd.

Holding Delilah tighter, I press a kiss to the top of her head. "I thought I maybe built up Windfall in my mind, that I remembered it with rose-colored glasses." I inhale Delilah's scent—sugar, spice, and everything nice—taking in the barbecue tent, the scarecrows on the lampposts, the kids chasing one another by the fountain as parents and teens smile and chat in groups. "But it's even better than I remembered. There's a peacefulness and warmth in this town that's irreplicable."

Delilah hums against me. "I think part of the reason I left Hugo, aside from him being a selfish dick, was because deep down I didn't want to leave here."

I move us in a circle, ending farther from the crowd. "I hate that he didn't treat you with respect, but I'm thankful you didn't get married."

She doesn't reply, but she hugs me so tight I feel the hard beat of her heart. We dance quietly, clinging to each other in a way that excites and scares me. Like we're both addicted to each other but worried this high will eventually crash.

I brush her wild curls off her face, try to read her eyes in the dimness. "Thanks for an awesome day and for making me take a break from working."

"Today was so fun." She runs her hands up and down my back. "I don't want it to end."

Not liking the melancholy in her tone, I lean down and lick a path up her ear. "The day's not over yet. I still have plans for us."

She whimpers and rocks her pelvis into me, a needy move that threatens my composure. Her admission about dirty talk stoked a fire in my gut. I'm more than eager to test Delilah's boundaries.

Licking my lips, I anchor her against my thigh, my cock already pumped with steel. "You like rubbing your pussy on me, baby? Does that feel good?"

"God, yes."

"How about this?" I grip her ass and grind her on my thigh, readying to give her all the dirty talk she can handle. "I'm picturing my cock sinking into you, Delilah, thrusting so fucking hard. Filling you up over and over. Is my thigh enough, or do you need more?"

"I need . . ." She trails off as her hands dig harder into my back.

"What do you need, baby? Tell me, and it's yours."

"You." It's just one word, but the way she says it—*you*—as a gasped plea, I'm not sure she's just asking for sexual release. "Please," she adds, and my brain shuts off.

I don't need to overthink. I don't need oxygen to survive. I just need the ability to give Delilah whatever she desires. "I'm taking you home."

I grab her hand to go, but she yanks me the other way. "We're not going home."

"We're not?"

She shoots a sultry look over her shoulder. "No, babe. *We're not.*"

I follow, confused, until she drags me into the alleyway on the opposite side of the street and starts kissing me. In public. Fulfilling *my* fantasy. I respond hungrily. Cage her against the brick wall, taking her mouth in a blistering kiss, moving deep and thorough, our hungry sounds louder than the music drifting from the square.

"Is this risky enough for you?" she asks against my lips.

"It's fucking perfect." Semidark and just the right amount of dangerous, the soft sounds from the festival reminding me people are nearby. But I'm not the only one with hidden desires. "You like it like this, baby? With my tongue fucking your mouth? Or does your pretty little cunt feel empty?"

Eyes blown wide, she takes my hand and guides it under her skirt. Guess she likes my dirty talk.

"That's a good girl. You want me to feel how wet you are, is that it?" I run my finger over her underwear, and *fuck*. She's more than wet. She's drenched, working her hips to get some friction against the soft graze of my fingers.

"E, please. I need this. Now. Please make me come."

For half a second, I debate dropping to my knees and setting up camp under her skirt. I'd happily move in there for a year (or fifty), lick up all that wetness and make her come on repeat. But I need her eyes tonight, her trust as she chases whatever it is she's after.

In case anyone comes too close, I angle my body toward Main Street and push her underwear aside. I nudge her clit with my knuckle, and she grips my arms. When I press harder, she lets out an almost silent cry and squeezes her eyes shut.

"Delilah." I slip one, then two fingers into her, stretching her wide. "Your pussy is so hot and tight, gripping my fingers. Watching you come is a fucking gift, so I need you to look at me while I get you off. Show me what I do to you."

She stills, breathing hard, but doesn't open her eyes. I don't move my hand.

I'm not sure why I'm pushing this. Maybe it's the balancing wire we're living on, strung together with a mix of baggage and possibility. I won't ask for answers she's not ready to give, but I'll ask for her vulnerability. For her to be as laid bare as I always am.

She finally opens her eyes, and my heart pumps in double time. I've seen Delilah let loose. I've seen her tease me and get mad and laugh so hard she cries. I've seen her fall apart around me, but I've never seen this much desperation or unchecked desire.

Blood rushing, I capture her lips in another bruising kiss, moving my fingers in time to my tongue, fucking her mouth and tight channel as she says *yes* and *more* and *I need you so much.*

"You have me," I pant in her ear. "I'm fucking yours. Just like you and this gorgeous pussy are mine."

"Oh, God." She clings tighter to me, her desperate eyes on mine, her walls clamping around my fingers. When I press harder on her clit, she tenses and bites my shoulder, coming so hard she crumples into me.

I ease my fingers out, lick them off, then kiss her gently. "Was that good for you? The dirty talk?"

"So good." She runs her hand over my stiff cock.

I groan but edge my hips away. "Tonight was just for you. That's all I need."

She blinks at me and traces my cheekbone. "That wasn't all *I* need. Your fantasy was only half-fulfilled."

"Delilah—"

She shuts me up with a kiss, working her hand over my aching length until I'm rocking in time with her, heat snapping up my thighs. I'm not sure when she unzips my jeans or when I lift her up and latch her legs around my waist. I'm so fucking turned on, so high on her and the air hitting my ass and the nearby sounds, that I shove her underwear aside and thrust in deep.

We moan into each other's mouths. The hint of danger propels my hips. It's an aggressive affair with more dirty words and gasping breaths as we work each other over into oblivion, cursing quietly as we shake and let go.

When we're both spent, I put her carefully down, my mind and body still fuzzy with lingering desire. "I just fucked you in an alleyway."

She laughs against my chest. "I can't believe we did that."

I smooth her hair back. "Was it as good for you as it was for me?"

She fixes me with an intense stare that clears the postsex fog from my head. "Everything with you is always perfect."

My chest heats and swells, filling with so much pressure I almost tell her I love her, but I don't. We may be opening up about our hidden desires, but neither of us has uttered those three words while the other has been alert. I'm not fully sure why. Maybe we're both afraid. Maybe our silence is like the secret she's keeping, truths tucked away until we're secure and safe enough to face them, but I'm okay with this for now—fun dates and wild sex. Us, building our foundation so we can weather whatever storm awaits.

# TWENTY-EIGHT

Delilah and I are roomies. My blue toothbrush is beside her yellow one. My black briefs are snuggled beside her lace underwear with the pretty bows. While I've spent less time in my pink apartment and we never formally discussed living together, gradually the past three weeks, more of my belongings have appeared in her place.

I'm at her dining table, hard at work on my graphic novel, putting the final touches on the last panels. I chose the happily-ever-after ending. The sunshine-and-lollipops version of our future with bird children of our own and a new treasure chest of memories we'll create. It's sappy and cheesy, but I could use some sappy cheesiness in my life. And this is still a novel—a story to sell. Grandiose happily-ever-afters win over readers.

I've gotten smarter in my old age and set an alarm before I started working. We're entertaining for our first time tonight. Ricky and Aaron are back from their belated Belize honeymoon. Avett and Naomi have a sitter. We're making beef fondue—*yes*, the pot has been decontaminated since the meat-soup discovery. My job is to run out and get wine and the beef. Avett's bringing a salad. Ricky's making some fancy potato-and-cheese dish. Delilah's got the apps and dessert and dipping sauces covered. I refuse to have another Eternity incident and ruin our first dinner party, hence the alarm. Not that I need it.

Delilah flies in before expected, flowers in hand, dropping them and her keys on the kitchen counter.

"How's your work going?" she asks while puttering around and pulling out a vase.

I can't answer. I'm smiling too wide. Candy Cane is doing her oh-my-God-she-came-back dance, wiggling up a storm. Delilah laughs and crouches, giving my girl a good rub. That's not enough for Candy. She stops, drops, and rolls, stretching out on her back and spreading her legs. My dog is a floozy.

"Such a ham," Delilah coos.

"If I jump around like a fool and wiggle my butt, will you rub me too?"

Delilah stands slowly and—embodying a drag star supermodel—sashays over to me and straddles my lap. She kisses me hard, rubbing herself all over my thickening cock.

"You mean like that?" she says against my lips.

I palm her ass. "Your body still makes me angry."

"Your six-pack makes me furious." She reaches between us and squeezes my dick. "As does this."

I'm done working. Done thinking. We're making out and grinding on each other like we've been told a nuclear missile is headed for this apartment and we're allowed to do one thing before we're incinerated. My choice will always be to do Delilah.

But my stupid alarm blares.

She squints toward the kitchen area. "Is your phone playing Carly Rae Jepsen's 'Call Me Maybe'?"

"Playing it around Maggie pisses her off." Because of the time I used it to pretend Lennon was calling. "But back to the part about my six-pack making you furious. Stripping needs to happen."

Laughing, we strip and kiss and grope our way to the bedroom, ignoring the alarm, getting tangled in each other. Then I'm all over her, tasting, savoring, using my tongue until she falls apart. The second I'm inside her, she knocks her head back. I grunt like the savage man I am. I hike her legs over my shoulders, dragging through all that wet heat, hitting her just where she likes. She hits me in the heart like always, deeper every time, those eyes locked on me as I thrust and murmur dirty words to get her off. Afterward, when I pull out, I kiss her deeply, then move down her body and kiss her scar, wondering if today is the day when she opens up. As usual, she runs her fingers through my hair and stays quiet.

A quick shower later, we're satiated (for now), hurrying to get dressed. Delilah tosses me my shirt. "I still don't get the 'Call Me Maybe' thing. Why do you and Maggie hate each other so much?"

"We don't hate each other." I drag my shirt over my head, making a mess of my damp hair. "Maggie and I are jealous of each other for having a piece of your heart."

"That's ridiculous."

I shrug. It's true. As a teenager I hated when Delilah had her girls' nights or scavenger hunt days with Maggie, leaving me to miss her. Maggie resented the amount of time Delilah and I spent together. Nights, weekends, and days siphoned from their friendship. As adults, we simply like to rile each other up.

"Maggie's also protective of you," I say.

Delilah's mood dips. The change is so sudden that I almost ask what's wrong, but she turns away from me and walks into the kitchen. "Maggie excels at micromanaging."

"And antagonizing me. But the feeling's mutual." I follow Delilah, taming my hair as I go. "Do you have any idea what happened with her and Lennon?"

"Lennon?" She pauses midreach for the sunflowers she brought in. "They weren't even friends."

Exactly what I thought. "Something definitely happened with them. They're both secretly obsessed with each other."

We stroll down that memory lane, Delilah back to bright and happy as we talk about how cliquey high school was, factions separated by style and music choices, hobbies and wealth. She fills a vase with water. I pull out the place mats for later, loving getting the apartment ready, dividing tasks. I'm even looking forward to the cleaning we'll do afterward. Simple domesticity I wasn't sure I'd ever have.

I grab my wallet and phone. "Don't worry about the table. I'll clear my stuff and set it when I'm back. Oh, and we want dog meat for the fondue, right?"

I mouth, *Just kidding*, to Candy Cane.

Delilah throws a dish towel at me.

I walk to the door and can't help but imitate Delilah's famous move, glancing over my shoulder. I watch her wipe down the counter, her moon necklace dangling as she works. She pulls out glasses and fusses with the flowers she brought, seeming as content as me to create a fun night for us and our friends. I'm starring in my own cologne commercial this time, for a new Calvin Klein scent meant to remind men of comfort and joy, with notes of angry lust added to warn them of the moments they lost. The times they screwed up.

A cologne called Second Chances.

I watch my favorite person, and that telltale push against my ribs returns, like my heart's a hot-air balloon again—too big, too full, so pure and bright it will carry me to Mars. I suddenly know. I have to speak before I leave here. Confess my deepest truth before this balloon pops.

"I love you, Delilah," I say roughly.

She whips around, her mouth dropping open. Something flares in her eyes. Fear? Shock? A hint of overwhelming joy? I can't be sure, and it doesn't matter.

"Don't say it back," I tell her.

My pulse is racing, my hands shaking slightly with the relief and happiness of finally speaking the words while she's awake, but she's not ready. If she was, she'd have shared her secret with me, and I didn't say it to hear it back. I said it because I had to.

She hasn't moved an inch. I smile at her and leave before she over-thinks this to death. I'll tell her I love her again when I return. I'll whis-per it in her ear while we're making love later. I'll croak out the words in the morning when I paw at her body and convince her to cuddle longer.

I'll say it for the both of us until she's ready.

Once outside, the early-November air is cool but not too cool, the freshness mixing with the sweet decaying scents of fallen leaves.

Mrs. Jackson sees me from across the street and waves. "The girls made a quilt to send to your mother."

"She'll love that." My hot-air balloon grows larger, filling with so much goodness. "Drop it at Sugar and Sips. I'll pick it up next time I'm there and make sure she gets it."

When I pass the hardware store, Dave Tanaka pokes his head out. "Got those antislip mats you were after. Came in this morning."

"You're a lifesaver." Without them, when Candy Cane runs full speed and lands on Delilah's area rugs, she becomes a dog torpedo. "I'll grab them in the morning."

"See you then." He salutes me and slips back inside.

Two women with strollers smile at me as I pass. I smile back. I get another wave, this time from an old pal of Callahan's. I'm so content I can't control the bounce in my step. Windfall really is feeling like home again. Welcoming. A place where I can plant roots and grow.

I'm strutting toward the butcher shop, humming "Call Me Maybe," when Sandra pops out of nowhere, blocking my path. "A woman's in town looking for you."

Honestly. Having Sandra on my side is a game changer. Not only does she dog sit for me as needed, but she's a veritable Sherlock Holmes. Just last week, she came up to my table at Sugar and Sips and told me my shoelace was undone. Nothing gets by her. "Is this woman from Windfall?"

"I didn't recognize her. She asked Angel if she knew you. Angel said no."

Maybe Angel should get employee of the month. "From what you observed, can you estimate the woman's approximate age? Height? Any physical descriptions you recall?"

"Early thirties, Caucasian female, my height." A.k.a. vertically challenged. "Blonde hair, definitely not her natural color."

"Was she holding a candlestick by any chance? Or a wrench? Did you see any ID that indicates her name is Patricia Peacock?" I'm incredibly curious who's looking for me, but playing Clue with Sandra's too fun to act serious.

She purses her thin lips in contemplation. "She didn't say her name, but her purse was exceptionally large. Any number of things could be hidden in there."

I place my hand solemnly on Sandra's shoulder. "I'll keep my eyes peeled. And if you see her again, tell her to leave her contact information. We'll do recon before I contact her."

Sandra nods. The move does zilch to dent the perm haloing her head.

This time, when I continue on, I'm not humming. I examine the pedestrians, wondering who's asking around about me. US Marshals would have shown their ID. Most blasts from my past have either gawked at me already or have come to say hello.

The town's taking down the sewn scarecrows from the lampposts, readying to swap them for holiday-centric decor. I smile, remembering my icing kiss with Delilah, the dancing and laughing, and us running around town following clues. That balloon in my chest puffs up again, filled with too much contentment to be safe.

Then I falter.

There's a kid staring into the bookstore's window. He's lean and lanky, looks about nine or ten. I only catch his profile, but there's something so familiar about him unease pokes a hole in my hot-air balloon.

Air hisses out. Fast. My lungs struggle to inflate. I focus harder, sure I'm making things up, seeing the impossible, when I hear, "E. Is that you?"

I turn and freeze. "Sadie?"

Desmond's lost love, the heart he lost ten years ago, stands before me. She holds her big purse close and bites her lip as memories crash over me: Sadie eating dinner at our family table, teasing Desmond for slurping his soup—a joke that would've earned me a cuff on the back of my head; Sadie shoving straw down his shirt at the annual tractor race, shrieking as he ran after her; Desmond picking a sleeping Sadie up into his arms after she'd fallen asleep on our couch, kissing her forehead softly. Fun moments. Simple moments. A hoard of memories that plagues Desmond daily, and I find my gaze returning to the young boy at the bookstore window, roaming over his familiar features—piercing eyes, thick eyelashes, wide mouth.

"Is that . . ." My voice cracks. I can't get the words out. *Is that Desmond's son?*

Sadie nods, tears gathering and spilling over. *Jesus fuck.*

I grab her. Or she grabs me. We grab each other and hug like our lives depend on it. It probably does. Sadie must have been pregnant when we left. Desmond not only lost the love of his life, but he lost a child, nine years of that kid's life as his son learned to talk, to walk, first smiles, first laughs, first cries, first and second and third and fourth triumphs and failures. He missed every single thing while he drank and wasted his life, and my father did this. He ruined my brother so thoroughly he'll never recover.

Her body shakes. *I* shake, unsure how to process what this means. The boy—*my nephew*—comes up to Sadie and tugs on her jeans. "Mom. What's wrong?"

Sadie presses her fingers to the inside corners of her eyes, stretches her jaw, then bends down and faces him. "Just adult stuff, honey. Nothing for you to worry about." She smooths the front of his striped shirt and juts her chin toward me. "This is E. He's an old friend." She locks eyes with me, an imploring look I take to mean she doesn't want him to know who I am. "E," she says softly. "This is Max."

Max is a good name. A strong name. And I feel myself cracking. My body's begging me to move. Run. Sprint so fast from this reality it can't catch me—the knowledge of what was lost and how hard it will hit Desmond, my brother who's already a shadow of the man he was. But I can't run. I promised Delilah I wouldn't disappear again. I owe Sadie answers. I need to be strong for Desmond, who can't be strong for himself.

Firming my jaw and gentling my voice, I say, "Nice to meet you, Max."

Sadie stands and ruffles his hair. "Go in the bookstore, honey. I'll meet you there, okay?"

Max eyes me warily. I don't blame him. As far as he knows, I made his mother cry. But he says, "Okay," and runs inside.

I rub my hands down my face. "Holy shit, Sadie."

"I know. Trust me, I know." Silence lingers. Ten years of silence I can't begin to fill.

Aside from her red-rimmed eyes, Sadie's as stunning as ever, with wavy sun-kissed blonde hair offset by darker roots—the dyed hair Sandra had observed. She still has the type of delicate bone structure a fairy or elf would flaunt, with a petite frame and fair skin to match. She was so much smaller than Desmond I used to wonder how sex worked between them. Then there's the big purse on her shoulder that might hold a candlestick or a wrench but most definitely holds my brother's heart.

"I don't follow the news much," she finally says. "Only heard about your dad's book the other day, totally by accident—some random couple talking about it in the grocery line—and I nearly lost it. You have no idea how hard I looked for Des, how many calls I made after you disappeared, the people I hunted down. I tried so hard, and when I couldn't find him, I had to leave." She takes a deep breath and wipes her eyes. "I refused to tell anyone here I was pregnant. They thought I was drowning my sorrows in food, getting fat, but I couldn't stay here and be faced with the questions, see all our memories every day. I wouldn't have survived."

I hear the self-blame in her voice, like she somehow didn't do enough to find him, or she should've stayed so he could find her. Painful ifs that drive a person mad.

"My father did this, Sadie. Not you. Not Desmond, who loved you so much losing you flattened him. My father stole the past ten years of your lives, and there was nothing either of you could've done to stop it."

Except that's not fully true. Desmond had planned to propose a week before our disappearance. If nerves and doubts hadn't thwarted him, Sadie would have been family. She'd have been in witness protection with us, the two of them raising their child together. How the hell will he live with that knowledge?

She covers her mouth with a shaky hand, closes her eyes briefly. "How's Des? Is he okay? I kept trying to find him after Max was born. Contacted every law firm I could find, across a bunch of states. I tried for years, but I guess he had a new name."

I don't know how to answer this without breaking this already broken woman. There's no softening this truth. I'm once again sucking on the noxious fumes of Desmond's banana Camaro, watching his angry fists grip the wheel, while his eyebrow piercing infects his face as viciously as memories infect his mind.

"Losing you was rough on Des," I say cautiously. "He took WITSEC worse than any of us, never finished law school. Kind of spiraled and made a lot of"—appalling, reckless, self-destructive—"bad decisions."

I can't say anymore. I'm a Yellow-Bellied Coward Bird, pathetically spineless, one word from flying straight into a window headfirst. I don't have it in me to watch Sadie fall apart. I'll have an epic *in*burst and might run after all.

She presses her lips together. "Can I have his number?"

I guess this *can* get harder. The rocks in my heart grind down to shards, cutting deeper with every breath. "We don't know where he is right now. He disappears sometimes, and Dad's book probably hit him hard. But I'll find him," I add when her face crumples. I grip her shoulders, being her Jake. Her younger-older brother who will keep her together. "I'll tell my family, and we won't rest until we find him."

She dashes at her face again. "Yeah. Okay, yeah." She focuses on me, smiles through her tears. "God, I can't believe how handsome you are. You're a man now, E. Are you back with Delilah?"

Despite everything, a burst of happiness hits me. My home. My love, even when things get hard. "I am. It was rough at first, but we're finding our way through this mess. You and Max should come over. We have plans, but you can join us. Or we'll cancel. I don't think I can entertain with this news."

She shakes her head and steps back, hiking her big purse higher over her shoulder. "We have a long drive home. Maybe next time."

These shell-shocked minutes haven't been enough. I need to know Max, talk to him, give him bad advice he'll hate, tease him about his crushes, teach him how to draw and how to cook my famous curry. "Can we have a family get-together? With my mom? She'll go nuts when she meets Max." Probably break down, but Jesus. He's her first grandchild.

Sadie fiddles with her purse strap. "Of course, but I'd rather Max meet his dad first, if that's okay. Once you find him."

Desmond. *His dad.*

I sag slightly, unable to pretend I'm not disappointed. Finding Des might not be quick. "I understand, but if it takes a while, maybe they can meet him sooner?"

"We'll talk, but please give your family my love." She presses her palm to my cheek. "It's so good to see you."

She blinks back more tears. We exchange contact information, then she goes inside the bookstore, leaving me staring after her, unsure what to do with myself. I've forgotten how to move. Walk. Speak. Swallow. Think.

Home. Delilah.

There's only one place I want to be. My feet move, speed walking and then jogging, desperate to get to Delilah, hug her, share this news so it doesn't consume me. I need to call my family, but I need Delilah first.

I'm breathless by the time I'm at her door. I'm empty handed, but it doesn't matter. We'll have to cancel tonight. Our friends will understand. I'll drive to Houston as soon as possible, hit the road after I talk to Delilah. Figure out how to find Desmond and give him the second-biggest shock of his life.

I burst into Delilah's place, expecting to find her busy in the kitchen, prepping the appetizers she planned, but she's at the table, staring at my computer, hand clutching the mouse. My stomach drops. I know what she's looking at: the screen I didn't bother closing. My story isn't a secret. I don't care if she reads it, but her face is so crestfallen I have the sinking feeling I've done something very wrong.

# TWENTY-NINE

Candy Cane is doing wiggly figure eights at my feet, clueless to the volatile energy in the apartment. "Not now, girl," I say as I approach Delilah.

Candy gets the picture and flops on the floor. Slowly, I take the seat next to Delilah, who hasn't looked at me or spoken a word. My insides are a shaken-up beer bottle, frothy, $CO_2$ pressurizing, one degree from detonation.

"It's your story," she says, flat. "Your life."

"It's *our* story. And I won't sell it if you don't want me to. That's not even why I started it. I actually have no clue why I started it, but once I did, I couldn't stop. And Sathya needs money for her family, and our publisher's being difficult, and I don't want my father's account of our life to be the only one in the world. So, yes, I want to publish it, but only if you agree. It's completely up to you. And my family."

She clasps her hands on her lap and faces me. "I'm not upset you documented our story. It's breathtaking—the imagery, the way you've fantasized all of us with those gorgeous wings. The pain on these panels is agonizing to read, and the story deserves to be told."

I reach for her clasped hands, but she doesn't let me thread our fingers together. All I can do is cover her hands with mine. "Then why are you so upset?"

Quiet upset. Eerily frozen upset. The type of upset that's so deep and severe the temperature in the room drops.

"Because this is *your* story, E. Not our story. Certainly not mine." She shakes off my hands and pushes back her chair. "You told me you loved me before you left, and I could barely breathe. I sat down and stared at nothing for a while, because I realized how unfair I've been to you. How selfish. I kept putting off telling you what happened to me, assuming there would be a perfect day, a time that wouldn't destroy you, but that time never came. Then I grabbed your computer, thinking if I wrote it down, it would be easier. I'd read it to you or let you read it, and that would be that. We'd maybe find our way through, or not. I don't know. Then I saw your story and the ending you wrote, and I just knew there was no way to tell you this without breaking us."

She means my final storybook ending. The sappy version of us with a happy family, nothing but promise in our future, and she's sitting there, rigid, telling me that ending isn't possible.

For the record, I am not okay.

Sadie's appearance and news shaved off a few layers of my resilience. The way Delilah's talking, I'm downright terrified.

"Nothing you say will break us. I'm not going anywhere. That ending is a reader's ending, overdone and overly happy. I don't for one second think our life will be without hardship. I know better than—"

"I can't have kids, E." She stands, clutching her stomach, right over that permanent scar. "I was a mess when you left. Drank too much, blew off curfew, did stupid, reckless things. And there was this night—a party at Billy Rivera's property—and I got wasted. Messy, stupid drunk. Avett was there and stole my keys, wouldn't let me drive. So I stormed out, because fuck him. I wouldn't get in his car and decided to walk home. I don't remember much after that, but I remember stumbling on the side of the road, seeing the headlights flash."

I'm on my feet. I don't remember standing, but I can't be confined. Can't sit. Can't speak. She needs to get this out, and I need to listen to

270

every word. Take her anger and devastation. Take it all so she doesn't have to continue carrying it alone.

"They say it was good I was so wasted when the car hit me."

I make an animal sound, grab at the front of my shirt.

"Intoxicated people have a slower reaction time," she goes on, her voice as stark as her face. "They don't tense up as much in anticipation of being hurt, and that stretch of road is so dark the driver didn't see me until it was too late. I was told I looked fine on the outside, but the accident shattered my pelvis. There was internal bleeding. The doctors rushed me into the operating room planning to do damage control, but there were internal lacerations, and the hemorrhaging was extensive. They had to do a hysterectomy to save me."

"Delilah." Her name's a whisper. It's all I can manage. My head's filled with violent images of Delilah's body connecting with a car, going flying, lying on the road, hospital rooms, scalpels, doctors, blood, her ability to have kids ripped from her.

She's talking again, saying something about recovery taking a year. Relearning to walk, intensive physiotherapy, but I can't latch on to her words. They float through my head, bumping against the image of the nephew I just met. Desmond's son he doesn't know. My father's words: *I had an opportunity and I took it.* That man stole my brother's child and all of Delilah's future children. He stole and stole and stole and never once apologized for his reckless actions.

There's a buzz in my ears. A ringing I can't contain. No, not a ringing. I'm tugging the back of my hair, bent forward at the waist, and I'm screaming. A vicious roar that bounces off the walls and lacerates my throat.

Delilah's on her knees in front of me, gripping my shins, telling *me* it's okay. It's not. Nothing is, but I'm not the one who lost everything. I got Delilah back. She'll never get the future she wanted.

"I'm so sorry." I drop to my knees too, press my forehead to hers, cup the sides of her tearstained face. "I'm so fucking sorry. If I could go back and kill my father, I would. Burn any evidence of him from the earth. Just . . . *fuck*. Delilah. I don't know how you dealt with all of that."

She clutches my wrists, the two of us heaving together. "I'm okay, E," she says on a hiccuped gasp. "Physically, at least. It was almost a decade ago, but this right now . . ." Agony haunts her eyes as she blinks. "Seeing you like *this* is why I took so long to tell you. Why I selfishly allowed you back in my life, when I knew how this would go."

Something darker flashes across her face.

I grip her cheeks tighter, forcing myself to hold it together. She may hate seeing my suffering, just like I hate hearing about hers, but learning about the hell she endured is the true start of us repairing what we lost. Her emotional and physical suffering was deeper than mine, I realize now. She's monumentally tougher than me to have come through. Most people are tougher than me, but this? To find the strength to go on, build a business, relearn to walk and smile and face life with optimism when she's lost so much?

She *is* the winged albatross of my novel, courageous and powerful, able to spread her clipped wings and soar.

I'll rewrite those panels. Hold her and listen and absorb every painful minute of her ordeal, give her story the darkness and devastation it deserves—and the inspiring perseverance. Show her I understand the horrors she's been through. Show *her* everything will be okay. Prove I don't care that we can't have kids of our own.

That deeper catharsis will start another day. Tonight I'll stay instead of driving to Houston. Bury my anger and devastation and be her rock. Then I'll meet with my family and upend their worlds once again.

I stroke my trembling thumbs down her cheeks. "Something happened concerning Des." Drama I don't want to heap onto Delilah's shoulders at a time like this. "I need to go back to Houston tomorrow, but I'll stay tonight and come back as quickly as possible. Promise I'll be less of a mess by then."

"You don't understand." She jerks her forehead away from mine, her jaw firming in a way I don't like. "When I said I knew how this would go, I wasn't just talking about your emotional reaction. I knew this would be the end of *us*. There's no going forward from here."

I blink hard, clear a portion of the fuzz from my brain. "What do you mean . . . *the end of us?*"

Unless I misheard her, shit's about to get emotional.

We're both on our knees, her face red and splotchy, mine probably looking confused and tortured, on the verge of furious.

She gestures angrily between us. "This has been a charade, E. We've been pretending since the wedding, acting like we can pick up where we left off. Like we don't have ten tons of baggage between us. You'll never be able to look at me the same again. Every time you see my scar, you'll remember what we can't have. Every time I look at your face, which hides absolutely nothing, I'll remember what I did, what I took from us. I can't live if I'm constantly reliving our history, and neither can you. We're done, E. We never stood a chance."

Oh, hell no. Absolutely not. Not while I have breath in my lungs. "How can you even say that? I love you, and you love me. I'm sick about what you went through. I'm *so* sorry you can't have kids, but I don't care. It doesn't change how much I love you."

"That's just it," she shouts. "Love has nothing to do with this! Being with you hurts *me* too much."

I cave forward, her brutal shot hitting me square in my gut. My instinct with Delilah is to yell. I'm angry at her for giving up so quickly. I'm livid with my father for all he's orchestrated—Sadie, Desmond, Delilah, and all we've lost—but that's any old day of the week that ends with *y*. There's so much helpless rage churning through me, but I don't want to escape on a run. I don't want to *in*burst and shut down, blocking everyone and everything out. I want to face this head-on with Delilah, but that's not what she wants.

I clamp my jaw, unsure what to do.

For some reason, my attention slides to Candy Cane. She's hiding under the coffee table in the living area, eyeing us fearfully. She doesn't like yelling or crying. She's sensitive like me, easily scared and ill equipped to cope with stress. Normally she bounces back after an episode, slinking closer when I hold out a treat and talk in soothing tones.

I could do the same with Delilah. Soften my voice, coax her to give me another chance, kiss her how I know she loves to be kissed, remind her of how much fun we have together, that love *does* conquer all, and I think it could work. When I returned to Windfall, I pushed and pushed and pushed, being so persistent she didn't stand a chance.

*For her*, I'd tell myself again this time. *I'm fixing us for her, so she can truly be happy.*

But that would be a lie. I'd be doing it for me. Like her ex, who disregarded Delilah's wishes, and like my father, who did everything to serve himself. Dad was single minded in his pursuits. Relentless, hiding his paper trails, lying to his family, going after what he wanted, no matter the cost. In his case, his doggedness was selfish and narcissistic. In my case, I thought my persistence with Delilah was for *our* greater good.

All the while, she's been hurting in private, showing me one face, dealing with another darker demon, letting me believe we could work. *Being with you hurts* me *too much.*

That pang in my gut twists deeper, and I gulp back a rising sob.

Missing Delilah these past ten years carved out a piece of my soul. Having her back has made me feel alive and happy in a way I never imagined possible, but if forcing our relationship hurts her this much, I'm no different from my father, and he's the last person I want to be.

I look at Delilah. She's crying. I'm crying. We're such a mess, and I don't want to do what I think I need to do. The thought of never seeing her gorgeous face again has bile rising in my throat, but I can't keep hurting her for my selfish needs.

"Okay." My voice catches on the worst word I've ever uttered. "If this is too hard for you, I understand. I won't push. I have to leave town anyway, like I said. See my family about something that came up. You can give my stuff to Avett. I'll grab it from him when I'm back. And I won't come to the coffee shop anymore. I'll—" My throat's on fire, burning like the fiery depths in the Gates of Ember underworld. "I'll finally let you move on."

She presses her hand over her mouth, more tears flowing. I can't stay a minute longer. There's no point telling her about Sadie or begging her to change her mind or reassuring her that her inability to have kids doesn't affect my feelings. I'll always remind her of the worst time in her life, the bad choices she made. And I'll likely lose my resolve, revert to the guy willing to steamroll her feelings to get what he wants—*her*— while she suffers in secretive silence.

Without waiting for her reply, I get to my feet and call for Candy Cane, who thankfully follows me out of Delilah's apartment, down the hall, into a beige future I can't begin to imagine.

# THIRTY

I've called a Bower family meeting. We're back in Lennon's and my apartment with our Invisible Man poster. After a round of hugs, Mom assumed her typical position, standing in front of the TV. I'm perched on our IKEA end table. Lennon, Cal, and Jake are crammed on the couch. The only person we're missing is the reason we're here.

"Out with it already," Jake says to me. "And if you rounded us up to tell us you're in Windfall shacked up with Delilah, save your breath. We all know."

My throat thickens at the mention of Delilah, a familiar ache that's plagued me the past two days. It's been hours of driving where I've done nothing but think about all I've lost. Gross motels where I've barely slept, staring at the water-stained ceilings, *thinking about all I've lost.* I keep second-guessing my decision to leave Delilah, trying to figure out if there's a way to get her back that doesn't end with hurting her. Every time I come up empty.

I'm oddly numb now. A husk that's been squeezed dry.

"I'm not here about Delilah." I can't rehash our breakup. Unearthing that mess won't serve me or them. The second I tell them about Desmond's son, they'll once again discover things *can* get worse. "I've learned something that's tough to say."

Mom freezes, readying for another blow. My brothers sit straighter.

Cal rubs his palms down his jeans. "Is it Desmond?"

"In a manner of speaking." I feel like we're a human bowling alley. They're the scarred pins, recently aligned after having been knocked down fifty times, waiting for me to toss another ten-pound ball at their heads. Such is my life. "I saw Sadie in Windfall. She came looking for me."

"Sadie?" Mom's eyes grow wide. "That's good, right? If anyone can reach Des, it's Sadie. I assume she's single? That's why she looked for you?"

I frown. I didn't ask about the single part, and I don't recall noticing a ring. Granted I was on the bewildered side of shocked at the time, but it's a pretty important piece of information.

"I'm not sure of her relationship status." And my news is more daunting than that. I've got the heavy ball in my hands, testing the weight, deciding if there's a way to toss it that will hurt my family less. Unlikely. "Sadie has a child. A boy. His name's Max, and he's Desmond's son."

Mom gasps. Jake stares at me like he wants to crush my head with his eyeballs. Cal's face slackens, and Lennon. I haven't seen him cry once since leaving Windfall. He's acted weird and cagey and generally pissed at times, but I've never seen his eyes glass over like this. Tears don't spill over, but his face trembles, which would normally make my face tremble, but that numbness creeps through my body, spreading wider. This must be what happens when you've reached your pain threshold. The excruciating agony kills your nerve endings, deadens your emotions.

"Fuck." Lennon bends forward, shoving his face toward his knees. "Motherfucking *fuck*."

Cal wraps his arm over him, tries to shield him from what this means for Desmond, but Cal's expression is severe, sharp. Our fixer's nowhere in that angry glare.

Jake shoots to his feet and paces. He jams his hands through his hair, muttering fiercely under his breath, then he goes to the wall and punches it.

"Jake!" Mom runs to him.

My stomach lurches. Apparently I *can* still feel.

Jake swivels around, wrathful, holding his hand awkwardly. "I will kill our father. Honest to God, I will drive to wherever he moved and bludgeon that disgusting excuse for a human to death."

"No one's killing anyone." Cal, of course, tries to diffuse, but there's no compassion or calmness in his voice. He wants to kill our father too. As do I. I have no underlying affection for Raymond S. Bower. No lingering little-boy wish to reconnect with my dad.

Lennon lifts his blotchy face, wipes his nose on his arm. "That man should've been tried and convicted and tossed in jail. I'm all for the killing."

The venom in Lennon's tone isn't surprising, but it makes me sadder. Of all of us, he was closest to Dad growing up.

Mom doesn't bother tempering their threats. She's checking Jake's hand, occasionally wiping the tears pushing from her devastated eyes. Cal and Lennon are wax sculptures of themselves—faces frozen in expressions of matching despair, skin red and shiny with rage. And here I am, watching it all, eyes stinging and gut twisting, but I'm not verging on an *in*burst or an outburst. I'm not an animal version of myself, mutated, vulnerable, the rocks in my heart grinding painfully. That numbness is doing its job, and I've known the news longer than them. I've had days to go through my cocktail of emotions, but there's something else at play here.

Something deeper holding me together.

For weeks, I've purged my lingering anger and heartsickness into my graphic novel. I didn't get the whole story right. Not Delilah's portion, at least. But maybe that outlet wasn't just a way to document my story for her as I first thought. Maybe those pages were the valve I've needed all these years. My way of downgrading the pressure, releasing enough steam so I don't burst.

Aside from a few sessions at our Safesite, none of us boys attended therapy. There was no point. We weren't allowed to talk about our situation. A decade later, I'm finally drawing, writing, purging. I've talked about my ordeal at length with Delilah. Even with a broken heart, I can stand here for the first time and be the strong one for my family.

Channeling my inner Captain Jake, I take Mom's spot in front of the TV and survey the wreckage that is the Bower clan. "We need to find Des. The best way is to divide and conquer. We'll start by making a list of any people who know him and places he's worked or visited. We'll divide up the list and drive around, make calls. Lennon, you had a beer with him at his last job, right?"

Lennon blinks at me, the glassiness in his eyes dissipating. "Who are you, and what have you done with my brother?"

"The scar on his lip looks off, doesn't it?" Cal elbows Lennon, mock whispering in his ear. "He could be an impostor. The cartel infiltrating our ranks."

I give them the finger and look to Mom for sanity. "In the early days, you had an emergency contact list, right? We could see if he's visiting any of his old friends." A.k.a. couch surfing with his drinking buddies.

She nods a few times, barely looking at me. "I'll find it. He also used to show up unexpectedly at the coffee shop near my apartment. He hasn't done that in a while, but I'll make sure I go there every day." While her voice is steady, her expression's dazed, like she doesn't recognize me either. Or maybe she doesn't recognize her horrible life. "Did you meet him?" she says, searching my face. "The boy?"

*Her grandson.* She doesn't say the word. I can't imagine how hard it is for her learning she's had a grandson for nine years and has never met him. "Briefly," I say gently. "But he didn't know who I was. Sadie prefers to introduce him to Des before he meets us properly, unless this takes too long. Max looks like him, though. Has Desmond's eyes."

Mom ducks her head, shading her face with her hand. Jake tries to hug her from behind, but she shakes him off and walks toward the windows, wrapping her arms around her stomach, giving us her back. I hate Dad all over again for hurting her, being so reckless with our lives, but there's no going back and murdering him in his sleep.

Jake mumbles words I can't decipher, but his savage expression indicates they aren't kind. "There's a massive problem with your plan, E."

Of course there is. It starts with a *D*, ends with a *D*, and rhymes with *Shmesmond*. "I know Des won't be easy to find."

"That's not it," Lennon says, adopting his full-body hipster smirk. His default setting when stressed. "He means we need code names and walkie-talkies."

Jake glares at him. "You're my second-favorite brother, but you and your stupid jokes are half the reason Des is gone right now."

Lennon balks. "Who's your first favorite?"

"Me," Cal and I say in unison, then shoot each other competitive looks.

Ignoring us, Jake clacks his teeth together and directs his fury at me. "You didn't find out if Sadie's single. If Des learns he's had a kid for nine years and that the love of his life is happily married to some other guy, do you think he'll be all 'Hey, that's so great for you. I can't wait to get to know my son, who some other fucker raised, so I can be a weekend dad in this super fun, super functional blended family'?"

Point taken, but I'm suddenly pleased I dropped the ball and didn't find out if Sadie's in a relationship. "If she's married or taken, Desmond will implode. I think we can all agree on that."

My brothers nod. Mom's back is still facing us, but she says softly, "It will destroy him."

It will feel like he's moving through quicksand, deadened limbs useless as he struggles through each day. At least, that's how I feel. "Which is why it's excellent I didn't ask Sadie if she's hitched or otherwise taken. I have her contact and could call her to ask, but I won't."

Jake curls his lip. "Why not?"

"If we find Desmond, can we all agree it's best if I break the news to him?"

Detonating that blast isn't a job I want, but I'm the one of us who chases him when he storms off, trying to understand his pain. I'm also the only one who lost his first love too, and I'm the only one who knows he planned to propose. Des trusts me the most, and they didn't exactly do a bang-up job at our last family tête-à-tête.

My brothers nod again. Even Jake, grudgingly.

Mom, whose back is *still* facing us, says, "It has to be you."

"And can we all agree I'm crap at hiding my emotions? And if Sadie is married or shacked up with some guy, I'll crumple, and Des will read me plain as day and freak out and make this situation miles worse than it already is?"

Lennon folds his arms and leans into Cal's ear. "His hair's different too. Less Justin Bieber and more Zac Efron. He's definitely an impostor."

"A smart one," Cal says. "None of us should find out. If he doesn't think he has a chance to be with his family the way he'd want, Des might vanish forever."

Mom finally turns, her face pale and eyes red. "Agreed. None of us asks."

Lennon and Cal agree to avoid the relationship question, but Jake's the holdout. His jaw bunches, his teeth grinding as he struggles to gain his composure. I do the only thing I can think of. I march over to him and grip his upper arms, usurping his oldest-brother move with flair.

"We'll be okay," I tell him. I'm not sure the prediction's true, but it's all I've got. "Des will be okay."

His breath wheezes through his nose, the tendons in his neck flexing taut. The longer I grip him, the less his eyeballs look like they want to squash my face. Gradually, the lines of his jaw smooth. Finally, he tilts his head, squints one eye at me. "Something's off with his chin. He's definitely an impostor."

At least the Bowers can find humor in horrible situations. "Thank you all for being supremely annoying. What do you say we get to work?"

Finally on the same page, we crowd around our small coffee table, pad of paper and pen in the middle, taking turns jotting down names of people and places. The list is short. I'm not sure it'll help, but doing something feels better than doing nothing, as has been our fate the past ten years.

When Lennon makes another crack about me being an impostor, I give him my smuggest face. "Maggie asked me to ask you if you'd like to play a round of truth or dare."

He turns to stone, eyes shifting nervously. "I have no clue what you're talking about."

"Really? Because Maggie and I have gotten close." In the way vipers and mice consider themselves pals. "She tells me everything."

Lennon smells my lie and says, "Fuck off."

I'll find another tactic to make him crack, on a day when we're not all hopped up on adrenaline, trying to play Battleship in search of Desmond's coordinates. And when I'm not drowning in my own misery. For now, we divvy up names and places and agree to keep one another posted. They all hug Mom extralong before they leave, everyone pretending like they're not breaking. Except me. The way Mom shakes against me and tells me she's so happy I have Delilah, I don't stand a chance. My dulled senses flare back to life.

I crumple, hunching over her, sucking in ragged breaths.

"E, honey. What is it?"

There's no one here but us. Lennon's outside, seeing the others off. I don't want to load Mom with more heartache, but I can't keep this secret from her. "Delilah and I broke up. Being with me is too hard for her."

She pulls out of my death grip and searches my face. "Too hard?"

I'm not ready to share Delilah's devastating ordeal. I've barely had time to digest what she suffered, and I've only heard a fraction of her nightmare. We were too raw in the moment.

Choosing my words carefully, I say, "While I'm part of her best memories, I'm also part of her worst. There's too much pain in our history to move past it."

"But you love each other."

"We do." So damn much, but according to Delilah, love doesn't conquer all.

"Then it's never too late. You fight for her, E, the way you fought for us just now. You're the one who held us together today. You said what needed to be said and didn't let us fall. Make her understand the pain's worth it. Make her see how much better you are together."

She's asking me to push again, bulldoze over Delilah's concerns and feelings like her ex-fiancé. Convince Delilah I'm worth the suffering. But I'm done with my Fifty Ways to Win Back Delilah ploys and turning relationships into checklists. I won't go back down that road, but I *was* the one who held my family together today. I was the strongest I've ever been, not because I have Delilah. The harsh reality of her loss didn't help me keep a level head. I helped my family through our latest setback because I've installed a release valve on my emotions. Or maybe my healing started years ago, when my family kept urging me to get outside, enter drawing exhibits, write my teenage Top Ten Bests in journals. A slow mending of my shattered innocence, years in the making.

The past months, I've pushed myself further, finally illustrating my story and sharing my burden with Delilah, but she's never had the chance to share hers with me.

Not truly. Not in detail.

An idea forms. A long shot—one that would be tough for us both—but I'm used to the odds being stacked against me. And maybe, just maybe, our story could have a happy ending after all. Not cheesy and idealized. Real. Flawed. But we'd be together.

"I'll call her," I tell Mom, allowing a stirring of hope to rise. "Try to talk things out."

First, I need Delilah to answer my call.

"That's my fighter. And I have something for you." She finds her purse and pulls out a small bundle. "Agent Rao dropped off our new-old identification. You're officially Edgar Eugene Bower again."

I open my passport, run my thumb across my shitty name, overwhelmed by the tiny book, as though it defines who I am. But it doesn't. Rallying my family to find our brother defines me. Messing with Lennon's head and gripping Jake's arms defines me. Finding a way to help Delilah heal defines me. The rest is window dressing.

# THIRTY-ONE

After our meeting, Lennon went out on a find-Desmond mission. I checked in with Sandra, who has Candy for the next couple of weeks. I hate not having my girl with me, but I'll be running around too much while here, and she's not a city dog. She thrives in the charm and quiet of Windfall. As do I.

Next up, I call Delilah. It clicks over to voice mail. I debate hanging up and trying again later, but I panic and say, "It's me please call me back we need to talk even if you think we don't we do so yeah just please call me okay bye."

Can you say *word vomit?*

I glare at my phone, hating my ineloquence, willing it to ring. It does not.

Two hours later, after *my* unsuccessful find-Desmond mission visiting one of his urine-smelling haunts, I'm back in my beige apartment, on my couch with Lennon. I've filled him in on my breakup with Delilah and my word-vomit message, still avoiding discussing her accident. We're now staring at the ceiling instead of watching TV.

"If there was a prize for most screwed up family," he says, "I bet we'd win."

"Hard call. There was that reality show where contestants had to be naked twenty-four-seven. They couldn't have come from solid families."

"Good point." He rolls his head over the back of the couch and looks at me. "But you'd win Most Embarrassing Voice Message."

"I panicked," I say, rubbing the heels of my hands into my eyes.

"I mean, it's not like Delilah doesn't know you're a bumbling fool. But you need to be more prepared next time."

I bounce my heel, nodding. "I'll write down a preplanned message. Something to guarantee a callback. I should do it now, right? Call her again?"

"Definitely. I need some good family news this week."

I grab the pad of paper and pen from the coffee table and shut myself in my room. Ten minutes later, I reread my planned message: *Please don't avoid me, Delilah. If our history means anything to you, call me.*

Trust me. I know how good it is.

Sitting on the edge of my bed, I call Delilah. The phone rings once, twice, three times. The line clicks over, but I don't get her message. I get breathing.

Then I get Delilah. "What do you want, E?"

*You,* I almost blurt. But that's too obvious, and I didn't consider this option. I assumed she'd ignore me at least one more time. Now my planned message no longer applies.

Without any appropriate words prewritten, I go with the blunt truth. "I need to hear your story, Delilah. Like this, while I'm away. You won't have to see how it breaks me. I won't have to try and hide my pain or witness yours. I can't move on until I know everything, and I think you need to share it."

The moving-on part is a partial lie. My plan is to offer Delilah a safe space to exhume her worst moments, vent and cry and say what needs to be said. If Life's truly on my side, if my instincts here are right, unloading her sadness will finally allow Delilah to see me without seeing all she's lost. At the very least, she might feel less burdened.

She's breathing heavy again. I debate making a phone-sex joke, but now's not the time. I wait for her to break my heart or give me hope. Finally, she says, "Okay. But this doesn't mean anything. We're not getting back together."

"I know."

She scoffs. "Stop trying to reverse psychology me."

"I'm not doing that." Really, I'm not. I'm careening down Hope Road, but I'm not the one steering this car. This must be how the boy who cried wolf felt.

She huffs out a breath, hopefully getting comfortable on her couch. I don't plan on hanging up anytime soon. "Where do you want me to start?" she asks, her voice hesitant.

As hard as this will be, I need it all. The guts of her pain. "You've talked about how worried you were after I disappeared, and then how angry you got, but not in detail. You must have been devastated and probably felt badly about yourself too. Tell me about that."

She does. It's not pretty. Nothing about our time apart is pretty. Those years are raw and ugly and painful, but this is when healing begins. She sounds stronger as she talks, less halting, her words coming quicker, like she's creating her own emotion valve, letting the pressure slowly escape.

"It all just tore me down," she says partway through, tears and sniffles stealing her words. "I never considered myself an angry person before that. Even when my dad died, I was devastated and hated watching how hard it was on my mom, but I didn't rage at the world. Having my best friend and love of my life vanish without understanding why . . ." This sob is more violent. "I didn't recognize who I was."

I squeeze my eyes shut, let her grief wash over me. I don't tell her I'm sorry. I don't try to soothe her with soft words. Comforting her would serve my need to be consoling, not her need to unburden herself.

An hour later, I'm lying on my bed, one arm flung above my head, my hand fisted and jaw tight as she describes her slow road to recovery after her accident, the hours of physiotherapy, the hardest moments when she felt like giving up.

"I thought about you so much those days," she whispers.

"Because you were furious at me for leaving?"

"That was part of it. Anger can be a good motivator, but I thought a lot about your nature and how deeply you feel and absorb other people's pain. How I used to believe you were an empath."

"I'm not an empath, Delilah. I'm just a really hot guy who has a killer six-pack and happens to be in touch with his emotions."

Her muffled laugh warms my heart. She doesn't joke back, but I take that as a win.

"After the accident," she goes on, "I forced my friends away. I was so ashamed about what I did, so disgusted with myself for drinking and acting so reckless, but I eventually realized I needed them. If I wanted to recover, I needed positive people around me so they could absorb some of my pain before I suffocated on it. Which, I don't know, sounds pretty selfish."

The past couple of months, I witnessed Windfall band together, protecting Delilah from me. They put on a fully cast, top-notch production of *Delilah's Getting (Fake) Married*. "I bet your friends were more than thrilled to be there for you. Except Maggie. She was for sure only there to poison you against me."

"She was vicious when it came to you. Exploded if I ever brought you up."

That news pleases me. I respect Maggie for taking care of Delilah when I couldn't. "You were lucky to have those supports. I'd have been lost without my brothers, but I could've used friends some days. People not directly affected by my dad's actions. There was nowhere I could be sad or angry without hurting the people I loved."

"I felt like that too," she says. "I always wanted kids of my own. I wanted to teach kids and have kids and be a mom. After the surgery, I was devastated, but I didn't want to drag the people around me down. There was a lot of pretending."

Both of us, two sides of the same rusted coin. "Is that why you didn't go into teaching? Being around kids was too hard?"

She pauses. Maybe she's squishing one of her pretty pillows against her stomach, or maybe she's curled on her side of the bed, imagining I'm beside her. "It played a part. I also lost a year of my life, and the idea of being in school again was unappealing, mentally and physically. Sitting for long stretches was hard on my pelvis for a while, and I hated the idea of everyone there learning what happened to me. The whispers and looks I'd get. Staying in Windfall was easier for a lot of reasons."

"I'm sorry." For a million and one things. "You would've been a great teacher."

"Maybe, but I have no regrets. I love my shop and what I do. Everything happens for a reason."

I can't imagine a good enough reason for us to have endured our suffering the past decade, but the fury that sometimes sneaks up on me doesn't flare, needing to be beaten down with an aggressive run. I'll never forgive and forget, but all this purging and talking has mellowed my anger.

Delilah yawns. I rub my eyes. We're both exhausted, but I don't want to hang up. I don't know what tomorrow will bring—if she'll answer her phone when I call. I can't be sure this talk has been as important and therapeutic for her as I hoped.

"E."

"Yeah?"

A rustle of sheets. Soft, delicate breaths. "Thank you."

"For what?"

This pause lasts longer. "It's just . . . I'm drained and sad, but I'm also kind of weightless, if that makes sense. Calmer than I've felt in ten years. Thank you for listening."

My heart stutters. Tingling spreads across my scalp.

I push up to sitting as tonight's biggest realization wallops me.

If I were still a list guy, this evening would have crashed its way onto my Top Ten Bests, shoving in front of *my* first time meeting Delilah, *my* first kiss, *my* first time having sex, *my* utter fascination when she yelled at me to get off her land. Always *my, my, my,* the same way I pursued Delilah doggedly because I missed her in *my* life. But this emotional moment has zoomed to number one because I've helped Delilah heal, regardless of how it affects *me.*

Jesus. I check my chest hair, wondering if I've sprouted more with this influx of maturity.

Nope. Still sparse.

Tomorrow I plan to work on my novel, begin the rewrite of the panels to reflect Delilah's truth. *My* safe place to be honest and feel what I need to feel. Remind myself that I'm not like my father. I can make good choices and put other people first.

Tonight is about her.

She's still breathing softly in my ear. My heart hurts from her admissions and how far away she is, but I'm honored she's trusting me with her pain. "I'll always love you to Mars and back, Delilah Moon. After all we've been through, I hope we can still be friends."

She doesn't reply. For a second I think she's fallen asleep or I've gone too far and upset her into silence. Then she whispers, "You can call me tomorrow, if you want."

We'll assume that's a rhetorical suggestion.

# THIRTY-TWO

The next evening, I visit two seedy bars. At the first, a three-sheets-to-the-wind woman offers to hook up in the nasty bathroom. At the other, I step in something sticky I'm pretty sure isn't spilled beer. Not only is Desmond nowhere to be found, but he's doing an impressive job of never answering my calls or texts. I suspect he changed his number, which is frustrating and deflating.

At my wit's end, I pull out the big guns and text Sandra for assistance.

E: From your experience, what's the best way to track a guy who doesn't want to be found?

Sandra: I'm not a tracker.

E: But if you were a tracker and really needed to find a guy, what would you do?

Sandra: Nothing.

E: You're being very unhelpful.

Sandra: You're not listening.

This is the level of attitude I deal with from Sandra.

Although today's a wash, I hurry home, feeling a buzz of adrenaline. Delilah said I could call her if I want. And I *want*. I want to hear her voice. I want to be there for her again, and always.

Lennon's not home when I get back, and I don't bother scrounging for food. I dial Delilah's number before my keys hit the counter, my heart beating in my throat. She could have changed her mind since last night. Our talk might have reinfected her old wounds. She might have realized cutting me out is the only way forward.

The phone rings once, twice. On the third ring, my adrenaline starts to crash, everything in me turning heavy.

"E, hi. Hey." She sounds out of breath.

My tension uncoils. "Delilah." I sigh and flop on my bed, ridiculously relieved she picked up. When it comes to her, I'll always be 199 percent pathetic.

"Sorry it took so long to answer. My hands were covered in batter."

"You're still at work?"

"No. I'm home." The sounds of a pot clanking, then running water carry through. "Baking helps when I'm feeling . . . off."

Because I pushed her to open her healed wounds. "Did our talk last night make things worse?" I ask tentatively.

"It's not that. I mean, yeah, talking about that time is always hard. I just also . . ." She trails off, her voice getting softer. Vulnerable. "I wasn't sure you'd call."

A rush of happiness floods my stomach, even on this frustrating day. "I'd have called sooner, but I've been running around."

"You never told me why you had to go back to Houston."

"Another family nightmare. Nothing for you to worry about." Not while she's dealing with her own mental health.

"E." She pauses. There's a soft swish, the rustle of what sounds like couch cushions. "Last night you said you hoped we'd always be friends. This is what friends do: try to be there for each other. If you're having a tough time, I want to know."

*Friend.* Not the label I want. *Soul mate. Her albatross.* Those would be a start. I'd even settle on *exasperating lover who annoys her with his antics,* but the edginess of the past few days pushes at my chest and throat. "Sadie came to find me in Windfall."

"*Desmond's* Sadie?"

I rub my eyes. "Yeah."

"Because she wants to reconnect with him?"

"In a manner of speaking." The bowling ball is back in my hands. This time it's covered in spikes, pricking my skin and sure to cut Delilah. Now that I know her secret, Sadie's truth is that much harder to share. A deep breath later, I say, "Des didn't know, but she was pregnant when we left. She has a nine-year-old boy. Desmond's son."

Delilah gasps. My eyes burn.

Her breathing gets ragged, shaky. I bite my tongue to stem the push of tears. I can't imagine what it's like for Delilah, hearing this news. I'm not sure how she copes in her everyday life when she sees children, knowing what she can't have.

"We're trying to find Des," I say roughly. "He's not making it easy."

"I'm so sick for him." She sniffles a couple of times. "For Sadie and all of you. And I really fucking hate your father."

"I'd say join the club, but membership is pretty full."

"God, E. I wish you'd told me."

"There was a lot going on." Our worlds imploding for a second time.

We're both quiet, but her soft breaths calm me. Awareness I'm not alone in the mess that is my life.

"How do you plan to find him?" she finally asks.

"By acquiring hepatitis."

She lets out a watery laugh. "Care to explain?"

"Des has some questionable hangouts."

We talk about the gross bars he frequents and my family's ramshackle efforts to find him. I make jokes about Sandra's annoying advice, drinking in Delilah's laughter like a dehydrated man. When there's a lull, I ask her more about rehab and her recovery after her accident. She talks with a stronger voice tonight, explaining how hard that time was, both on her and on her mother, my understanding of Hayley Moon's wrath gaining clarity.

Near the end of the call, she gets quieter—longer silences filled with weighted beats.

"Don't call me tomorrow," she says suddenly, so quietly I almost didn't hear her.

But I did.

My heart plummets into a free fall. "Do you have plans?"

"No. I mean, sort of. I just need a breather, I think."

"Yeah. Sure. Whatever you need."

Unfortunately, what she needs seems to be less of me.

~

I'm half-focused the next day, looking for Des while desperately analyzing my talk with Delilah, wondering if that was a we're-done-thanks-for-helping-exhume-my-trauma breather or if it was truly an I-just-need-a-breather breather.

One night passes with no word from her. Then two.

When not hunting for Des, I throw myself into revisions, burning every candle at every end as the new panels develop: Delilah, midflight on her beautiful wings, wasted on her misery, getting hit by a passing shuttle and flung through a cloud; Delilah with her abdomen slashed open, eyes wide, crying, as a doctor removes her ability to have kids; Delilah's wings having shed their splendor, dragging on the ground, unable to lift her into the sky.

Each new panel wrecks me in ways I can't describe, but pouring them into existence sands the edges of these new rocks in my heart. They're there. Always there, but the pain is less acute. Maybe one day, the rocks will dwindle into soft beach pebbles, the kind that shift under your feet, reminding you they were once fierce cliffs that bowed to water's persistence.

Or Delilah won't call me again, and the rest of me will turn to stone.

On the third night my phone *finally* rings.

I trip over nothing on my bedroom floor, rushing to grab my cell. At the sight of her name, I blow out a rough breath. "Delilah, hey."

She doesn't say hi back or do that thing she did at the end of our last call, quietly breathing and not talking much. She immediately says, "God, it's good to hear your voice."

"Even if I talk like a proper wanker?" I say in my horrible English accent, unable to contain my relief.

"Blimey. Your accent's rubbish," she says, using her congested Australian voice, laughter in her tone.

I fall happily onto my bed, unprepared for Joking Delilah.

"I'm sorry it's been so long," she says before I can ask how she is. "There was just so much stuff in my head. But I got together with Maggie and we talked until, like, three a.m., rehashing my accident and you and recovery and how angry and sad I was back then."

She takes a huge breath, as though her mouth is having trouble keeping up with her thoughts. "Then I took a long walk with my mom last night, and we talked about my reckless choices before I got hurt. I hadn't done that, I realized—apologized to her for my behavior. I think I've been living with a lot of guilt over my actions, among other things. And we talked about losing my dad, which we don't really do, how losing you after was tied to those crushing emotions. Anyway, the whole thing was intense. We cried a lot, but we hugged and laughed about good times with my dad too. And I just feel so lucky to have a mother and friends who've been here for me when I needed them. And you," she says as she takes another big breath, the air slowly leaking out. "You'll always be my best friend, E."

For the first time in a long time with Delilah, I'm too moved to speak.

"You still there?" she asks quietly.

"I'm always here for you, Delilah."

Her contented sigh is a gift. "I saw Candy, by the way."

The change in topic is jarring, but I can't get enough of the lively lilt in her voice. "If she was walking on her own without Sandra, I'll be reporting her to the dog police."

"You should be *thanking* Sandra. They were in town square, and a guy playing Frisbee almost landed on Candy, but Sandra stepped in the way like a football lineman."

This is why she's my go-to dog sitter. "Sandra didn't get hurt, did she?"

"The only thing that got hurt was the Frisbee player's pride when she ripped him a new one for not looking where he was running."

"I'll have to send her a fruit basket. Or maybe a selection of perm haircare products." I scratch my scruffy cheek, which hasn't seen a razor since I left my heart in Windfall. "Or those microscopic listening devices she can plant around town."

"Or you could just thank her."

"Delilah, she saved my dog's *life*."

She snorts. "So dramatic."

What I am is *happy*. Happy and thrilled we're back to chatting and joking together, even with our traumatic history. "Tell me more about your past few days."

She obliges, sharing more about Maggie and her mom and work, less emotional when hitting on sensitive subjects. She asks tons about me too. About Des and my family and my art, telling me again how amazing my work is, like we're still teens and Delilah's determined to boost my creative ego.

"Can we talk again tomorrow?" I ask eventually, my voice quiet in my dark room.

"I'd like that."

"But we should only talk in English accents."

"Aye, mate," she says, butchering the intonation. "That's a brilliant idea."

I shake my head at her dramatics, smiling at my ceiling, not wanting to hang up. "Thanks for calling tonight," I say softly.

"Thanks for listening, and for giving me the space I needed."

"Whenever you need to talk, I'm always here," I murmur, imagining her head is cradled on my chest, her arms wrapped tightly around me. "That's what friends are for."

That's what relationships are for too. Being a sounding board, instead of forcing your wants and opinions on your partner. Being there to learn, not just lead. Attributes I hope Delilah considers before I return to Windfall and ask if she'll give us another chance.

# THIRTY-THREE

After two unsuccessful weeks searching for Desmond, I've resumed my Head of the Family spot, standing in front of my TV. The faces turned toward me are resigned. No one knows when or how we'll find Des. I'm starting to think Sandra wasn't grinding my gears with her advice to quit looking for him. If someone doesn't want to be found, the best way to find them is to wait. Do nothing, because doing something might push them further away.

"So," I tell my family, less firm and confident than the last time I usurped this spot of power. "I'm leaving today, heading back to Windfall." Where I may or may not have my heart rebroken. "Before I go, I have something to show you."

"If it's that beard," Lennon says, "we've all seen it, and it's pitiful."

I don't react. He's pissed I ask him to play truth or dare daily. I also refuse to shave until I have Delilah back. "You're just jealous I can grow a better beard than you."

He scoffs. "In your dreams."

"E's beard is definitely better," Cal says, "but you'd still win a hipster contest."

Lennon crosses his arms and glowers.

I massage my dark beard, smirking. "While I do have an exceptional beard, I also have a new graphic novel to show you all."

"E, that's so great." Mom isn't facing the window, giving us her back. She sounds pleased for me and my professional progress, but she looks tired.

"Does that mean Sathya's not still avoiding you like the plague you are?" Lennon gives me his best suck-on-that face.

"Better question," Jake says, butting in, "why do you look as nervous as the time you asked me if getting a rash on your dick after shaving it means you have syphilis?"

First, I was fourteen and had a fear of STDs. Avett told me, while privately laughing his ass off, that his cousin's penis shriveled and fell off from syphilis. Second, I read an article that said women only liked men who manscaped, and I was determined for Delilah to like me. The article didn't say shit about some men having sensitive skin and needing to moisturize.

To Jake, I say, "Fuck off." To the rest of them, I say, "Sathya and I are cool. She didn't want to do the prequel and has some family stress. Long story, but she backed out of our contract, which left us in a tight spot. My new project will smooth those waters, but I won't publish it if you don't give me the okay."

Sathya knows the deal. We've talked a couple of times this week, mostly so I can ask how her mother's doing. While her prognosis is good, bills are piling up. I want nothing more than to help her and her family, but I can't throw mine under the bus in the process.

I hold my satchel against my chest, my laptop tucked safely inside. Sharing newly finished work is always daunting. Having my family read the depths of my despair in those early days and learn about Delilah's suffering is extra tough, especially when I don't know where Delilah and I stand.

For the past week and a half, we've talked daily, laughing together and sharing more about tougher times. I ache with how much I miss her. I know we've made progress, but neither of us has broached the topic of our future. Regardless of our undeniable friendship, I might always remind Delilah of her worst days.

Either way, I told her I couldn't talk again until I returned to Windfall. The rest of what needs saying has to be said face to face. Before any of that happens, I need to share my graphic novel with my family.

"The story I wrote is about me," I tell them, forcing my spine straight. "It's about all of us."

Silence drops. Actually, no. Jake's wheezy breaths from the time he broke his nose on Desmond's fist fill the room. That fun-filled Bower boys' night was the eve of Desmond's first date with Sadie. Jake thought it would be funny to superglue Desmond's jar of hair gel shut.

"Publish whatever you want," Jake says. "Better you get in the last word than our piece of shit father."

Lennon smirks his hipster smirk. "Publish that baby. At least your tell-all will come with pictures."

Mom's cheeks have more color in them. "One hundred percent."

Cal stands, walks over to me, and grips my shoulders. I obviously opened the door to this move. Now we're all arm grippers. "I'm proud of you, E. Writing that down couldn't have been easy."

"It wasn't, and there's stuff in here that will upset you all. Stuff about me and about Delilah. Please read it before you agree."

They trade wary looks. The last thing my family needs is another painful shock, but they've had two weeks to acclimatize to the Desmond bomb. It's time they learn about this.

Cal gently pries my bag from my grip and leads my family to the kitchen counter, where they extricate my laptop and hunch over my work. My words. My panels. My lingering pain. I don't watch the screen as they scroll. Mom's gasp tells me when they've reached Delilah's accident, as does Jake's *fuck*. Lennon glances at me with so much emotion not even his beard can cover his trembling chin. Cal presses his fist to his mouth as he reads, rubbing at his eyes periodically.

I pace. I yank at my hair. I chew my cuticles raw until they get to the new ending I wrote. The image of Delilah and me, our wings wrapped around each other, with yet-to-be-colored sunbeams hitting our faces as we kiss. A simple panel. A close-up of just the two of us, because that's my nucleus. The pit at the center of it all, and I seriously don't know what I'll do if she still pushes me away.

Mom's happy sigh signals they're done.

Cal murmurs, "Goddamn."

While they don't look upset any longer, they're not saying much. I can't tell if they're still as gung ho on me publishing my story. Then they move as a unit, coordinated, as though they share the same beating heart, crowding me and embracing me in the family hug of hugs.

"So talented, man." One of Jake's hands finds my upper arm and squeezes. No way will he let us all steal his arm-gripping thunder.

"He gets it from me." This from Mom, who still draws people with four straight lines for limbs.

"It was okay-ish," Lennon says, being Lennon-ish.

The pressure in my chest feels good for once. "So . . . you're all cool if I publish it?"

They disperse, my brothers crossing their arms as though we weren't just hugging it out like a group of preteen girls.

Lennon slits his eyes. "Only if you change my character."

That's not happening. "The Dong Tao chicken is highly prized in Vietnam for its delicate meat and was once only bred by royalty."

"It has lumpy old-lady legs and needs to change."

His irritation is almost as fun as it was drawing those gnarly limbs. "Those legs give your character strength and power. Plus, those chickens are incredibly rare. It'll impress your hipster friends."

He curls his lip. "For the millionth time, drinking craft beer doesn't make me a hipster."

He'll never win that battle. "If you want, we can play truth or dare, and the winner decides if your character changes."

He mouths, *Fuck you.*

"I'm fine being the eagle," Jake says, head tipped up. Proud.

"Love the barn owl version of me." Cal puffs out his chest like it's full of feathers.

Mom, who embodies the small but resilient wren, glances around at our messed-up family, this group of boys who *in*burst and outburst and needle one another to cover our discomfort, and she smiles. "If you and Delilah want your story out there, it's your choice. I'll be the first in line to buy fifty copies."

Best mother in the world.

No one discusses how Dad will feel about being a bullying grackle who gets shredded in the end by a troop of vultures he deceived. Spoiler alert: we'd all pay to watch that movie. We don't debate how this will affect Desmond. I've purposely kept the details about him limited. There's no mention of Sadie's reappearance or of Max—those aren't my secrets to share—and I didn't feel right about harping on how far he's fallen. He'll have to find his own emotion valve to purge his demons.

With the publishing issue settled, Mom walks me to the door and gives me another warm hug. "Tell Sadie I'm here if she needs help or money or a babysitter—anything at all. Tell her I'll hop in a car and drive across the country if she needs me."

I resent Des for causing all this turmoil. All this searching and waiting. I'm also just sad for him. "You'll meet Max soon, Ma. Des will resurface. He always does. And if any of you hear from him, make sure he calls me."

They nod and grunt. Lennon salutes me but still looks pissed about the Dong Tao situation. He had his chance to play truth or dare. He passed.

I don't love leaving them with this limbo hanging over our heads—the uncertainty of when they'll meet Max, a kid who will be smothered by uncles and a grandmother he's never met, along with the stress of how the news will clobber Des—but I need to get back to Windfall.

I may have held my family together during this latest crisis, and I can now grip shoulders like nobody's business, but don't let my profound maturity fool you.

I can't handle losing Delilah again.

I'm almost out the door, when Mom says, "Make sure you go straight home to Windfall."

Normally, I wouldn't think twice about the comment, but there's electricity in her voice. Excitement, when nothing about our situation warrants excitement. I turn toward her. "Is there a specific reason I should go straight home to Windfall?"

"Nope. Nothing. Just call me when you're close. So I know you're safe."

The wattage in her grin betrays her. She's up to something. Or maybe Delilah is? I don't let my mind go there. I've already overthought my conversations with Delilah more times than is healthy, and I don't want to rain on my mother's parade by asking questions. It's too nice seeing her smile. "I was debating taking a road trip to check out the world's largest rubber band ball, but I'll pass this time and call you when I'm close to Windfall."

"Excellent choice," she says, keeping her lips neutral, trying to hide her giddiness. Doing a crap job of it. "Have a safe trip."

I do my best not to let her brightness infect me. But it does. Something's brewing, and my mind goes where I said it wouldn't. To Delilah. To us and happily ever after, and I really hope I'm not reading this wrong.

# THIRTY-FOUR

My drive into Windfall feels different this time. Instead of furtive and anxious, crouching in my seat to avoid detection, I relax at the sight of the town-limit sign: **WELCOME TO PARADISE**. I'm not having trouble swallowing, imagining people's reaction to my resurrected-cockroach self, or slowing down, unsure if the lost love of my life will shoot me in the nuts. She won't. I don't know what reception I'll get, but we're past nut shooting.

I called my mother as promised, and she gave me nothing. No hints as to why she's tracking my arrival to town. But yeah. I probably lied about the not-feeling-anxious part. As I park behind my building and realize today will be another tipping point in my life, for better or for worse, I'm decidedly nervous. I stare through my windshield, trying to convince myself to move. It's not working, but my phone rings.

Delilah's name on my cell has me fumbling with it, trying to answer quickly. "Delilah, hey."

"Why are you sitting in your truck?"

I glance out both side windows, then look in my rearview mirror. I don't see Delilah, but I do see Sandra, standing there, resuming her role as Eighties-Permed Private Eye. "Why are you still using Sandra to spy on me? And why isn't Candy Cane with her?"

"Candy's with me. I've had her for a few days, and Sandra and your mother offered to help so I'd know when you got back."

I think about what all this means—Delilah and Sandra narking on me together, Delilah caring for my dog, Delilah reaching out to my mother. That rush of hope grows into a landslide.

"Where are you?" I'm moving as I talk, phone pressed to my ear as I leave my bags in my truck and head for the narrow walkway that leads to the main street.

"By a bench in the town square."

"Don't you dare move."

"I'm not going anywhere, E." The way she says this, with emotion thickening her words, I can't help but read into the meaning. *I'm not going anywhere without you. We'll never be apart again.* Goddamn it, Hope. If you ruin this for me, I will . . .

Nope. No other scenarios are possible.

I strut toward the main street with one thought on my mind: *Delilah Moon, Delilah Moon, Delilah Moon.* Like I'm in the airport departure lounge again, fixated. Consumed. Desperate for the sight of her. The daylight's dimming, but I spot her standing by a park bench, phone pressed to her ear. Her curly hair is wild, her intense eyes searching for me. Candy Cane is perched beside her on the grass, sitting like the bestest dog she is.

"Thing is," Delilah says through our phones when she spots me, rooting me in place. "I thought being with you would be a constant reminder of my worst days. I thought I'd be happier letting you go and starting fresh. But the second you left my apartment, I felt pain so deep it was like I was reliving your disappearance all over again. Except this time it was worse, because I caused it. I'm the one who sent you away, but I still wasn't ready to believe we could work."

"Delilah." I'm not numb anymore. I'm a barrel of emotions on rough waters, my insides sloshing around, ready to spill out and pool around her feet. But she's still got her phone against her ear, like she wants or needs to say this from a distance. "What about now?" I say, hoarse. "Are you ready to believe?"

She bites her lip. A few cars drive by. I sense a bit of an audience, the town of Windfall always up for a new episode of *Edgar Gets Shot Down*, except there's no chance this episode ends with me leaving here alone. I plan to give them the season-ending shocker: "Edgar Gets the Girl."

Delilah steps closer, still hovering on the other side of the street, talking to me through our phones. "I don't want to hurt anymore, E. Not like this. And I don't want to keep hurting you. The way you called and let me talk out everything from my past—it was exactly what I needed. All that opening up pushed me to talk to Maggie and my mom. Unearth issues I didn't even realize were issues. So I'm done lying to myself, pretending I'll be happy without you. Because I won't be. I'm *not* happy without you. Not in the way a person can truly be fulfilled. I'm sure I'll have setbacks, and there's stuff we need to talk out, but I don't want to do it over the phone. I want to do it together, preferably in your arms."

That's it. I'm toast. I've never needed anything as badly as I need her right now.

I shove my phone in my pocket, ready to sprint to her. Delilah shifts on her feet, looking equally impatient, but another car drives by, this one crawling at ten fucking miles per hour.

Something in Delilah's face changes. Her posture straightens, the lines on her brow smoothing out. She hits me with her solar eclipse grin and plants her legs firmly. I know what's about to happen, and I'm here for it. We're finally ready for it, but I won't let this attack hug be one sided. The second the Sunday driver slides past, I'm running. She's running. We're two meteors hurtling through space, about to collide in a burst of stars.

I catch her like I always will, crushing her close. Feeling whole for the first time in ten years. No more secrets. No more waiting for the other shoe to drop. We're here, we're together, and I'm kissing the daylights out of Delilah Moon. She moans into my mouth. I clutch her closer, swipe my tongue against hers, moving deeper like the greedy man I am—the ending of "Edgar Gets the Girl" is R rated—and I suddenly have no clue why I was nervous. As rocky as our journey has been, our story only ever had one ending, and this is it.

I move to her ear, give her a filthy lick. "You, Delilah Moon, are devastatingly sexy."

She makes a needy sound that undoes me. "I missed you so much. And since when do you have a beard?"

"This is my I'm-heartbroken face," I murmur.

She pulls back and runs her fingers through my unkempt scruff. "The beard's pretty hot, but I was heartbroken too."

I rub my cheek against hers. "Enjoy it while it's here, because it's getting shaved tomorrow. And we'll never be apart again. Not like this. From now on, we fight together or feel sad together or do whatever we need to do, as long as we're together."

"I'm so sorry I freaked out, but *yes, yes, yes.*"

Our lips collide again, our kisses more frantic this time.

Someone whistles and calls, "You two are gross. Get a room." Definitely Maggie.

Without glancing at her, I give her the finger, but I notice something odd. Candy Cane is still sitting by the park bench. From what I can tell, she's not tied to it with a leash. "Delilah, did you staple Candy Cane to the grass?"

Arms latched around my neck, she laughs. "I trained her to sit and wait patiently."

"Oh my God."

"I know, right?" Delilah beams with pride. "She's a natural."

"But she hasn't seen me in two weeks. Then I ran and you ran." Excited running is a blatant invitation for Candy Cane to go berserk. "Are you telling me you trained our dog, who gets deranged excited when she hasn't seen a person in two minutes, to sit calmly and wait to greet me?"

Instead of confirming my claim, she says, "*Our* dog?"

I brush our noses together, my heart beating wildly, still playing catch-up to all that's happened. "*Our* dog is brilliant. We should have her IQ tested. Get her enrolled in advanced linguistics."

Now that I'm looking closely, there's nothing calm about Candy. Her body is pitched forward, her eyes wide and searching, desperately waiting to be told she's allowed to move. Unable to resist, I call her and she bolts, taking a running leap at me. Her exuberance knocks me down, but I don't mind. Delilah hits the grass with me, both of us being smothered by dog licks and love.

"We could sleep out here tonight," I say as I rub Candy's ears and stare into Delilah's Sonic eyes. "Wake up with a bunch of kids staring at our faces."

"E," she says, her expression sobering. "I promise to never push you away again like I did. But"—she swallows hard—"I'm still worried you haven't thought this through."

I trail my finger down her pinked cheek. "Which part?"

"The not-having-kids-of-your-own part. You might grow to resent me." Her voice thins with worry. "As you get older, you might have regrets. So many times, when you talked about Candy, you mentioned being a dad."

I sift through our conversations, the moments I noticed Delilah pulling away from me: in the shelter playroom after playing with the dogs and in the elevator at the Sheldrake Inn. Both times I made off-the-cuff comments about being a crap or overbearing dad, clueless to how those remarks affected Delilah. They were nothing but that for me—remarks. Jokes to keep things light. There's only one truth for me, my holy grail at the end of this turbulent path.

I brush a wild curl behind Delilah's ear. Her eyelids flutter. "When I saw you in the airport lounge," I say, still awed by fate's hand guiding us together that day, as though Life was on my side this whole time, doing all he could to right my father's wrongs, "and thought you were married, something in me atrophied. I wasn't thinking about the kids we wouldn't have or the family picnics I wouldn't experience. I was thinking about us, the woman I love more than anything, officially having slipped out of my grasp, and I was devastated."

Her breath catches.

"Learning you can't have kids also devastated me," I go on. This is the part I planned to say to Delilah's face before she stole my thunder with her reconnaissance work and attack hug. Words said with imploring eyes, a wildly beating heart, and open sincerity. "Not because we wouldn't have children of our own. I was tortured because of the pain the accident and outcome caused *you*. I don't care if we live a life with a brood of dogs or if we adopt kids who need homes, or if we're just the cool aunt and uncle who buy our nieces and nephews alcohol when we shouldn't and take them to get tattoos to piss off their parents." Better ones than Desmond's. "The details don't matter to me. Because they're just that—details. I won't live another ten years without you by my side, let alone one day. Nothing's more important to me than us being together."

Her eyes glaze. "I love you so much, E."

"Because of the abs?"

Her laugh is watery. "Because you're you. I'm so lucky to have you."

"We're lucky to have each other. Also, there's gonna be a lot of the Sex in our future, Mars."

She narrows her eyes at me. "Stop calling me Mars."

Squinty eyes aside, I hear the smile in her voice. She still adores that nickname. "Sorry. There's gonna be a lot of the Sex in our future, Uranus."

"You're impossible."

Candy Cane lies at our feet while we talk about the Desmond situation and Delilah's reconnection with my mother and how brilliant and cute *our* dog is. Townsfolk call out greetings as they pass our reclined bodies. We smile and wave back. We don't talk more about her accident and its repercussions. We've done that plenty the past two weeks, and I have no doubt those tough topics will come up later. For now, we kiss periodically and touch chastely, the trauma of our history settling into a deeper understanding. This togetherness. Our bond, unbreakable no matter what drama is tossed our way.

When Candy gets up and pees on a kid's toy fire engine, we decide it's time to go.

Delilah clambers to her feet and brushes grass from her jeans. I jump up, which causes Candy Cane to prance around my legs and bark. I'm clearly not the alpha in our threesome. I'm the runt she bosses around and plays with.

Before I can grab Delilah's hand and finally head home, she steps in front of me. "Since this reunion has gone as well as I hoped"—her shoulders hike up in an excited hitch—"we have plans tonight."

I smolder at her. "Do these plans involve multiple rounds of the Sex?"

She shoves my chest playfully. "Not right now. I have a surprise for you."

"Does this surprise involve my six-pack and your mouth?" I ask.

Delilah rolls her eyes. "It does not."

I grab her hand and swing it like we're in grade school. Seriously. We're still this cute. "Does this surprise involve lemon curd carnage and my face between your legs?"

She laughs. "Wrong again."

New decor is on the lampposts, bouquets of evergreen cuttings and pretty bows, half of them adorned with red holly berries, the others with blue dreidels—a reminder that Windfall's holiday celebrations are just over a month away. More people wave at us as we cross the street. Hopefully they're pleased with how this episode of their favorite show ended.

"I finished rewriting my novel," I say hesitantly. "My family's fine with me publishing it, so it's up to you. Maybe you'll read it tomorrow?"

Delilah stops walking. My stomach does a nervous drop. "I don't need to read it to give my permission. I trust you and think it's important to have our truth in the world. The answer's yes, but I'll still read it tomorrow."

"Thank you." For being the best person I know. "You can help me brainstorm the title. I'm kind of stuck on it." Continuing to her place, I lift our hands and kiss her knuckles. "Does this surprise involve us reenacting our first time, with Eternity and 'Pillow Talk' on the stereo?"

She tips her head back, grinning. "You're too much."

Or just enough.

When we get to her apartment above Sugar and Sips, music drifts out. And voices.

"Delilah." I stop and spin her toward me. "Are we filming our own porno? Do I need to wait outside, then you'll answer the door and tell me I'm not your usual repairman?"

She's downright cackling now. "We're not filming a porno, goof. We're having fondue night."

Baring her teeth in the widest smile I've ever seen, she swings the door open for her surprise. Our friends are there: Ricky and Aaron, Avett and Naomi, even my nemesis Maggie and her boyfriend, Thomas, glasses of wine in hand, hanging out around the coffee table with the appetizers Delilah planned for our canceled evening. Fresh sunflowers are on the kitchen counter. The table's set with mismatched colorful napkins and blue ceramic plates. Melted cheesy goodness of some kind wafts from the oven—probably Ricky's fancy cheese-and-potato dish—making my nose exceedingly happy.

*I'm* exceedingly happy.

As much as I want to devour my woman and would have given my all for any of my surprise guesses, especially the porno one—with our improved acting, we could take the adult-entertainment world by storm—this surprise winds me in the best way. This is us being a real couple, sharing our home with the people we love. This is the life I would have imagined for myself ten years ago, and I can't believe I'm lucky enough to live it.

"Look what the cat dragged in," Avett calls, lifting his wineglass in salute.

"Dog, not cat. Now you've insulted Candy Cane and need to apologize."

"Sorry, Candy!" His grin is crooked. This must be glass of wine number two.

At the sound of her name, Candy bounds over to our friends and accepts a round of gentle, not-too-vigorous pats. I drag Delilah into my arms. "This is the best surprise."

"Sorry it's not filming a porno, but I wanted to show you how serious I am. That I want a future with you and all this." She gestures at the festive room. "Our friends. Our home together, whatever that home looks like. I'm not scared anymore. I won't shut down and block you out again."

There's nothing left to say. Not when she's given me everything I want. I kiss her, going for chaste and sweet, but Delilah's not having it. She digs her fingers into my hair, deepening the kiss, being naughty with her tongue.

"You two are still gross." Maggie, always there to needle me.

I wrench myself away from Delilah, keeping her tucked close. "Lovely to see you, too, Margaret."

Naomi is mooning at us like we're a pile of puppies. "Y'all are still too damn cute."

Ricky kisses Aaron's cheek and nips his ear. "We're cuter."

Aaron blushes ten shades of red.

I laugh. "They're definitely cuter."

Delilah pours us wine as we catch up on the newlyweds' honeymoon and Avett's recent pet patient—an old rottweiler who peed on his shoes—and Naomi's most headstrong student, who has an argument for everything Naomi says.

"Sounds like someone I know," I say, staring at Maggie.

Maggie cocks her head and tugs her ear. "Did you guys just hear that? Whatever it is, it's the most annoying sound I've ever heard."

We eventually move to the table and eat and laugh and tease one another. Whenever possible, I brush my hand along the back of Delilah's neck and am rewarded with goose bumps spreading across her skin. She squeezes my thigh. We trade soft looks and hot looks and you're-my-favorite-person-in-the-world looks, and I realize how much better fondue night is now than it would have been two weeks ago. How relaxed and easy we are with each other and our friends. I also finally have the perfect name for my graphic novel, the only way to describe my last ten years: *To Mars and Back.*

# EPILOGUE

*Five Months Later*

I stretch out my arms and clasp them behind my head. "It's obviously a penis."

"It curves too much," Delilah says.

"Some penises curve."

"They don't expand into a fan shape."

"Excited penises do. That's the ejaculation."

We're stargazing in my truck bed. Even though I'm not looking at Delilah, I'm pretty sure she rolls her eyes. "Not every constellation is shaped like a penis, E. At least once, you have to choose something else."

"I have mutant eyesight. Don't doubt this superhero vision." I roll toward her and stare at her profile. "Now I see a princess with flowing hair, half-albatross, half-human, with blue eyes the color of Sonic the Hedgehog, who makes kitchen-sink bars like a top chef, trains dogs like a dog whisperer, and is not excellent at using English accents."

It's a cool night for late April. We're under two thick blankets, wearing hats, our noses red from the crisp air. She rolls toward me. "I see a handsome prince with a badass scar through his lip, and much cooler hair than when he loved Justin Bieber, and chestnut eyes that remind me of holidays and cozy nights, who creates fantastical worlds with his hands and loves like there's no tomorrow, and is not excellent at stargazing."

I scooch closer to her. "I'm insulted."

"No, you're not." She kisses my cold nose.

I kiss hers. "Speaking of fantastical worlds, I got the page proofs of my novel." Due to the time crunch, my editor expedited our revisions, hiring a letterer to finalize the written font and several colorists to flesh out the images under my direction, pulling this off in record time. The pages arrived with a card signed from him and my agent, which read, *Thank you for your bravery and sharing your story with us.*

"Is it amazing?" Delilah asks, a twinkle in her eye.

"I haven't opened it yet. I want you to be the first to see it." I also have a surprise for her at home: a framed print of the final panel in full color—the close-up of Delilah and me, our wings wrapped around each other, sunlight cresting over our faces as we kiss. "I'll just watch you while you read it."

"That won't be creepy at all," she says dryly.

I settle on my back, fitting her into my side. "Sadie called today with some great news."

"Yeah?"

I relax into Delilah, relieved as hell about Sadie's decision. "She's moving back to Windfall with Max. Since she's not close with her family, she thinks it would be good for Max to be close to us."

"E, that's amazing. We'll get to see him way more."

We will, which is awesome. With school and distance, we've only seen Max a handful of times. The first get-together was intense. Mom cried a pile of tears, while the rest of us barely held it together, slowly getting to know our nephew. Having Sadie and him here is the best news possible, but seeing them is always a reminder that Des is still out in the world, miserable, clueless that he's a father.

This isn't the longest he's been MIA. The longest was after one of his anniversaries with Sadie. I don't think it was a special number. I'm not sure why that moment hit harder than the others, but he dropped off the grid for seven months and returned with the amoeba-lion ink on his neck, more hair stuffed into his man bun, and less life in his eyes.

I'm not sure what to expect this time.

"I was thinking we could do something at our place, once Sadie and Max move," I say. "A simple lunch with her and my family."

By *our* place, I mean Delilah's cozy apartment over her business. As sad as I was to see my Pepto apartment go, I gave up the lease. My home is officially with Delilah.

She rubs her cold nose along my neck. "I'd love to have them to our place."

I also secretly want my family to visit Windfall again. I think they'd be happier living here. Mom could reunite with her quilting ladies, have a supportive group of women on her tough days. Lennon could build an amazing outdoor education business here, with hiking tours and programs for kids, instead of struggling to fill his programs in Houston. Cal's too nice for city living, and Jake's too serious to have fun there, but they're all too scared or scarred to return here full time. In Lennon's case he's terrified of a feisty redhead.

If they saw this place, though. If they were forced to drink the small-town Kool-Aid and breathe the cleaner air and remember the comfort of living in a community bound by gossip, filled with pseudo-family determined to protect their own, even performing plays if necessary, they might rethink their lives.

"We'll invite your mom too," I say. "Since she loves me now."

Delilah huffs out a laugh. "She tolerates you."

Not true. After Delilah and I spent a week in hibernation having lots of the Sex, her mother called and thanked me for being patient with Delilah, giving her space while we worked through her pain. Then she said, "You better treat her like the queen she is. I taught her how to skeet shoot."

The Moon women are the best.

I maneuver Delilah on top of me. "We should sleep out here."

"We left Candy Cane at home."

I growl. "Damn that adorable dog for thwarting my plans."

"Maybe we could get her a friend, though? If you wouldn't mind having two."

If I wouldn't mind?

If Delilah wasn't lying on top of me, I'd jump up in my version of Candy Cane's deranged excited dance. Still, I go for unaffected and starfish under her. "I don't hate it, but we'd have to suffer through another afternoon in the shelter playroom, touching and petting all those"—I make a disgusted face—"*dogs.*"

She wrinkles her cute nose. "It would be awful."

"I mean, we could suck it up. Just once. If you want."

"I guess I could muster some interest. To make you happy."

We grin at each other, and I hug and kiss her like she deserves to be hugged and kissed.

I stick my hands under her layers of tops, about to warm my hands on her breasts, when my phone rings. I groan in frustration. She bites my earlobe and rolls off me, giving me no choice but to answer. My phone's always close, in case Desmond finally calls. In case my family needs me, but if this is Lennon, I'll be sending him a lock of Maggie's hair in the mail with a note that says, *I dare you.*

Prepared to yell at whoever's on the line, I say a curt, "Yup?"

"I can hang up. Call again in another five months."

I freeze, my heart shoving its way into my throat. Delilah moves in front of me, eyes wide with worry. She mouths, *Who is it?*

*Desmond,* I mouth back.

She clutches her hands to her chest. I shove off the blankets and stand in my truck bed, wanting to pace, to run. But Delilah's arms slide around me from behind. She presses her face into my back—a second spine to hold me up, reminding me I'm not alone.

"Someone at Sandy's bar said you were looking for me." Des sounds distant and groggy.

I feel like I mainlined three cups of coffee. "That was five months ago."

"And?"

His tone's as flat as ever, and I'm worried he has more infected piercings on his face. Regardless, I need to be on my A game. I can't tell him this devastating news from a distance. This is face-to-face news, meant to be shared with shoulder grabs and a team of medics nearby. I owe it to Sadie and my family to make sure Des doesn't fall apart.

The only way to make this happen is to lie. "I need your help, Des."

"Ask someone else. I'm busy."

Busy my ass. "Dad reached out to me," I say—total lie. "What he asked was a shock, and I can't talk to anyone else about it." More lies. "He keeps calling and I keep putting him off. I'm about to lose my shit on this and need to talk to you." So many lies. Whatever works.

"What could that asshole possibly want from you?"

"Not over the phone, Des. I'll come to Houston. Just tell me where and when."

Delilah gives my roiling stomach a squeeze. I whip off my hat, suddenly too damn hot. If he doesn't agree, I'm screwed. I'm not sure how else to make him stay put long enough for me to find him.

Enough seconds drag that I'm doubting my success. Then he grunts. "Fine. I'll text you."

He hangs up. Typical Desmond, cutting himself off from family as quickly as possible, but I spin and hug Delilah. "He agreed."

"Holy shit."

"Holy shit." I'm freaking out. This wasn't even the hard part. The hard part will be facing Desmond and watching him crumble when

I tell him he has a son. I'll need Delilah with me for that gut punch. Not for the conversation. Des won't want her there to witness his pain. Maybe she'll tag along in disguise, loiter in whatever seedy bar Des suggests we meet at. Or she'll wait for me at a nearby shop, my personal safety net. As long as I know she's close, I can get through anything.

# AUTHOR'S NOTE

Thank you for reading E and Delilah's story! If you miss them already, I have a treat for you. Visit my website, www.kellysiskind.com, for a *FREE bonus chapter*. You get to experience their steamy afternoon at the Sheldrake Inn from Delilah's point of view.

And make sure you snap up Desmond's book, *10 Signs You Need to Grovel*. Holy heck is that grump about to get the shock of his life!

# ACKNOWLEDGMENTS

I wrote this book during a difficult writing time for me, when I was struggling with where I was in my career. Then E jumped into my head and staged a coup.

I've never drafted a book as quickly as I did this novel. I fell in love with E and Delilah as they *re*-fell in love with each other. I credit E for reminding me that writing is *fun*, and every brother after him has solidified my love of the craft. I hope you laughed and cried with E as much as I did.

I can't thank my agent, Maria Napolitano, enough for her hard work on this manuscript. She has a questionable plant collection, but her editing prowess and ongoing support are the reasons more people are reading E and Delilah's story. Thank you, and the whole Bookcase team, for all you do. I feel so fortunate to be part of such a synergetic agency.

Nabbing Maria Gomez and Angela James as editors is like winning the lottery. Their collaborative approach and intuitive feedback have made the revision process seamless. They both understood what I wanted to do with this novel and pushed me to take E and Delilah exactly where they needed to go. Thank you so much for your insight and for fighting for this book!

I'm incredibly thankful for the whole Montlake crew, from my copyeditor (Stephanie, the comma wrangler and grammar guru) to the marketing and production teams. Releasing a book truly takes a village, and it's been a pleasure living in yours.

Although I drafted this book quickly, my books are never editor ready until I've gone through revisions with my critique partners and beta readers. Sending all the thanks and chocolate to J. R. Yates (my partner in crime and in Italy), Jennifer Hawkins (whose words put mine to shame), Michelle Hazen (my talented sounding board and fellow travel lover), Annette Christie (who swept in at the last minute to save my butt), Sandra Lombardo (such a thoughtful reader and friend), Nena Drury (an artist whose enthusiasm and kindness are invaluable), and Michelle Pike (a kind soul who is incredibly generous with her talent and time).

Readers! You're why I write. Thank YOU for reading this book. Thank you for spending time in this world I've created. I hope you had as much fun stomping through E's head as I did. I cannot wait for you to read Desmond's story next! Writing that gruff man as he fumbled through the trials and tribulations of being a dad and winning back his lost love, Sadie, flattened me in the best way.

Bloggers and vloggers and Instagrammers and BookTokers: my books wouldn't be what they are without all of you. *You* put the time in. *You* help spread the word. Thank you for taking the time to read and share your thoughts with others. What you do is invaluable and hugely appreciated.

I'm excited to see you all again soon in the quaint town of Windfall!

# ABOUT THE AUTHOR

*Photo © 2015 Eirik Dunlop*

Kelly Siskind writes romantic comedies and contemporary romance novels for daydreamers and fantasists everywhere. She is the author of the One Wild Wish, Showmen, and Over the Top series, among other titles. Kelly's novels have been published internationally, and she has been featured on the Apple Books Best Books of the Month list.

Kelly lives in charming northern Ontario, where she alternatively frolics in and suffers through the never-ending winters. When she's not out hiking or home devouring books, you can find her, notepad in hand, scribbling down one of the many plot bunnies bouncing around in her head. Sign up for Kelly's newsletter at www.kellysiskind.com and never miss a giveaway, a free bonus scene, or the latest news on her books. And connect with her on Twitter and Instagram (@kellysiskind) or on Facebook (@authorkellysiskind).